The

I0685144

Zionist

James Berry

Dedication

The Zionist is dedicated to my late, beloved wife, Judith, whose Jewish ancestry comes from the country where *The Zionist* account takes place. The gentle and powerful force she carried in life came from her faith in Jesus, the Jewish Messiah, and the essence of what she was now lives in the minds and hearts of those she touched in this life.

Author's Note:

Romania was an ally of Nazi Germany from 1940 to 1944 and had a Jewish population of 750,000 before World War II. In four years, one-half of the population had been killed, starved, and robbed in the most horrific, barbaric ways. Romania caused more deaths of Jews than any other country in Europe except Nazi Germany. Unlike other countries in Europe where German military killing squads carried out its genocidal acts, in Romania much of it was done by the indigenous citizenry and gendarmes.

For 60 years following the war, the Romanian governments under communism and post-communist regimes carried the mantra of Holocaust deniers, making it one of the best-kept secrets of the war. It wasn't until 2004 that an official government statement was issued acknowledging there had been a Holocaust. Today in the country of Romania, the core Jewish population is less than 10,000.

In recent years, great concern has risen over attempts to rehabilitate the images of convicted and executed Romanian Nazi war criminals. This speaks to the country's continued systemic anti-Semitism. Knowing these historical facts will help the reader follow the story in book one of the *Zionist Series*.

Contents

Dispatchers were sent by couriers to all the king's.
provinces with the order to destroy, kill, and annihilate all
the Jews—young and old, women and little children.
(Esther 3:13)

Prologue

Above the rooftops of the German military headquarters in Bucharest, the Nazi Swastika Flag waved briskly in the wind. A clear blue sky had pushed away the gray cloud covering leaving a pristine overhead picture for those now on the streets shopping and plying their trade. Everything outside the walled compound came to a sudden stop when its steel doors opened with the sound of roaring military vehicles leading the way onto the public street followed by a battery of army escort cyclists clearing the roadway for the prestigious figure ensconced in an upscale Mercedes. Military protocol was underway with all the pomp and ceremony that went with a newly assigned field commander who was now on his way to a large military encampment where he would debut in a formal military exercise.

Dark clouds of war covered much of the face of Europe. Now it had come to Romania. The war machine of Nazi Germany had crossed her Rubicon and there was no turning back. In need of an Eastern land bridge to access the underbelly of Russia, German troops had joined the forces in Romania, a Nazi ally, for a common effort in their march to Moscow.

The general Berlin appointed to lead this region's war effort had arrived in the country with advanced instructions that he be honored with an official military troop review. The general's reputation for pretentious military ceremony had preceded him and when the upscale Mercedes

1

drove out of his headquarters surrounded by a military escort team, it was a picture showing the image of power and war with a distinct insight into the general's imperious nature. For the public who watched the scene, it would be remembered in history as a day of infamy.

The young and old, those destined to bear the scars and pain of war, filled roadsides and village streets to watch the moving scene of the general's ostentatious motorcade. Nazi flags waved briskly in the wind above the vehicle transporting the pompous-looking figure in the back seat. The public stood mesmerized. Faces gripped with fear were telling a story before its time.

Inside the Mercedes transporting the field commander, another kind of drama was in play. Alongside the general sat an elegant-looking lady, the wife of the general, whose musings were fastened on the passing peaceful countryside. Mother Nature chose to give her best with overhead majestic cerulean skies accompanied with gentle breezes that ruffled leaves of towering trees in the open fields, all a symphony playing to the audience of one. Eyes that welcomed the calm of nature turned toward the poised, pompous-looking general seated nearby. She followed the outline of his well-cut German officer's uniform showing creases that marked a crisp, tailored fit. Official medals hung prominently across his chest, medals rumored to be given, rather than earned in the heat of valor. Her eyes followed the outline of his proud, jutted-out chin tipped upward, then down to his manicured fingers with palms resting flat on his thighs. The proud, portentous image the general carried accentuated dominant eyes that spoke of power, control, and vanity—all part of his air of importance and station in life—the essence of what he was: narcissistic and vain. The general was self-made, with emphasis on self but not with the effort of gallantry or honor.

His position came from his talent to use the corrupt side of man: bribery, treachery, and disloyalty. He had no loyalties—only a show of them. Today, at his insistence, his trophy at his side was on display, his wife of great beauty, elegance, and wealth. At his request, she sat beside him knowing she was being used to bolster his vanity for a show of masculine prowess. Though husband and wife, hands were not held, eyes did not meet. Her delicate fingers that held large diamonds came from her reserves, not his, and for his benefit, her exquisite beauty and notoriety were used, put on display and worn like the medals carried on his chest—all outside his heart.

Today was show time for the general—an elaborate ceremonial display of a troop review and inspection. The sum of his life had been to make others think well of him, and today the maestro would bow to the audience of his vain ego: he would use his talked-about wife, known for her beauty, charm, and gentry to bolster his public image.

The ride from the general's headquarters to the military encampment where formal ceremonies would be conducted was scheduled to take thirty minutes. The general's trophy-wife sitting alongside found solace in nature's scenic beauty of green, rolling hillsides dotted with grazing sheep and cattle. *There would be more grandeur to it, she thought, if it weren't for the noisy army trucks and personnel carriers in front of them, but this was the style of the man who sat beside her. When it came to him, it was all about him. She would be glad when this was over. Her arranged visit to see her husband in Romania during wartime was certainly irregular, but he had a way of getting something when others failed. She hoped his ceremonial inspection of the German forces stationed alongside the infamous, indigenous Romanian Iron Guard was brief so she could return to her husband's*

3

headquarters where they could discuss her concerns of their troubled marriage. For this reason, she had agreed to come to this country at his request and act the part of a loyal, supportive wife. Both were on a mission: his was self-aggrandizement; hers was for the noble cause of their marriage.

The general and his escort pulled into a large, open space just outside a village where everything had been set up for the formalities of troop-inspection regalia. Attendants opened the door assisting the general out of the vehicle, now wearing white gloves, followed by his wife.

Throughout the formal exercise of reviewing the troops, the general's elegant wife performed beyond expectations in bolstering the image of a man empty of character and nobility. It was from there that she chose to take a stroll toward the nearby village knowing her husband would spend time conferring with his officers on the field.

Approaching the outskirts of the village, she thought it strange hearing no sound and seeing no movement. It carried an aura of quiet. Where were the people, the wagons, the carts hauling wares and produce? Moving closer, she could see down one of the main streets. The quiet made everything feel like it was a ghost town, then, her eyes turned down the walkway in front of the stores and homes. There appeared to be bodies lying on the ground scattered about, even in the open street. She stopped. She couldn't believe what her eyes saw. Human bodies lay everywhere. She ran where they were strewn about. It was horrible, mothers and fathers with children in their arms, all bloody with grotesques images on their faces, all killed with guns. None was alive, it was as if they had been herded into the street like cattle and shot. She recoiled in revulsion, began to shake and tremble at the sickening scene of wanton killing of innocent people. She

4

had the need to escape what her eyes beheld, to flee the hellish sight of evil. At the command of her emotions, she ran and ran, her lungs gasping for oxygen to meet the body's demand. She had no destination, just the need to flee, to escape, to be free from the memory of what she saw. Her mind and emotions were erratic, each pulling in its own direction. About to collapse from exhaustion, she stopped to catch her breath, leaned up against the side of a wagon behind one of the buildings. Unable to hold herself together, she leaned over in agony and heaved until her stomach muscles throbbed with pain. The body's demand for purgation left her bereft of strength. With all the might she had left in her weakened state, she forced herself into an upright position, sought to steady her shaky frame leaning against a nearby, one-horse-drawn cart full of loose hay. She kept her eyes closed wishing the world she'd just seen never happened. Why did she allow herself to visit her husband in this country? Deep breaths were again taken, this time slower. She was coming to herself, was about to turn and leave in a hasty retreat to the safe haven of the vehicle that brought her here, when she heard a whimper coming from underneath the hay inside the wagon she leaned against. *Those were sounds of a child, surely it couldn't be! What she heard was like the voice of God whispering peace in the dark.* Her hands flung back the hay brushing nature's gift of covering from the face of a small child. Suddenly, the mental image of a world gone mad was replaced with the face of God—a child, God's gift of innocence, a gift to remind man what he was when he entered earth.

The general's wife who could not have children, and yearned with gnawing hope every time she saw one in a baby carriage, lifted the little one-year-old up into her arms, saying to herself, *his mother and father are among the dead, and*

5

they hid him here in the hay for his safety and was now orphaned with no one to care for him. She noted a special gold locket showing a Star of David around his neck like it was something that would identify him.

The vehicle that brought the general and his wife on this tour to inspect his troops was on its way back to his headquarters. Now, the man who sat beside her was no longer the self-confident-looking person he was in coming to the site for inspection. His captured beauty, his trophy to show off, had convinced him to allow her to return to Germany in the company of an orphaned Jewish child believed to be their own. The infant would pass as a German child. His light coloring with blond hair and deep blue eyes would allow acceptance by the Aryan race into which he would be introduced. The general had learned before today that the lady seated by him had power beyond what he controlled, that when she wanted something badly enough she achieved it either by the energy she possessed or by the power of her fortune. Though he ruled over men and used his wife as a trophy, she had the power of money, the only thing the general respected in his wife, something that had eluded him.

The beautiful woman of gracious character now held in her arms a Jewish orphaned child whose life would mark destiny for both of them. She had come to a foreign land to evaluate her marriage to a man of reprehensible character; however, if she could be a devoted mother to the orphaned child she held in her arms, she would gladly suffer the indignities that may come to her marriage.

Chapter 1

The Dream

The year was 1967. Israel had just won the Six-Day War and taken the Old City of Jerusalem, an event that stunned the Christian Messianic world. It was the second great awakening of the twentieth century, the first being the creation of the state of Israel in 1948.

Hans Baughman would always use this event to mark the time when he went to work with only eight weeks left to complete his residency at the local general hospital, to be followed by private practice in the same city, the place he grew up and where his mother still lived. His three-year internship had gained him respect with his mentors and those he worked alongside. He was precocious, full of questions with the weakness of showing boredom with the mundane. He had spent his day mostly on his feet, and after calling his mother to check in on her, he went to bed. But sometime in the early morning, Hans found himself shaken from a deep sleep, traumatized by a recurring, tormenting dream. He lay quiet on his bed staring into what looked like an abyss of personal darkness, a darkness made especially for him. The rumpled, damp sheet enveloping his sweat-covered torso was pushed away. Peering at him from a crack in the window shade was a small trickle of light from outside street lighting. His damp body, clenched fists, and beaded drops of sweat spoke of the stygian shadows that gripped him moments earlier in a nightmarish dream. Part of him was still hinged to that dream in the other world, a world that seemed more real when he was there than the one he was reentering—the one he lived and worked in. He lay quiet, gave reason and emotion time to finish their battle. Reason would always win, but emotion tied to his nightmare tonight would die a slow death. How could he easily forget the vivid scenes of an infant crawling about looking for someone in the midst of a threshing crowd of mothers, fathers, and children, hearing gunfire, screaming, yelling and crying, watching the child crawl over dying and bleeding bodies that lay in the street. Worst of all was the scene of dead children, children the little toddler knew as playmates.

The nightmare never changed. It was the same visual script each time and always arrived at the same hour of the night as if it were programmed as a special kind of torment. Tonight's dream was a repeat performance—one he'd seen so many times he'd lost count. It was a dream that left disturbing memories throughout the day.

In the darkened room, he forced himself to roll over in his bed wishing he could see something besides another blank wall of darkness. It had been another night of déjà vu horror. He looked at his watch—was four o'clock. The dream was right on schedule. The rapid beat of his heart spoke of the mental images that had performed on the stage of his emotions. In real life, seeing the same horror in a movie repeatedly would have a desensitizing effect and become boring, but not his dream. Every time it came his way, it was like a first-time event. He was a medical doctor in real life and knew this recurring dream had deep-seated meaning of something in his past.

The longer he lay in the quiet of darkness, the faster his mind traveled over the events of his life. He was an only child, his father having passed some years ago. His mother had not remarried and had fulfilled her life with her only son. He knew there were mysteries surrounding his family, only because his mother rarely spoke of her life prior to his birth. She was a devoted mother who had always been kind, gentle, and caring. Though she lived a quiet, sequestered life with friends, she put him in the middle of everything that provided optimal social and educational growth. People on the outside, neighbors, friends, and visitors never thought of them as wealthy, only an average family that seemed to have everything they needed or wanted. Volunteers who worked with charities would often find their way to their door knowing she gave generous donations to worthy causes. His father had been out of his life for so many years he could not remember what he looked like. His mother rarely spoke of him, and when she did, it was always in a neutral vein, never praiseworthy or negative. He was always the center of his mother's life—everything revolved around him. He knew his father must have left her well off because of her standard of living, but she never talked about money, and his inquiry about her finances was forbidden. He was always told, "You can be assured that when I'm gone, you'll have plenty of money to live on." She saw to it that he wore the best clothes, went to the best schools, and played with the right kids. There was no escape from wondering why these ruminating thoughts about his home life always followed this recurring dream. They seemed to be associated in that one followed the other, like it was the second chapter. In his state of emotional fatigue, he was about to drop off to sleep when his alarm rang. It was six o'clock.

Hans forced his eyes open. Light was beginning to creep through his east window facing the sun. It was a welcomed site, the dawning of a new day, an exit from his horrifying chamber of darkness. He managed to raise himself to a sitting

9

position on the bed, throw his legs over, and make his way to his chest of drawers where hospital scrubs were stored. He always dressed for work in his scrubs at home—he hated changing at the hospital. By the time the coffee pot had finished its brew time and beeped, he was dressed, ready to make toast and rush off to his work at the hospital. He had just sat down when his phone rang.

The moment he heard the voice at the other end of the line, he knew something was wrong. It was the lady who assisted his mother with chores and cooking—his mother had been taken to the emergency room with a fast heart rate, dizziness, and shortness of breath. She had been in perfect health, having just passed her annual physical. Hans' world was shaking beneath him. For the first time since he was a small lad, he thought about what life would be like without his mother, a permanent state of not talking or visiting with her. In times like this, one couldn't control the paths the mind walked down. He knew the hospital employed one the best cardiologist around. In fact, they had gone out to lunch together on several occasions, and he knew he was on duty today.

Pushing his way through the crowded emergency room at the hospital, he saw his cardiologist friend with another doctor at his mother's bedside. They had her connected to a defibrillator machine, a device that delivered bursts of electrical shocks to the heart to change its erratic behavior. He took hold of his mother's cold hand, looked at the heart monitor showing that her heart had deteriorated to the ventricular fibrillation stage. His mother's heart was having chaotic electrical activity, was unconscious and dying.

With a controlled command in his voice, the cardiologist said, "Quick, apply the defibrillation shock!" He stood at the bedside holding his mother's limp, flaccid hand, feeling guilt having to release his grip so the device, which brought people back, wouldn't bleed off on him. He avoided speaking. Life and death procedures in the hospital required intense focus and concentration. His mother's body lifted itself with each sudden burst of electrical energy. He cringed, closed his eyes at the unbearable sight of what his mother was going through. The scene was that of his mother's body being desecrated, misused, and tortured as if being punished for wrongdoing. Only doctors with loved-ones in this condition would think such life-saving procedures as acts of brutality. Emotion and efficient medical treatment were separate entities inside a doctor's psyche and should never be symbiotic when pursuing the patient's best outcome. Hans looked at his mother in repose. He was not here as a doctor but as a son. His eyes fastened on the monitor—it was now showing a flat-lined heart. What would define life and death today, would be a machine, an object without emotion and feeling. Hans' eyes bounced back and forth from bed to monitor—it was still flat-lined. The doctor stopped applying the shock, looked at his friend, saying softly, "She's gone, Hans." He'd already exceeded the number of jolts customary, and Hans knew it. A solemn, dark veil covered Hans. The son lowered his head releasing his will and spirit to the demands of the cycle of life. It was the final part of the signature of mortality.

The living around his mother's bed said nothing. The hand he couldn't hold during the shock treatment was now lifted to his lips and kissed. Across from where he stood at his mother's bedside were two grim-faced doctors who had fought to save her life. The doctor assisting his cardiologist friend closed the curtain for complete privacy. Encased within the curtained wall were our people, three were doctors, each called to save life. Today they had failed. Defeat was written on their faces, but with Hans, something

11

came over him that gave strength. From down inside, a little boy of innocence emerged holding a golden chalice full of unforgettable memories, memories that now offered strength, strength to be alone, strength to face life without the one whose love and care nurtured him to become what he was. That golden chalice holding all those memories would stand by his side even as the one who created them had done in life.

It was a time that demanded reverence and quiet without interruption. Those within the curtained room saw him gently caress his mother's hand and arm, then lean forward to touch his cheek to his mother's, a mother who was beautiful in life and younger than her years. Tears fell from his eyes onto the hospital bed. She was gone, but he would never forget what she gave him in life: her love and a reason to live. The doctors wanted to leave so he could be alone but thought it best to stay. They were used to hospital sorrow, it was part of their work, but this was different, the deceased was the mother of their colleague. Like sentinels standing guard, they showed respect watching sorrow take its course as warm teardrops continued to fall from the face of a faithful, loyal son. Hans raised his head. Two faces showing eyes of sympathy spoke louder than words, followed by hands touching the bereaved. With vision but a blur, Hans could tell that the doctor standing alongside his friend was one of the new interns and that she wore a unique, special-looking, gold locket that had on its front the imprint of the Star of David. Their faces soon faded, but the lingering image of the locket remained. He had seen that locket somewhere before.

Chapter 2

In Memoriam

Hans was finishing his third year of medical internship at a hospital in the town where he grew up. At the time he signed on to begin a career in the medical field, his mother still lived in the family residence, and for convenience, he chose to rent a modest cottage near his place of work. Now with his mother gone, the family home sat alone in bleak darkness, and the burden of being its caretaker fell on him. It held everything that marked their lives together. He would keep it as she left it, except for those items that carried deep emotional connections. They would be packed and stored for safekeeping, and because she had already planned her entire funeral, he'd be free to do most of the packing and storage before the day he wished would never come.

Before going to his mother's home to pack her valuables and personal effects, he stopped at the hospital to arrange a leave of absence. Everyone who knew Hans and worked with him thought highly of his professional skills, that he was honest, demonstrated effervescent joviality, and mixed well in individual and group social functions.

Hans pulled up and stopped in front of his mother's home, and before getting out, the force of memory came at him like it was a piece of history that should be honored before continuing. While she lived, life was all about him; now that she was gone, it was all about her. Death had brought a twist of fate, good fate, like it was designed that way by the Creator. Hans remembered one of the many discussions they had together about his personal life and the goal of marriage and having children. His mother was never generous in giving opinionated advice, but on that day, she didn't hold back.

"Hans, when you are serious about marriage, let the one you've chosen believe you are as poor as a church mouse, and conduct yourself in a way that she will believe it."

"Are you saying women place more value on money than what a marriage is about—a relationship based on love?"

"Only some women, not all. If a woman marries you knowing you have nothing, then you'll know it's about you and not your assets. In saying this, I must be fair. There's the other side of that coin. Sometimes men marry women for the same reason."

Hans remembered the look on her face when talking about men marrying women for their money. Until now he never had the freedom to explore some of the "yank" moments, those times when a bump in the road happened but knew it was a place he should avoid.

Today, Hans was without his best friend. In life, he never had a father to look up to, and he never saw his mother date men. She was a beautiful woman, and many men were interested in her during his lifetime and would sometimes use him in their efforts to gain her attention.

Hans' still sat in the car looking at his mother's home. His world was upside down. His mind was left to wander about seeking answers to questions he'd raised during his lifetime. He knew there were private areas of his mother's life that had pain and intrigue, but it served to her advantage if left as such. His mother carried a burden, one that had a mission attached to it, as if she were here in life for a special reason. Death had removed boundaries and restrictions. Hans now had the freedom to roam the open field and pursue unanswered questions. His mother often mentioned that someday there would be no need to ask questions, that there was coming a time when she would be free of something she carried around inside, something mysterious and foreboding. When alluding to this subject, it was usually when she was reading a book, magazine, or newspaper about the war, the Holocaust, or the politics surrounding it. He remembered during those times she would become morose and depressed, and it would take several days for her to rebound. Before his mother's death, he never felt the freedom to reflect on her attitude toward those events. Now, he was in a different world and a force of energy was pushing him forward to explore, to roam about the landscape. However, in this freedom, there could be unintended consequences: the matter of guilt. Was he desecrating the memory of his beloved late mother? Was he being disloyal, disrespectful? Death had a way of opening doors. It allowed the mind to explore, to seek answers to life's issues. But death could sometimes be a two-edged sword. It had the power to cut both ways. One side of the sword had already made its swath in the loss of his mother. In pursuit of unanswered questions, he now ran the risk of the sword's backstroke.

Hans silenced his memory, pushed his car door open, and made his way to the task in front of him. For three days, he acted and practiced the role of caretaker packaging and boxing items that were part of both of their lives. The fourth day brought the activity of the traditional public viewing at the site of the mortuary. It was there he met and greeted his mother's many friends and acquaintances. Among those in attendance were her contemporaries before his time. It was those he didn't know that awakened the voices he'd put to rest about his devoted mother.

The evening following the viewing was long and sleepless. Even Epicurean food dishes neighbors brought in went untouched. He had wished for relatives to show up on the day of the viewing, but none came. Two kinds of darkness ravaged Hans throughout the night: one came from nature, the other from the pain of hurt. Nature showed her other side at the break of early dawn. Music was heard from chirping birds preparing for the day's workload of building nests for those who would follow. It was a moving, descriptive message showing the cycle of life: some must go, others must stay and build the nests for those who would follow. Hans slipped off into a deep sleep.

―――――――――――――――――

It was one o'clock when Hans' neighbors saw a Limousine pull up and stop in front of his cottage. The driver got out, opened the rear door, and waited for his passenger.

The young doctor was not known as a connoisseur of modern fashion, but when he stepped outside in full view and began his walk toward the waiting transport, neighbors peering through cracks in window shades thought otherwise. The suit he wore showed an upscale, high-end pinstriped brand. What the onlookers didn't know was it was the only suit he owned, and that was at the insistence of his late mother who picked it out for him.

The formal attire Hans wore couldn't hide what his eyes and face were showing, a world in disorder with painful forces flashing memories of a beautiful life taken from him. Sitting by himself in the back seat of the limousine without friend or relative was a picture of where he was: alone without his best friend. It was she who supported his efforts of going to medical school, gladly providing funds to cover every expense. However, she practiced tough love. When home for summer vacation, she insisted he get a summer job to help defray college costs, and though he enjoyed his temporary jobs, he often wondered if it were really about money. She would give him birthday parties with his friends and cater lavishly. It was in those days of innocent partying his friends would give a look of askance at each other because of the appearance of opulence. His friends came from every walk of life, some unaccustomed to those kinds of parties. His mother had one major rule: alcohol was never served. He wasn't sure if it were because of her religious beliefs or she didn't want the liability it might bring. When the party was over, so was the show of sumptuous living. Everything she did was for his benefit.

Death had opened Hans' memory floodgate. Time seemed to stand still. It had been five long days since his mother passed. He had gone through her personal effects and moved them into a storage site. He wanted to secure everything that made her what she was to him—her clothes, jewelry, watches, and little collections from her travels. He especially wanted to put in safekeeping their letters of correspondence and the small things he sent her from time-to-time. After going through everything, he found nothing that indicated she had a history before he came along: no pictures, birth certificate, marriage license, not even a photo of his father. It was what he didn't find that left a gnawing cloud of mystery. He was at a loss about what to do. If something didn't develop soon, he would be forced to seek legal counsel.

His mother was turning out to be a paradox. She was close to him on all issues, was free to discuss any subject, except the matter of her estate. *The closest she got to it was when she made the statement that there existed a will, that she had finalized her funeral arrangements with the local mortuary and that an attorney would contact him upon her demise.* The word demise surfaced a memory in Hans. He remembered the way she looked when using the word "demise." It was a term meaning death, but it implied death with legalese attached to it. It was her face that mirrored something inside. It carried a look of comfort, an air of serenity as if she looked forward to the event. Hans held back tears thinking of her looking forward to her death.

When the Limousine door was opened for Hans in front of the church, both driver and the open door went unnoticed until the driver spoke.

"Sir, we have arrived at the chapel. Do you wish to get out?"

Hans lifted himself to a standing position alongside the driver. His eyes went toward the front entrance of the church where guests were gathering, then remembered last evening's public viewing at the mortuary where there were so many floral arrangements around the bier that there was hardly room to stand.

"Driver, how do you live and cope with all this sadness around you every day?"

Hans intended his question to be rhetorical, and after a long pause, he was impressed with an unexpected response.

"I think, Sir, that's a question for you to answer, you being a doctor and always around pain and suffering."

"You've given an incisive answer, but sometimes the heavier pain isn't physical. How is it that you know I'm a physician?"

"I take time to review the public records in our office. I like to know a little about those I drive about."

"And what do you know about my family?"

What had been animated dialogue fell into silence, the kind of silence that demanded a circumspect response.

"Very little, Sir, and what I do know is forbidden to be discussed. That's company protocol."

When Hans turned around to go up the walkway leading to the church, he thought of the doctor-patient confidentiality and gave a closing remark: "We both share the burden of that protocol."

The brief interaction with the driver had served to quiet the voices coming from his mother's shrouded mystery.

The driver closed the door to the limousine and watched Hans walk up the church steps holding a special flower in his left hand. For five long days, Hans had dreaded this hour, the hour he would give his final farewell to the only person of his life. Today, he wasn't his mother's grown son. Down inside he was a little boy, the little boy she dropped off at school and read to before bedtime, the little boy his mother brought to this church he was now entering.

At the entrance, Hans wondered why he was greeted by name by mortuary attendants who offered to usher him to the family pew. Why would they know his name when the mortuary office couldn't give him a record of the party making all the finer details of his mother's burial. Pushing the mystery of his mother into the background, he refused the ushers' offer and began the torturous journey toward his mother's resting vacated mortal form.

Standing in front of the open casket that held his mother, Hans leaned over with tears in his eyes and gave her his last kiss, placing her favorite flower in her folded hands resting over her heart. Kneeling down, he said a prayer like she always did for him when he was a child. His mind swirled with tangled helplessness, a smothered feeling of useless struggle in a vast ocean without a life vest and no one nearby to throw a lifeline. When he thought his world would end, he felt a hand touch his shoulder. He looked up in his kneeling position and saw his lifeline: it was Karl, his cardiologist friend.

Karl knew Hans had no family and needed someone to be at his side. Both sat together in the reserved family pew. Karl was Jewish, married with two small children.

Hans felt the void of having no relatives present. His mother had lots of friends, some of which had already entered the chapel—but no family, at least none close enough to read or hear about this very important religious cultural event. Parishioners who attended her church were making their way up to the front to greet Hans, extending expressions of condolences, but no relatives were among them.

The empty pews behind Hans kept filling up while the one he sat in had only one friend. He knew his friends from college years would be here along with hospital colleagues and would welcome any of them to sit in the family pew. The awkwardness of having no family kept him looking toward the front door. Eventually, two of his old college buddies who used to go home with him on weekends were seen signing the guest book. His mother had thought highly of them, and with Karl at his side, he made his way where they were standing at the front of the chapel, greeted them, and insisted they sit with him and Karl in the family pew. It was most appropriate—his mother considered them part of her family and had been generous to both by helping with their tuition cost at the university.

By the time the clergyman commenced the funeral liturgy the chapel had filled leaving standing room only. Someone had given the minister an armload of information about his mother, and with the cloud of grief blanketing the filled chapel, it was refreshing for Hans to hear the testimony of the record of his mother's life. She couldn't speak for herself, and if she could she would have edited much of what was told, not because of inaccuracy, but from self-imposed modesty. It was like a financial report at a board meeting. Without giving numbers, her record of charity giving extended to mission organizations in Africa, India, and other parts of the world. Her generosity was kept hidden from her son. This was a strange experience for Hans—others knowing more about her finances than her son. Something else hit him hard, which created further mystery: he wasn't aware until today that she had chosen to be put at rest in a section of the cemetery apart from where her late husband was buried. This was another matter never discussed with him. Loud bells sounded. Unfolding events made Hans wonder if there would be an end to this enigma.

The service was a traditional formal exercise of church liturgy conducted by the cleric of the church she attended. Hans' early religious instruction was encouraged by his mother with regular church attendance. As he grew older, his attendance and interest waned, but his mother never wavered, even involving herself in women's auxiliary activities.

Hans dreaded the minister's final prayer. It would turn the event into history, a history lacking continuity. Death had brought silence from the one he loved in life, but it had awakened, like a light in darkness, a picture puzzle with missing pieces. Those in attendance slowly filed by the casket, one-by-one. Some were close friends, others were acquaintances, but all came to pay their last respects to a person of pristine and noble character. When half the crowd had shuffled down the center aisle to reach the bier at the front of the sanctuary, a man being pushed in a wheelchair by a smart-looking, well-dressed lady caught Hans' full attention. The man was looking toward Hans, his face

21

showing a graying beard with a matching full head of hair, all in contrast to his wrinkled eyes set in a mask of age. His bright, blue eyes stared at Hans with a smile—the only smile he'd seen that day—a strange scene for a time of sadness. Hans' eyes followed him until they stopped in front of the casket where he stood to his feet. Using his wrinkled, feeble-looking hand, he placed a deep-red rose alongside his. Then to his surprise, the lady attending him took a similar rose and laid it beside the other two, and holding his mother's hand, he saw her weep like they had been close friends. *The red rose...that special flower...the old man and the lady had to know his mother in a close, personal way—the roses gave them away. Were they unknown relatives? Who were they?*

His thoughts of the man in the wheelchair were suddenly interrupted. A tall, beautiful woman with long-flowing, wavy, dark hair stepped up to where he was seated and greeted him with a handshake. At first, he thought her to be one of his mother's friends, but when he saw the gold locket about her neck with the Star of David, he realized she was the intern helping Karl at his mother's bedside. Doctors can sometimes look quite different in scrubs than in street clothes. She introduced herself, saying, "My name is Sheena Reznik, and I want to extend to you my condolences in the tragic loss of your mother. Everyone tells me she was a wonderful person, and from what the cleric said today only underscores her reputation." Before she walked away, she left him with the words, "I hope we can get better acquainted in view that we'll be working together in the hospital."

"I'll look forward to it," Hans said as she moved with the flow of the crowd. He was impressed by her warm, sincere condolences. *Lingering in his thoughts was her beauty, adorned with the gold necklace bearing the Star of David. He had seen that locket somewhere before.*

Karl rode with Hans to the cemetery for the final act of putting closure on death. Neither spoke. There were two groups at the gravesite: his mother's friends, and his. He looked for the old man in the wheelchair but was nowhere to be seen. Hans considered the bright spot in the whole group was the lovely new intern wearing her gold locket, and he took comfort in her acceptance of his stares.

At the close of the burial service, he told Karl and his friends who sat with him during the chapel service that he wanted to spend some time alone and would join them later at the post-internment luncheon. Though the luncheon was a customary event, he didn't look forward to it. Seated under the overhead canvass covering the burial site, the history of his mother rushed through him. Moments earlier the entire area had been filled with people. *Now seated by himself in front of the casket, he thought of the two homes his mother had vacated in death: one being where both lived throughout his life with all his childhood memories; the other was the one resting inside the casket in front of him, soon to be lowered and sealed until a later time when she would return and take up residence—the church called it the resurrection, his mother called it the blessed hope.*

Hans had the need to be alone with his thoughts, meditations, and personal history. Though he spent much of his time away from home during his college years, he and his mother remained close up to the day she passed. His meandering thoughts were distracted by the appearance of a dark vehicle moving slowly up behind the limousine waiting to carry its single passenger to the luncheon wake. The sun was bright and gentle, cool breezes were beginning to rustle the green leaves hanging in the trees overhead. It was the best nature had to offer as a balm to quell the pain of hurt. Hans had become mesmerized by nature's serenity of calmness. It was giving its best performance possible. Again, he was distracted by the dark car. A large man dressed in a black suit emerged from the vehicle, walked up to the driver of the limousine, then turned and came in his direction. He couldn't overlook his slumbering, rhythmic gait, which spoke of rigidity and purpose. As he came closer to the canopy that covered the burial site now emptied of people but shrouded with the air of grief, the man's eyes angled to the ground, making it appear he was showing respect. When he reached the large corner post of the overhead canopy, he stopped, leaned his heavy frame against it at the point of his shoulder, as if he needed to rest after his effort of reaching where he was. He stared at Hans, saying, "Please accept the condolences of those I represent."

Hans' eyes turned back to the sterile, dark scene of the casket in front of him.

"Who sent you to invade my privacy?"

"I'm not allowed to give you that information. I have been given the assignment of telling you that your life is about to be changed in a dramatic way."

He spoke the words with a slow, deliberate flow that carried the tone of a prophet announcing disaster. The heavy man pulled away from the pole he was leaning on, straightened himself up and scanned the perimeter of the well-manicured cemetery as if he expected someone he knew or was being cautious over someone who might come along he didn't know.

"Does this have to do with my mother's death?"

"It has everything to do with your mother's passing. Please don't ask what that change is because I don't know."

Hans was offended by the man's presence. His private space was being violated while grieving and saying farewell to his mother who would soon be lowered into the earth.

24

"You have a strange way of announcing whatever your message is. Of all days…today is my mother's funeral!"

"Yeah…I'm sorry…I told them it was the wrong day, but they said this was important. Look, I'm a private detective and was hired to come here and give you certain information."

"And what information might that be?"

"All you will get from me is what I've been asked to deliver…only a telephone number."

The overweight man struggled as he reached into his pocket and pulled out a card with a handwritten telephone number.

"You are to memorize this number and burn the card so no trail will be left. It is your contact number to reach a man who will meet with you about your mother's estate along with other matters. It's the other matters I'm told that will shake your life."

"When am I to make this call?"

"When you feel up to it, you are to call and leave a message. A party will return your call and arrange a time to meet. I have never met the big man who is requesting this meeting. When they need my service, they use intermediaries who pass on to me their directives. I've been told that you should know that all this has been ordered by your late mother."

Hans was reaching inside himself trying to find something that would help define what was going on. He found nothing.

"This sounds clandestine, totally out of the norm for my mother to make these kinds of arrangements. Why such secrecy?"

"All I can tell you is these people are law-abiding, upstanding people, and you will find this out when you meet with them. I must confess, I've been involved with a lot of crazy things in my line of work, but this one beats them all. I'd like to give you an answer to your question, but I can't. It would be interesting to return someday just to see how this turns out—it carries mystery and intrigue."

The bearer of tidings stepped closer. His rounded face and hanging jowls were as limp as the cold hand he extended to Hans. "I'm sorry about your loss; they told me your mother was a great lady and a smart business person."

My mother wasn't a business person, thought Hans. The man's veracity was now in question. The bereaved son watched the harbinger-carrier extricate himself from his assignment. He turned and faced the casket, paused for a moment to show respect, and without looking back, he continued his awkward stride back to his darkened car. He had accomplished his mission.

Hans was shaken from two worlds. It wasn't enough to lose his mother, but to have this person from who-knows-where to invade his space of grief with some cloak-and-dagger yarn was a bit too much to handle in one day. He noticed the maintenance truck coming in his direction to attend to the finality of the burial. Not wanting to have as the last memory the sight of the casket being lowered into the earth, he began a slow walk to the limousine waiting to take him back to town. Hans had pulled enough death sheets over faces in the hospital to know that mortality always gave birth to another form of pain some called grief.

The parking lot at the reception hall was full. He was late arriving because of lingering at the gravesite and the arrival of the uninvited guest. Once through the door, he was met by ushers who escorted him to a special table where his friends were seated. Something inside Hans lurched with excitement: Karl had taken the effort to invite the beautiful Sheena to sit at his table. He sat between her and Karl.

Everyone at the event seemed to know each other better than they knew him. A large picture of his mother was the centerpiece of a collage commemorating her life, the part of her life with Hans. There were no photos of his father, or pictures of his mother prior to his birth. He wondered if they had been lost during the war, or was this his mother's wish? She always told him her funeral had been put in the hands of someone who would take care of everything through the local mortuary. He had been in a state of numbness from the beginning of this ordeal and was now awakening to the experience he had with the private detective at the gravesite. Was the heavy man real, or had he dreamed what memory was telling him? If he didn't know better, he'd say someone was playing a joke on him—it seemed so sinister. He was saved from further musings on the matter when the food server arrived to take orders.

The catering agency provided no written menu, and guests had to remember what the server was saying when going over the selections available. After a couple of orders were taken, Sheena submitted a question: "Do you have anything kosher?"

"We do," replied the server. "It's an order overseen and prepared by those who keep kosher."

Hans looked at Karl. "Karl, you're Jewish, do you practice kosher?"

"I'm Jewish, but I don't follow the dietary rules. I have bacon at least once a week, and the Rabbi knows it."

Up to this point, Sheena had been a wallflower, but she knew how to deliver a punch line, saying, "And the reason the Rabbi knows is that he supplies the Rabbi from his own source."

Chuckles came from those at the table. Even Karl enjoyed the jest. Something rippled inside Hans that gave heightened interest in the new young intern seated beside him. He'd been around a lot of beautiful women before, dated them, ran after them, and even ran from them. She carried a certain clean, wholesome persona, different from most attractive women he'd known. Her beauty was compounded by what she was inside. She reminded him of his mother—she was like that. Thinking about his mother pushed him back into the familiar rut of ruminating over the unknown part of her life. Growing up at home, she gave him so much emotional security he never thought about unanswered questions. However, when away at college he often reflected on these matters but never had the freedom to ask questions knowing it would upset her. Only on one occasion when he was fifteen-years-old did she open that door, and it was but a tiny crack.

"Mother, why don't you ever talk about yourself when you were young?" He remembered seeing tears come to her eyes as she walked over, looked him in the face holding his cheeks between her soft, delicate hands, saying, "I don't have the strength to do that—they're too sad." From that moment on, he never opened that door—it was the look in her eyes he never wanted to see again.

As the day wore on, Hans found in himself the strength to avoid self-introspection and joined in the celebration of the life who made others better. However, he noticed the crowd was becoming more party-like. Some even brought adult drinks and was passing them around. He knew everything was his mother's money, except the alcohol. Someone had taken the initiative to liven the celebration.

Hans wasn't much for crowds; he preferred close, individual connections. Outside his role as a doctor, he carried the look and sound of a compassionate counselor who listened rather than give advice. Advice was reserved for his patients, sometimes leaving him almost friendless among those he was qualified to help most. He always saw individual health care as a package of two parts: one was mechanical and treated with the highest standard of healthcare; the other had to do with the mind and emotions. If the latter were damaged, then the mechanical took a back seat. It was a lot like the vehicle and its operator. Of all the deaths, accidents, and injuries the percentage caused by mechanical failure was minuscule. In too many cases, the patient's mind and emotions needed fixing. This was why he almost went into psychiatry.

His analogy of patient care carried over to other compartments of his life. Beautiful women attempted to get close to him. They presented themselves as a complete package, but he saw them as a dichotomy, like a car and its driver. Though they had multiple parts to the whole unit, it was the driver part, the real self, that chose destination that interested him. When they found this out, interest waned. This part of his nature could be credited to his late mother who had made an environmental transfer of influence by the way she modeled her values and principles in the driver-part of her life, and his mother was known as a very beautiful woman.

Hans and Sheena engaged in small talk at first, then, moved into common subjects of interest. Sheena found Hans could be entertaining and knowledgeable. She wanted to hear about his background and home life.

"Hans, will you show me the memorial collage of your mother?"

"I'd be glad to." Turning to others seated at their table, he said, "Karl, if you and the others here at our table will excuse us, Sheena and I will be right back."

They stood in front of a professionally created outlay of large photos giving a timeline from the time Hans was a child down to recent events of this year. There were pictures of his mother with friends, award ceremonies honoring her for her service on the school board, community activities, and sponsorship of missions. The pictorial scene was as much about her son as it was of her. In all the photos on display, none showed her late husband.

"Your mother was a beautiful woman," Sheena remarked.

"Men thought so, but she never remarried after my father passed."

"I'm assuming by the photos that you were the only child?"

"I had no siblings."

"How old were you when your father passed?"

"My mother never talked about my father. I can't even remember what he looked like. Her world with him seemed sad and I never probed."

"I'm sorry, but I think I've crossed the line of propriety in asking these questions."

Sheena saw Hans pause at her statement. Showing deep reflection, he responded, saying, "It's comforting to talk to someone about a subject that was never discussed in my home, knowing if I brought it up it would sadden my mother. I never had the need to look into those matters because my mother gave me all the emotional reassurance and security a child needed. But I do have questions now that she is gone."

When they returned to their table, they found Karl and Hans' college friends still animated in conversation. After being seated, interaction resumed with normal banter and dialogue. Though Hans appeared as vocal and responsive as the others around the table, he couldn't keep his mind and eyes off the beautiful, unique-looking woman seated beside him. Her chiseled features with dark wavy hair against her light skin coloring gave a compelling appearance. Something else impressed Hans about her. She wore no makeup, and her clothes were plain but carried a persuasive inner wholesome beauty that had a commanding appeal.

Unknown to Hans, she was attracted to him as most beautiful women were, but her interest was on a different level. Hans carried pain, pain beyond the grief of losing his mother. This was what others overlooked, a sealed chamber of desert silence, something hidden that even Hans couldn't uncover. To Hans benefit, Sheena was gifted. She possessed intuition having worked with children who carried physical symptoms caused by underlying issues.

Underneath their overt joviality, laughs, smiles and small talk, Hans came to feel that she was seeing something inside him others overlooked, that she was pushing herself into areas of his life where other women failed to go. As a doctor, he could sometimes just look at a patient and predict what much of the lab tests would reveal. He detected Sheena was another kind of doctor, one who was creating a lab-test prediction about him. Her eyes spoke messages to that part of his nature never touched before. Now, it was her turn to separate the driver from its carriage.

Sheena knew social interaction provided opportunity where hidden parts of a person's life could be exposed without the knowledge of it being passed on. Tonight, the social functions in play were serving as a Rorschach inkblot test and were uncovering parts of the real Hans. *The longer Sheena was around Hans, the clearer certain things became,—he carried mysterious hurt beyond the loss of his mother.*

The afternoon cultural event of food and visiting ended. It was four o'clock, and most of the people had greeted Hans, extended condolences, and left. Those having already departed included Karl and his college friends. The mortuary's limo was no longer available, and Sheena saw Hans in need of a taxi.

"Hans, it appears you have a choice of requesting a taxi or accept my offer of giving you a lift in my vehicle."

"I'd much rather sit alongside a colleague discussing matters of medicine than in the backseat of a cold taxi."

He was pleased she offered. She was pleased he accepted, even though she knew medicine wouldn't be discussed. They walked together crossing the street to a public parking facility where they passed shiny, late-model cars before reaching hers. He was surprised when she stopped at a vehicle that looked ten years older than the others nearby. It carried the look of dull paint, worn tires, and small dents on the fenders.

The old car reminded him of the time before going off to college. His mother had told him if he worked the summer, she would help him buy a car. He got a job for the summer, saved his money, and when it came time to leave for school, he and his mother went to a used car lot to purchase a vehicle. All the vehicles he saw on the lot looked like Sheena's. Then to his surprise, his mother took him to a new car dealer, and together they picked a new one off the floor. His mother wanted him to know what the real world was like, and from then on, providing he worked the summer months, she bought him a new car every two years.

"Hans, you don't object to riding in my old car, do you?"

"Of course not—looks just like the one I once was going to buy."

"A status symbol is important to a lot of people, even doctors, but I try to live within my budget."

Hans assumed the well-used vehicle she drove probably reflected the size of her school loan. He did what he sometimes was known for: he asked an impertinent question.

"Sheena, do you owe much on your school bill? Tuition cost is out of sight!"

Before he could put a soft touch on the invasion of her privacy, she shot back, "I owe nothing. My folks paid all my expense in full at the beginning of every school year." It left him embarrassed and withdrawn. However, he did wonder about the old car she drove.

He thanked her when he was dropped off in front of his home, making a mental note that the only piece of jewelry she wore was the gold locket with the Star of David. He knew she was Jewish, not because of the locket, but by her ordering kosher food.

Hans opened the door to his home feeling calm and serene. He was away from the crowds and alone. He could always tolerate being by himself as long as he was accompanied with a good book. One of his oft-repeated sayings was, "Being alone was not loneliness." But now he was alone inside a long tunnel of darkness without his best friend in life, and it remained to be seen if the two terms, alone and loneliness, would come to mean the same thing. Then coming to him was the flash memory of his recurring dream: the little boy running, crawling through the mayhem of shootings, killings, screams, and crying. Nobody could have been lonelier than that lad. He wished for a night's sleep without the dream.

Chapter 3

The Lawyer

It was Monday morning, two days after the funeral and Han's world was still spinning over the strange events of his mother's passing. He followed the instructions of the mystery man at the gravesite and dialed the phone number given him. The formal closure of his mother's passing had been finalized, but legal and emotional trauma lingered, all cloaked with mystifying strangeness. Hans had not memorized the phone number as suggested and considered his experience with the messenger an over-dramatized stage performance for the benefit of someone besides him. Earlier, Sheena had called offering expressions of goodwill in his tragic loss with the conversation leading to Hans inviting her to dinner.

The phone continued to ring, and Hans was about to hang up when it activated an answering machine: "Please leave your number." *Well, Hans thought, that measures up to what he was told by the stranger at the gravesite*. He left his number, hung up, and went to get a book to read. No sooner had he sat that his phone rang.

"Hello."

A long pause ensued. Then a voice carrying a tone of authority asked, "With whom am I speaking?"

Hans, thinking it could be one of his patients, answered, "This is Doctor Baughman."

The voice was cryptic: "Last Friday, someone gave you the message to call the number you just dialed. I hope you have destroyed the number as recommended. This is a matter of your mother's passing and cannot be discussed on the phone. Someone will pick you up in thirty minutes and take you to an office where everything will be explained. You must avoid mentioning anything of this to anyone."

The voice abruptly stopped, the party hung up without giving Hans time to respond. He thought the experience was chapter two of what started two days ago at his mother's gravesite.

Thirty minutes after Hans hung up there was a knock on the door. He cracked the window curtain before opening the door. In front of his cottage was a large, dark vehicle parked in the street with a driver behind the wheel. When the door swung open, a tall, burly, head-shaven, bar-room-bouncer type stood in front of him in an imposing way. Without introducing himself, he gave his first order.

"Let's move quickly, they're waiting for us at the office."

He seized his arm and started walking almost lockstep toward the vehicle. At first, the man was thought to be a sergeant by the way he was giving orders. Now, he was performing like a jailer leading one back to his cell. It would be an embarrassment if the neighbors saw this. The scene would remind them of how the police looked and acted when they went to homes to remand someone who had an outstanding arrest warrant.

The man opened the door to the vehicle and with a light shove pushed him into the back seat. The driver quickly sped off with a speed dangerous to one's health. Now he sat next to a man in a speeding car who looked twice his size dressed in high-end clothes. The driver behind the wheel was the big man's opposite: short, with a rumpled look and a full head of hair. His power was not in size but from the controls in his grasp. Hans said nothing, and after three minutes on the roadway, the dour, ruffian-looking man seated at his side softened, as if some kind of danger had passed.

"I hope you understand, Doctor Baughman, we're on a mission to deliver you to a party whose intent is to keep your meeting confidential."

Talking like this made the oversized man look more human. He continued.

"I'm usually assigned to more stealth operations in information gathering with overseas assignments. I know we came off pretty rough-looking, but in our business, crazy things happen to innocent people."

"Do you work for the government?"

"Far from it! I can't tell you who hires me, but I can tell you I'm off the books, well paid, and attend to keeping bad guys from hurting and disrupting our legitimate business interest around the world. I'll say no more and answer no questions. What you've heard from me is an introduction to the main meeting where you're being taken. What the general public doesn't know is that there's a sinister underworld activity attempting to disrupt the flow of our money to the causes we support."

Hans didn't know what the big man was talking about. Right now, his concerns were around his mother's legal affairs.

Before the Burley-One started his dissertation, Hans thought him to be a Neanderthal, not a homo sapiens—his own kind. But his prejudice was declared unwarranted after listening to him articulate his mission. One might look like a Neanderthal, but looks alone weren't a determinant on intelligence.

No sooner had the Big-One finished talking that the driver pulled into an underground garage with little lighting.

Someone near the elevator was coordinating his arrival motioning where to stop. The outside spotter opened the side door.

From inside the vehicle, Hans felt a large hand pushing against his back. "Let's go quick, Doctor, we mustn't linger."

The spotter now walked with the Big-One moving quickly to the elevator. Once inside with the door closed, they seemed to relax. When the elevator stopped, the Big-One left and returned two minutes later, saying, "Follow me, Doctor!"

Like an obedient, well-trained puppy, Hans was led from the elevator down a hall that led to a door over which was written: Board Room.

"You're on your own, Doctor. When you walk through that door, you'll meet the man who brought you here."

Mission accomplished, thought Hans. What an effort to go through! Now he suffered mental fatigue—worse than a long day at the hospital on his feet.

The big guy, with his massive frame and glistening baldhead, took hold of the door and opened it for the invited guest. Hans took two steps, stood in the middle of the threshold holding the door open. In front of him was a room above his grade level. He could see and feel what went on here. It echoed the aesthetic aura of opulence, power, and intrigue. In front of him was a long, beautifully finished table, around which were leather-padded armchairs, neatly in place. The walls held costly paintings, revealing the level of art appreciation of the people who frequented this room. The visitor's eyes fell upon a figure seated in a wheelchair at the end of the long table. Alongside the chair leaned a beautifully carved walking-cane lauding its carver's sculptural talent. It spoke of its user's emphasis on detail. The occupant in the chair, dressed in a dark, tailored suit, carried the octogenarian image with a well-worn, wrinkled face, a face showing wisdom, kindness, and generosity. His hair was full, making a younger man envious—and was white as snow.

Hans felt a strange mystery forming itself like eerie vapors over a dark, cold swamp. This man, the old man in the wheelchair in front of him with those deep-set, wrinkled blue eyes was the same man at his mother's funeral two days ago. Those furrowed hands that placed the red rose alongside his inside his mother's casket were the ones now resting on his lap. He had attended the funeral in disguise. His mother's death continued to cast long, foreboding shadows.

Hans released the door. It slowly returned and closed with the sound of an ominous click. Its loyal service in keeping what went on in this room private would continue with the new visitor. He stared at the old man until the face that was crowned with white hair gave a smile—a smile that confirmed his presence at his mother's funeral.

"Doctor Baughman, I presume!" The voice didn't match the frail, fading figure in senescent decline. It was robust-sounding, spoken with self-confidence. His eyes showed clarity and authority. Before Hans could reply he was given an order, but unlike the sergeant who brought him here, it was mellow, fatherly, and kind.

"Come, sit by this old man who won't be around much longer. I know a great deal about you. I have followed your development from childhood clear through medical school and residency at the hospital. I can give you facts about yourself that you've forgotten."

Hans was now taking short, slow-moving steps toward the old man at the other end of the table, holding onto each chair as he steadied himself in the unbalanced, strange world he found himself. A vortex of swirling confusion was portending to something ominous. He was never short on questions and answers, but now was bereft of answers and only had questions.

Again, before he could respond, the man sitting in the wheelchair continued. "My name is, Gustov Klein, a long-time friend of your late, beloved mother. In some ways, I have acted as a father to your mother. You have been brought here to begin the process of finalizing your mother's affairs. Before we continue, I will give you a brief overview of history you know nothing about, a history that makes your mother one of the noblest people who ever lived and walked this planet. What you're going to be told will inspire and crush you at the same time. Our journey together will take time and will come in several phases. I have been your mother's attorney all her life and had she outlived me others younger than I would attend to this business, all at the direction of her last will and testament to the minutest detail.

"I am at liberty to say the following in our first meeting because it involves the estate of your mother. Your mother's father was a very successful German industrialist. In the rise of Nazism, he got crossways with its leadership and knowing that government restrictions would bring disaster on his company, he quickly transferred much of his wealth out of the country to safe havens. Your mother, an only child, was enrolled in a university in England studying economics. No one knew the details, but both parents were killed, and those in the know believed it was carried out by orders coming from those high in the government.

"Your mother returned to Germany, took up life there, met an important military officer and married. You'll find more details of this and other matters in her handwritten letters. Your mother had studied economics, was savvy on how to invest her father's wealth. Using her aggressive marketing skills in a changing modern global economy, she became one of the wealthiest women in Europe. Her estate became so vast that she maintained a company of lawyers just to oversee and manage her business affairs.

"By now you are probably asking, 'Where does Gustov Klein fit into all this?' I was a friend to your mother's father, and after he and his wife were killed, I helped your mother in her loss and stayed by her side as a family friend, and am now the one who heads up that company of lawyers that manages her wealth.

"Now, for the bombshell of your life: you are the sole heir of all her estate and are one of the wealthiest men in Europe. This massive office building you entered today takes up a city block with its four stories and is the central hub of your mother's vast enterprise. In terms of our relationship, I am now technically your employee."

Hans said nothing. The wrinkled face of the old man holding deep blue eyes faded in-and-out. Was this another form of his frequent nightmarish dream about the little boy. He felt detached from his known world. How could this be...his mother being one of great wealth? He knew his mother carried a burden of mystery but nothing like this. He never suspected this...they were an average family...lived a middle-class lifestyle. He worked at odd jobs to go camping, she gave him allowances for doing chores around the home, yet she was wealthy, and now this man was telling him he had inherited everything and was one of great wealth.

Hans' catatonia left him stunned, speechless, and silent. His eyes stared at one of the expensive paintings hanging on the wall, but it wasn't the painting he saw, it was something beyond, something in his mind, a picture of a different sort— one that spoke of the mystery of his mother. He had a question that begged an answer. He struggled to reach across the chasm that separated his known world from the one the old man was offering. The young doctor's eyes were now staring down at the table in front of him when he asked, "Mr. Klein, why did my mother choose to hide her financial world from me and live a modest lifestyle?"

The old man looked at the young doctor. Hans saw a generous, warm smile spread across the lawyer's face. Riveted in momentary silence, two people stared at each other from two different worlds. Both had needs: one had the need for answers, the other, the release of a burden he'd carried for his mother.

"You have asked an important question, and I will take time to answer it along with others I know you have. After the war, your mother became an ardent supporter of Zionism. She used her wealth to support the return of Jews to the land of their ancestry. At the same time, underground Nazis inside and outside Germany began to threaten those who used wealth to support the newly formed state of Israel.

"Knowing this would endanger your life, your mother and I agreed that I would become the front image of her vast enterprise. I would be the chairman, the figurehead of her company, and she would be an invisible party. From that point on, we were never seen together in public, and I learned to live in a walled compound under tight security. This gave your mother the freedom to live a normal life with her son. Your mother and I both felt that God had placed destiny on us for the good of Israel. Your mother had two major goals in life: support Israel with her wealth and maximize her son's best outcome by living a middle-class lifestyle.

"The reason you were brought here to my office under the cloak of secrecy was to keep you under the enemy's radar until everything is securely transferred to your control. Until then, I will continue to carry the position of chairman of Katharina Enterprises. This was your mother's verbal agreement with me. You have the power to interdict this, but it will not serve you or the company by doing so.

"Now you know why I attended your mother's funeral in disguise. I could never be seen in public with her or you. We always met in secrecy behind closed doors among loyal employees when dealing with major issues."

Hans' world was churning. Known for his cognitive powers, he now sat without the skill to control the flow of his impulses. Rational thought eluded him in his state of confusion. He could only sit and listen in a world turned upside down.

"Your mother designed and structured her final affairs when you were young, and it was her intent that you continue following her uncompleted tasks after she was gone, but she knew for you to do this you would first have to have a personal birth in finding yourself. For you to reach that point in your life, she has left you handwritten letters, letters I have never read, and to have done so would have desecrated her memory—they are for your eyes alone. They will tell you her story and will lead you through steps intended to make you into another person. After you have read and worked your way through them, I will address any further questions you may have.

"When we have concluded our meeting today, I will give you a key to a safe-deposit box that holds those letters. The originals are stored separately in the company's vault of which you will be given the key when everything is finalized. Inside that safe-deposit box you open today, there will be certain items of importance apart from the letters. Please understand that everything I'm telling you is at the direction of your mother, and if you are in question of it, I will show you her extensive and detailed directive.

"Your mother did her best to prepare you for a mission only you could do, and that it would be revealed to you when your time came. She could have had many suitors, even re-married, and had fulfillment in life in an honorable way. She was a very beautiful woman, this you very well know, but she chose the pathway she felt called to walk down. Some clergymen take the vow of celibacy, denial of having a companion in life to give more time and effort to God's work. God's work for your mother was you. For that work, she denied herself by living below her standard and not re-marrying. To her, this was God's call on her life. She knew if you lived in wealth, and everything that went with it, it would destroy something inside you and thwart the purpose of your personal destiny."

The lawyer handed Hans an envelope containing the key and authorization to collect the contents of the box, then looked sternly at him with his piercing blue eyes, saying, "I request you honor and respect what you find in that box by not opening it until it arrives with you in the privacy of your home. It is important you follow her written instructions inside the box. When you want to see me for further directives, you can call my private number written inside the envelope I gave you.

"Some of my staff will be contacting you about matters you need to know, and it will be up to you to move into the role your mother had before she left us. Your meeting with me today is designed to leave you confused and disoriented. A wise man will use these conditions as tools to build a bridge to go somewhere."

Hans had settled enough to communicate a question to the Old Man who had shaken his world. "I have one last question, Mr. Klein. Who was the smartly dressed lady with you at the funeral?" The old man looked away giving the appearance of not wanting to answer his question. He turned his face back toward Hans. "Sonje's her name, Miss Sonje Shuster, someone who knows everything there is to know about this company and works closely with me in management. She will be in charge of the staff who will be working with you to get your feet on the ground, and when you reach that point, you need to make her your Executive Administrative Secretary. She's a financial guru and acts as a consultant in our corporation."

The same people who picked Hans up dropped him off on a downtown busy street from which point he walked two blocks to the bank with authorization to collect the contents of the safe-deposit box. Hans was left void and empty. He had entered a strange new world of wealth, all because his mother trusted and believed in him to do the right thing with it. He felt awkward, yet unmoved by it all, except for the heavy burden of responsibility he would carry managing it. He would still live in his modestly rented home until he finished residency. His mother's values were already moving his thoughts about life and money. He remembered he had a dinner date with Sheena.

The bank was a typical bank. Hans stood in line holding the envelope containing the authorization to access the box along with its key. When it was his turn to be served, he took the key from the envelope and handed the authorization to the bank teller without looking at it. She looked it over carefully, glanced up at Hans, then walked over to her department manager and handed her the form. After reviewing it, she proceeded to take it into the office of the senior manager. He noticed a group gathering together whispering and glancing in the direction where he stood. When the senior manager came out of his office, he appeared nervous, walked over where he waited.

"Mr. Baughman, would you kindly come to my office?"

Hans assumed something was wrong with the authorization form. After entering the office, the manager shut the door, still showing a state of uneasiness.

"It's highly irregular for someone of your importance to come into the bank and personally make this kind of request."

Hans had been confused about everything today from the moment he made his first phone call, and now it continued here in the bank.

"Would you kindly explain yourself, Sir?"

"Mr. Baughman, this affidavit is from the chairman of the Bank Board, and he indicates you are the new owner of the bank."

Hans sat in a cubicle behind a private, closed door. It was the place where customers viewed what they kept in rented boxes. In front of him sat the box the lawyer said contained copies of letters his mother had written. It seemed to be staring at him in a haunting way like destiny was contained inside, and when he remembered the somber tone of the words of the lawyer about opening the box in the privacy of his home, a dark, foreboding cloud settled around him.

Thoughts rushed through his mind about the number of times his mother had come into this same cubicle to place personal things inside this box for her son. Her fingerprints were literally on this box. She was a whiz in business and knew how to utilize people, but when it came to matters about her son, she always left her own fingerprints by doing everything herself. When driving him to school, she could have hired a driver, or the times when he needed help with his homework, hired a tutor. *It was her fingerprints on his life and not her wealth that made her different from those who used wealth to replace the live touch. He wondered if he would have the strength and will to open the box.* He called for the manager.

"Find me something this box will fit in, then call a taxi—I'm taking it home with me!"

Chapter 4

The Letter

Hans looked at the safe deposit box resting on the seat alongside him. Since his mother's passing, everything seemed to come wrapped in ambiguity. He was still reeling from the news that his mother was a person of wealth and had left everything to him. Why the box? If she had something to say, why couldn't she have said it in life? He was close to his mother—she was all he had, yet the mystery continued.

The longer he sat with the box in the taxi, the bigger it grew. It was fear that increased its size, fear of the unknown, fear of finding another part of his mother's world he knew nothing about. He was still reeling from his meeting with the old man in the wheelchair, and now it was a box doing the bidding of his late mother. Relief came when he arrived home and placed the box inside his bedroom closet. He reminded himself he had a dinner engagement with Sheena.

Hans stopped in the driveway of Sheena's rented residence. The neighborhood showed signs of age but was clean and quiet. She had been watching for him and came out as soon as he stopped. He got out and politely stood by the car to open the door for her. Sheena never wore makeup, and Hans never noticed because of her natural coloring. Her skin was smooth, showing rosy cheeks and striking ruby-red lips, all the physical qualities women helped along with the use of cosmetics. Other women dressing in this manner lacking her qualities would come up short.

When Sheena saw the new high-end car he drove, she made a comment about it, saying, "Hans, you're spoiling me with this fancy new car—it's gorgeous! It looks brand new—when did you buy it?"

He was opening the door for her and was about to answer when he remembered what his mother once said: "If you are ever interested in a woman for marriage, let her think you are as poor as a church mouse—it will then be about you and not the money." At this point, Sheena was certainly the marriage type, then, he remembered the old vehicle she drove when he rode with her a couple of days ago. If he conformed to her standard, he would walk on ground he'd never been.

"Oh, this is not my car! A friend of mine loaned it to me for a couple of weeks until my mother's affairs are settled."

"I'm glad you told me that—it puts us more on the same footing if you know what I mean."

Wow, he thought, I missed that one by a hair. Integrity was his code word, and it didn't go down well lying about the car, but it was for a good cause. To continue this ruse, he would be forced to live in two worlds: the one of wealth his mother left him, and the one he had given birth to tonight, which meant he'd have to trade in his new car for an older one.

When Sheena got in the car her eyes scanned the interior. Special attention was paid to the leather seats, the sleek new technology, and its smell of newness. They were now on the roadway, and Hans noticed that the beautiful, new intern suddenly turned quiet, forcing him to carry the conversation. Then, like it was a well-thought-out chess move to establish her territory, she asked Hans, "Were you a happy child growing up?"

Where did that question come from? He knew she was a resident pediatrician, her specialty being children, but where was she going with this? At least he could be honest with the answer. What he didn't know was she asked this question to every man who was successful enough to take her out. Tonight, it was an elementary step in understanding the man taking her to dinner.

"I had the happiest childhood that could be desired. My father died when I was very young and my mother filled in the gaps. She put me above self-interest, attended every sports and school activity I was in, listened while I practiced the violin, read to me at night and had prayer before I went to bed—just some of her qualities as a mother."

She saw he was comfortable talking about his childhood memories, and for him to do so at this time of his loss probably helped in the grieving process, but he continued.

"My mother and I were very close; however, we parted ways in religion. She saw to it I received religious studies at her church, and I attended every Sunday with her until I was a sophomore in high school. I know it saddened her, but it didn't change her love for me. She always said I would return someday."

By this time, they'd reached the restaurant he'd selected, and because it was an upscale eatery, he thought she might think the cost wouldn't match the budget of a resident doctor. However, it was a one-time splurge, an acceptable choice.

After being seated, Sheena continued her probe. "What would you say the happiest event of your childhood was?"

He snapped a response almost before the question ended:

"When my mother read to me before I went to bed."

"What did she read?"

"Bible stories, fairy tales, and the classics written by Charles Dickens."

"And what would you say your saddest experience was?"

"Oh, you are probing here tonight, aren't you? Is there method in your madness?"

She gave a hearty laugh putting Hans at ease.

"Of course there's method and I hope no madness."

He was walking right through the door she had opened, the door leading to the inner part of his greater self, the part speaking of hidden memories and unsolved issues. *Oh, that he could have a transcendent enlightenment the next time his dream revisited. Perhaps he would then gain understanding and be released from its grip.*

With a serious look in his eyes, he said to the beautiful, plain woman who sat across the table from him: "Does it have to be something during my childhood?" He was rushing to tell his story about the little boy in his dream. Sheena read his eyes and saw something big coming, and wasn't sure she was prepared for it.

"Every adult has a child down inside, and I think you would qualify."

For fifteen minutes Hans graphically detailed his recurring dream about the little boy, how it left him limp, lifeless and depressed after he awakened. Sheena had tears in her eyes. He looked away showing embarrassment of telling someone for the first time his inner secret. Skilled hands that performed physical exams and sutured open wounds were now twitching. She watched him remove his nervous hands from the table and place them on his lap to hide his tenseness. Cold silence like a blanket of ice covered them.

What Hans told her about the little boy was now a story showing on his face. She saw a little of that on the day of his

50

mother's funeral—something children sometimes experience and display when inner conflicts aren't brought to a satisfactory conclusion. Hans wasn't a child, but there was a child inside him with the need of coming out. She was first to speak.

"Who does the little boy look like?"

The question bothered Hans. Reluctant to answer, he looked down at his hands now resting on his lap, lifted them back to the tabletop. He wanted to avoid answering Sheena, but he had come too far. He feared unknown consequences, but the woman he was with had built a bridge and was now beckoning him to cross. His answer was slow and deliberate.

"The little boy in the dream…he looks like me, even has blond hair."

Sheena had forced him to acknowledge something he had refused to accept. Something strange happened between them at that moment, and from that point on she would own part of Hans' private life. What she had done was to treat Hans as she would a child who was undergoing bad dreams: she listened and helped fill in gaps with pertinent questions. Then she remembered somewhere in unpacked boxes she had a couple of books on dreams, required reading in her course of study.

"Hans, I have two books on dreams, books I was assigned to read in my study of pediatrics. They are somewhere in unpacked boxes. If I can find them, I'll drop them off on my way to the hospital tomorrow morning."

"Great, I'll give them a read! I'm planning on being home all day."

When Hans stopped in front of Sheena's modest rental, they found themselves recovered from the seriousness of the evening. She wanted to invite him in but thought it too brash. They'd known each other only a few days. She chose to compromise with a certain message as a caption for the evening.

"If it weren't so late, I'd invite you in. Thank you for such a delightful evening! Enjoy while you can this fancy vehicle."

Oh no, thought Hans, why did she have to mention his new car again? He continued ruminating. This lady certainly covers all her bases.

When Hans drove to his cottage he knew he had been smitten by a woman he couldn't let go of, and in pursuit of her, he knew there could be turbulent waters ahead. His mother had made them worlds apart with his inherited wealth, and though he would accept her into that world, would she be willing to go? Sheena was much like his mother who had wealth but chose not to live in it for the sake of her son. At least this was what he saw at this point, but human nature being what it was could make people appear to be something they weren't. *If Sheena found her way into his life, would it come about because of who he was or because of his wealth? Only time would tell.*

In going to bed for the night, he passed by the closet where he stored the safe-deposit box, opened the door for a final look before retiring. There was something about that box he dreaded. It wasn't his mother's estate he inherited that brought the Sandman that gave sweet dreams that night, it was the memory of the evening out with the most beautiful, plain woman he'd ever met.

It was seven o'clock. Hans was lying in bed staring at the ceiling, allowing thoughts of being with a beautiful woman the day before to compete with what awaited him in the closet. He knew he was avoiding the box. Too much had come at him at once, and it all evoked memories of the way things used to be—like two days ago. What the lawyer had told him stood out in his mind. His mother was a survivor, a survivor after the tragic death of her mother and father. She must have believed in him, else he wouldn't be given the responsibility of her wealth, and knowing her, she had outlined directives in that box. He quickly got dressed, put on the coffee maker, and went to the closet. The box and its contents weighed about ten pounds and held legal-size folders. Access was by removing the top cover. Hans felt tension of the unexpected.

After removing the top cover, he saw a handwritten note in his mother's writing resting on top. It read:

Hans, my wonderful son,

You are reading this because God has chosen to take me to His abode, an event I prepared myself for through His Son, Jesus. I'm requesting that you go through this box reading the packets of materials in numerical order. After reading the first few pages, there may be the need to put it down for a day, two days, or a week before you resume. By now, you know you are the sole heir to my estate. The reason I have made you my sole heir is that you are my beloved and faithful son who has given me joy and happiness throughout our lives together. You have the energy, intelligence, and wisdom to carry on in my absence. God gave you to me for a special reason, and in time you will know the reason.

Your loving and devoted Mother

Hans took the top packet identified as number one and replaced the cover on the metal box. He was not prepared for what he read:

My Dearest, Hans,

I met the man known as your father in Munich. He was ten years my senior and was a high-ranking Army Officer. He swept me off my feet and married me more for my money than for his love. He was ambitious, would do anything for promotion and recognition. When the war broke out, he was promoted to the rank of general and sent to command a segment of the German forces in Romania in 1940. After arriving in the country, he made arrangements for me to have visiting rights. I chose to go hoping it might improve our troubled marriage. Several days after arriving, we took a tour to a site where he did a troop inspection with his commanding officers. I was along more for the show than anything else, and to break up the monotony of waiting, I took a stroll to the nearby village they called Ediniti. As I entered, I saw dead bodies of several hundred Jewish men, women, and children. The killings were carried out two hours earlier by the Romanian Nazi Iron Guard and German SS soldiers. The ghastly scene was more than I could bear. I fled, ran until I had no strength left to continue. Nauseous, I vomited and vomited, and needing to steady myself, I leaned up against a wagonload of loose hay to rest. From under the hay,

I heard the sound of a child whimpering. It was a sound of life, the life of innocence, and it was like the voice of God. I quickly removed the straw and saw a toddler with blond hair and blue eyes looking straight at me. When he saw me his whimpering stopped, and he gave me a smile only God could put on an innocent face. I took him up into my arms, and from that day on I never let go of him. I persuaded my husband to allow me to take the orphaned child back to Germany under the pretense he was ours. By now, you have probably figured out you were that little one-year-old Jewish baby I save from the Holocaust in Romania. Before your parents were killed, they hid you in the wagonload of hay, and I was the fortunate one to find you. I lived inart fear someone might come to know you were Jewish. Because of what I found out about the man I married, and his involvement with the Holocaust, I have tried to expunge the guilt of my marriage to him by using my wealth in helping the Jewish State of Israel.

You may be upset with me for not telling you sooner, and if you are, I understand. This is the first step in your journey to know the rest of the story. It may take you days, or even weeks to recover from this news. If I have ever done you wrong in your lifetime, it would only be this one thing of not telling you what you now know, and knowing you, when the pain settles you'll forgive me.

I have avoided discussing at length the man you were told was your father for a reason. He will be discussed later. The next packet you examine will contain the clothes you wore when I found you. It also contains a gold locket, which was around your little neck.

Your loving mother

Hans was a doctor trained to diagnose human physical conditions and prescribe treatment. Now, he was the patient with symptoms no doctor could cure. His tangible memory world was shattered. Like a skilled artist who works the empty canvass to create a masterpiece, Hans' adoptive mother bore that reputation with the son she saved from the Holocaust. The work of art in his life, performed by the skillful, purposeful hands of his mother was admired by everyone. He was the painting of a life she had created who now suffered damage.

His healing was beyond the reach of a doctor; it required a healer of a different order.

Hans sat on the edge of his bed, bent-over, with his face buried in the palms of his hands. The reality he knew anything about was upside down. *His mother was not his birth mother! He was adopted, saved on that dreadful day by a wealthy German lady. He wished he could weep, but his sensory world was gripped by dark shadows of numbness.* All that worked in him was memory, the memory of the little boy. Now, he knew the identity of that little child in his recurrent dream, the little boy with blond hair crawling about over dead and wounded bodies. However, his dream showed a different story of how he arrived at the wagon of hay. The German lady who became his mother in this life was wrong about how he reached the wagon. In his dream, someone dressed in white would always pick him up and carry him through menacing-looking soldiers with guns, place him in a wagon and cover him with hay.

For thirty minutes Hans sat in the same position. The phone rang and rang. It went unheard. Memory was his only working part, and it was channeled to the little boy. He stood up quickly remembering the details of the dream. In the dream, there was something around the little boy's neck, and his mother said that when she found him he wore a gold locket.

All of his senses were now functioning as he tore open packet two. Lifting from what was inside, he held in his hands the very clothes he had seen on the little boy in his dream. *"Where's the locket?"* he said aloud. Taking the packet, which contained the clothes, he ran his hand inside and felt something small with a chain attached to it. At the sight of a gold locket with a Star of David, he broke into a therapeutic downpour of tears.

The therapy of weeping sharpened Hans' senses. Someone was pounding on his front door. He wiped his face and eyes the best he could. Distraught with a strange weakness, he staggered toward the sound of the knocking. Unconcerned about his disheveled appearance, he opened the door with swollen, bloodshot eyes. It was Sheena holding two books.

Without saying anything, Hans stood like a statue, stiff and expressionless. The only life showing was his puffy, laser-fixed eyes peering at Sheena's gold locket with the Star of David. *It was identical to the one just found in the packet taken from the box.*

"Hans, I've been calling you—what's wrong? What's going on—your eyes, they're so red and swollen?"

With only the movement of his lips, he said, "Come."

She followed him to his bedroom, saw an unmade bed with an open metal box on the floor and handwritten papers on top of rumpled bedcovers. He reached over, picked up the letter he had read earlier and handed it to her, saying, "This was written by my mother." Hans walked over to the window and looked out while she read the letter.

As she read the letter, her eyes widened, her jaw dropped, and a grimace appeared causing wrinkled lines across her smooth face. She sat down on the bed and began reading the letter again, placing the palm of her right hand on her forehead. Tears were forming in her eyes from feeling the hurt and pain Hans was going through.

She slowly stood to her feet holding the letter in her hand, saying to herself, *he trusted me enough to see and read this private matter that has shaken his universe.*

Hans continued looking out the window into space. Sheena placed his mother's letter on the bed, was at a loss for words as she stepped quietly toward him. His pain and agony compelled her to place her hands on his back shoulders. Leaning close to one side of his face, he heard her say, "I'm so sorry, Hans."

The energy from her spoken words pushed Hans into a state of deep sobbing, compelling her to hold him tightly in her embrace, an embrace that spoke of strength and friendship.

Life experiences had taught her that bonding in relationships was a result of a series of events and experiences: conversation, going places, doing things, and even arguing together. These had one thing in common—the element of time; however, sometimes tragic events short-circuited time. Hans and Sheena were in the throes of one of those events.

He looked at the gold locket hanging around her neck. "I have something you need to see," he said, leading her over to the rumpled, unmade bed. He took the gold locket he wore when he was found in the wagon in Romania as an infant, placed it in Sheena's hand, saying, "This locket was found on my person when I was taken from Romania. It looks much like yours."

Sheena gasped at the sight of the locket. Momentary silence couldn't conceal her astonishment. A dropped jaw and widened eyes were like words spoken aloud—a look found on the face of a teenager without makeup and pretense. Hans wasn't used to seeing beauty and innocence shrouded with such simplicity. In her speechless state, he heard a soft, quiet whisper-like voice, saying, "They look just alike…you can't tell any difference between the two lockets." Then looking up at Hans with a raised, excited voice, said, "Look, Hans, they're made to hold small pictures...here, take mine, open it and you'll see my mother and father's inside."

He placed his hands near Sheena's beautifully formed neck, opened the front side of the locket. Inside were two small black-and-white photos.

"Perhaps there's something inside your locket—why don't you look?"

Hans had livened up and felt comfortable having Sheena around. He didn't know how she felt being in his bedroom with him, but being a doctor she went into men's rooms all the time at the hospital. He wondered if the locket would open after being in storage for so many years. Gold always looked gold. It had been in storage for twenty-five years and was as bright and shiny as the one around Sheena's neck. It opened easily, and inside were two black-and-white photos.

With Sheena's presence, a balanced world was returning, but upon seeing what was in the locket, the strange world of detachment returned—it was the pictures—the two people who might be his biological parents—he held them in his hands—his heart sank. His world was out of control. He belonged nowhere. The reality he knew anything about had become tangled with the revelation of everything foreign. It was another world, another time, like a phantasmagoric dream without a connection to reality. His newfound history had made him a non-person—he belonged nowhere—he was a wandering soul without a body to occupy. *Who was Hans Baughman, this German-reared man, adopted by a German lady who in her death was telling him he was the child of Jewish parents.*

Sheena grabbed one of his hands, saying, "Hans, these are pictures of your mother and father—oh, how wonderful!"

He heard Sheena's words, but memory spoke louder: the only parent he ever knew was the one who reared him. Now, he was looking at photos of two people who were his biological parents, yet they were foreign to him. However, though foreign, the thought of the anguish they suffered on that fateful Holocaust day riveted Hans.

A new dichotomous world awaited the young doctor. The letter he'd read from his mother had forced on him a seat in the Coliseum to watch two gladiators do battle for his soul. One came with being German and the embellishment of wealth, the other was from the Jewish world of the Holocaust. He felt like calling out to God for help...but he had left God and was now the Prodigal who had lost his way. Though he was rich, he was poor, though clothed in finery, yet he was naked. The journey back to his Father's home would be a long trek. He had traveled far, and it would take time to reach the place he once knew as home. He had never felt this alone in his lifetime.

Hans needed help. In desperation, he said to Sheena, "Can you stay with me until I settle down and find myself? I have no one to help, no family or relative, and I don't want my friends to know about this. You're the only person who can understand what I'm going through."

She saw eyes and a face of a man that once carried the look of strength and confidence now showing hurt, pain, and weakness. Sheena said nothing, picked up the phone, and called the hospital and told them she would not be in today.

"Hans, I want to help you any way I can, and probably the best way to start is talking. Tell me about yourself, who you are, your late mother, and even your friends. It's important you tell me about your inner feelings."

The longer he talked with Sheena, the calmer he became. Her presence served as a balm, a sedative that pushed voices coming from his mother's letter into distant shadows. Cognitive rational thought began to return, and Sheena shifted the conversation to include herself.

"Hans, you and I could be good friends. The letter you gave me to read from your mother tells me you are Jewish."

The letter...the letter from his mother, he let her read the letter in his state of confusion and disorientation! Now she knows! She knows his mother had wealth. Sheena saw him take the letter he handed her earlier. He held it a long time attempting to understand how she would interpret its overall meaning. Because she had wealth at the end of the war didn't mean she did twenty years later. The extent of her wealth wasn't defined in her letter. Perhaps he could convince her by giving her a tour of the middle-class home where he grew up. She must not know of his inherited wealth. If she were drawn to him, it had to be because of who he was and not his wealth.

After talking for two hours, Hans took action to convince Sheena he inherited little from his mother's estate.

"Sheena, I need to go to my mother's home to check for items that may have been overlooked. I would like you to go with me if you feel up to it."

Hans was smitten by Sheena before he met with the lawyer downtown about his mother's estate, so he knew his attraction to her wasn't out of needing someone to lean on from the shocking news of his mother's letter. He wanted and needed this woman in his life and would do anything to bring it about. Perhaps the convincing key that his mother wasn't wealthy would be to show her the home she owned and lived in. If she had an attraction for him, it had to be because of him and not his money.

"Of course, I'd love to see where your mother lived."

"You'll see it's not much, but it was a happy place growing up. I want to take my locket with me, so if we have time we can get a goldsmith to examine them and explain why they are so similar—do you mind? "

"It's a splendid idea."

"What's the history of the locket you always wear?"

"It was given to me by my mother," she said, "an heirloom in the family, it came from my grandmother who bought it at a faire from a well-known goldsmith, and I'm to leave it to a daughter someday."

"Do you have siblings?"

"No, I'm the only child."

"And your parents are both living?"

"Yes, they're still living."

"I'm sure they're a big support for you."

Hans noticed Sheena was beginning to withdraw and become reclusive. Something was disturbing her.

"Hans, if I'm to be a friend to you, I have to be frank and upfront in matters of my personal life."

He stopped everything that had internal motion going on when she made this statement. He knew she was speaking of interest she had in someone else.

"I wasn't completely honest with you the other day when I left the impression my father paid my medical school cost. It wasn't entirely true. You see, my parents were Holocaust survivors and qualified to participate in submitting my name for a scholarship and was accepted after sending in my academic records. The funds came to my father who had to countersign before they were paid to the university. I left the impression that the source of funds came only from my family."

Hans slowly released a held breath, saying, "You have remarkable qualities: you are honest, wholesome, and beautiful. I'm sure you don't have a lack of suitors knocking at your door."

"They knock, but I don't answer the door."

She either didn't know how or didn't wish to turn the same subject back to Hans, so she remained silent. She knew there were beautiful professional women at the hospital always making complementary remarks about the handsome unattached doctor, a normal thing when a group of unattached women got together. She thought he was all of that, but it was his reputation of character that first impressed her.

"I like your first two descriptive adjectives."

"I like the last one, the one about you being beautiful."

"You embarrass me, Hans."

He paused just long enough to deliver a stroke of intent. "Sheena, I will forever embarrass you by calling you beautiful."

"Am I blushing? I do that when I'm embarrassed."

"When you blush, it shows innocence—not many can lay claim to that."

"If I'm innocent, it's only because God has made me so."

When she used the word innocent, he remembered what his mother had written in the letter about what he looked like as an infant when she found him in the hay—*that he had the face of innocence. He was no longer innocent and no longer a child. Something told him he needed a new innocence, the kind of innocence Sheena had, the innocence he had as a child.*

"In what country did your parents survive the Holocaust?"

"They survived the Holocaust by getting out of the country where you were born—Romania."

Chapter 5

Gold Lockets

Hans pulled up and stopped in front of the house he had lived in for as long as he could remember. *It was now quiet, empty, and lifeless—gone was the spirit of the noble lady who plucked him from the burning embers of the Holocaust and made him her son. Why was he singled out to be saved while his birth parents pictured in the gold locket perished?*

Hans turned off the key, found it difficult to stay focused on the purpose of his mission. Childhood memories rushed through him. He was in front of the home where they were created, but today those memories were in conflict with another world vying for equal opportunity, the world he knew nothing about, yet he belonged to that world and its demands were being heard from the voices coming from photos inside the gold locket.

Caught in the dilemma of two competing forces, Hans found comfort in Sheena's calm, nurturing spirit. *She welcomed that dependency knowing that he had the need to thrive in the world he knew before he confronted the one he didn't know.*

Sheena reached over and touched his arm. "Hans, I think you were very fortunate to live in this house until you were an adult. You must have a lot of warm memories of your experiences being here so long?"

Hearing Sheena's voice, feeling her touch and looking at her calm, beautiful face brought a restored equilibrium. Hans was now following Sheena closely for her reactions to his mother's home, neighborhood, and anything associated with the standard of living in the community.

Sheena knew Hans needed diversion, a voice outside his inner psyche, something to soften and dilute the energies now competing with his known world. Perhaps, if he knew the story of her parents who were survivors of the Romanian Holocaust, it might be helpful.

"Hans, you and I have a lot in common in that our ancestry goes back to Romania. My mother and father went through the earlier part of the Holocaust inside the country, were always running, moving, and hiding until they went to Palestine in 1942 where I was born. My father was a gemologist and diamond cutter, worked at his trade on a kibbutz until 1950 when a German diamond company came to what was then the new nation of Israel looking for diamond cutters. My father took the well-paying job and moved us here to Germany. I was eight-years-old at the time, could speak Romanian, Hebrew, and Arabic. I learned German and English in this country and did well in school. When my father retired, he and my mother stayed here to be with me, their only child.

"Most of our relatives perished in the Romanian Holocaust. My folks never talk about it, and I know they carry a lot of sadness and emotional pain. Sometimes, when they get together with other Holocaust survivors, I think they discuss it together when no one else is around. My folks used wisdom and thought it best I be reared in an environment that offered the lowest level of stress possible. Also, the human psyche has a way of dealing with tragedy sometimes by sealing it off, as if it belonged to another world and another time."

"Hans, are you religious? How much does faith influence your life? The reason I'm asking you is that I am very religious. I am a Jew, but God has revealed himself to me in a special way through my parents.

"I said earlier my parents rarely spoke of their experiences in Romania, but they have frequently shared with me an experience they had when they were fleeing to the forest, running from the Romanian soldiers who were rounding up Jews to send them off to camps. While they were cowered together in the brush, they heard soldiers coming toward them yelling, pushing those they had found in front of them. My mother and father, on the ground wrapped in each other's arms, prayed. Expecting the inevitable, they saw a figure stand between them and the soldiers. The person had a white garment on that covered him down to his feet. He wore no shoes or sandals, his feet were bare, and each foot showed an ugly, fresh, deep wound. He remained standing until the soldiers passed, then He faded like a mist evaporating in the sun.

"This event changed their lives. They came to know He was Jesus, the Jewish Messiah, described and prophesied about in Isaiah fifty-three. Later, they became affiliated with other Jews who were called Messianic believers. They retained their Jewish heritage, practiced Judaism in the traditional manner, and believed He would return as King David's descendant to rule in Jerusalem.

"Hans, I said earlier I wanted to be upfront and honest with you, and this is why I am telling you these things. You asked me earlier about suitors knocking at my door. I don't answer the door because of my faith. I follow the same faith as my parents, a belief that Jesus was the Messiah and Savior of the world. Those I open my door to must have the faith I have. I want to be your friend, Hans, your special friend, and as much as I want it to be more, I can't open that door of my life."

Hans was respectful, said nothing, got out of the vehicle and opened the door for Sheena. A somber, silent atmosphere settled over them, and neither spoke as they made their way to the front door. Gone were the voices competing for Hans' attention from his other world. Once inside, He began his perfunctory activities of looking in drawers and opening closets, all as a show for Sheena.

Hans carried a downcast look, and Sheena knew she had set him back on his heels. Now she wondered if it could have waited considering his mental and emotional state. She was first to break the ice.

"This is a very nice home. What will happen to it? Will someone buy it, or will you be living in it?"

"I'm not sure yet. A lot will depend on where I choose to do my private practice. What do you think of this home? Do you think it's above or below the standard for a doctor?"

"Well, I suppose that would depend on the salary of the doctor. One certainly couldn't afford a home like this being an intern, but I suppose if a person had his own practice and all things were equal, this would be a home commensurate with a doctor's income."

Hans felt good about himself. He had lived in a home Sheena considered a middle-class residential home. He avoided going into the garage, knowing his mother's upscale vehicle was parked inside. If anything showed his mother living beyond a middle-class level, it would be her vehicle.

Now it was his time to feel guilt. She had been up-front with him about the matter of her medical tuition being paid from a scholarship rather than from her family, and he had just passed off an image that didn't represent his new financial status.

Hans and Sheena took time to check the yellow pages for goldsmiths who designed and built jewelry. One was found who specialized in restoration and duplication of existing pieces.

Both were excited as they entered the shop. When they told the manager of the shop what they wanted, an elderly man came from a back room who had been a long-time, skilled artisan. The lockets were placed on the counter.

"What can you tell us about these two lockets?" asked Hans.

The old gentleman took time to look the couple over. He turned around, went back into the shop, brought out a special optical viewer, and proceeded to examine the lockets one-at-a-time. When he finished looking over the exteriors, he opened both faces and continued looking at the workmanship in a slow, methodical way. When he finished, he closed the faces of the lockets and placed them on top of the counter.

"Now my friends, what is it you wish to know about these lockets?"

"Everything you can tell us," said Hans.

"Well, to start with, I will tell you they were made by the same person. The individual who made them was a very skilled goldsmith. Products like this are rarely found. One can tell by the workmanship on these lockets the artisan was never without work and probably was patronized by people of wealth. These lockets indicate they are a European product. Well, that's about it, unless you have further questions."

Hans called the goldsmith to one side, slipped him twenty Deutsche Marks knowing Sheena might consider the amount too exorbitant. They left the shop pleased with the information given them by the old tradesman. Now, they knew that the goldsmith who made the lockets was Jewish and had lived in Romania.

The day ended with Hans taking Sheena out to eat. Both had established markers for a relationship with each other—Sheena had verbalized hers—Hans had presented his in a more subtle way. One tried to convince the other he wasn't wealthy with the motive of being accepted for what he was rather than what he had; the other openly shared her wealth of a different order that permitted a relationship only to a defined point.

Hans had made the best effort possible and figured he was successful, but came to believe Sheena was more interested in her faith being her life's principal, which led him to think all his effort, might be in vain. However, they had common interest: both were Jewish, both were doctors, and each had a gold locket made in the country of their ancestry.

Sheena struggled through the evening. She had strong feelings for Hans, would always be a loyal friend, but unless he possessed the faith she had, she could only remain a friend. She retired for the evening wondering what their futures held.

Chapter 6

The Journey Back Home

After Sheena drove away from Hans' cottage, the voices from his strange world returned. He was now alone to face what he had pushed into the shadows throughout the day with Sheena. His confused identity rushed at him with swirling energy. Being with Sheena had masked and anesthetized what his mother told him in her letter. Now, he was alone and his new world was coming from the shadows re*gistering its full impact. His mother was not his mother; he was not German, but a Jew, born in Romania.* As an infant, he had been circumcised according to Jewish custom. This was why he wasn't allowed to swim with his friends and be part of a sleepover until after the Nazis were defeated. Now, he understood many things he had wondered about, and it was shaking his world.

Hans had the need to flee, run, and hide. He didn't belong anywhere. There was no living relative he could turn to. The ones who brought him into this world lay in a silent, unmarked, mass grave somewhere in Romania, and the person who became his mother was gone. The knowledge of who he was made him an alien in the world he knew anything about. There was the need to find himself in this new universe.

He threw blankets and an extra heavy coat in his car, locked his house, and drove away. He drove and drove, not knowing where he was going. The first night he slept in his car, went hiking in the highest mountains caring neither for the wonders of nature or the beauty his eyes beheld. Sometimes, in exhaustion he would fall asleep with his blanket under a tree, only to awaken in the middle of the night to see the stars peering at him overhead. In those times, he thought of Nebuchadnezzar's bout of mental illness living in the wild. He saw how trauma could make one break and lose connections with reality. All his medical training and experience could not assuage the forces pushing him into the dark abyss of untraveled dimensions that could leave him without strength to return. He and the disabled king of Babylon had something in common: both were handicapped and both were rich. The king's illness came as a curse from God—his from the knowledge of who he was. Because of the righteous lady who adopted him, he was among the wealthiest in Europe but the poorest and most empty inside.

He remembered Samuel Coleridge's classic poem, *The Rime of the Ancient Mariner,* the story of an old Mariner who shot the white albatross, the bird of good fortune. Everything good and favorable died with the bird and his curse was to sail the dark, bleak seas with the dead albatross tied to his neck. From the Mariner's ghostly experience, he uttered the legendary words:

> *Water, water, everywhere,*
> *And all the boards did shrink;*
> *Water, water, everywhere,*
> *Nor any drop to drink.*

He was now the Ancient Mariner in another kind of foreboding sea, created by the box he'd opened. It was his albatross. What the sea was to the Mariner, his inherited wealth was to him. It was everywhere, but none of it could give relief to the agony of his special kind of thirst.

Like the Ancient Mariner, Hans' psyche became detached from rational thought. Without a sense of time and space, he wondered about the countryside in need of being found. He drank water from flowing creeks, and sometimes hikers would see his haggard condition and give him something to eat. His beard grew, he lost weight, and his clothes became tattered and soiled. Gone was his quick-witted, ebullient nature. In his pursuit of finding himself, he had become lost. He possessed neither the mental nor the emotional capacity to care for or understand what was happening in the real world he had left.

The morning following Hans' departure, Sheena called to check on him. When there was no answer, she went to his cottage, found it locked and his car gone. She returned morning and evening, and on the third day began to make inquiries. She talked to the neighbors, called all the hospitals, and even checked with missing persons knowing he had no one to report him missing. She even visited the gravesite of his late mother several times thinking he might be there.

Hans had been gone eight days. After finishing her schedule at the hospital, she drove to his home as she had done that morning. His vehicle was still gone. Her heart sank knowing he was somewhere suffering from what he had found out about himself. He had no one. She cared for him deeply, even loved him, if one could use that term. It was something never felt before about anyone. But feelings could not supersede fact when it came to faith. The sun had just set when she arrived home. The heaviness of seeing Hans' vehicle gone from his driveway still hung over her.

Water was put on the stove for tea when the sound of a car was heard outside, then a knock at the door. She never answered unless she knew who it was. The curtain was moved slightly so she could view her driveway. Her heart leaped—it was Hans' vehicle in the driveway, but it was hardly recognizable with dirt covering it from top to bottom.

73

She ran to the door and pulled it open. She couldn't believe what she saw.

She said nothing; the gesture of her hand covering the mouth over her dropped jaw spoke everything. She hardly recognized him, unshaven, clothes tattered, and gaunt-looking. Hans spoke first.

"I'm sorry I never told you I was leaving."

"What has happened to you? Are you all right? Where have you been?"

Hans answered none of her questions. He had not been invited inside and still showed a lost look. He turned to walk away, but Sheena grabbed him by the arm, saying, "No, no, you can't go!" pulling him inside and shutting the door.

Once inside, his eyes roamed from wall to wall examining her small, humble dwelling. Her furnishings were substandard. He remembered her old car. Detachment showed on his face. Slurring his words, he muttered, "I'll buy you a new home, the nicest one in town—and a new car."

One week earlier, Hans had gone out of his way attempting to convince Sheena he had nothing. Now, he was flaunting his wealth.

Sheena thought him to be near delirium, speaking dribble, looking disconnected and confused.

"Hans, I don't want you to say anything. Give me your coat and sit down here on the sofa while I get you something to eat."

Hans was brought a glass of milk with a serving of cottage cheese and applesauce. He said nothing as he ate, just stared, and looked around.

"Your place is warm, Sheena, warm like you. The lady who raised me was warm like you."

"Do you resent your mother for not telling you sooner?"

"No. She was, and is, the only friend I ever had. Were it not for my memory, there would be no one."

Sheena took his hand. "I want to be your friend. I told you this before—I want to be your special friend."

Hans was so wiped out from mental and physical exhaustion he spoke with a slur.

"A special...friend...to me! I'm friendless. You should be a special friend to someone who has friends. I have everything most people desire, but no friends, no family."

"Listen to me, Hans, I want you to stop running from yourself, you are to go home and go right to bed. I know you have an extra key hidden somewhere outside your house. Give me the one on your key-ring and I'll let myself in tomorrow and cook you breakfast."

"How do I rate, having the most beautiful woman in the world come to my abode and fix me breakfast?"

Hans talked like he had been drinking, but she knew that wasn't the case, he was tired, exhausted, and needed rest.

"Hans, do you have a Bible?"

"Of course I have a Bible."

"Will you please promise me something? Tonight, before you go to bed, I want you to read chapter fifteen in the book of Luke, then pray to the God you knew as a child and ask Him to help you through your pain."

"I usually don't make promises like that."

"You will for me, won't you?"

He thought of his long journey he had taken from his Father's home. This lady who had come into his life was his mother speaking to him. "Sheena, I would do anything for you."

Like an energetic teenager, her face exuded the radiant show of pleasure.

"Hans, you're the best friend I've ever had, and I hope you will remain so."

Hans found the key to his front door and entered what he abandoned one week earlier. He looked in the mirror and saw what neglect had done to him. Sheena was on his mind and so was his promise.

He found his Bible, turned to Luke 15, and read the account of the Prodigal. It was a story that fit his description. He knew the story well from his youth. He had read it, heard it from others, and now he was the essence of the story itself, the man who left home to live in a far country. When he finished reading the account, he knelt, beginning his prayer with the Prodigal's words, "Father, forgive me for I have sinned...." Hans paused, reflected on his life, then, continued: "I have traveled into a far country and spent myself in the world of empty rational thought. My inner condition matches what the mirror shows. With your help, I'll turn my life around and be your son with honor."

He shaved, showered, and dressed in clean, fresh clothes. When he looked in the mirror again, he saw a new man. He not only looked new, he felt new inside. God had removed the curse of the Mariner's albatross from around his neck. His simple prayer had made him what Sheena was: innocent.

For the first time in a week, he slept a full night. What awakened him was not an alarm, but a noise in his kitchen and the smell of bacon and coffee. Then he vaguely remembered leaving his key with Sheena and her saying she would fix breakfast at his place. He was anxious to join her, but he lay pondering what happened to him last night. He had returned to two homes—one he'd been away from for a week—the other for several years. He never had a father in this life, but he found one in death, the death of self when he prayed, "Father forgive me...."

He didn't want to tell Sheena about his spiritual experience, his conversion. In doing so, she might think it a shallow whim just to get her attention. For now, he would be a friend, and let God be the one to tailor future events. He would still maintain a modest lifestyle and go no further than the halfway point in social connections with Sheena. He needed to complete his residency and work on the box that had issues to be settled. The lady who had saved him from the Holocaust was waiting for him—at the box.

Sheena was in the kitchen with an apron on cooking eggs and bacon. The table was set for two. She heard a door open and a voice say, "Good morning, Miss Beautiful!" A chill went up her spine. *Why did he affect her like this? Her thoughts were running wild; this was a new life experience for her. She must keep herself in check.* Then he appeared. She just stared. Hans was first to speak.

"Am I privileged or what?"

"What you are is a new man. Wow! You look a lot different than last night!"

"You look great yourself with that apron on. You're going to make someone a wonderful wife someday."

Hans was back to his old self, full of personality, teasing her emotions by the things he said. To keep control of herself, she had to act professionally.

"Hans, when will you be returning to the hospital? People are asking about you."

"In a couple of days, I'll be back giving everyone a bad time as usual."

"Everyone likes you; they think you're a good doctor."

"So are you, and a good cook to boot."

Sheena's returned smile was what he remembered the rest of the day as he commenced his journey to make life meaningful for himself and others.

Chapter 7

The Nazi Husband

Hans returned to work at the hospital to finish the last three weeks of his contract. He maintained a close connection with Sheena, calling her every two or three days to see how she was doing but never made overtures of getting together and was always careful to act professionally. She responded in kind, sometimes wishing it was as it had been in the beginning. It was important for Hans that his inherited wealth not become public knowledge. He could have easily broken his contract of service with the hospital, but that ran the risk of raising questions, which could imperil his confidentiality. Great effort had been taken by his mother to conceal her wealth from the public so she could live a private, middle-class lifestyle with her son. For Hans, it would be a challenge to continue that role in view of the vast amount of wealth being transferred from one party to another. However, the same battery of lawyers that attended to his mother's affairs would see to it that the new generation enjoyed the same outcome.

Hans felt comfortable working at the hospital. It was something he was trained to do, and he enjoyed his work. However, his interest was divided. Hanging over him was the responsibility of filling the empty seat at the helm of his mother's enterprise, a vast network he knew nothing about. Therefore, when Mr. Klein's associate called him from the central office, he welcomed the intervention.

"Doctor Hans, this is Sonje Shuster here at Katharina Enterprises. Mr. Klein has assigned me to lead a group to assist you in making the transition into the chairmanship of the vast holdings your mother has passed on to you. If you are going to be home within the hour, I would like to drop by your place, introduce myself, and leave some materials for you to study."

"I welcome your intervention," responded Hans, "and I'll be awaiting your arrival."

Thirty minutes later, Hans heard someone drive up and park in front of his cottage. He pushed the drawn curtain back slightly, saw the lady who was with Mr. Klein at his mother's funeral coming up the walkway leading to his front door, followed by a man carrying several boxes.

Before the doorbell rang, Hans opened the door, saying to his guest, "Come in Miss Shuster."

"Thank you, Doctor Hans." After crossing the threshold, she held out her hand for a friendly greeting. He made note that her manner of dress matched the exquisite look she carried when in attendance of his mother's funeral.

"Doctor Hans, we've brought by some materials for you to review before we come together to discuss them. We have a long journey in front of us and this batch of folders is only the beginning. The people who will be meeting with you will be from my office, and if you have questions they cannot answer, please contact me personally."

"Miss Shuster, how long have you been with Katharina Enterprises?

"I've been with the corporation twenty years."

"Did you know my mother?"

Unlike her snappy, quick statements and remarks up to this point, Hans saw a slow, calculated response.

"I knew your mother through Mr. Klein, and we loved her dearly...Doctor Hans, I must get back to my office. Please study these files carefully so when my office contacts you, you'll be in a position to move on for additional information."

The lady who had paid Hans a visit departed as briskly as when she arrived. He was impressed with her professional persona, and when he delved into the folders she left, he was further awed that they were largely reports put together bearing her own signature. Then he remembered the words of the old lawyer: *She was a financial guru, and acted as a consultant in the corporation.*

The days following Miss Shuster's visit, others came from her office delivering materials to be studied. Hans was giving himself a crash study of the company's holdings and operational systems when one evening he came across a sealed metal box labeled: Health Industries. Upon close examination, he found documents showing that Katharina Enterprises owned several large hospitals, one being the unit where he was doing his residency. He was sure it was by design, an unbelievable irony: he owned the hospital where he was doing his internship.

Because of the coming-and-going of visitors in fancy cars and dark suits, the neighbors expressed their concerns to Hans. To avoid attention, he rented an office building away from the neighborhood where he could meet with his tutors until his own office was built at the main complex downtown.

Hans came to realize when he was with Sheena, she gave something that was missing in his life, something that made his world broader, and more complete. Now, he struggled with the burden he inherited and its weight was compounded by his decision to keep that information from Sheena. *He*

81

wondered how his mother had done it. Where did she get the inner strength to carry on all by herself? The answer was to come in the packets awaiting his inspection.

It was the first two packets from the box that left Hans broken and devastated, but with the help and support of Sheena and his return to work, he was on the road to recovery. The first packets had involved him personally, but the unknown awaited him. Everything in the box was a process. Each packet required personal growth before moving on to the next one. His mother designed it that way knowing he would follow the outlined instructions.

Today, he would discover the cause that energized her life from morning until night, as well as the mission for which he had been groomed.

The box had become friendlier, easier to deal with—it wasn't about him—at least he hoped so. Fear and trepidation were gone, and though unknowns hung overhead, the old Hans was returning to take charge.

Hans was never a meticulous housekeeper. Sometimes he would leave an unmade bed, dishes in the sink, and open drawers. There were times when he came in from the hospital and wished there was someone waiting for him. This was his mother's strong point when he was still at home. She was always there somewhere in the home. How did she run a financial empire without him finding out about it?"

It was after he had eaten breakfast and briefly talked with Sheena he went to his bedroom and took from the closet what awaited his attention. After removing the top of the box, he looked at packet number three, opened it, and found five pages of copied handwritten notes on the same order as the previous packet. It showed his mother's handwriting with her clear, distinct, artistic style. She had a way of talking and writing where concepts were always succinct and well organized. She could type and had access to a thousand secretaries, but she wanted her son to have that personal grab of her presence with handwritten pages.

On top of her first page, she had scrawled in large letters the words, "MY HUSBAND." The words were underlined. This was the man passed off as his father. Today, he would learn about his dark side, the side he was never told about, the side that motivated his mother to go underground and join forces with a consortium whose goal it was to use their combined wealth to thwart and undo the havoc inflicted upon the Jews during the Holocaust. The handwritten letter read:

My dearest, Hans,

I met Eckhart Baughman in Munich, Germany in 1938. He was ten years my senior and held a high rank in the military. It was the worst decision of my life to commit myself to him in marriage. He was aware I had inherited wealth, wealth I'd greatly added to with good business investments in a changing economic world. Looking back, I'm sure he married me for that reason. He was materially and egocentrically ambitious and would do anything to improve his rank or establish himself in a higher social status. His activities often took him to inner-circle Nazi party gatherings, which he attended either by himself or with the accompaniment of another woman. His lack of integrity and the reports I had gathered from private investigations led me to hide my fortune beyond his reach. It was a fortune that came through my father. Life is strange. Even

83

after making wrong decisions, and I made a major one in my marriage, God allowed good things to happen. Your life was saved, and you became my son because of this marriage. It was only after the war that the world came to know millions of Jews had been killed in Europe, and your parents were among the first.

When I returned with you from Romania, I discussed with my husband why he allowed the Iron Guard and the SS to massacre the villagers, and by the time I finished the question, it was written on his face that he had sunk to the bottom of depravity. He had looked the other way because in doing so, he ingratiated himself to those above him.

I further learned he sank even lower by continuing the practice of looking the other way, allowing the specialized SS troops to slaughter thousands in the territories where he was stationed. He was so well regarded by the top leaders in the SS command that they made him the manager and controller of all the wealth taken from the Jews. He was responsible for converting gold and valuables into currency and hiding it in Swiss banks for the SS. From these, he skimmed a fortune for himself placing it in his own name.

I knew nothing of the fortune he had absconded with until after he died at the close of the war. It was then I found hidden secret documents showing a list of Swiss accounts. I was able to access and gain control of these accounts because at the time we were still legally married, though not living together. Divorce was considered earlier, but because of the war, it was put off—a blessing in disguise. At the end of the last page is a list of Swiss bank accounts held in your name. They total more than fifty million dollars, all of which belong to Jews who used to live somewhere in Europe. What you're reading now is a copy. The originals are stored in a safe-deposit box registered in your name in the bank you now own. Therefore, when you have studied these pages destroy them so the information will not be available to those who are constantly watching our movements. My lawyer, Gustov Klein, knows the extent of all my assets; however, this matter is known only to you and me. I leave it to your discretion on how you use the money to benefit Jews.

My husband had two major weaknesses: women and money, not necessarily in that order. Evidently, he collaborated with others in this miscreant act and refused to divide the spoils. Before the war was over, they found him dead from what appeared to be an accident. However, the body was severely bruised leading some to believe he was murdered before the accident. These rogue elements within the SS continued to harass me, which turned out in the end to be a good thing. You and I went into hiding in an area that would eventually be taken by the US forces and saved from having to live in East Germany under Soviet domination.

My wealth was not held in Germany, but mostly in industries and companies in England and America, countries doing business within the military industrial complex during which time it markedly increased in value.

While in hiding from rogue elements of the SS, I had a spiritual conversion that changed my life. You were three at the time. I was fearful, knowing that all the wealth I possessed couldn't help me. I held you tight in my arms one night and began to pray aloud. Suddenly, a light filled the room and warmth came over me that took my fears away. I never heard a voice, but something was saying to me that the little boy at my side had been saved for a special mission in life.

That night I told God I would do everything in my power to reverse what my husband had done to the Jewish people. As I write this, I see myself as a modern-day Pharaoh's daughter, a Gentile, who pulled you from the bulrushes in the river so you could become a modern-day Moses to lead His people to the Promise Land.

Let what you have read today settle well inside you before going to packet four. It will tell you how I started down the road of reversing the evil deeds of the man I married. Knowing you, you will find your family name as Moses found his, and when that happens, you will free both of us from the curse of my husband.

Your loving mother

When Hans finished reading the last page, he could do nothing but stare at the paper that spoke of pain a gentle, noble person had carried in life. Though she didn't give him biological life, she was his mother for earth's journey. Her heart was as big for him as if she had pushed him through her own birth canal. Love had a way of defying natural law.

A knock at the front door interrupted his thoughts. He quickly placed the packet in the safe-deposit box, closed it, and returned it to the closet. Upon opening the front door, he was surprised to see Sheena standing without a smile, showing a distinct look that she had come for a friendly confrontation.

"Hi, Sheena."

Part of Hans was still in the box he'd put in the closet. Without inviting her in, he stood in the doorway giving the impression he was treating her as a salesperson who had come to sell him something.

Sheena saw his eyes drifting and after a long pause of silence, said, "Hans, if you don't want me to come in, we can talk standing here."

"Oh, I'm sorry. I'm preoccupied with some very serious matters. I apologize! Please come in." He was glad he had returned the box to the closet and everything was put away.

He led the way to his living room and she noticed it had a different look, not with its furniture, but in the books and magazines scattered about. Instead of medical journals and reference books, there were religious magazines, books, and an open Bible. A strange feeling came over Sheena. This was not Hans, and not wanting to be drawn into a topic of discussion until she had finished her reason for being here, she sat down and commenced her mission.

"Hans, I want to apologize for taking up your valuable time, but I feel I must express my feelings about what appears to be an attitude you have toward me. I was under the impression we were to remain friends, but it appears it hasn't happened. I'm sorry I offended you in discussing my faith, and matters about my mother and father."

Sheena notice Hans was unresponsive, appearing almost bored. His world was divided. Two people were talking to him at the same time: one was Sheena inside his living room, the other, his mother from inside the box.

"Hans, are you listening to me, have you heard what I said?"

"I'm sorry Sheena. Before you came, I had just read a letter from my mother, a letter about a very unpleasant subject."

She remembered the other letter, the one he let her read, the one that made them close. She would never forget those moments, she dreamed about them at night. There must be another letter, but he was keeping it from her, not opening himself up as he had done before...perhaps his feelings had changed about her. He's aloof and unconcerned about her presence. Perhaps she shouldn't have come.

While Sheena struggled in herself over the reason she came to see Hans, Hans was giving his energies to the ripples coming his way from the letter he just read from his mother. Both were like two ships cast upon stormy seas with lots of coal to fire the furnaces, but with broken rudders. They were torn between two dilemmas: she wanted a relationship with Hans, but was tormented by his lack of faith; he wanted her, but on the right terms of acceptance. Each needed and wanted each other.

Hans thought his burden to carry out his mother's intended wishes, whatever they were, were impossible to do by himself. All he inherited from his mother had only made him lonelier. He wondered how his mother managed to carry the load all by herself, but she was a woman of steel, hardened by the gruesome atrocities of the war. He was her Moses and she was the king's daughter who had pulled him from the river of doom, the ash pile of the Holocaust. She believed he was destined for some event that would be revealed. *His thoughts turned to Moses' loneliness in the desert for forty years. Would this fortune he inherited send him to the desert?*

Sheena was sitting in the chair that Hans used when he read the Bible, made notes, and wrote out prayers. In plain view, her eyes caught a recently written prayer on the table alongside an opened Bible. She knew whatever was written was private, but couldn't resist the temptation to read the first line—then couldn't stop:

Lord, thank you for bringing me back to your fold from which I wandered. I was lost, but you found me and carried me to the sheepfold. Lord, help me to know the paths I should take.

What she had read in front of her eyes was a confidential statement of his faith. She knew something had happened and that it was a recent event, something he had never discussed with her. She was elated, pleased, yet sad in that he never shared what happened in his life. *Why would he avoid speaking to her about his new commitment to God when he had already shared the secret of his life—that he was adopted and was Jewish? Why had he shut her out? Things were not adding up.*

"Hans, the prayer you have written out was in front of my eyes. I couldn't help but read what it said. How did this come about?"

"It was the night you asked me to pray to the God of my youth. I read the story of the Prodigal and prayed the prayer he prayed when he came home."

"Hans, why didn't you want to share this with me?"

"Because I thought my telling you would make it appear I was doing it as an act to persuade you to come into my life."

"I would never have thought that because you're known as a man of integrity—everyone tells me that at the hospital."

She saw Hans stand up. He appeared nervous, walked over and stood at the bay window looking out with his hands cupped together behind him. His eyes were facing the outside scenery, but what he saw was the person seated in his living room.

"Sheena, what I'm going to say is something I have given much thought to. I have a special mission in life, and it's not in private medical practice. What I need from you is an answer to a simple question, and I know I'm sounding academic about this, but I need to know...."

Hans stopped in the middle of the sentence, his hands still held rigidly behind him, then spun around looking at Sheena.

"Knowing that all I have to my name is my mother's house, will you marry me? Not today, not tomorrow, but at the right time. You have occupied my space so much I can think of nothing else."

Hans stood looking at Sheena like a lawyer in court who had finished his argument. She was unprepared for this—

never saw it coming. When she came here today, it was out of a feeling of rejection, and it ends up being a marriage proposal. She tried to collect her wits—it was slow coming and Hans waited.

"Hans, love is a dynamic energy, a creation of God, but it can only be validated as it flows through the laws of God. I fell in love with you the second time we met, but there was no channel through which the exchange of love could flow because we were not together in faith. What I have been praying for has happened. I came here today thinking your interest in me had waned. Now, you're asking me to marry you...."

"Sheena, I have asked you a question. Do I have to ask the question again to get an answer?"

Hans saw Sheena taking advantage of what was going on. She was playing for the memory of history.

"Yes, I would like to hear that question asked again, Doctor."

"Sheena, Will you marry me knowing I have little material worth?"

"Yes, I would marry you, Hans, if you didn't have a dime to your name."

He quickly moved to where she sat, pulled her up into his arms, saying, "You are the most beautiful woman I have ever known and now you're going to be mine."

"You're embarrassing me again, Hans, and I'm blushing."

"I will embarrass you the rest of your life. I need a partner in life today, and a wife tomorrow. Will you be my partner and in the days to come be my wife?"

"Of course I will, I've already told you that!"

"The first thing I want to do is meet your mother and father and ask them for your hand in marriage."

"And the first thing they will ask you is, 'Will it be a Jewish wedding?'"

"And I will say, 'That's up to the bride, it's her wedding.'"

In the days that followed, Hans met Sheena's family, finished his residency, and told Sheena that his mother's luxurious car now belonged to her. Though she refused to accept it, he convinced her it was a lady's vehicle—too feminine for him. In the meantime, the box would continue to be attended to with a veil of secrecy over his inherited wealth.

Chapter 8

The Consortium

Hans was in close contact with his staff of financial advisors and legal minds responsible for running his late mother's empire and was coming to see how incisive and resourceful she was in creating wealth. Some people were prodigies in music, others in the arts and sciences. His mother was one in finance. She seemed to have had special insight into good investments. Those skills carried over into how she planned the future with the little boy she saved from the Holocaust in Romania.

The central control site for his mother's vast empire was a massive office complex consisting of four stories covering a whole city block. He met with an architect on the top floor to go over plans for his new office. Included in the plans would be an office adjacent to his for the Administrative Executive Secretary, and upon Mr. Klein's suggestion, he would request Miss Sonje Shuster to fill that position. He needed her to guide him through rough waters until he got a handle on everything.

For the time being, it was Hans' intent to keep from Sheena the knowledge of his wealth. To do this, he had to maintain the image of a middle-class lifestyle by staying in his rented cottage. Weekly, he entertained Sheena with a catered-in dinner, after which they would take in a movie or attend the opera. Sheena was a violinist with an appreciation of the arts. He no longer volunteered at the hospital, but would often meet Sheena there for lunch. Soon everyone knew he wasn't working in the medical field. When having lunch with Sheena in the hospital cafeteria, she raised the subject.

"Hans, people keep asking me, 'What are you doing now that you're not with the hospital and not in private practice?'"

"Tell them I'm starting a business."

"What kind of business?"

It was time for Hans to be creative. He was good at using the left side of his brain with analytical stuff, but now he needed a fast response for Sheena. He didn't care about how others thought, but Sheena was a different matter. He remembered one of his companies dealt in business machines, the new high tech office equipment coming on the market.

"I'm opening a store that will be selling the new office machines on the market."

"That sounds interesting, will it make a living?"

He saw the nesting instinct coming out in Sheena—could he support a family doing that? It warmed his feelings, and the moment he left he put his people together to open a storefront business selling office equipment and business machines. After it was set up and in operation, he took Sheena by and she was quite impressed, even made a comment about the number of customers in the shop. Now, he had a front that would insulate him so he could function in both of his worlds.

The initial information from Hans' mother about his adoption and the events surrounding it had left him devastated, but the time for healing and recovery had run its course, and Hans was now ready to continue with packet four. He was beginning to understand the design his mother put in this box. It was a process for him to go through so he could be morphed into what he needed to be to carry on the vision for which his mother shaped him.

He took from the box the packet showing number four. It was thin, nothing unusual, and when he opened it, he found handwritten pages titled: The Consortium: Christian Zionism.

My dear son,

You are about to hear the story of my life that played out behind the scenes of our warm, middle-class home and happy existence, and I hope it was for your sake because I worked hard at making it so. However, behind what people saw of us, there was another world going on that only I knew about. In my spiritual growth and study of the Bible, I came to understand there would be a kingdom set up and ruled over by a descendant of the ancient King David, that His seat of authority and capital would be Jerusalem, Israel. These pages will give you the untold story of how I and certain other people of wealth created a secret underground consortium to promote the future King's arrival. Our objectives were to reverse the evils of Nazism that tried to destroy the descendants of ancient Israel who were destined to inhabit the soon-to-be-created State over which the Messiah would rule. Not only did I find a certain personal release of guilt from being married to a man who participated in the evils of genocide, I found I could be a sword in God's hand to help pave the way for His coming kingdom. Nazism was only one form of underworld darkness, and though the West

95

defeated it in its military and political forms, the energy it carried descended into the dark, lower chambers of evil only to be transitioned into a more acceptable form in order to influence and shape the world community under the guise of fairness and human rights. The systemic anti-Semitism of Europe that carried Nazis to power is still alive and well. It is the underbelly of evil with the objective of preventing the arrival of the coming Messiah. Lacking a political state with boundaries and a people to occupy those boundaries, the Messiah cannot come.

Herein is the consortium's mission statement: Use wealth to promote population growth in Israel through immigration, support of pro-Israel programs and politicians. The coming kingdom for which we are doing battle will be a physical expression of the kingdom He now rules over in the hearts of men.

Now my son, like Queen Esther, you have been brought to the kingdom for such an hour. When you were plucked from the burning embers of the evil Holocaust, you were sealed to go and find yourself as Moses did on the backside of the desert. Some take the vow of poverty to serve God, others, the denial of a family, but rarely does one take a vow to use and accept as a burden in fulfilling God's will the abundance of wealth. You are a son of Abraham, it is for you to find yourself, and when that happens, it will be time for you to read my last and final letter contained in the box. Your journey in finding yourself will take you down unmarked paths. They may be lonely, difficult, even devastating, but in the end, like Moses, you will appear in the courts of Pharaoh to make your demands for your people. You will know when it is time to read my last and final letter.

Your loving Mother

Hans saw everything falling into place. The cloak-and-dagger events of his concealment to reach the lawyer's office and the secrecy of the phone calls spoke of the level at which the consortium operated. Paid security specialists wrote the script for the board. If the truth were known, he and his mother were under the watchful eyes of these agents when he was growing up.

Today's letter from his mother was like the finger of a prophetess pointing at him. She had the strength of a lion to achieve what she did in life, had groomed him carefully to step into her shoes by leaving him everything, except the one thing that was beyond her power: the matter of a personal journey he alone must make in finding himself and the reason he was saved from the Holocaust.

In finding himself, Hans knew it would start at the beginning—at the wagon where he was found in the village of his birth. Would Sheena help him? Would she need to know of his mission? How could she help him if she didn't know the whole story? He had the need for her to go with him, but he would have to convince her. It was a country still clinging to its history of championing anti-Semitism. There would be only one way he could get into the country and probe for information about his ancestry: using the power of money under the guise of business. His German name would serve him well in that effort.

Chapter 9

Using Business as Cover

The facts were on the table. Hans had gathered all the information he could on the Holocaust in Romania during the years of 1940-1944. Some of the materials had photos of such gruesome scenes he had to look away. Over three hundred thousand Jews had been killed by indigenous Romania Iron Guard and Nazi German soldiers. Even civilians had become part of the killing and robbing sprees. After one village was slaughtered, they would move on to the next. The extent of systemic anti-Semitism was reflected in the government's refusal to acknowledge there had been a Holocaust. Hans remembered the words written by his mother: *Nazism was the underworld of darkness to derail the coming event of the birth of the State of Israel.*

To embark on this grandiose venture of going to a country to find himself by uncovering his past was against all rational judgment. To get in the country was one thing, but to start asking questions would be quite another. It had been some twenty-seven years since the Jewish villagers were killed, villagers that included his mother and father. Since the people were not a mobile population, it was possible there could be people still living there who were witnesses to the event, even Gentiles who might open up and discuss the past. It was a country ruled by a communist dictator suspicious of foreign elements and was rife with poverty and corruption. Foreign investment had been thwarted because of political instability and lack of Western progressive thought. Some parts the country carried a tinge of medieval presence. A great deal of planning would be required, and he would need a trustworthy person to act as an interpreter who knew the purpose of his efforts and be able to independently ask the right questions without raising suspicion. In a country where its inhabitants were suspicious of others, the interpreter would need to read eyes and physical gestures to get a complete picture or answer to a question. He knew Sheena could speak Romanian but it would be with an accent making her appear foreign.

There were other issues complicating the matter of convincing Sheena to be part of his mission, the major one being her leave of absence from the hospital and loss of income. He could cover both of these, but the issue of being paid for her leave of absence, which was against hospital policy, ran the risk of Sheena uncovering his position of wealth. Pushing aside Guilt that hung over him for not revealing to Sheena his inherited wealth at the time of his marriage proposal, Hans came to realize his wealth was a double-edge sword. It had the power to cut in both directions, and at this stage, he was unsure about Sheena's commitment to marriage if she knew of his wealth. Most women would welcome this encounter, but she was unlike others, which was the magnet that attracted him to her. For now, he would avoid any situation that might expose his position of wealth and allow the vicissitudes of life to bond them together so when the time came for her to be told, she would accept a marriage and his inherited wealth.

While Hans sat on untold wealth, it brought no solution to his need of finding himself by returning to the land of his birth and the discovery of the reason why he lived and his family perished. Then it came to him like an awakening—the big guy, the one who pushed him along to meet with the lawyer. He had the experience of moving in large circles in dangerous areas and now worked for him. It seemed somewhat oxymoronic, the tail wagging the dog. His life experiences matched his size and he would have access to resources that were needed. Hans quickly sent a message to the old lawyer requesting a meeting with the big guy.

The next day Hans received a call from the big man who was larger than life and noted that it was clandestine time again, something he'd have to get used to—a repeat performance: a large black car with a driver. He jumped in the car and they rode around without stopping while Hans explained his dilemma. The well-experienced man who took up more than his share of the back seat, didn't take long to respond.

"This is what you may want to do to get into the country. Your mother had controlling interest in a large oil company where oil-drilling operations were ongoing, and it would be a piece of cake if the company were allowed to do geological research in the area where you want to go. It would be a quick, in-and-out event involving light, minimal gear using the typical seismic blasting sonar. The government would require a contract to be drawn up before you begin. Governments like the one you're dealing with are eager to find oil reserves because when the oil flows revenue finds its way right into their pockets. Sometimes it helps expedite these matters with a little money upfront if you know what I mean."

"I'll look the other way on that one," said Hans.

"This kind of testing in the countryside will allow the team to move about in a casual way and shouldn't create suspicion. We can even employ locals in your geographical areas of interest, which usually helps lower the resistance of locals talking to strangers. Money always loosens the tongue. The biggest problem is to get the approval from the government. After all, we might even find oil."

Hans was overly impressed. This guy had been around the block a few times.

"I want to take a woman with me. Is this a problem?"

"Man, you're pushing me into a corner, would your mother approve of something like that?"

"It's not what you think. This person's father and mother are survivors of the Holocaust in this country and she will be my guest in an honorable way."

"Whew, you had me worried for a moment! We'll try to work from a centralized city that can accommodate our group with food and lodging. If we're required to work in remote areas, we'll sleep in tents, and if we're in and around villages, we'll get lodging inside homes. Money always opens homes. Just be sure you take your own bed clothing.

"If you want to go down this road and assign me for the task I'll get someone on it right away. Your mother used my experience on a lot of her projects, but we never met together like this, it was always by phone using a form of abstract code."

"Well, I think you should get used to this venue because I'll need your services with what lies in front of me. Proceed with the matter discussed unless otherwise instructed."

Hans took a piece of paper and wrote something down, saying to the man, "Written down on this piece of paper are the names of two villages that are close to each other, and we want to make a thorough visit of each one. There may be other sites, but these are the principal ones. We need to be in the area for three or four days to gain the confidence and respect of the villagers."

The driver dropped Hans off. He walked one block and drove to his new business venture that acted as a front for his second life. The business was actually doing well, and to demonstrate its success to Sheena, he bought a new car. She was impressed, but what preoccupied his mind was how he would deal with Sheena if this arrangement of getting into Romania were successful.

He could put it to her that the oil company doing the testing invited him to go as a physician for the team, and she would be along as his guest. This would sound logical, and in reality be truthful. The new business he started could handle her reduction of income from being off work.

Only time would tell how all this would go down. In the meantime, his attention would be given to working with his staff of attorneys and accountants. To run an enterprise of this size, he would have to know the details of every facet of operation. Only when he reached that point would he feel comfortable meeting with the consortium to plan strategy in preserving geography and a people for the coming Messianic kingdom rule.

Chapter 10

The Desert's Backside

Hans was missing the satisfaction he derived from working with patients. Whether out of wanting to reconnect with helping patients or be closer to Sheena, he began volunteering one day a week at the hospital. It was always a day when Sheena was on. He made sure his breaks and lunch times always synchronized with hers. When he pulled into the hospital parking lot for his scheduled day to volunteer, he saw Sheena walking to work. At break time, he would find out why.

They sat across the table from each other drinking coffee in the doctor's lounge when Hans raised the issue of her walking to work.

"Sheena, I saw you walking to work this morning, is there something wrong with Mother's new car?"

Sheena looked embarrassed. "You know there's nothing wrong with that beautiful, gorgeous vehicle. People are wide-eyed every time I pull into the parking lot—they think I won the lottery!"

"You're too svelte to require exercise, especially, when you are on your feet here at work."

"I'm embarrassed to tell you. My folks are struggling financially, and I try to help them with what I can, so I'm cutting down on my gas consumption by doing a lot of walking."

Hans didn't say anything. The people who had given life to the girl he loved were now suffering financial stress. He

104

looked at the delicately folded hands across the table from where he sat. Neither was adorned with an engagement ring. Staring at her hands without a ring, his lips and mind were divided in thought. Without moving his eyes from her hands, his lips spoke to her parents' need.

"Are your folks buying or renting the home they're in?"

She thought it strange that Hans was so disconnected in conversation, staring at the table showing such a mechanical response.

"They rent, and this is one of their causes of stress—it's been raised."

Continuing to stare with a fixed, unmoving look, he finished his statement. "…I want you to take the rest of the day off—we're going shopping, and I want you to call your folks and ask them to move into my mother's house and be its caretaker. I'm not going to sell it, but keep it in her memory."

It was now Sheena who appeared detached. Taken by surprise at Hans' offer, she collected her thoughts, saying, "Hans, they have a lot of pride and independence and won't take kindly to a gift like that."

"It's not a gift. I need it taken care of, and there is no one more caring than your folks."

She looked around the room. No one they knew was present, then reaching over she touched his hand, saying, "You're the kindest and most generous man I have ever known."

"Tell them to start packing. Tomorrow, I'll send a moving van to their place. Now, let's go shopping!"

Sheena had no idea what Hans had in mind, the term "shopping" could mean many things, but when he pulled in front of the most high-end jewelry shop in town, her heart began to pound.

"Your hand is going to be adorned with the biggest diamond we can find in this store."

She couldn't restrain herself. She pulled him into her embrace kissing him while passersby took notice—and smiled. One of them was a little boy with his mother who had been in the hospital as a patient and had been cared for by Sheena. He recognized the doctor.

"Mom, there's my doctor inside the car kissing a man."

For the mother, it was interesting tabloid. She stopped and watched the couple get out of the car and enter the jewelry shop.

"It's alright, son, for a doctor to kiss a man who's going to buy a ring for her."

Inside the shop, Hans told the clerk to bring the largest diamond rings the store had and place them in front of her on the counter.

"Now Miss Beautiful, it is the ring you decide on today that your finger will carry when we leave the shop."

"You are giving me too many choices."

"Blame it on the store, not me!"

"Don't be funny, Mr. Hans, this is a once-in-a-lifetime experience."

He leaned over and whispered, "No ring will ever match your beautiful face."

She stopped cold and looked at him. "You're making me jittery and weak inside—I can't concentrate when you say those things." She could see he was taking pleasure in moving her feelings and had it not been in a public place, she would have encouraged more of the same.

Hans yelled over to the clerk, "Are you sure you don't have some larger diamonds?"

"More rings will only add to my confusion," said Sheena.

When the clerk returned from a back room, he carried on a velvet pillow one ring with larger accompanying diamonds. Hans saw her face beam when she saw it. He knew what her choice would be.

"Does it fit well enough to wear, or does it need to be ring-sized?"

"It fits perfectly, and I will wear it everywhere with great pride."

There was no price tag showing its cost, but she knew it was one of the most expensive pieces in the shop. "Are you sure you want to spend what this ring cost? You do have a budget, don't you?"

Hans took his index finger, touched her lips that looked like scarlet ribbons. "Don't let these lips say anything more about the cost of this ring—okay!"

It didn't take long before gossip mongers were spinning tales over the new diamond ring Sheena wore, and she was as vivacious showing it as the mongers were talking about it. It was the size of the diamond that commanded attention. How could a doctor who wasn't gainfully employed afford a diamond that size? They also noticed Sheena's zest and new spring in her step.

It had been two months since Hans had given Sheena her engagement ring. He continued volunteering his service at the hospital, had moved her parents into his mother's empty home, and Sheena was back to driving her beautiful car. He would rarely go to his store that was used as a front and did so only when he needed others to see how he made a living. Outside of his time spent at the hospital and with Sheena, he focused entirely on his staff of legal experts and financial managers. Miss Shuster, the lady who attended his mother's funeral, was in charge of bringing Hans up to speed and worked tirelessly with him and his staff. He realized the extent of the mental grasp his mother had of the financial world, and the intensity of his studies learning about it was every bit as grueling as medical school. Sometimes, he was up late at night working with overtime staff solving an issue halfway around the world. His staff would tell him, *diligence was his mother's motto*, and he could see that her work and life not only lived in him but in others, she touched.

Hans' new office downtown was still undergoing renovation. In the meantime, he continued to use the building he rented after his neighbors complained about strange visitors coming around. It was his classroom where he went every day to be schooled in matters of running the global enterprise he now owned.

He had worked late, went home, and was preparing to go to bed when he received a call requesting him to come right over.

"Is this an important matter? I'm getting ready for bed!"

He didn't recognize the voice, but voices sometimes sounded different on the phone than when spoken in person.

"Yes, it's a very important matter because it concerns you."

When he arrived, he noticed the security guard was visible and appeared to be on special alert. Someone opened the door, and he was immediately ushered to a secluded conference room away from the night staff. When they opened the door, he saw seated at the end of the conference table the Big-One with a shaven head and all.

He was short on formalities, stood to his feet, and shook Hans' hand, saying, "I have a report to give you. Our men have rung some bells where you want to go, and everything's set up and ready. After reaching the country, we may have to do a little gambling by taking a chance on using their internal airline, which is known to be a little short on safety. We'll get the team all set with the necessary gear, and when you give us the word, we'll swing into action."

"What name do you go by, and how shall I get in touch with you?"

"I go by the name of Max, but other names are used depending on my assignment. I have to survive in what I do, and remaining nameless is sometimes part of the job. You can reach me by contacting the Old Man, the chief of the whole caboodle, the man I took you to meet. He left you a number in the briefcase, so let him know when you're ready to go."

"I want it clearly understood that no one is to know who I am outside this financial esoteric group. I intend to maintain a middle-class standard of living without the opulence of wealth, even as my mother did. The lady going with me on this mission is engaged to me, and we both have common histories in the country we'll be visiting. She knows nothing of my wealth, and I want it to stay that way. We are to be treated as medical doctors on this mission, nothing more and nothing less. Is that understood?"

The Big-One was taken aback by the authority Hans demonstrated. It was then he knew the wealth of the Noble Lady, the name Hans' mother went by, had been given to the right heir.

"Doctor Baughman, you can be assured your privacy will be kept even as it was with your mother. Loyalty is what we're known for in our group."

Hans now had a problem. He was at a loss on how to approach Sheena about his mission to visit the village of his birth. They would have little responsibility other than subjecting themselves to the indignities of being foreigners. For Hans, there would be no surname change, but Sheena's case was different.

Sheena always welcomed Hans' daily phone calls, but Saturdays were very special. It was the Sabbath, the day of the week she and Hans worshiped at a Messianic Jewish synagogue. It carried all the formalities of most liturgies, but the music and worship extolled Yeshua HaMashiach. Today in shul, Hans had difficulty focusing. He had to convince Sheena to go with him to Romania. His thoughts centered on the woman seated next to him, the person he would spend the rest of his life with, and she had to know at some point about his duel life. *The question was when should he tell her?*

One hour later, he sat across the table from her in a restaurant looking at the large, beautiful diamond on her finger. It wasn't a question about the trip to Romania he would open the conversation with, but one that had been with him even before he asked Sheena to marry him.

"Sheena, if we sank to the depths of poverty, how do you think that would affect our marriage? How would it change you?"

"Hans, since I've already been there and done that, and am presently not far from a state of poverty, that question should be addressed to you."

"Are you telling me I'm wealthy?"

"No, but you are higher on the economic ladder than I am!"

Hans had carefully framed his question in a way that would lead to the question he really wanted to ask.

"How do you think wealth would change us if we won the lottery and could buy anything, go anywhere, or do anything we wanted?"

Hans could see it was difficult for her to transition to his hypothetical question. Material wealth had never been part of her space. The only wealth she knew anything about was what she had created inside herself—values that transcended material worth.

"In a marriage, both parties would have to come up with some common basic values, put them on the table and reach an agreement that would be best for both. If I personally came into wealth and it was up to me, I would give it to my people who have no homeland so they could move to Israel or to a country that would accept them as Jews. You will never know the pain my folks carry in their memories of those times in Romania of not belonging, not being accepted because they were Jews. Thank God for the nation of Israel!"

Hans could see in her eyes the pain she carried for her family. He was awe-struck by her answer.

"What would you do with wealth?" Sheena asked.

"I'm doing exactly as you said you would do."

Hans framed his response to her question that made it truthful. She chose not to un-parse the tense structure of the sentence, and Hans congratulated himself on truthfulness in obfuscation. But the turmoil of when to tell her the whole story still weighed heavily on him.

"Sheena, you are a beautiful person, and I have come to see that your beauty inside matches what's outside."

"Well, I won't blush today because I'm preoccupied with a big question for you!"

"You look serious about whatever it is."

"Hans, when are we getting married?"

The question shook Him. *How could he answer when she didn't even know about his other life—the one of wealth?*

He looked at her ring hand, reached across the table, and held it in both of his, saying, "I'm going to hold on to this hand as long as I live, and I will never let it go. First, I want you to make, create, order, or whatever women do to get a wedding dress and have it ready and waiting. Arrange the wedding party, do everything necessary for the event—let not one thing be left undone, so if I call tomorrow, assuming you have everything prepared, you'd be ready to go. Don't worry about the cost, I will pay for everything." *This was the best response Hans could come up with at a moment's notice. A wedding date couldn't be agreed upon until she knew about his inherited wealth.*

"Hans, you're generous but impossible! Are you playing with me, or do you really want this done in this manner? Usually, a girl likes to plan and organize things like this…you know… dream about it."

"Are you telling me you haven't been dreaming about it?"

"It's all I've been thinking about."

"Well, isn't that dreaming?

"Of course!"

"But a date would help you dream better?"

"Mr. Hans, you're being impossible again!"

"Your mother lives nearby and she will gladly help you plan everything out."

"Thank you for the advice, but I'm very capable of planning my own wedding!"

"Are you sore with me?"

"No, I'm not sore; I'm just madly in love with you." Then reaching across the table she placed her open hands on his cheeks, smiled, and added, "Has anyone ever told you that you are very handsome."

"Yes! My mother used to tell me I was handsome, but probably all mothers tell their sons that."

"Well, in your case, it was fact, and from now on, I'll take over from your mother in that department."

The subject of the wedding had a slight bittersweet closure to it when referencing a mother calling her son handsome. Both said nothing, *but it entered their minds: how many times did his biological mother say those same words to him for the twelve months he was with them in that village in Romania?*

After lunch was served, Hans opened a new topic. "Sheena, there's an oil company that does seismic geological testing, and I have the opportunity to go along and provide medical services as needed. They are offering very good benefits, and I would like you to go with me. The benefits they're giving me would cover what you would lose in taking a short leave of absence."

"That sounds adventurous," said Sheena. "To what country will you be going?"

"Romania."

He had a controlled fix on her countenance. In most cases, a face would show the truthful answer before the verbal response. None showed, and no immediate response came. He continued to wait. Soon a flicker of life showed, but it didn't have the picture of an answer—only a show of compassion.

"Hans, are you trying to find out who you are?"

Now Sheena's hand covered his in a show of empathy. He saw the broad world of compassion she lived in. It was one that demonstrated extra powers to understand people who felt hurt. How could he be so lucky to have a person like this to stand with him in life?

One week later, Hans and Sheena were onboard a chartered jet with his handlers and the professional team of geologists and technicians. They were scheduled to touch down in Bucharest, then on to Chisinau where they would stay overnight in a recommended hotel. From there they would move about the area of operation in heavy-duty overland trucks.

The pilot of the chartered plane broke in over the intercom stating they were flying over Ploesti. Their flight route, which was closely monitored by the government, took them directly above the airport. From the air, the pilot could see a few smaller planes parked near hangers.

When the pilot mentioned Ploesti, something came to Hans. His mother kept books in her library that covered the war in this region of Europe. She read everything about Romania, and he now understood why. It was the country she had visited and found him. Being an avid reader growing up, he'd read the same books.

"Sheena, below us is the site of one of the biggest bombing raids made in World War II by the Americans, and one wrought with great loss of lives and planes. In 1943 over one hundred and seventy B-24s left Benghazi, North Africa, for Ploesti on a bombing mission to destroy Hitler's oil supply with just eighty-eight planes making it back to base."

"Yes, I remember my folks talking about it after the war. There were Partisans in the mountains, some of them Jewish, and they helped rescue parachuting airmen." A long pause ensued. She was thinking of her mother and father being Holocaust survivors, and now their daughter was entering the country from which they escaped, a country with a history of having killed three hundred thousand of her people. She knew coming to this country would be emotionally debilitating, but she must overrule her feelings and garner strength if she were to be of any help to the man she loved.

Her musings were expressed to Hans. "There are three kinds of people in a war: those who live, those who die, and those who suffer the results of it." *She had come on this mission to support Hans, and it had already shaken her. She was one of the victims who suffered from the results of that war.*

The charted jet aircraft holding the equipment and team members landed at the Chisinau airport. Original plans were to take a local carrier out of Bucharest but were able to change the flight route with a hefty prepaid gratuity eliminating the need to unload and reload all the equipment. Rented overland trucks were waiting for them at the airport terminal.

After disembarking, Hans could tell palms had been greased by the way they gave little scrutiny to passports and luggage inspection. They were quickly rushed out to a rented top floor of the best hotel they could find. Hans, Sheena, and Max had private rooms; the others bunked together. When money flowed, respect and courtesy followed. This was a country struggling under communist dictatorship. Funds that should have gone to build the infrastructure went to suppressing internal democratic movements, and finding wealth in petroleum energy became a dictator's national bank account. Hans was hopeful that greed would serve to distract the government from the real reason he and his crew were in this land.

Sheena didn't come with Hans to discover who she was, or where her relatives lived and died. That would be another day and another time. She was here in a country to support a forlorn man trying to discover his identity by connecting with his family's history in a town scarred by a Holocaust of plunder, murder, and rape. Together, they would wade into the foul, murky swamps of history that would leave their memories scarred forever from the ravages of an evil kept hidden from a modern world. She would stand by his side until he discovered why he was saved by a woman who became his mother whose husband was a Nazi general.

The first night after everyone was in bed and the lights were off, Max came to Hans' room to go over maps he collected from the archives of government offices. They were valuable in that they showed detail that modern maps didn't, and this was important for their kind of research. The official state position on the Holocaust in Romania was that it never happened. They would be searching for two things: witnesses who would tell their stories and physical evidence. Hans had stepped over a threshold to enter a desert in search of a burning bush. Both, he and Sheena had on their person their gold lockets.

Chapter 11

The Burning Bush

Recruited to help with the Romanian language were two westernized Romanians who traveled the globe working with oil companies. Sheena could speak five languages, Romanian being one of them, having learned it from her parents. She required the interpreters to speak to her in Romanian to sharpen her skill, and Max, the Big-One, knew how to organize and manage events using people. Everything was running like clockwork. Max's involvement in this project was more perfunctory in that everything was out in the open and above board, except for the work that would be done later under the cover of darkness. One of the interpreters had the responsibility of acting as a booking agent, preceding the group to arrange overnight lodging and food. The geographical layout of the terrain being tested allowed the party to centralize themselves in cities and drive from there to their testing sites. Medical supplies brought in by the two doctors would serve to maintain the health of the team and act as a lubricant in building relationships with the locals, especially, in their targeted villages.

The geological team understood their professional activities were serving as a cover for something else and the results of their tests had no bearing on the success or failure of the project. They were not told the mission but knew that certain members among them would be coming and going, and if government people moved in and asked questions, they were to be told they were at the next site preparing for a test. The team was informed the vehicles would be bugged, and when referencing the government in conversation, the wisdom of sycophancy should be practiced.

Each truck had magnetic plastic signs attach to the sides of the doors displaying the company's name—all for showing that it was a government-approved project. The truck taking the lead held Max, Hans, Sheena, and one interpreter. The restriction on what they could say inside the vehicle gave long periods of silence, which forced them to do a lot of facial and hand gesturing and sometimes whispering in each other's ear. They took in the cultural surroundings, which stood in sharp contrast to West European countries. It was like a bad painting that gave the feel of an unnerving screech. The centralized planning and government-run communal farms told the story of failure here in this land. Parts of Medieval Europe stood out in the landscape with spotted plots of gardens, family farm animals, women with headscarves and long dresses down to the ankles, each living in and around a hovel without running water. These were people made into peasants by the system of government forced upon them.

Seeing firsthand the economic hardships of the people living under this government left the crew with a greater appreciation of the political and economic freedoms in the West. The bright spot was found in nature with rolling hills and natural foliage twisting in the breezes, effusing gentle, scenic tranquility. Nature had succeeded in a country where man had failed. After driving thirty miles, the two trucks stopped. There was the need to talk, stretch, and study the maps. They were nearing the location for their first test, a site about twenty miles from the village where Hans was born. The doctors wore rugged outdoor clothes like the rest of the team, and Hans saw Sheena put on her golden locket showing the Star of David. Then they took a short stroll together.

"You're being brave wearing your Star of David."

"You don't approve?"

"Oh, I approve, I'm just saying you're being brave doing so."

"I take pleasure knowing you are here to take care of me."

"I'm sure there's still systemic anti-Semitism in this country, a permanent fixture in the cultural landscape. They have built their cathedrals to honor the founder of their faith with one hand and used the other to kill His brothers. Only repentance and forgiveness from God can change a man's heart. This applies to a nation. This country will never prosper economically until the leaders acknowledge and confess its sin of genocide against the Jews."

Sheena rushed to take his hand and pulled him up close, saying, "I'm so proud of you, Hans, the things you said are like prophetic words."

"They are words from the Bible. God said to Abraham, 'I will bless them that bless you, and I will curse them that curse you.'"

"How is it Hans you know so much about the Bible? You quote and refer to it all the time."

"It was Sunday School, my mother, and self-application. I was a good student and retained what I read. Besides, children never forget what they learn."

"Hans, you are a miracle! You were pulled from the jaws of death by the hands of a Gentile, a Gentile whose husband was a Nazi general. God had a purpose in that event, and I will be with you in support of that cause."

He put his arm around her shoulders, walked her back to the waiting truck. *What couldn't escape his thoughts were that he took great effort to keep from Sheena his double life, and now there was a lingering fear that when she found out she might have second thoughts about marriage.*

The team of Petroleum Engineers on this project would apply the typical seismic waves that penetrate the earth allowing a virtual map to be made of the earth's underground geology. Seismic waves would be sent out into the earth, then, bounced off at different underground points returning at varying speeds for the engineer to analyze. The reports would give a good indication if potential oil reserves were below.

The pathway they had mapped out would take them near Hans' village of birth. He wasn't looking forward to this but knew it was something he had to face. It was a mountain he couldn't go around, one he couldn't go through—it had to be climbed. He informed Max he and Sheena would take a ride and scout out the village area, introduce themselves and attempt to build a rapport with the villagers. He instructed Max if they weren't back by the end of the day they should return without them, and they would follow later. The Big-Man didn't like that part of the arrangement but complied with the directive.

Unknown expectations settled over Hans as he pulled the truck away from the worksite onto the main roadway. It was the first step in bringing closure to his mission. Working in their favor was Sheena's skill in the spoken language. Not using an interpreter would help create an informal climate which could potentiate conversation.

The drive to Ediniti, Hans village of birth, took forty-five minutes over poorly maintained chug-hole roads. They knew they had arrived at the outer edge of the village with the appearance of scattered clusters of buildings. It hadn't grown much in twenty-six years.

"Sheena, this is the same road my mother walked down that iniquitous day when she came upon the dead. This was the section of town where most of the Jews lived."

"Yes, and the buildings we see standing are most likely the same ones that were here when your mother came upon the site."

Hans pulled to a stop and left the motor running. He wanted to absorb the physical site his mother took that changed both of their lives.

He looked at Sheena. "You will never know how much your being here means to me. I could never do this by myself."

"I'm proud of you, Hans. You're doing fine, just keep on moving through this cauldron of pain and you'll achieve your purpose for coming here."

The large truck bearing the name of the company doing the geological tests started moving again down the main road leading to what used to be the Jewish sector. Buildings stood as they did before the Holocaust, the only change being the occupants. Locals had confiscated the homes and businesses. Old homes and storefronts dotted both sides of the street. Most shops and stores had a second floor that was used as a place of residence for the shop owner or manager.

Hans brought the truck to a stop in front of a building with large glass storefront windows that spoke of another time when variety needed to be seen by passersby on the streets. Both got out and stood by the truck.

Hans was first to speak. "Let's walk up and down the street just to get the feel of the physical layout. The more I can absorb the physical placement of buildings, the greater capacity I'll have in the arrangement of disconnected pieces that will invariably come later."

"That shows wisdom on your part," responded Sheena.

"I'll need more than wisdom to complete the task I've begun. The intervention of Providence is preferred."

"But Hans, sometimes Providence comes in the form of wisdom."

"That is a statement of heavy truth, and your being with me is a gift of both. It is Providential that you are with me, and you come packaged with mountains of wisdom."

"Hans, you are taking me out of my league! I'm a physician, not a theologian."

"However you come, you fit perfectly the occasion."

"And you, my future husband, are great with words."

The main street that lay in front of Hans and Sheena was empty of human life. Evidence of yesteryears was everywhere: old dilapidated Soviet-made cars that looked inoperable, draft animals tied up nearby and some hooked up to wagons filled with farm produce. There was more evidence of the use of draft animals than anything mechanized.

"We've stepped back in time," said Hans. "Things haven't changed since the war. These buildings are the same structures that were here when my mother ran about them trying to escape the horrors she saw. Until today, I only had my mother's written script filed away in memory, but now, seeing the street close-up, memory takes on vivid life form. This is something that will haunt me for as long as I live."

"It is better it haunt your memory in the daytime than in dreams of dark-harrowing nightmares," remarked Sheena.

"Your lips again have spoken from the fountain of wisdom."

"Where are all the people? Everything looks like a ghost town," remarked Sheena.

Hans knew what was going down. "Sheena, don't look! The people are inside buildings watching us from behind curtains."

"But, why the hiding?"

"That's normal, we're strangers, and people who live under the dictatorship of this country have reason to fear strangers and strange vehicles. May I add the supposition that fear of strangers could also be from the guilt of the town's history. The buildings around us were taken from Jews killed in the Holocaust, and it is rumored that hired assassins are easy to come by in this land. Money has legs and travels easily across international borders. History is a great teacher and leaves the record that avengement is an ancient custom and is more prevalent in a community without equal justice under the law."

"Wow! You are informative today, Doctor Hans. Let's stroll back and visit the shop near our truck."

Everything grew quiet between them knowing eyes were viewing their every step. *Rushing through Hans was his mother's letter describing this street filled with the dead. She ran to escape the morbid scene and found him, an orphaned infant, somewhere on a back street in a wagon of hay. Today, that orphaned infant walks the street of infamy where family members bled and died leaving microscopic blood DNA hidden somewhere among the cracks, crevices, and dust of earth, all calling for justice.*

Sheena, trying to find words to fill the vacuous atmosphere, whispered to Hans, "Let's go inside this store near our truck and see what they sell."

With one hand, Hans took hold of Sheena's arm, and with the other, he opened the door of the shop. Confidence and bravery were hanging all over the two strangers. A quick view of the store's inventory on the shelves made them think they were in a time machine. It was a shop without manufactured goods; everything came in pieces, made to be put together. No hanging clothes, just products with which to make them. Food items were in open bulk bags, and the public brought their own containers for whatever they purchased. The strong garlic odor, blended with other spices, seemed to act as a symphony that characterized the culture of a people who lived on little, wished for more, but found that change never happened, and for the reason that change didn't happen, anti-Semitism would continue until the government intervened.

Strong feelings gripped Hans. The village was full of people who were here when genocide happened, the calamitous day his adoptive mother saw the dead. It was the day that scarred her memory but one that gave life to an infant who now stands in a building that could be the very building his birth mother and father owned or perhaps had often visited.

A strange new world was coming at Hans. He was German in language and culture, but on a voyage of finding himself on the waters of rough history. Today he was in a port where it all started, where his mother and father gave him life and was found as an orphan by a noble lady of great wealth.

The two strangers moved further inside the shop. Behind a large counter where customers were checked out, there stood a lady who appeared to be the cashier and proprietor.

The customers in the store upon seeing the strangers stopped looking at what they wanted to buy. They stood staring at the visitors. The one behind the counter joined in, creating a choir of zombie-lookers. All were showing concern. Their village was never frequented by visitors and large commercial vehicles.

Speaking Romanian, Sheena attempted to put them at ease, saying, "We're with the geological people here in this area doing tests for oil deposits, and we wanted to come by and visit your village."

Sheena moved closer to the lady behind the counter. Both saw her eyes go to the gold locket that hung about her neck. She tensed up at the sight of the locket. Then her eyes went to Hans. Fright filled her face as if she'd seen a ghost. Both would later confirm that she actually shook. In an act of boldness, Sheena lifted the locket up toward her face, saying, "I see you're looking at my locket, do you like it? I think it's beautiful!" She made sure she saw the Star of David.

Hans and Sheena didn't know if she were frightened or angry, but both knew she was disturbed. Before she could respond, a man came running into the shop almost yelling, "What medicines do you have? My daughter is sick with a high fever!"

"We have no medicines in our shop,"

"What is he saying, Sheena? He seems distraught about something."

"He said, 'His child has a very high fever and needs medication.'"

Turning to the distressed father, Sheena said, "Sir, this man and I are doctors and can help your daughter. Do you want us to look at your child?"

"Oh, please doctor, please!"

Hans went to the truck and picked up his medical satchel containing several meds including broad-spectrum antibiotics. They walked several blocks with the father, went up a pathway to a home that carried the typical picture of the landscape: a small, four-room house with luscious green gardens of tomatoes, cucumbers, squash, beans and domestic animals. They were led inside where they saw two children standing side-by-side showing concern over their hollow-eyed, ten-year-old sister lying on a bed languishing with a high fever. Sheena explained who they were and that they were there to help her. After checking her temperature and examining her throat, she instructed the mother to cool the surface of her body using damp cloths until the temperature decreased. In the meantime, she was diagnosed with inflamed tonsils and given painkillers for the fever and a regimen of antibiotics.

"We'll come by tomorrow to check in on your daughter. The pain medication will lower her temperature. If her fever is still with her, give two tablets every four hours."

"Thank you, thank you!" said the mother. The father took hold of Hans' hand, his eyes showing tears of gratitude. "Thank you! God has been good to us sending you our way. You will never know how much your help means to us."

Hans and Sheena took note that in all their exuberance of showing thankfulness, they were distracted by the gold locket around Sheena's neck. The mother's name was Maria, and the father was called Mario.

On their way back to their hotel, they were exhausted but pleased with the introduction they gave themselves at the village. They disregarded the rule of talking inside the truck but practiced discretion when referring to the villagers' interest in Sheena's gold locket with the Star of David. There was something about the locket that seemed to take on the voice of a harbinger.

The next morning Max had the breakfast tables downstairs at the hotel arranged so he could talk privately with Hans. He needed the agenda for the day, and Sheena sat with them with guarded conversation in play. Everything was open game except any reference to the other side of Hans' confidential life that she knew nothing about. After Max left to take care of other matters for the day, Sheena raised a question about him.

"Hans, Max seems to be the chief among all the Indians here, but he shows deference to you. He acts like a sergeant to them but treats you like a superior officer."

"It's because I'm a doctor, and he knows if he gets ill I'm the only one who can help him. Also, we're along for the ride and have no one to give a report to when we get back home—therefore Max can be more relaxed in our presence. Everyone on the team is performance driven except us. Our measurement of performance will come in the village before we leave this country."

Hans wasn't quite sure he gave a satisfactory answer, but that would soon be dispelled when he got a chance to whisper in Max's ear.

After breakfast, the geological team was off for their second day of testing for oil reserves. Hans and Sheena were to tag along until they reached the first testing site, then take one of the vehicles for their second visit to Ediniti to attend to their little patient.

Upon arrival in the village, they stopped in front of the shop they had visited the previous day. They found it locked and no one around. Instead of faces hiding from behind closed curtains, today they were peering out the windows and doorways in plain view to get a look at the visitors. They left their vehicle parked in front of the shop, took their medical kit and headed in the direction of their patient several blocks away. Sheena saw Hans take from his pocket his own gold locket and place it around his neck. Then taking her hand, they continued their walk.

The door was open when they approached the house, and upon seeing them, everyone showed excitement and pleasure to have such important people visit them. Their ill daughter was now sitting up in a chair talking excitedly. Sheena checked the medications and reminded them to follow instructions when they were to be taken. The mother and father offered them chairs. When they saw that each wore a gold locket, it registered dramatically in body language. Hans was first to speak.

"What do our lockets mean to you? You keep looking at them."

The father looked at his wife, then at the children, then back to Sheena. "I would like to go outside and talk away from our children."

The children were told not to follow them, but stay together in the house because the adults wanted to talk. The father began his story. Sheena was the interpreter, and because Hans knew how to read her face, he sometimes knew the story before it was told.

The father pointed at Sheena, saying, "When this lady came yesterday wearing that locket, and you standing by her with blond hair, I saw the wife of the person who used to own that shop twenty-five years ago. I was eighteen years old. In fact, I would work for him sometimes helping clean up and run errands. There were people in the village who didn't like him or his people because they were Jewish and ran a lot of the shops in town. He always treated me well and paid me well too."

"What kind of shop was it?"

"It was more like a little factory than a typical shop. I worked with his father who was a well-known goldsmith. The father told me he had emigrated from Russia where he had been patronized by wealthy nobles because of the quality of his workmanship. After coming to this country, most of his clients were Jewish people. They would come from everywhere to buy his merchandise, and sometimes the father

128

would travel to fairs and sell his products that were very much in demand. Sometimes, he took me along to help carry the loads of merchandise."

Sheena saw Hans remove his locket. Holding it in his open hand, he asked, "Is this one of the pieces he made in his workshop."

The man had memory he had to process, a memory that lived with him like a nightmare. He looked down, then away from the doctors who had treated his little girl. He didn't want to see their eyes when he gave the answer.

"Yes, he and his father made those pieces in their shop."

Hans opened the face of the locket.

"Do you know the people in these two photos?"

The man looked at the photos, then, turned his face again from them. Cold silence like a fog settled over Hans and Sheena. Everything from the time Hans first found the locket in the box pointed to this moment. The drama of silence broke when the man spoke.

"Yes…I knew those two people. He's the son of the goldsmith, and the lady is his wife."

"And what were their names?" asked Hans.

"Isaac and Rachael Isler were their names. Mrs. Isler's maiden surname was Pencovich. Her father owned and operated a prosperous lumber mill and had a son who helped manage the business. The son often came around to visit his sister and little nephew."

Hans' world was spinning. Though it all happened over two decades ago, he was reliving the event like it was in real time. He would never be the same. *Sheena saw Hans struggling like an innocent bird caught in a hunter's net, he walked away and stood alone at the edge of Mario's property. With laser-fixed eyes beamed toward the village nestled in the valley below, he saw a community, a people, a culture, and a way of life unchanged from what it was when his family perished on that fateful day. Nothing had changed.*

From behind, Hans felt two arms embrace him, followed by the words, "Hans, I feel the heat of the flame you're walking through. This is your mountain you have to climb, and I want you to know that I'm with you all the way."

Hans turned his gaze from the village back to Mario and his wife still standing where he left them, saying to Sheena, "Shall we go and listen to the rest of the story?"

"Yes, but only because it's your story, one that will soon be told to the world."

Mario felt the dark weight of history gnawing inside when he saw Hans and Sheena walking in his direction. It was history that he was a part of, and it all happened in front of his eyes. Whatever the facts were, Hans was prepared to continue his journey in finding himself with Sheena at his side.

"Mario, are you going to tell me the rest of the story?"

"Only if you insist!"

"I insist," replied Hans.

They saw Mario look at his wife, then back at both of them. "It all happened the day I was cleaning the workshop in the back of the store, the same store where we first met yesterday. It sounded like thunder shaking the buildings. German army trucks, soldiers, and the hated Romanian Iron Guard troops were converging on the whole town pulling out the Jewish storeowners, their families with their children, making them stand in the street. They forced me out, told me to go home. I ran, hid, and waited to see what would happen. I felt an eerie quietness. Then, an evil as I had never seen or heard burst forth. Someone gave an order to open fire. The Jewish townspeople started to run, mothers with children in arms, soldiers running after them firing their rifles and shooting them down. They walked around those lying on the ground, and if anyone were alive, they were shot again. I buried my face in my hands, I couldn't watch. When the shooting stopped, I saw soldiers and some of our own villagers with sacks go into the stores and buildings and loot the valuables. Later, I was told some of the locals had participated in the killings."

This was Hans' recurrent dream, the nightmare that haunted him in the dark of night. That was the clamorous night when someone in white picked him up from among the dead and carried him through the line of soldiers to the wagon where he was covered with hay.

All four parties stood grappling with their emotions. The wife of the husband reached over and held his hand as he continued.

"The dead now have no memory, but for the living, the memory of that event is imprinted on every mind that was forced to dig an open, mass grave, forced to carry the bodies of mothers, children, and fathers to their final resting place without marker, name, or prayer. I never go to that site, nor walk near it because of its haunting memories."

Hans was in a torture chamber hearing the testimony of someone who saw the slaughter of his family. Though He began his journey over his mountain with many questions, he was finding strength and purpose the further he traveled. Knowledge and the report of the event from an eyewitness stiffened his resolve.

Reaching a point of anger, Mario and Sheena saw Hans' body stiffen, then demanded the unthinkable. "I want you to take me to the burial site!"

The husband's sympathy suddenly turned to fear. "Oh, I can't do that, Sir, with you being a stranger and all; it wouldn't go down well with me in the community. There are people here who were complicit in the killings, and some are in possession of their property."

"Is the storekeeper one of them?"

"Yes, it was she and her husband, but he died a violent death not long after they seized the property." *When Hans heard this, he said to himself, that sometimes natural law distributes poetic justice.* '

"Can you show me the mass burial grave site tonight after dark? I'll make it worth your while! Your children will go to the best private schools and attend the most prestigious universities in Europe. Sir, your act of kindness will be rewarded."

Sheena thought Hans' promise was a bit overreaching considering his nebulous financial future. He had no private medical practice established and his new business was barely off the ground.

"Tonight, at nine o'clock, I'll meet you a half-mile outside the village on the road you came in on. We'll go from there on foot. It's a place away from everything—everyone knows its history and won't build near it."

"I would like your full name and mailing address," said Hans. "I'm leaving you my card with a mailing address where I can be reached." Hans saw everything falling into place. Information was the key to his being in this country, and the man who stood in front of him was about to unlock that door.

Hans and Sheena walked back to their truck holding hands, neither talking—it was like being at a funeral. What the man didn't know was his entire conversation had been recorded. Hans was almost at the top of his mountain. There were different kinds of pain, some resulted in ruin, and some gave life, like the birth of a child. He had been in labor with his climb to the mountaintop, and birth pains were getting closer together with the feeling that new life was about to begin. Perhaps tonight, the delivery of new life would occur. Most births do come at night unless the doctor gives the mother a shot of terbutaline to delay its arrival, but this doctor would welcome a nighttime delivery.

Before pulling away from the shop formerly owned and operated by his family, they gave the building a hard look. It was still locked, the occupiers apparently fearful of history coming back to bite them hard. Many in the town carried guilt for the sins of omission and would never be free, nor blessed economically until it was acknowledged and confessed as evil. The village was a microcosm of the nation.

Chapter 12

The Mantle

As a lone survivor on that eventful day in the village of Ediniti, Hans grappled with what seemed like another kind of ghoulish nightmare: the need to find evidence of a mass grave where his mother and father lay.

Two trucks would be going to the mass gravesite, the first arriving at nine o'clock with Hans and Sheena, the second would follow thirty minutes later and would hold four people with high-tech photographic cameras, shovels, and specialized digging tools. Hans had a major objective: reach the top of his personal mountain and obtain evidence of a Holocaust in his village of birth. Tonight, they would attempt to uncover Holocaust human remains, photograph them and the site.

As Hans and Sheena approached the place where they were to meet with the man who would take them to the gravesite, they turned off the truck lights, slowed to the speed of a crawl and stopped. Sheena would be his interpreter for the evening. Soon, they saw someone move toward the truck coming out of tall weeds by the roadside. His hand could be seen waving. He appeared nervous but was willing to help. They grabbed their flashlights and followed behind him in single file, Sheena in front of Hans. They walked over a large open field moving their feet through damp, knee-high grass for a half-mile, then, the man slowed his pace and began taking short steps, feeling the ground with his feet as he moved along. He was attempting to identify the area by the configuration of the ground surface. The villager knew soil, it was his life, and what he was doing was performing the skill of a trapper. He knew that several-hundred bodies buried in a mass, shallow grave would settle, creating uneven demarcation lines on the surface of its periphery.

When he found what he wanted, he made a ninety-degree turn to the right and continued to walk taking short steps. He stopped, turned to Sheena, and spoke softly.

"We are on the outside rim of the grave. We'll walk its perimeter single file and trample down the grass so you can see the extent of its size."

"Hans, hold my hand. I know this is hard for you, and I'm sorry you have to go through this."

"With you, my love, I can go through anything."

When she heard those words, he felt a tighter squeeze on his hand. After walking the perimeter several times, Hans had them stop, then pulled the two close to his face so he could speak in a low voice.

"I would like to be left alone from here on. You go to your family and forget everything tonight. As an expression of my appreciation for everything you've done, I'm leaving you something in this envelope to show my gratitude. Buy each of your children something special."

He had not discussed this gift with Sheena. He had Max, who usually dealt with matters like this when money was involved, to carve out what would be equivalent to a year's wages in this country with an address in Germany where he could be contacted. The man quickly left moving in the opposite direction they took to reach the gravesite.

Now they were alone. Hans knew he would carry this experience in memory forever. *Held in this grave, a grave that bore no marker, were his mother and father who loved him with an eternal love, and had it not been for the man in white who carried him to safety, he would be among them. Order didn't exist here: husbands, wives, and children were apart and no rose went with them to the grave. It was a grave created from the darkness of hell, and he was pulled from it for a reason.*

These were the thoughts surging through Hans when he turned and faced Sheena. "Before King David's Son, the Branch, comes to this earth to rule, He will need two things: the Promise Land and a people to fill the territory. A spectacular event happened this year, Jerusalem, the centerpiece of biblical geography, came under the control of a people who came to life from Ezekiel's valley of dry bones, and we are being put in the middle of it all.

"There are Egypts still holding our people in slavery that need to be freed to return to the land of their fathers. Sheena, I'm standing at the top of my mountain, and I can see beyond. Now I know why I was plucked from death by the hands of a lady of nobility, a righteous Gentile who was chosen to take my birthmother's place."

Sheena drew Hans up close, saying, "Hans your feet are on top of your mountain, you have completed your journey in finding yourself!"

"Yes, and the vision up here is clear. I now have my own mantle, my own call for service. My sorrow will be turned to strength and my loss will be gain for others. My earthly mother prepared me all my life for this event, but knew I had to wear my own mantle, have my own vision."

"We'd better get to our vehicle, our party will be here soon," said Sheena.

"You're right, I'll lead the way."

They didn't speak as they walked briskly under a brilliant moonlight, but as they neared their truck, Hans stopped and turned around. "Sheena, I am destined to become a Zionist. I was born a Jew, raised a Gentile, and am becoming a Zionist, one who will work for the nation of Israel in preparation for the Messiah's rule on earth!"

"Is that what you saw on top of your mountain?"

"I saw that...and more! Moses made two trips to the dessert. On his first trip, he found the burning bush and his calling. The second journey included the rigors of leading his people to the gates of the Promise Land. On my visit to this land of pain and tragedy, I have found the burning bush and with it comes the commission of leading Abraham's posterity back to their homeland."

The flickering of flashlights around their truck gave the message that their backup team of people had reached the site using only the light of the moon.

"Sheena, I see our people have arrived." When they reached their truck, they found Max, a photographer and the two Romanians pulling equipment from their vehicle. None of the geological team was among them. Knowing time was of the essence, they quickly unloaded shovels and equipment like it was an everyday event, saying nothing. They had come to do a job and wanted to get on with it. Hans carried two shovels and a pick; Sheena managed one shovel. Hans led the way, followed by Sheena, Max, and the rest of the party.

Four areas inside the perimeter of the mass grave were evenly selected and marked. Two teams of three worked together. The bright moonlight helped expedite the digging process, but concerns were raised when a barking dog off in the distance let the party know he was apprised of something going on. It soon became intermittent and stopped. The only sounds at the digging site were from the swishing movements of the shovels with the accompaniment of grunts. They found the first remains at the depth of one foot.

Once a discovery was made, smaller delicate tools were then used to expose just enough bone material to be photographed. Everyone took extreme caution not to lift or move the remains. Each site was left open and exposed until all four had been excavated. They were then photographed extensively as evidence of a mass grave and would be kept on file for future use in exposing the country's Holocaust record.

After the final photographs were taken, the unearthed soil was replaced and smoothed over. Before leaving, the party of six paused in reverence to pay respect to those entombed in the shallow mass grave. Silence marked the memory of each person on his walk back to the trucks. It was now two o'clock in the morning. Everyone would be in bed by four, and the next day they would congratulate themselves on a mission accomplished. It would be a night to be remembered as they honored the dead by giving them a place to live in history.

Because the mission was so successfully carried out in their first village, Hans decided to forgo further operations. The geological team would spend two more days in the country testing and compiling reports on their findings.

When their private chartered jet was in the air on their return flight home, Hans' thoughts were on the future of nations like the one they just left. There was coming a day when anti-Semitism would be nonexistent, a time when the righteous Ruler would bring peace and goodwill to earth, and nations that now denied the Holocaust would give of their material wealth to build and support the country of Israel. He opened his Bible and read the sixtieth chapter of Isaiah, then meditated on what the Scriptures were saying about Israel and the Messiah's new world order:

Nations will come to your light, and kings to the brightness of your dawn...your sons come from afar and your daughters are carried on the arm...the wealth of the seas will be brought to you...foreigners will build your walls...you will drink the milk of nations and be nursed at royal breasts...and they will possess the land forever....

His German mother who adopted him was a picture of what the future held for the nation of Israel. She saw the promise God made to Abraham as a unit of two elements: geography and posterity. The two were inseparable. Land and Abraham's descendants were fused together forever. He was one of those descendants, pulled from the bulrushes of the Nile by a noble Lady and given a life in the palace. Today, he was making his journey from the desert where he had found himself, shrouded with a mantle and a mission to plead for his people and their cause in the courts of Pharaoh.

Chapter 13

Five Smooth Stones

When the flight from Romania touched down, Hans knew God had fitted him for battle. He remembered David's conflict with Goliath. The shepherd boy refused Saul's armor, choosing to do battle with the familiar tools of a sling and a stone. He would apply the same principle by using what he had within his reach—his inherited fortune. The major difference would be the battlefield. David saw his enemy and the ground Goliath walked over. The enemy he would meet was difficult to measure; the battleground was always moving and changing. He and David weren't the only ones who had something in common. Goliath, David's enemy, and the enemy he would do battle with came from the same cut of cloth: both used violence as their modus operandi.

Sheena had taken off a week from the hospital and needed an immediate replacement of funds. After taking a taxi to her modest rental, Hans carried her luggage inside, kissed her goodnight, and handed her an envelope, saying, "Here's your payment for a week's work as a doctor."

Before closing the door, his eyes gave special notice of her humble dwelling, yet she was comfortable, peaceful, and contented. He had been around beautiful women before he met Sheena whose lives reeked of affluence, but always wanted and needed more than what they had. *How could he be so lucky to have found a woman with his mother's values?*

Then came the force of reality, something he wished he could avoid: how would she respond when told about his wealth?

Sheena didn't tell Hans, but she was glad to be home. Her modest dwelling was like being wrapped in a warm, comfortable blanket on a cold night. After placing the envelope Hans gave her near the phone, she carried her luggage to her bedroom and decided to call her mother and tell her they were back from their trip. She hadn't told her the specifics of where they were going, lest she would worry. While talking with her mother, she noticed the envelope Hans left was quite full and wasn't sealed. Holding the phone in one hand, she used her other to examine the envelope's contents. She stopped speaking in the middle of a sentence.

"Sheena, have we lost connection, I can't hear you?"

"I'm still here Mom! I'm overwhelmed with what I was paid to cover my week from the hospital. Your future son-in-law is really generous; he just gave me three months salary for one week's loss of work."

"If you ask me, Dear, he has more than he lets on. He seems to go out of his way to tell you he has nothing. Have you ever looked at the size of that diamond on your finger recently?"

"Well, he does have a successful business. Besides, he was hired by a very wealthy group for this trip and added me to the payroll."

"Does it bother you, Sheena, that Hans isn't Jewish?"

"Oh, he is Jewish, Mom! Both of his biological parents were Jewish. Hans was adopted when he was one-year-old!"

Everything went silent. Sheena's mother was in pause mode trying to understand what she just heard.

"Mother, did you drop off the line?"

"No, I'm here trying to take in what you just told me. Why haven't you told me this before now?"

"I wasn't at liberty to tell you, but Hans recently said you and Papa should be told—but it's to be kept confidential for public relations reasons—and for the record, I would have consented to marry Hans even if he weren't Jewish because I love him, and we both have the same commitment to our Lord."

"My wonderful daughter is very lucky indeed to have Hans, and so are we!"

"I wouldn't want to use the term, luck—that sounds too much like the lottery. I'd say God had everything to do with it, and if he ends up poverty-stricken, we'll love each other all the more."

"What if he ends up very wealthy, Sheena, what would you do then?"

Everything inside Sheena was put on pause—the room room lost its oxygen. She remembered Hans alluding to this subject, and now her mother was asking the same thing. For the first time, she considered how wealth could influence their lives together. There wasn't a quick answer—too many unknowns, so she stuck with an age-old truism.

"As long as God is the center of our lives it doesn't matter whether we're rich or poor, life will go on in a normal fashion, but I don't expect to be rich or poor, so we'll survive just fine together."

On his way home from Sheena's, Hans was reflecting on his agenda for the week. Not wanting to leave the safe-deposit box at his home while away on his mission to Romania, he had returned it to the bank. This week he would pick it up and resume the final stage of the process his mother had programmed him to go through. As his mother requested, he had destroyed the Swiss bank account records, something known only to him. At the right time, he would deal with the matter of how to return the money to help the

Jewish people. It was money from Jewish assets from all over Europe and would have to be given to benefit the whole of Jewry. It would be a heavy burden to carry. He was already missing Sheena.

It was eight o'clock when Hans pulled into his driveway. Darkness had settled in, and he noticed the nightlight was out. He always entered his home from a side door adjacent the driveway, and tonight was no different. There was nothing like home, he thought, as he opened the door, turned on the entry light, and moved inside. Thoughts were running through his mind about how familiarity caused certain nostalgic feelings when coming home from a trip. The human psyche preferred routine.

Hans was focused on domesticity until he turned on all the lights. Everything came to a stop. Something was different. Objects, big and small had been changed. Someone had moved items and didn't put them back where they were. He continued to go through the rest of the house paying close attention to details. The whole scene was consistent with inconsistencies. Somebody had been in his home looking for something and lacked the skill to replace what they moved as they had found it. Hans wasn't a good housekeeper, but he had a photographic memory for detail—like a camera. He felt like Papa Bear who came home and found everything rearranged, except the party who visited his domicile was not as benign as Goldilocks. The telephone rang interrupting Hans' inspection.

"Hello, this is Doctor Baughman."

"This is Max, I'm taking a chance calling you like this, but it's an emergency. I have two messages for you. First, I am told to inform you the consortium board wants to meet with you as soon as you process the box. I don't know what that means, but they told me you would. They want a confirmation from you that you will continue your mother's policies with the consortium. The second message is one I wish I didn't have to address. A report was just handed me from security, and I must warn you to take all necessary precautions when moving about. You have become an object of prey by our enemies because of the wealth you inherited. The danger extends not only to you but to all those in your inner circle. I'll send some people over to patrol your area until you can find better defensible living quarters. You might consider providing a safer living site for Doctor Sheena and her family. Everything about her place, the neighborhood, road configurations, and the home layout makes it a difficult place to defend, and besides, she has to know there are certain things she must comply with to make security work. Kidnapping is one of their ploys in achieving their goals."

"What are their goals, Max?" said Hans.

"Mr. Baughman, their mission is to create fear and intimidation through violence among wealthy contributors to the cause of Israel. There are underground Nazi cells that support and sponsor a renewed Holocaust effort. You are now their target, and danger is heightened because we've learned that they've enlisted trained Middle East terrorists."

Max kept talking, but Hans stopped listening. His concerns were about Sheena. She had become a victim of his inherited wealth! It wasn't fair! Now, as in any war, she could suffer collateral injury or death, an unintended consequence. Unknowingly, he had endangered her life.

"Max, you listen to me good! I want Doctor Sheena put on the highest level of security detail. In the meantime, I'll work something out about getting her into a more defensible place to live."

"No need to worry, Doctor Baughman, that was done immediately upon hearing the security report an hour ago. I also ordered the same for you."

"When I was away last week someone entered my home and searched it thoroughly. As far as I know, nothing was taken, but it gives confirmation of the report you mentioned."

"Our security people assigned to you and Doctor Sheena will consist of plainclothesmen and drive-bys. With Doctor Sheena, we may move someone in next door where she lives, but you need to get her out of there as quick as you can."

"Max, tell your contact, 'I'll be in to see the consortium soon.'"

When Hans hung up, he felt another weight heavier than the load of the inheritance—the safety of Sheena. Events had forced his hand to tell her everything. His mother who had put him in this predicament would support him in what he was about to do.

Hans thought of David's conflict with Goliath. Before he did battle with the giant, he picked up five smooth stones in the brook. Intelligence and experience go hand-in-hand. Experience required David to use only one of those smooth stones, but intelligence told him he may have to do a second or a third sling at the big man. He would do his best to combine those two qualities in his battle with the Goliaths he'd face. The cool brook awaited his visit in search of smooth stones. First, he must square everything with Sheena about his wealth, then, take measures to move her and her parents to a well-secured compound.

Chapter 14

For Richer for Poorer

Hans was awake on his bed unable to sleep. It was the bed he slept in when his nightmarish dream came to him leaving him distraught and depressed the following day. He no longer suffered that recurring dream after reading his mother's letter telling how she found him in the wagon of hay. His insomnia was from another kind of nightmare of his own making. He should have been forthright with Sheena early on instead of prolonging the concealment of his inherited wealth. Sheena had fallen in love with him for what he was, but he had to keep pushing the issue, perhaps out of fear of rejection if she knew. Now, he had to level with her and pick up the pieces. How would he go about doing it? But the greater question was—would she still want him? She wasn't like other women. He looked at his watch—it was ten-thirty. He had to call Sheena.

The phone rang and rang. He was about to hang up when he heard the click of a receiver being lifted. The voice was slow coming on, and Hans knew he had awakened her.

"Hello."

It was Sheena speaking, and he didn't want to leave her upset for the rest of the night after a long, weary flight from Romania. Jet lag and lack of sleep would really do her in.

"This is Hans, I'm sorry to awaken you, but I need to talk to you for a moment."

"Oh, you didn't, I talked to my mom for quite a while and was late taking my shower before going to bed."

He must make the issue about "him" and not "them."

"I'm at a crossroad in my life, Sheena, and there's a matter I need to talk to you about. Are you free tomorrow morning?"

"I'm on schedule at the hospital from nine until three. I'll be free after three o'clock."

"Work until twelve, and I'll pick you up at the hospital."

"I'm not sure that can be done, having been gone last week. The hospital intern chairman may not approve taking off early."

"Just don't you worry, love, I'll take care of it. He will come to you personally and give you leave."

"You seem to have a lot of confidence in what you say. Why is our getting together so important that I have to take off work? Is this about you, me, or both of us?"

"It's all about me, and when I pick you up we will either go to my place or yours."

Hans went back to bed thinking, with that off his mind, he would have a better night's sleep. His first chore tomorrow morning would be to call the hospital Residence Chairman. In view that Sheena would know everything, it no longer mattered that his ownership of the hospital be kept private.

At twelve o'clock Hans was waiting for Sheena in front of the hospital. She was almost skipping with a generous smile on her face. She looked lovely, Hans thought. He was a lucky man, and he hoped he would still be lucky after today.

She jumped in the car seat alongside Hans, saying, "Hans, you were so right. The chairman came up to me two hours before noon and told me it was fine that I leave at twelve, but he seemed to be in a trance. He looked like he'd seen a ghost. Wasn't he the chairman when you were doing your training here?"

"Yes, and that's the reason he looked like a ghost."

She laughed, taking it as a point of humor. He smiled along with her, knowing the chairman's reaction was from being informed about the ownership of the hospital.

Hans decided to bare his soul in familiar surroundings, so he went straight to his own home. He said a silent prayer as they walked to the living room and sat. He didn't choose to sit alongside Sheena, but directly across from her—she in the big armchair—he on the sofa. He wanted to be able to look at her eyes when he spoke. Before he said anything, she saw how nervous he was. He leaned forward placing his forehead in the palms of his hands, then, slid them across the top of his head like he was pressing his hair down.

"I don't know how to make my opening statement, other than start by saying, I love you very dearly. When you first came to know me, all I knew about myself was that I had a wonderful mother who lived a middle-class lifestyle and provided for my every need, sometimes restricting what I asked for, not because she couldn't afford it, but she wanted me to learn restraint and discipline. Part of this discipline included my working at summer jobs for college tuition and expense. When she passed, my world changed. There was the funeral that became the opportunity for us to meet, then came the most startling event of my life. I found out my mother, who pulled me from the fires of the Holocaust, was one of the wealthiest women in Europe, and she had left everything to me. I inherited so much that to this day I'm still unraveling her assets."

Hans wasn't looking at Sheena, but at the floor. Her face had frozen with the look of being in a trance. She had come here thinking Hans had issues of a psychological nature he wanted to talk out with her, but never something like this. She felt insecure. If what he said were true, she was engaged to marry one of the wealthiest men in Europe! What was going on here? How could this be happening to her...perhaps it wasn't true, maybe it was a mistake. Hans was never wrong about anything. Her mind raced to her love of books and the great writers of intrigue, those who wrote stories about the very thing happening to her, and it wasn't like the writers' description. She wanted to flee, run, and hide—it was a world her feet had no place to stand—a world foreign to her experience. She continued to sit dumbfounded and numbed as he continued.

"The woman I wanted to marry was to be one who loved me for what I was and not for what I had. I lived a double life trying to convince you all I had was my mother's house. I moved these duplicitous acts so far down the road I didn't want to tell you, being afraid you would say no to me in marriage because of my wealth. I feared it because you are so much like my mother. She denied wealth to herself because of a higher value of creating a son who would be unspoiled and prepared to face life.

"Her story doesn't end here, Sheena. She allied herself with a consortium of Zionists, people of great wealth whose efforts went to support the causes of the restoration of ancient Israel and the return of her people. She supported the belief that the Messiah must have a nation and a people before He can return to rule the world. Her wealth went to support that cause."

Sheena's eyes were staring at the floor. She was confused when Hans asked her, "Now that you know the whole story, will you still marry me for what I am?"

Things were falling into place. Everything fits! This explains his strange behavior, awkward responses about money—even her mother noted he was always talking about not having money.

She raised her head slowly, took a deep breath, saying, "Hans, your mother knew what she was doing when she reared you. Your histrionics came off perfectly because I suspected nothing but what you implied you were. As long as we remain the people we are now, we will be happy in whatever state we find ourselves, and to answer your question, yes, I will marry you for what you are and not what you have."

He stood to his feet, pulled her to himself, saying, "You are the most beautiful woman in the world."

"You just want me to blush."

"From what I see, I've been successful!"

Hans decided to allow his lifted burden and the atmosphere that surrounded them be savored for several hours before dealing with the more serious matter of living in the dangerous world he had created for her and her family.

That evening Hans explained to Sheena what his mother's fortune was about, that its profits would continue to join the forces of others to support a land and a people for the coming Messiah, the one who would rule the world from Jerusalem. She was told the evil forces that created the Holocaust were still active and that she and her family's lives were to be changed with unpleasant disruption. They would live in a gated, wall-secured home with security people acting as gardeners, attendants, and drivers. For their safety, they would be driven about by a security-trained driver.

Hans went on to tell her that if her parents chose to live in Israel he would provide a home where they could live normal lives. Sheena placed her ring hand up close to her face admiring its beauty and size. It spoke a tangible message of a promise. Her deep blue eyes didn't move, only her lips spoke her thoughts.

"Hans your mother has changed our lives forever, and not only us, but everyone you touch in life. She used the greatest force known to man: it's called love—the energy that's like created matter that can't be destroyed. She wrapped a mission in that package, and now you're giving it to me. My natural person doesn't want that burden, the weight of being separated from life as you have described it, but love with a mission gives purpose for living. Love is a creation of life itself and is a flag that waves from the deepest part of a person." She stopped speaking, then turned and faced Hans, saying, "I see your flag, Hans, waving briskly in the wind. Do you see mine?"

He took her hand holding the large diamond ring, raised it to his lips and kissed each finger, saying, "The ring on your hand is an expression of the time when I first saw your flag waving at me, and as you have so adroitly said, 'Love is a creation, like life itself.' A special new life was birthed when you became part of me."

Sheena's mother and father chose to stay near their daughter, so arrangements were made for them to live in a large, walled compound with two homes and separate quarters for security personnel. Each preferred this, rather than living apart, especially with the security restrictions they were under when traveling outside the compound. Drivers, gardeners, and attendants were all trained security people with the mission to monitor cameras on everything going on inside and outside the compound. Though there were three security men present at all times, and the occupants of the homes knew they were present, they rarely saw or heard them, even when outside walking in the garden. It was the lack of freedom outside the compound that was difficult—attendants always hovering over them.

Hans found himself under similar conditions at his own new residence, smaller in size, but under the watchful eyes of men experienced in providing security.

Sheena chose to continue her internship at the hospital using taxi-looking vehicles with drivers who were trained security men. People she worked with noticed that the administrators were showing deference to her, and soon it became public knowledge that the man she was engaged to marry owned the hospital. The lowly doctor, who in training took orders, would now be giving them through his administrative team. This was a shakeup throughout the whole system. The laws of social stratification took its natural evolutionary change. Sheena was no longer a part of the group she worked with. Han's sudden wealth had abruptly changed their social standing with their friends. Though Sheena still dressed in the same plain and simple manner, they were now looked upon with suspicion. People would greet her only if she greeted them first, and some who would be friends avoided her for fear of others ostracizing them.

Now, she saw the wisdom of Hans' mother in rejecting a wealthy lifestyle for the common life. This was why Hans was who he was and why he could handle wealth. But as for her friends and friendships, she would work against the tide and live by the royal law: that love was the greatest positive force known to man. Using it, she would move that mountain that was created because of wealth. It would start with Karl, Hans best friend at the hospital, the doctor who stood in as a family member at his mother's funeral. She would invite him and his family over to her place for dinner along with two of the single nurses. This would be the beginning of a weekly event that brought small groups to her place with Hans always present. The walls of her compound and the heavy security gate would continue to stand while she worked at taking down other kinds of walls, brick-by-brick, using the power of the greatest force for good.

Chapter 15

Seat of Power

Hans stood in front of the safe-deposit box that had placed destiny over his life. He watched the bank attendant insert her key and turn the lock, then followed using his own key to open the second lock. Hearing the snap of the lock opening, something inside told him this was his final walk down a path where he would hear his mother's benediction and final words. He didn't dread it, but would be glad when it was over. She had groomed him for this moment. There were no more surprises, and he could predict what she would say to him today. He removed the box and made his way to his vehicle where his driver was waiting. At the insistence of Max, he now used a driver who was a trained security officer.

It was now easy for Hans to include Sheena in everything he did; however, he never burdened her with trivial matters. She had been his anchor from the beginning, and tonight they would be together for the final reading.

When he arrived at her compound and went to her door holding the box in his arms, he was greeted by her beautiful face, ruby lips, and long wavy black hair.

"My, you look lovely, a beautiful sight for my tired eyes."

"What are you carrying in your arms?"

"Tonight, I want you by my side when I read my mother's final letter. My mother said, 'I would know when it was time.' I have reached that point, so I've chosen tonight."

They sat on the sofa together as Hans opened the box that had shattered and reshaped his new world. Tonight would be the doxology of his mother's last words. It would register finality. Holding the single-page letter written in his mother's beautiful penmanship, he read it aloud as Sheena looked on:

My dearest, Hans,

What one says in death doesn't mean much if it hasn't already been said in life. Every day I told you I loved you. You were God's gift to me in life. By now, you have made your journey across the barren stretch of desert that has brought you into your own. I would take great pride in you bearing your own Jewish name, a name given you by loving parents, who, by the events of life, gave you to me for my personal life's journey.

You have met my dearest friend, Gustov, who has been like a father to me and is a genius in legal matters of business. Because of the paths we have chosen to take, he will not be able to attend my funeral, and if he chooses to do so, it will be at his own peril. I called him Uncle Gustov all my life. Because of him and others running my affairs, I was able to be a mother to you in the home. He will soon make his journey to his new world of light, leaving you to carry on.

You now have your own mantle to wear for what God has called you to do. You were the child plucked from the bulrushes, trained in the courts of Pharaoh, but will choose to lead your people to the Promise Land. I am now onboard that ship leaving the harbor of life. You see it as a ship sailing into the night. Where I stand on the bow, the sun is rising in bright splendor, and this final letter from me is my hand waving with the message that I shall return to rule and reign with Him.

Your loving Mother

Hans and Sheena said nothing. It was a time to let silence be the reverent farewell salute to a noble person who made people better in this life. Both had tears in their eyes. Hans felt like an eaglet having been pushed from his nest to fly on his own. He would learn to stretch his wings and use the wind to stay aloft.

The first to speak was Sheena. "Hans, no voice will speak louder from the grave than your mother's. The Bible says, 'That they may rest from their labors—and their works do follow them.'" Hans would remember those words in the days, months, and years that would follow.

The next morning Hans called Gustov, the old gentleman in the wheelchair who went to his mother's funeral in disguise.

"Uncle Gustov, I want you to know I have finished the journey my mother has taken me on. I am now prepared and ready to assume the responsibility she handed me."

The Old Man, a title given him by loyal employees, upon hearing the endearing term, uncle, allowed his wrinkled face to accept the tears that came to his eyes and rolled down his cheeks. The voice he heard carried a vibrant tone of confidence—something had happened since their first meeting. Change had taken place. The lawyer heard someone who was no longer a shocked heir having just heard that he had inherited a fortune.

"My son and I say that affectionately on behalf of your dear mother, you have arrived at the opportune time to give me relief. You must fill my shoes as I have done for your mother. The next and final phase in finding my shoe size is to meet with a group of people we call the consortium. Your final commitment to your mother's work will be realized when you give them your allegiance."

One week later after a day's work at his office, Hans' driver pulled through the metal front gate of his compound. Max was waiting for him.

"Doctor Baughman, do you want to talk in the vehicle or inside the house?"

"Inside the vehicle is fine."

"Driver, I'll take over here," said Max.

"I have a message for you from the Old Man. You are to meet with the consortium in two days. Someone will pick you up here at nine in the morning and take you to the airport where a private jet will fly you to Brussels. There, someone will meet you and provide directions where you're to go. Also, you are not to wear a suit but dress in old clothes, and it wouldn't hurt to leave off shaving. You'll be meeting where low-lifers hang out."

"Why the down-dressing and low-lifers?"

"I only follow orders, Doctor Baughman, and asking questions to a superior is not germane to my role. Regarding security, I ask more questions than they like to hear."

It registered loud and clear with Max that Hans wasn't on board with the idea of down-dressing. Hans felt like ancient Naaman who wanted healing of his leprosy but preferred to dip in the beautiful clean rivers of his homeland instead of the muddy Jordan River. To encourage Hans, Max gave him a slight push.

"Doctor Baughman, your mother instituted this in the consortium as an annual event to show that the wealthy had a responsibility to the poor"

A long, silent pause followed Max's shove. It was a light verbal push but was as forceful as he was big.

"Max, my mother's voice coming from you today has the ring of a prophetess. I'll comply, go to the event, and dip in the muddy Jordan River.

Max was trying to make sense out of what his boss just said when Hans shot back: "Will my return trip be the same route?"

"That's a variable," said Max. "Present plans are that you'll be taken to the top of a hospital where they have a helicopter landing pad and leave from there to an airport you didn't fly in on."

Hans was reminded of what he was told at the cemetery in front of his mother's casket by the visiting harbinger, that *his life was about to be changed as never dreamed it could be.* Those words were already fulfilled!

It was a small jet aircraft that seated twelve that Hans had boarded. He was the only passenger and was dressed in a way that would qualify him to be in a soup line: a scrubby beard and well-worn, faded clothes. He had no problem wearing an unshaven face. That came naturally without effort, but the clothes were another matter. His normal casual clothes didn't qualify. He remembered telling Sheena his dilemma and how she came to his rescue. Her father, about the same size as Hans, enjoyed working in the garden with the flowers and had some old clothes that would serve the purpose. When he came out to model them for her, she giggled at his appearance.

"Do I look that funny in these things?"

"Don't move! I want to get your picture for our scrapbook I'm putting together."

"I'll fit in it very well, because that's what I look like—a piece of scrap."

"That's alright, as long as you're my piece of scrap."

"I'll never know why this attire is required for my appearance before the consortium. Perhaps it's a hazing event required for membership."

He remembered his last words to Sheena: "Is your wedding dress on the assembly line?" Coming back at him was the tilt of her head with an amused look, saying, "I'm working on it."

He also remembered why he wouldn't encourage a specific wedding date when she first asked him. But now that she knew of his wealth, there was no reason to put off a date, but the subject was not pursued—he had to leave for his flight.

When he disembarked the aircraft, he saw a Yellow Cab waiting for him with a man standing alongside. He knew right away, the man was part of the security team. He said nothing, proceeded to open the door allowing him to enter. Silence between the two made it appear the cab driver was doing a Christmas Eve charitable act by giving an inebriated vagrant a ride to his homeless shelter. Hans remembered the giggle coming from Sheena at the sight of him dressed in clothes fit for a soup line. He'd always remember that giggle.

Not one word was said between the two until the taxi stopped in the part of town known as skid row. He crawled out of the taxi keeping his head lowered. He had entered a strange new world. The passersby on the street paid him no attention.

"You walk two blocks in the direction we're headed," said the driver, "and you'll see a mission on the right-hand side that reads overhead, Hope Mission. You go in and ask, 'When do you serve the bean soup?'"

The driver drove away, bringing to Hans' mind what Shakespeare said in Hamlet: *"Brevity is the soul of wit."* The driver must have a lot of wit because his conversation was certainly brief, but so was his. It remained to be seen if he had any wit for the meeting in front of him.

On his walk, he passed several soup kitchens managed and sponsored by churches and philanthropic groups. Slow, shuffling foot-traffic became even slower as the needy neared the soup kitchens, waiting for the doors to open. Hans was amused watching human nature in play. People arriving were asking what mission served the best meal. The gourmet tastes buds, whether on a Grecian Epicurean level or at the homeless soup kitchen on skid row, were always the same— selectively discriminating. Hans wondered what would motivate a group of the wealthiest people in Europe to meet in a place like this.

He stopped at a door over which was written: Hope Mission. The sign in the window told the public hot meals were served daily from 5:00-6:00 p.m. He tried the door. It was locked. He knocked on the door, looked through the cleanest spot on the front window. Someone was coming to answer. After hearing the click of the lock, the door opened six inches with a question coming from the man inside, "What is it you want?"

"I would like to know when the bean soup will be served."

The man opened the door, saying, "Come in—they are waiting for you, follow me."

The gentleman he followed wore soup-line-looking clothes, and between the two, the one leading the way appeared even more homeless. Perhaps even in this dressed-down event, there were social gradations.

The aroma of the mission kitchen permeated the entire building. The structure was used to cook almost the same thing at every meal using strong spices including garlic and onions. The smell brought back a memory he had when his mother took him with her to visit a mission she sponsored. The building here had the look of being a man's world. Walls lacked the warmth of pictures, tables bore no touches of softness. It was the picture of what the world saw outside on the street: a cold barren look of man's failure to take care of himself, a stream of people beat up by life's events, some self-inflicted, some by the fate of the vicissitudes of life.

He followed the man to the back part of the mission that led to a door over which was written: Conference Room. Squeaky sounds from rusty hinges were heard when the door was pushed open wide. The threshold awaited his passage.

Hans stood at the entry of a room that looked much like the rest of the mission, drab walls in need of paint, a room lacking the touch of life from the décor of hanging pictures.

Humble uniformity had been the theme at the mission up to this point for Hans, but that suddenly changed when he saw the towering wall at the end of the room. A gifted artist had painted a beautiful mural bearing the theme of the mission. It showed the majestic figure of a Man riding a great white horse with a sword in his right hand followed by other warriors on swift steeds of power.

Over the top of the painting were the words that gave title to the One in command: *Lord of Lords and King of*

Kings. At the bottom of the painting were prophetic, futuristic words showing the results of His battle: *The kingdoms of this world shall become the kingdoms of our Lord.* Hans stood mesmerized by the mural's artistic quality and its thematic impact. Coming to him was a picture of truth. He had down- dressed for this occasion to be taught humility and equality with humankind, but another message was framing itself from the scene of the mural: it will ultimately be the Man riding on the white horse who will change the physical and spiritual state that man finds himself in.

The voices of truth coming from the visual message of the mural had competition: someone was calling his name. "Doctor Bauman…Doctor Bauman!"

Looking across the room, Hans' eyes fell on a homemade conference table around which were thirteen unpadded, armless chairs holding homeless-looking men dressed much like him, men of great wealth abasing themselves in what they wore. Curious eyes were fastened on a young man who had inherited his mother's wealth. At the far end of the table, sat a man who ran Katharina Enterprises: his mother's longtime friend, Uncle Gustov.

"Welcome Doctor Baughman to our group."

The lawyer looked older than he did in their last meeting, but his eyes and voice still carried the ring and look of erudition. He sat in his wheelchair with his ever-faithful walking-cane nearby.

The old lawyer opened the meeting. "Gentleman, I want to introduce you to Doctor Hans Baughman, son of the late Lady Katharina. I avoid the use of any surname in honor of her wishes. The man standing among us is not the son of the name he bears but is the son of a young Jewish couple killed in the Holocaust in Romania. Please be seated, Doctor Baughman.

"First, let me say the reason we are dressed as we are is because a certain lady, your honorable mother, started this tradition. Once a year, she wanted this consortium to leave plush offices and ivory palaces and walk among those who had been bruised and injured by life's unfortunate events, to touch and feel the pain of want and need of those in deprived conditions. Today happens to be that time of the year. What we have done is a reminder that we are but mortals and are responsible for our brother.

"Doctor Baughman, we are all here today because of your mother. She brought together people who had great wealth whose commitment was to Jesus, the Jewish Messiah. We all hold the belief, as the sacred Scripture teaches, that He will return to earth to rule in Jerusalem. Our purpose and calling in life is to use wealth to promote His return by supporting the state of Israel and her people. Geography and His people are two immutably connected entities. The people you see around this table make possible activities that are far-reaching beyond your imagination, and it all points to the theme of the mural on the wall. Your mother has already informed you what our objectives are and to reiterate them in detail would be superfluous.

"We wanted this meeting with you to establish where you are in support of this consortium. You are the sole heir of your mother's vast estate, an enormous volume of wealth, making you one of the richest men in Europe. Your mother's purpose in bringing all of us together was to use wealth to support the people of Israel and its borders. The Messiah's first kingdom was in the hearts of men. His next kingdom will be over Abraham's geography and his descendants. He

163

will be David's heir to the throne in Jerusalem and will rule the world in truth and justice.

"Throughout the years, I have stood here in place of your mother while she prepared you for this hour. I say to you as Mordecai said to Queen Esther, 'Who knows but that you have come to the kingdom for such a time as this?'

"Now my son, would you care to address this consortium that has stood with your mother in support of the land of Israel and its people? Please tell them of your intent as the new proprietor of Katharina Enterprises."

Hans stood to his feet. He took time to move his eyes around the table looking at each member as he spoke.

"Gentleman, I have returned from a long journey in search of myself. My name is no longer Hans Baughman, A name that declares my legal position and all rights therein. It was given to me so I could be saved and reared by a German woman who found me orphaned in the middle of the Holocaust in a village in Romania. She lived in fear someone would find out I was a Jewish child. After she passed, she told me the whole story in her own handwriting. This was the starting point of my journey. As you well know, my mother denied herself the pleasures of living in affluence but maintained a middle-class lifestyle in order to raise me so I wouldn't be ruined by wealth. In her heart, she knew I was saved from the Holocaust for a special purpose. She has fulfilled her mission in this life, and I stand here to walk in her shoes. Until my mother passed, I never knew she was wealthy. She loved me in life as much as if I'd been her own biological issue.

"Upon her death, the greatest legacy she left me wasn't her wealth, but a box of letters. That box was a ticket that put me onboard a train in search of myself. She was not only successful in rearing me by her self-denial—she was the cause of me finding myself. My mother's wish was that I find my name given at birth so we could be free of every trace of him who brought such shame. I now know the names of my parents who birthed me, and the name they gave their son. I am Jacob Isler, and for the record, I want the consortium members to know that what my mother started, I will continue to give my support."

Hans sat down. The old man slowly rose to his feet, held his cane to support himself.

"You have spoken well, and we could have expected nothing less knowing your mother. The amount of funds coming from you will keep our current operations in full swing."

Turning his eyes away from Hans to the men seated around the conference table, he continued.

"In view that I have just been voted in to serve one more year as chairman, I am recommending to this body today that Doctor Hans be appointed to the advisory committee to serve with the other three members. There are ballots in front of you...."

Before the chairman could finish his sentence, one of the members interrupted, saying, "I believe a public acclamation of this appointment would better serve us!"

After unanimous approval, the chairman directed a few words to Hans. "It will take you a little time to grasp the extent and scope of our operations around the world. Today, we want what time we have left to be spent in getting acquainted. Lunch will now be catered in by the team of people who do the cooking here at the mission. You will be served what is on the menu tonight at five.

"Now before we're served lunch, our security team tells us we should be cautious about our personal safety. Our enemies know they are losing the battle because of people like us who can use money off the books, money that can't be traced, to fund programs and activities that accomplish our objectives. They are focusing on anyone who gives of their wealth to support Israel."

Each member of the consortium came up to Hans and welcomed him as a member. He had just finished lunch when someone from behind whispered in his ear, "It's time to go." It was the driver who picked him up at the airport, then added, "For security reasons, we don't linger when it's time to go."

He was ushered out to the street to a waiting car. On his way to the helicopter pad, he drove by people on the street that were lined up waiting to go into the soup kitchen of choice. They thought of themselves as prisoners, locked up, confined to a station in life from which they could never escape. Yet, when he was on the streets moving about he felt unconfined, free from the restrictions he was under at home, free to move and be himself and remain anonymous. It was a paradox. For one class of people who had nothing, it was a prison, but for him who had everything, it was freedom. Now, he knew how Sheena felt. Wealth had made them prisoners and had forced them to be subject to rules and laws that governed survival, a different kind of survival than those on the streets.

After arriving home, he called Sheena to tell her that if her father didn't mind, he would keep the old clothes he wore as part of their scrapbook memories. They would remind him they were part of his journey in finding himself. He had found the door that opened to a place where he could retreat, live in another world and be alone with himself without the trappings of wealth, security, and close scrutiny. Perhaps Sheena would join him on these escapades from their prison of wealth to the down-dressing ventures of soup kitchen anonymity. On these streets dressed in poverty, he was more secure than when surrounded by all his security personnel.

Chapter 16

High Stakes

It had been two months since Hans appeared before the consortium and had subsequently met twice with its advisory committee. It was a group that used wealth to influence what was in the best interest of Israel and her people. It included the support of politicians in the West favorable to Israel, patronization of Zionist companies, and support of resistance movements in countries that suppressed emigration of Jews to Israel. Covert missions that required funding that intended to leave no paper trail were known only by the chairman and committee members.

Hans and Sheena had changed their weekly event of getting together while security hovered around them, to that of down-dressing, visiting soup kitchens and parks where the homeless strolled. A security officer would drop them off in the morning and pick them up at six o'clock. The place they visited was a prison for those living there. For Hans and Sheena, it was freedom. They could walk the streets, window shop, and even buy ice cream from vendors, then in jest assign a grade on their performance in pretending to be homeless. Even a passerby once offered them money by the way they looked and performed. They took his money—then gave it away. People would sometimes give them strange looks when they saw them reading books on the best sellers' list, and of course, Sheena's diamond ring was never worn. Soon it became a challenge. They were learning the names of the regulars, some of whom had been successful in society at one time, but alcohol and drugs had devastated them. What the homeless and vagrants didn't know was that the soup kitchens where they ate were stocked by one of their own who ate alongside them.

It was when they returned to Hans' walled fortress after one of their homeless outings, that they saw Max, the Big-One, waiting for them. He was still in his vehicle with his driver.

"Hans, I'll go in and put on some coffee and you can talk with Max."

"He usually doesn't talk, just brings information, but maybe today is a special day."

By this time Max was on the move, almost in a leaping stride with a slight bounce with each step, making his way in the direction of Hans.

"Doctor Baughman, as you know the mailroom examines all mail to be sure it's secure and free of any hazards. I have a letter here from Romania, addressed to you but without a return address. They apprised me of this, and I thought it may be an emergency."

No two men standing face-to-face could have looked more opposite. Hans wasn't small, just looked small alongside Max, but where they really stood in contrast, was in their dress. Hans, still in his vagrant street clothes, looked like a pauper, and Max, with a pin-stripe suit and starched shirt, like a corporate lawyer.

He took the letter from his vest pocket placing it in Hans' hand, turned to walk away when he heard Hans say, "Wait Max! Let's see if Sheena can read this for us. It may be important."

After entering the front room, Max saw Sheena dressed like a peasant. He almost gave comment but thought better of

169

it. Though she looked like a pauper and played the role on the streets, these people had the power to turn him into a real one without the acting part. One thing he learned in his line of work: do your business and don't step over the line. He'd done that a few times and gotten into trouble and didn't want to learn that lesson again. He watched Hans open the letter.

"Sheena, I have a letter here written in Romanian, do you think you can translate it for me?"

She spoke the language better than she could read it, but her skill in linguistics enabled her to parse the Latin syntax. Instead of reading the interpretation, she sat at a table and wrote the translation out on a sheet of paper.

Hans watched her eyes and facial expressions to get the preview of what would follow. Nothing came until the second sentence when it registered its full impact. He remained quiet waiting for the complete translation. When she finished the last sentence, she said nothing for a moment, then handed him the transcription.

"This is terrible news to come our way," she said, then thought how terribly depressed Hans would be when he read what she transcribed:

Mr. Baughman,

When you were here in our village, you were very kind in treating our child for her illness, and we returned that kindness by helping you understand what happened to your family. My husband took you to the mass burial site that you and others later examined. Someone found out what happened that night and with other villagers went to the regional authorities. They have arrested and imprisoned my husband charging him with slander and if money isn't forthcoming, they'll refer the matter to the central court. A friend of mine is taking this letter to the German Embassy to be put with their mail leaving the country. Can you please help us?

Maria

Hans' face turned away from the letter and his eyes looked out into space. Sheena, seeing the pain he was going through, put her arm around him to lend support. Then, he snapped quickly into taking charge.

"Max read this and tell me if we've had this kind of issue before."

After reading it, he said, "Not exactly, but similar. Most likely, this is just a local issue, and sometimes they like to keep it that way so they can control the outcome. There are two ways to go about solving this: deal with it at the office of the dictator himself or at the local level by offering a bribe. Either way, it will make family life miserable living in the village afterward, and in that country it's not easy to resettle elsewhere."

Hans asked, "Can we get them out of the country?"

"That's a high-stakes game. The cruel dictator in that country will do nothing on a humanitarian level."

"Will he trade the family for the threat of losing Western investment or the country's credit rating with Western Nations?"

"That's another high-stakes game you'll be playing," said Max. "There are a lot of variables connected with that approach, and there are the never-ending exchanges of talks."

"As I see it," said Hans, "our only alternative is to get him out of prison and bring the family to this country."

"If that's the way you choose to go," said Max, "we'll work at moving them across the border into the neutral country of Yugoslavia with a fake passport, and once we get them into that country we can easily move him to Europe. We'll need key players in the country who know the culture and language and who can make it appear to the regional authorities that the bribery money is coming as a collection from indigenous nationals. If the local authorities know it's a big operation from outside, they'll not take the bait for fear of reprisals coming from above them. The bribery money will be miniscule compared to the rest of the operation."

"Money is not an issue here," Hans said. "I recommend you get on this right away and keep me updated. If we can get them here, you can fit him in somewhere with employment."

"That will be no problem."

Hans realized if what they were attempting to do were successful, it could be duplicated in other countries in moving Jews to the homeland. This might be a problem coming his way that could end up being a blessing in disguise.

Before leaving, Max left a positive note for Hans. "If we can pull this off, it will guarantee the relatives still living there a certain level of safety, because if higher authorities find out he got out of jail, then out of the country, it becomes a political issue beyond the borders of Romania and heads will roll locally."

Before leaving, Sheena called her folks to tell them she would be home shortly and to put on water for tea. She gave Hans a goodnight kiss, got in the car with her driver and wished she were behind the wheel.

When she drove away, he waved bye, then reflected on how many Jews were in countries that didn't want them.

There had to be ways to help these people free themselves to go to the land of their ancestors. If this could be done, it would make the hardships of having wealth worth it all. His inherited wealth had to be wrapped in a mission, or it would be a curse to him in this life.

Chapter 17

Inner Circle Tragedy

Hans was scheduled to be at the consortium's advisory committee meeting at eight o'clock in the evening. He would meet with the group, place before them a proposal that had been given much thought. He had hoped he would have information on the project in the country of Romania. It had been two weeks since the operation was put in motion, and no news had come from Max. Hans was nervous and concerned about its success or failure. He had already drawn up plans in his mind of a new broad operation that would include a global enterprise of using freighters as a business front to pick up Jews in ports, open seas, and at any point they could be reached. The countries targeted for pick-ups would require inside people to organize and assist those fleeing the country. This would call for the use of secret agents working through contacts in Israeli Embassies. The operation would begin small with two or three freighters, gain expertise, and if successful, expand the project to include additional ships. Under the cloak of darkness in open seas, smaller boats could move undetected to an awaiting freighter. Tonight, he would present this to the committee.

Security was always high in these meetings. Sometimes they were held in hovels, the countryside, even on tops of skyscraper buildings taken there by helicopter. Tonight, the meeting would be held in the basement of one of the many banks owned by a committee member. When Hans arrived, he found the other committee members present. After the financial report and operations review were submitted, it was opened up for new business and deliberation. Seated around the table were men of experience, men who had succeeded and failed several times over but had ended up as some of the most successful in Europe. Hans addressed his issue when it was open for discussion.

"Gentlemen, I'm before you tonight as a new member of this committee serving among men who have proven themselves to be smart, capable, and above all, wise. Your wealth came through your own efforts after many years of hard work. I am here tonight with none of those qualities. Yes, I bring wealth, but wealth that has been inherited. This does not mean I come with less vision or purpose, and knowing what I have experienced so far, I would gladly have my old life back without wealth, the life that allowed me to take a walk any time of the day, go anywhere during the night, all without the fear and trepidation now lurking at every corner and crevice. I never wished this to touch my espoused and her family, but events have made it so.

"I have been appointed to this advisory committee and have said little in our previous meetings. However, tonight I wish to present to you a concept that fits into our paradigm, a plan that will move Jews from lands where they are unwanted and are not allowed to leave. In reality, it will be a smuggling operation on a large scale using registered freighters doing legitimate business to pick up Jewish families who would then be delivered to Israel. They would be smuggled aboard the ships at Ports, offshore, wherever they may be found and wherever they can be reached."

As Hans spoke, the Old Man in his wheelchair kept his head facing him while his bright blue eyes darted from one member to another to measure their response to what Hans

175

was presenting. The reception he saw on their faces allowed him to settle in with his eyes calmly on the one he hoped would be his protégé.

"I will match," said Hans, "whatever the committee puts up for the purchase of several freighters to begin this operation. It is my intent to see this be an operation that carries itself perpetually by it breaking even on the financial bottom line. It will require someone with expertise in purchasing these ships and overseeing the staffing. Another alternative would be to purchase a smaller, established shipping line using existing infrastructure to start with and make changes as we see fit. I know this is a big leap into an area where we've not been before, but it fits into our stated goals and makes us mobile and stealth in moving people to the homeland under the cover of business."

The chairman was the first to address the subject. He carried certain mannerisms unique to his persona. One of these was always displayed just before he would speak, a certain shifting movement of his body, like it was a tic. When others saw him in that state, they would stop talking and listen. Today was different. He showed his typical gesture, but behind his rugged, aging face pleasure could be detected in what he heard coming from the young heir.

"Hans, it appears your business acumen is ahead of ours when we were your age. This committee never rejects any new idea outright, and neither does it accept one without considerable thought and research. You know as well as the rest of us on this committee that you have the power and resources to do as you wish independently of us, but we appreciate your willingness to involve this committee in your proposed project. We will give it much thought and consideration. On the surface, it appears to be a viable operation, and now that I have spoken, other members can speak."

The first to speak was an American. The committee called him Chuck. He was independent, opinionated, and demonstrated the typical unreserved affable characteristics of many Americans. Everyone liked him. He was not as well educated as the other members of the committee, and unlike Hans, he came from a poor family but had used his natural wits to invest in oil in Texas, then moved his company around the world. His tall, thin frame always looked angular but sitting at the table leaning forward accentuated the look. Men, his age would be distracted by his trim frame and a full head of hair, done in a short, crew-cut style, making him look ten years younger than his age of sixty. Chuck carried a strong instinct for business and knew how to get things done. He was never a middle-of-the-road person, usually strongly opinionated for or against an issue. One never had to guess where he stood. Even with his less formal training, people highly regarded his skill to size things up. He allowed common sense to be out in front of everything he did. So, when he addressed Hans' new venture, the rest of the committee welcomed his insights.

"Doctor Baughman, have you any idea how many potential pickups are out there? This would be the bottom line for any project like this."

"This is a variable. There's no way of knowing the answer to that question. I will say that whatever the potential, the end result will be how the groundwork is laid and carried out. The people working on the ground are just as important as the ship itself."

The Texan continued. "I would highly favor this innovative effort by starting with one ship and work out the inevitable wrinkles before adding to the fleet. Making an operation break even is secondary to the project. If it's a worthwhile endeavor, and it works, we'll lose money gladly. The consortium must never allow itself to be tempted by profit."

"You are right about that, Chuck," said Hans, "however, a program that functions and carries itself, and at the same time accomplishes the objective, will always guarantee greater perpetuity. You and I may not be here tomorrow. Wealth may not always be in the hands of people who sit where we sit, and if something's in place that's self-sustaining, it will guarantee continuance. I concede to your point of commencing with just one ship until the yanks are straightened out."

The lawyer was impressed with Hans' skill to disagree with someone without being offensive doing so. Hans had already shown something of his late mother's people skills. The next to weigh in on the subject was the banker, Erhart Schmidt, who owned the building they were meeting in. He stood in contrast to Chuck. He was short, round-faced, with a sharp, pointed nose, the kind that if he were a grade-school teacher the kids would make fun of him behind his back. He brought to the table more of a CFO's skill than that of a CEO. He used his skill to oversee, disburse, and account for the millions that went from the consortium to their varied programs and operations. He spoke English with a blended European accent.

"First, may I say, Doctor Baughman, that your mother must have had a lot of faith and trust in your ability to leave everything she had to her only son..." Hans sharply interrupted, saying, "Mr. Schmidt, My mother gave me everything she had while she lived and it wasn't money—she gave herself. It is easier to give wealth away in your death than it is to give yourself while you're alive. I believe this is why we dressed as we did when we all went to the soup kitchen recently. Pardon me for interrupting, please continue...."

There was a pause. No one spoke. *The old lawyer raised his eyes upward toward the ceiling with a slight smile on his face, saying in himself, Lady Kathy, you did well with this boy.* The banker collected himself enough to respond.

"Doctor Baughman, I can see you have not only been trained to help cure bodies, you are adept at straightening the mind out about life. I shall always remember you in a positive way by this appropriate rebuke I deserved."

The lawyer saved Hans from having to respond, saying to the banker, "Well, Erhart, what do you think of Hans proposal?"

"I approve wholeheartedly. We all know this is a method already in use to smuggle less fortunate Third-World people to wealthier nations. Unlike the treatment they receive, the ones we pick up for Israel will be treated as our guests. However, there is a problem here with starting a new venture. Our enemies are quick to notice change, especially a new small change. Operating a new company with just one or two freighters may raise a flag; however, if we bought a small viable company already in operation, it could go undetected by those who oppose us. In banking, we carry a lot of notes in the shipping industry and have contacts in financing new loans. We know the people who take inventory, inspect, and evaluate ships for purchase. We use them when commercial loan applications come in."

The Texan broke in after the banker spoke.

"I can see the wisdom in what the banker has said. If the infrastructure already exists, we can save time by not reinventing the wheel. However, the top management must be controlled by our people who have expertise in this field."

William, the last member of the committee to voice his position had made his wealth in the booming new business of electronics and business machines. He had major contracts around the world with governments favorable to the West and was on the cutting edge of guided missile systems. He was an Englishman who practiced counter-culture-ways that offended some of his compatriots, one being he rarely wore a suit—thought their formal society should look more like the common person. He and the American got along very well.

"Hans, I think your idea is a splendid concept. My company will provide advanced technology for each ship. This'll give the captain an edge in critical situations."

"Today is historical," said the lawyer. "It appears everyone concurs with Hans in the implementation of a boat rescue operation. Let it be the record that we'll search for a viable, well-run shipping company for the sole purpose of smuggling Abraham's posterity into ships that will disembark them on the shores of Israel.

"We will commission Erhart to research the availability of small shipping lines that will be coming on the market. The rest of us can do our own independent work of finding a viable line that will serve our needs. Hans will be putting up fifty percent of the cost, and I'm sure the balance will not be a problem.

"Unless there's someone else in mind, it falls on Hans to be in charge of this program and will report its progress to this committee. As a closing note, may I remind everyone security has been tightened and great caution should be taken when moving about. Success always raises the danger level. I know you came in your own vehicle, Chuck, but we have a driver outside to take you to the airport, and I suggest you return with him."

"You fellows are too uptight about this. I came here in a rented vehicle and I'll return the same way."

"Remember Chuck," said the lawyer, "you're not in Texas, this is Europe!"

The committee closed with prayer and prepared to leave in their normal fashion. They never left a building grouped together, but separately at three-minute intervals after each called his driver. These were the security measures implemented by Max. Chuck had rented his vehicle and parked it near the bank. He was first to leave. Three minutes later the Englishman called his driver, and before hanging up, a massive explosion was heard coming from outside the bank. Silence gripped the room. Still connected by phone with his driver, William gave instructions to his driver. "There's been an explosion outside the bank! Proceed with caution and send for the police! Apprise the other drivers of what's happened."

The old man took control, saying, "We all know security protocol! We remain inside until our people tell us it's safe to move on. It could be a ploy to get us outside."

The room was tense. The old man sat down, stared into another world at another time, mumbling to himself in soliloquy. "In the war they used violence to intimidate us, today they enlist radicals from the Middle East to do the work they used to do themselves. When the Nazis came through Holland, they used cruel acts to intimidate the public into submission. Nothing is more sacred than life, and they knew how to threaten it with violence."

He stopped speaking to himself, turned, and faced the others with the look of a seer. "There is a stronghold of evil facing us as never before. When the enemy sees Israel established and the city of Jerusalem in the hands of its ancient people, they know the time is short before the King of all kings will come."

The old man who had spoken like a prophet slowly raised himself to a standing position. Others in the room saw the pallor hanging on his aged face. "Gentlemen, I believe we have lost our dear friend and colleague, Chuck."

The sound of sirens from the police and fire trucks could be heard in the heart of the basement. The old man now bore the weight of the news he just gave the others.

"Friends, we can view only from a window. We are never to be seen together in public, and when we leave we will keep this tragedy to ourselves."

They moved to a room overlooking the street scene. All wanted to look away but forced their eyes to view what was left of the car Chuck had driven. They watched his body being placed on a gurney and covered with a white sheet. As a group, they were anonymous to the outside world, couldn't be seen together or connected in any way. Even in death, they were forced to view everything from afar. Isolation was part of their calling. Before leaving, prayers were said for Chuck's family.

Chapter 18

Bread That Returns

Every morning and evening Hans and Sheena would call each other. They had made a pact together that they would avoid talking about anything negative until they exhausted themselves with the positive. It was a point in humor but it served to ingratiate each other's presence. Sheena had gone full blast chiseling at her mountain: class separation. Attempting to prove to herself that love was the greatest force for good in changing people, she had entertained three different groups in her home, each having a common interest: married couples, singles, and those near retirement. Hans was always present and saw to it she had help with food preparation and housekeeping management. When a guest arrived in a vehicle, they parked in a lot outside the walled compound and walked through a security clearance gate attended by a security person, who then escorted the visitor to the residence.

It was an evening for another scheduled group from the hospital. The party of seven guests was seated for dinner with Hans and Sheena appropriately placed at opposite ends of the table. Above the conversation, a knock was heard coming from the front door. Hans' eyes quickly went to Sheena. Both knew it was security. The home came equipped with a doorbell, but Max had imposed a rule that it never be used by his people. This way the residents could differentiate between security and invited guests. Security never came to the door unless it was a matter of urgency.

With conversation buzzing around the table, Hans showed a hand gesture to Sheena that he'd answer the door. He excused himself, went to the door, and found the security gardener waiting with a message.

"Sorry to bother you, Sir, but our Big-Man said you would want to hear the news about Ediniti. He's on the security line in the guard house."

"Thank you, give me a moment and I'll be right out."

Conversation was still brisk at the table when Hans returned. The only one not talking, but carrying a concerned look was Sheena. With everyone attempting to get a word in edgewise, Hans gave Sheena a phone call hand-gesture pointing outside. She acknowledged the message, and Hans went with the security person to speak with Max.

Security had private phone lines in the guardhouse, and it was there Max waited on line to hear from Hans. This was his first time being inside the guardhouse here at Sheena's place. One pulling into the front gate would never know there was a building like this sequestered in the back. It was clean and well kept—the phone was out in plain view. Hans always kept a formal front with security, and it extended to Max.

"Hello Max, this is Doctor Baughman. I understand you have news about our project in Romania!"

"Yes, in fact very good news! It has been tough going from the beginning until now. They've just crossed the border into Yugoslavia with their family of five. It'll be downhill from now on. Our people in the country made the bribery money appear to come only from family and friends. The five of them are happy and in good health."

"Excellent! Relocate them nearby with some degree of anonymity. They will be an invaluable asset in exposing the country's Holocaust record that continues to be denied twenty-two years after the war. When you get them settled, let me know so I can meet with them."

Hans was by himself in the guardhouse when he hung up the phone. He remained standing with a faraway stare reflecting on Mario Nicolescu's history in the village where he was born. *This person, now free from prison and on his way here, knew his mother and father when he was a young man. He had even seen him as a twelve-month-old child learning to crawl and walk around the shop and helped his father and grandfather by running errands and cleaning up. He knew them by name, and while hiding watched them die along with others, just because they were Jews. He didn't have to jeopardize his position in the community by telling him anything, especially, about the mass grave. Whether he could be considered a righteous Gentile remained to be seen. However, if he followed through and supported the cause of exposing his country's involvement in the Holocaust, he would deserve the right to be remembered as a righteous Gentile.*

He continued his reflections whispering aloud to himself, "Solomon, the wise one, said, 'Cast your bread upon the waters and it will return after many days.'"

On the day he and Sheena treated Mario Nicolescu's daughter for her illness, he didn't know at the time it was a small piece of bread placed upon the waters that would come back a hundredfold. *Does this fit into the paradigm of, "Give and it shall be given?" Perhaps it does, provided one doesn't give for the purpose of getting.*

Sheena saw Hans enter the area of the dining room with a smile on his face with two clenched fists showing a thumbs-up. She didn't know exactly what that meant, but whatever it was, it was good. The group around the table was still trying to establish their space in conversation and hardly knew Hans had been away.

Sheena had worked hard planning the evening. As soon as the group finished the main entrée, she and Hans cleared the table in preparation for a fun event. Everyone noticed the doctor assisting Sheena with the dishes. It made him look like one of them, narrowing the distance of the unconscious class-chasm. One of the guests, a manager of a department at the hospital whose name was Ruth, was a candidate for a class-chasm change. During the evening her stiffness had softened and she became brave enough to be herself.

"Doctor Baughman…" Before the guest could complete her sentence, he turned around, saying, "Ruth, in my house and on the street, we are on a first-name basis. You call me Hans, and I'll address you as Ruth…okay!"

Sheena looked back over her shoulder, saying, "And that goes for me as well!"

Hans quickly retorted, "Ruth, before I broke in, you were saying…."

"I must say this is the first time a doctor has ever broached me requesting friendship on a first-name basis."

"And I hope it won't be the last," said Hans. "You were saying…"

"Is helping Sheena with the dishes one of your methods of enticing her to marry you?"

"It's only one of my methods—the others are top secret."

Another guest who worked in Human Resources jumped into the fray, saying, "Men will do about anything until they get what they want, then they fall off the wagon."

"Whoa…but that's where the wisdom of the woman comes in," said Hans. "You see, the female is more insightful than the male in deciphering motives. She knows he's going to fall off the wagon, but he doesn't know that she knows, and until that time comes for him to fall, she gets everything from him while the getting is good. Now ladies, don't tell me you didn't know that. That's one of the secret weapons in your arsenal."

They joined in laughter together while Sheena was saying to herself, *that's a side of Hans I never saw before.*

After clearing the table, Sheena took over. "Friends we're going to play a challenging game called, '*What Person Said This?*' and the first one who gets the right answer to the statement I read wins a wrapped prize from this box I've placed here on the table. If we're ready to go, I'll commence. What person said, 'Religion is the opium of the people?'"

"Nikita Khrushchev," someone said.

"You're close, and he probably used that statement a lot in his political writings." '

"It was none other than Karl Marx, a German philosopher," said Ann, a ward clerk.

"Very good!"

"Ann," someone said, "how did you know that?"

"I may be just a ward clerk, but I do a lot of reading and took a couple of courses in philosophy."

"Right now, you're the smartest one among us," said Hans.

"You can open your gift if you like," Sheena said. In the presence of everyone, she opened her gift and found two tickets to the symphony orchestra.

"Now, on to the next question. What person said, 'Neither a borrower nor a lender be; for loan oft loses both itself and friend?'"

One of the younger nurses among them answered, "William Shakespeare."

"Good answer! There's a bonus offered with this question." Sheena looked at the young nurse, saying, "What was the name of the play and the character in the play who spoke those words?"

"I believe it was in Hamlet," said the nurse, "but I don't remember the character."

"Well you got half of the question right, and because it was so difficult, you deserve two selections from the gift box. By the way, it was Polonius who gave that advice to his son."

The evening went on with more trivia questions until Hans interjected something that was not part of the agenda.

"This is the last question of the evening. Who said, 'Cast your bread upon the waters, and it will return after many days.'"

No one answered, but Hans continued. "Bread is the symbol of life, and waters, the symbol of people. Wise Solomon penned those words after years of studying human behavior. I have found this to be a principle in life. When it's not about us, and we give ourselves, eventually, what we give will come back to us in one form or another. This principle applies in all areas of life, but especially to us in the medical field. We help people in a way no one else can and reap its benefits when the streams of life flow our way."

When the evening closed and everyone left, Sheena felt she was making headway in breaking barriers between them, and with Hans around to give punctuation with his jest, only added icing to the cake. She couldn't wait to hear what the good news was about with Hans' thumbs-up statement.

"Hans, you know I'm waiting to hear why you were beside yourself earlier tonight!"

"Do I have a surprise? Our team of people in Romania managed to get the father out of jail and the whole family smuggled into Yugoslavia. It took some doing and some paying, but our people made it happen. They will be a force to reckon with when we show the world Romania's Holocaust."

"Hans, you did it, you really did pull this off! I'm so proud of you! This deserves a big hug from me."

"I'll welcome that."

"Now, if you haven't fallen off the wagon, you can help me with the dishes."

Chapter 19

Prison of Wealth

Hans had moved into his newly refurbished office located on the fourth floor of the corporation's headquarters building that covered a city block. With the help of Miss Shuster, he was learning to oversee and administer the large enterprise his mother had built, and when Hans offered her the position of Executive Administrative Secretary, she accepted. He needed someone with her skills and knowledge to represent him in board meetings and conferences. Miss Shuster became Hans' gatekeeper in a front office with several secretaries carrying different portfolios. Though he addressed her to others as his secretary, everyone knew that with the old lawyer retiring from the scene, she would become the second most powerful person in the corporation.

He remembered the Old Man's contribution, first to his mother as a father, friend, then as a major contributor in running the front office of the business so she could be a mother to him. He also remembered his wise advice when learning the ropes of becoming chairman of the company…"Don't rely entirely on your management team. Learn enough to know when they aren't doing a competent job. Ask questions that are open-ended. You rarely want to ask yes-and-no questions. Though questions invariably lead to that point, they must justify the answers. This is a method of interrogation. It makes them think you know more than you actually do; however, don't let them think you're a know-it-all, otherwise, they'll not be creative in their answers, which doesn't help you. The people working here are very incisive, and if you stymie their freedom and creativity, you'll lose a lot of their work value and expertise."

As Hans settled in at the helm of the corporate ship, he solicited the Old Man's advice in tough matters. However, when it came to fiscal issues, he would always direct him to lean on Miss Shuster's expertise. He was a man who was wealthy in his own right, but what kept him in his mother's employ was from two commitments: to God, and loyalty to his mother's family. Later, Hans would learn the Old Man had given a promise to his mother's parents that if anything ever happened to them he would take care of their little girl. Something unfortunately did happen, however, the little girl was no longer a child, but an adult prepared to build an empire from her father's wealth. He also learned that upon the news of his mother's death, the old man asked his personal secretary to leave for the day, and turning to shut the door to his office, she saw him weeping. It was a known fact around the office that after his mother was buried, he went disguised to her gravesite to place flowers,

The Old Man had no family, and his late wife bore no children—he was alone, and when he called Hans, "My Son," it was with affection. He belonged to the family, yet he couldn't sit with Hans in the family pew at his mother's funeral. The only time she ever mentioned him was in her last letter explaining why he couldn't be present at her funeral. It was a sacrifice for the Old Man to be the face of her wealth in running her enterprise, but it kept her and her son hidden from those who could endanger their lives.

"The office" was what Hans called the place where he went to work every day. It was filled with people in cubicles making calls around the world, collecting data, creating reports, and management conferencing. The group that handled global affairs was the largest staffed segment of the enterprise, with most of the activity involving Canada and the U.S. Many who worked in that division were Americans and Canadians. Each major division had a regional director who reported to the corporation's CEO, who in turn reported to Hans and Miss Shuster regularly.

It was Friday afternoon and Hans had worked all week with global affairs, conferencing with managers, staff, and going over reports. He was tired and about to leave for Sheena's house for dinner when his administrative assistant, Miss Shuster, informed him he had an important call waiting. When he lifted the phone, he heard Max's voice.

"Doctor Baughman, this is Max. The good news I have for you is our party of five has arrived and is settled in at an apartment where there are Romanian immigrants. I thought this would be best for their adjustment to this country."

"Excellent! See they have spending money and tutors to teach the children German. To succeed in this society, they must learn the language. Break it to them that they will be requested to help in corroborating as first-hand witnesses the Holocaust in their village during the war, which will also include the mass grave we found. If they still have family there in that area, we'll provide the funds to establish them in another region so remote in Romania that no one will know where they've moved. This will be done before we show the world the evidence we've found. Our objective is to spotlight the evidence of the mass grave and use our Romanian witnesses to corroborate the country's dark Holocaust history."

"I'll get my contacts on this right away after I consult with the couple we just got into the country. A list will be made of family members who may be affected by your actions here in Western Europe."

"Before we hang up, give my executive assistant the address where you've put this family, and tell them Doctor Sheena and I will visit them soon."

Before Hans left his office, he checked the address where Max had settled the Romanian family. It was two-hundred miles away, which meant he'd travel by plane. He was glad it was the weekend with a Friday evening dinner with Sheena, and her parents.

One week later, Hans and Sheena sat side-by-side in a private jet on their way to visit the Nicolescu family he managed to get out of Romania. The flight plan the pilot filed on record was changed after reaching the halfway point to a small airport near the community where the family was staying. They changed into clothes that would match the typical working person, and when they disembarked, there was a taxi there to pick them up. They carried no luggage on their way to the waiting taxi.

"Is the driver one of your men, Hans?"

"He's one of Max's men. No one can run the security organization like him—he's the best."

"Does he get paid well for what he does?"

"He's paid twice what I would be paid as a doctor in private practice, plus health benefits and a bonus. His job performance is motivated more by what he believes, than what he's paid. He's one of us."

The driver opened the door without saying anything. Max had a rule. Drivers were allowed to greet their passengers, answer questions addressed to them, but never initiate conversation. Their business was security.

"Are you nervous?" Hans asked.

"No, not any more than when we visited the soup kitchens."

When they arrived at the address of the family, Hans recognized a security person dressed in plain clothes loitering nearby. The apartment unit Max selected was off the street and on the bottom floor. The people living in the area appeared to be from Eastern Europe. Children were running about playing nearby. One of the children stopped and stared at the two strangers walking down the sidewalk between the apartments. She left her playmates, ran up to Sheena, took her hand, saying, "Doctor...Doctor!"

"Look Hans...our little patient from Romania!"

The spirited child took the hand she held, kissed it, and put it next to her cheek with a big smile all over her face. The doctor leaned over, gave her a hug, and then spoke to her in Romanian. "Can you take us to your Mommy and Daddy?"

"Doctor," Hans said, "she's a little piece of bread who has washed up on your shore."

"That she is Doctor...she's all of that...and more."

The three were standing together when the door opened. The family knew they were coming. Excitement was written all over their faces, and the aroma of fresh coffee and baked sweets filled the home that was spotless and well kept. They filed the other two children in and had them speak in German. "Thank you for coming to see us here at our home." Sheena pulled all three of them into her arms and kissed each one on the cheek.

"Doctor Hans, someday we're going to have three girls in our family."

"What about boys—don't we get any boys?"

Sheena tilted her head slightly, rolled her eyes, saying, "I believe whatever we have will be entirely up to you, Doctor, if you know what I mean."

"Oh, I know what you mean. I happen to be a doctor and have studied genetics and know all about the Y chromosome!"

"We'd better get down to business instead of discussing science," Sheena said.

The wife of the house broke into their conversation, saying to Sheena, "Would you like coffee or tea to drink?"

"We'll both have coffee, thank you."

Out came a tray of coffee with cream and sugar and two plates of freshly baked sweets. After being seated on the sofa, the tray was placed in front of them on the coffee table. The couple looked happy with their three beautiful children sitting on the floor nearby.

Hans asked, using Sheena as an interpreter, a series of questions before reaching the real issue of visiting the family.

"Are you comfortable in this house?"

"We are very comfortable, especially with the washer and dryer."

"These living quarters are only temporary. In time, we'll have a job for Mr. Nicolescu where he will make a good salary to provide for his family. Have the tutors been instructing your children in our language?"

"Thank you for the job," said the father. "Many Romanians would want to be where we are. We were poor, but now we have been made rich. Thanks to you! Yes, the teachers come two hours a day, and they can already speak a lot of German."

"When you get settled in your permanent home your children will attend the best private school in town as I promised. Until you start work at your own job, someone will bring enough money every week for you to buy anything you need. I will leave my office phone number with you, and if you have to go to a doctor in town, there is a clinic nearby. All you have to do is walk in and tell them who you are and give them the name, Max. They have already been paid, so you don't pay anything. You are never to mention my name to anyone. You don't know me, nor do you know Doctor Reznik, okay! Are there any questions?"

The wife responded, saying, "We don't have any questions, we just have a lot of thanks to give to you for everything. We are free of the terrible people who mistreated us and put my husband in prison. We can't thank you enough."

"Now, I want to talk to you about some serious matters the children should not hear. Would you mind sending them outside to play until we finish our discussions?"

The mother gathered them up and explained that the adults wanted to talk about adult things, and they could return after they finished.

"First, what close relatives of yours live in and around the village of Ediniti?"

"They've all moved to work in the oil fields near Ploesti, and I think that's why they picked on us like they did—we had no one to stand up for us."

"Mr. Nicolescu, I'm going to ask you to give a statement at another time using the same words you used when you told me about my parents and grandfather being among many others in your village who were forced out of their homes and shops and killed in the streets, and that you saw it all from the place where you hid. Also, I will ask you to tell your story about burying the dead in the mass grave. This will all be filmed for the world to see what the Nazis did in the Holocaust in Romania.

"Mr. Nicolescu, will you go on film saying all the things I just mentioned, a film that the world will see. It will be just you and not your family?"

"I will most gladly go on film and tell the world the terrible things they did that day when they came into our village, but not only our village, there were others nearby."

When you do this, Hans thought, I will call you a righteous Gentile.

Before inviting the girls back inside to say goodbye, the parents were told not to talk to anyone about what they discussed.

On their return flight, the fates of both parties were discussed. The family from Romania would live in freedom, but those of wealth would return to voluntary confinement behind walls that kept them imprisoned. However, both on board the plane took heart knowing that within those walls they were free to carry on the work of preparing for the Messiah's return as a conquering king to rule over His people and the world.

Chapter 20

Operation Prince Henry

Upon returning from their visit with the Nicolescu family, Hans and Sheena went back to work in their new world of wealth and self-imprisonment, a world they were now accepting as a calling. Until now, they had not realized the extent of devotion the Old Man, now called Uncle Gustov, had for Hans' mother and her family. He and his late wife had through the years deprived themselves of a normal life by choosing to live in seclusion behind gated walls attended to by ever-present security personnel. His remarkable traits and skills extended to his home-away-from-home, the Katharina Enterprise headquarters building in downtown Munich.

It was at the central headquarters building where Hans went to work every day that he learned the extent of influence the Old Man brought to the company. Through the years, he made his life easier by putting together a management team second-to-none. His outstanding virtue was that he felt unthreatened when he brought in someone who knew more than he did. He learned from them and became as good as they were. His breadth of knowledge of corporate law commanded respect from his staff of lawyers. The umbrella corporation, now owned outright by Hans, increased the Old Man's generous annual salary plus a bonus, all with the approval of Hans.

The Old Man intentionally kept his distance and watched the young upstart learn by trial and error. He knew Sonje

Shuster, Hans' executive secretary, would be there to help when there were rough waters. He saw Hans demonstrating skills of quick analysis, could think fast on his feet and was good at articulating job descriptions. His training and experience in the medical field had taught him as a doctor to look for symptoms that were measurable to the eye before drawing blood for the lab. He worked from the general to the specifics. Also, being a doctor he had learned to have a good bedside manner while enforcing strict compliance. When the Old Man visited the office, he would always walk around with his cane and a smile on his face showing approval of his watched-over prodigy. He acted as if he owned the place, and a few knew he did own part of it, ten percent of the whole enterprise. Hans' mother gave that to him when they were getting the corporation going in the beginning, and it mushroomed into what it was now.

This was the beehive Hans came to work at one early morning following their visit to the Nicolescu family. Each employee had to show ID before entering the main lobby. The executives had a private entrance at another location, but both had security guards stationed at these points.

When Hans entered his office, he found an urgent message on his desk from his executive assistant: "Doctor Baughman, a Mr. BK called and left a message. I asked for his number, and he said you had it in your files. He said it was important you call him right away."

Hans' eyes brightened when he saw the name BK. All the committee members of the consortium used code names and unlisted phone numbers known only among its members. BK was the banker who was researching small viable shipping lines going on the market. He used a private office line to return the call.

"Hello Erhart, this is Hans. I got your message to call."

"Yes, we must meet over the matter discussed recently. There's a parking garage two blocks down from where we last met. I'll meet you on the third floor where you can jump in with me, and we'll use my vehicle as an office. When we finish, my driver will return you to the garage."

"I can be there anytime today," said Hans.

"Nine o'clock is fine," said Erhart.

Hans called his standby driver downstairs who worked with security during his downtime. As part of security, drivers were never told where they were going until he boarded the vehicle.

When Hans' vehicle reached the third floor of the garage, a dark vehicle with flashing lights pulled out of a parking space and stopped alongside him. A window came down, and a hand motioned him in. He instructed his driver to pick him up at this site when he received his call.

After shutting the door, he saw a thick folder on Erhart's lap. The banker began the conversation, saying, "This information just came across my desk from my contacts overseas. In Japan, a small merchant shipping company is going on the market, and from what I've been told, it has been well maintained and carries a profit margin.

As I said in our last meeting, a company we use specializes in ship evaluations. They will be able to go on board, examine the ships and everything significant to their condition. After evaluations are all done, the seller will put in escrow an agreed amount to cover any undisclosed or hidden defects. This is a form of insurance. Our lawyers who will deal with this will cover all the legal ramifications to protect our interest. We could keep the ship's registration in Japan and our management and operations elsewhere."

"How many freighters do they have in their fleet?" Hans asked.

"Information that I have here indicates there are eight freighters. I think this fits the number we had in mind. The Japanese are known to take care of their equipment and run clean ships."

"I suggest," said Hans, "we pursue this by getting your people to give us an evaluation of the fleet. If what you're saying turns out to be fact, that it's a viable shipping line and has a positive bottom line, it would be an ideal opportunity, providing everything else fits together."

"I concur," said Erhart. "I'll leave this folder with you containing the information on the shipping line, and in the meantime, I'll get right on this matter of having the fleet evaluated so we can be in a position to submit a fair offer. Inside the folder, the company submits an evaluation by their own evaluator, but I never go by what a company tenders. I always use my own inspection team for more accurate reports."

"I'll wait until you get an evaluation of the fleet," replied Hans, "and if everything looks good and the committee approves, we'll proceed with our plan. Buying the company will allow us to keep the Japanese name, making the operation and change of ownership stealthy."

Hans was dropped off at the garage where his driver was waiting. It was nearing noon, and he called Sheena to tell her he'd meet her in the hospital cafeteria for lunch. When his ownership of the hospital became public knowledge, Hans stopped volunteering one day a week, and the only time he was seen was when he met Sheena for lunch.

The driver pulled into an inconspicuous spot in the hospital parking lot. Both were wearing casual clothes, and when entering the dining room the driver separated himself from Hans. Because he had grown a beard, he went unrecognized until he joined Sheena who was waving at him near the end of the line.

"How did your morning go Mr. Hans?"

"My morning went very well. In fact, it went great! I received news about a very important matter that I'll tell you about later. What about your day? Is your labor of love demonstrating any results?"

"Oh yes, very much so."

No sooner than she finished her sentence, two nurses walked by and saw the two together. One was Ruth, a department manager. She showed excitement at seeing the two together.

"Doctor Hans, I didn't recognize you with your beard. I've been telling everyone how your sense of humor entertained us on the evening we were with you and Sheena. We all had a delightful time, and I look forward in getting together again, but the next time it will have to be at my place. And on that occasion, I'll call you Hans."

"Ruth, you're free to call me by my first name anywhere you see me."

Ruth leaned closer, saying almost in a whisper, "When is the date of the special event—you know, the tying of the knot."

"We're working on it."

After she walked away, Sheena looked at Hans. "Who's working on it? I'm the one that's working on it!"

"How is the dress coming along?"

"Oh, I can't make up my mind about a lot of things."

"Well, you made up your mind about the most important part of the wedding."

"And that would be...?"

"Me, of course!"

"You love to catch me off guard, don't you?"

202

"Only when you're not looking."

As they progressed through the cafeteria line, others passed by them showing friendly exchanges. One came up to Sheena knowing the man beside her was Doctor Hans, but pretending she didn't, said, "Doctor, who is the stranger here with the beard, is he your new man?"

"Yes, this is the new man I'm now dating, and I'm afraid the other one is going to be jealous." Laughter followed.

When they sat at an empty table, others joined them. Hans saw on Sheena's face a relaxed expression leaving the message that her labor of love had produced the intended results—her mountain had been moved.

Two weeks after meeting with Erhart, the banker, Hans went to his office for his workday and found a written message from Miss Shuster. "Mr. BK called wanting to speak with you. He left no number—said you'd return his call."

He was preparing to call the banker when his private line rang. Only a selected few had his number and any ring on that line took priority over any pressing matter. It was the banker.

"Hello, this is Hans."

"Hans, this is BK. I have some very good news about the Japanese shipping line that's on the market. The company we hired to do the inspection analysis has completed the project and has telegraphed a report of their findings. The company flew their men to ports around the world and inspected each ship with a team of two inspectors for each ship. These people know what to look for and are good at what they do. Because they are in such demand, we pay high prices for their services, but in the end, it is well worth it."

"Is their report complete or partial?"

"It's a complete report consisting of about one hundred and fifty pages with approximately fifteen pages per ship. It comes so detailed that it even rates the condition and quality of the silverware.

"One part of the package analysis shows the collective synthesis of the eight ships. The overview uses the numbers between one and ten to mark their standings. All combined together, they average out at an eight. Individually, they come in with two ships at nine, four at eight, and two at seven.

"This company we hired sent in their financial field people to look at their inside books to verify their public records, and they all check out. It appears to be a go from my point of view."

"In that case, we'll pay the company's asking price and I'll put up sixty-percent of the total purchase, and the balance can be carried by other interested parties. The commercial management of the shipping line will be handled by my company, and the exercise of implementing the on-land and people-smuggling operations will be supervised by the committee."

"I think you have everything laid out well, Hans. Knowing your company's history, you will have a long trail of lawyers with expertise in these matters handling the minutia of detail and legalese. I'll send you the originals and copies to the Old Man and William in England."

"I commend you on your expertise," Hans said, "and it's clearly telling why you were chosen to serve on the committee."

"We're all called to serve using the talents God gave us for the purpose of keeping a land and a people together for the coming Messiah. Some serve to spread His Word, others like us are called to bless Israel by doing what we're doing."

"My late mother would have said, 'Amen' to those words. I profoundly appreciate your depth of character, knowledge, and experience. Erhart, do you know anything in history about Henry the Navigator?"

"No, I can't say I do."

"Prince Henry of Portugal was a forward-thinking leader of his day. He contributed to the Age of Exploration in the fifteenth century by building ships for Portugal to explore the countries across the oceans creating commerce and trade. This project in front of us will be called, 'Operation Henry.'"

"That's a clever theme, and I know it will go well under your direction."

Hans hung up after expressing appreciation for his support. It would take a month to finalize the legal transfer of the shipping line, but in the meantime, its management could be organized and put in place and be ready to go when that time came.

The consortium committee met with top members of the Israeli secret service on a regular basis to be apprised on where to place the millions sent out every month. Hans made contact with the point man in Israel by visiting the Israeli embassy and posting a hand-carried letter:

General,

Our organization is taking on a special project that complies with our objectives in giving aid and assistance to Israel. I am not at liberty at this time to reveal this to you, but will at a later date. We are purchasing a Japanese seafaring shipping company and will replace all members of the top management team. To fulfill our reasons for purchasing the company, we will require the top management person to be a committed Zionist. He is required to have broad knowledge and experience in every aspect of the shipping industry but does not have to be an Israeli.

The prospective candidate will be required to have high-level management skills. The salary is market driven and commensurate with experience and qualifications. If you can recommend any qualified candidate, it will greatly benefit our efforts in helping the country of Israel.

For the cause of Israel,
Dr. Hans Baughman

One week later, Hans had a sealed message from the Israeli embassy that required his signature before the courier would release it. It read:

Dr. Baughman,

Great effort on our end has been made to find someone for the management position you described. At this point, we have only one lead. A man who fits the prerequisites you have laid out is emigrating from South Africa. We know everything about his personal history, which is impeccable, but not his intent for employment. Our embassy in South Africa has one of our special service people making contact, and as soon as we hear, I'll get back to you. In matters of this nature, my name is not revealed. Good luck.

Three days later a courier from the Israeli Embassy showed up with another sealed letter to be released only after he signed for it:

The gentleman of whom I spoke in my last memo will be contacting you about the position you need to fill. He comes highly qualified and is a patriotic Zionist in the strictest sense.

It was Friday afternoon, and the news Hans had received from the Israeli Embassy would serve as a news piece for conversation at the special Friday Shabbat with Sheena and her family. It would be a time when candles would be lit before sunset with the traditional recitation of a blessing, and in this Jewish home, it would include the Messiah.

Hans didn't have to ring Sheena's doorbell. She opened the door as he stepped up and the three family members were standing in line to greet him. He hugged and kissed the beautiful woman he was engaged to, and then kissed the cheek of his mother-in-law-to-be. Last, he embraced his soon-to-be father-in-law. Tonight, was a special event— everyone was dressed out, even the men wore white shirts, ties, and donned a yarmulke skullcap. The aroma coming from the traditional Jewish cooking permeated the home and served as a pleasant memory marker. The Shabbat dinner in this Jewish family was modified to apply its symbolism to Yeshua, the One who came to give rest to the soul.

During the formalities of lighting the candles, the women covered their heads with a scarf, saying traditional Jewish prayers, followed by the senior male taking a loaf of bread, breaking a piece of it and giving it to each family member, saying prayers of blessing and quoting the words of

Yeshua, "I am that bread which came down from heaven, and if any will eat of Me he shall live forever."

The men remained seated together on one side of the dining room table while the women brought the piping-hot dishes off the stove and out of the oven. The atmosphere was serene and a night to be remembered with Hans sitting across the table from Sheena, acting like a teenage flirtatious boy, and Sheena taking it all in with a look of peaceful elegance.

The Sabbath had begun, the work had stopped, but conversation that involved action continued. Hans was first to speak.

"The three of you are all the family I have. I have no one else to take into my confidence, and there may be unguarded moments when I will say things that are matters you shouldn't hear because they may involve people's lives, programs, and policies that are highly sensitive, and sometimes even clandestine. Therefore, I want you to know that whatever you hear me say in your presence is never to go further than your ears. Never discuss what I do with your friends and even your relatives in Israel.

"My inherited wealth has made all of us prisoners. I will never be a doctor in private practice, neither will Sheena. Every day I fear for her safety when she leaves and returns home."

"But, Hans, I feel safe with the driver we have."

"Yes, I know, he does a good job, but we need to change the scheduling so your leaving and coming are unpredictable. We have a policy at work that doesn't allow a driver to know where I'm going until I get inside the vehicle. It would be wise to change your route to and from the hospital every few days."

"You are offering very good advice, and to please you, I will adhere to your recommendations." She reached across the table with her soft, delicate hands and held one of his, saying, "You're under a lot of stress, aren't you?"

With a sigh of frustration, he added, "There's so much to be done…so much to learn and act on. I'm just at the point of understanding all the intricate details of my mother's holdings, and then I go and buy a cargo shipping line."

Realizing he'd spoken out-of-turn, he looked at Mr. and Mrs. Reznik, saying, "I just spoke to my family in my unguarded moments about a business purchase that should be kept secret."

"Hans," said Mr. Reznik, "I never dreamed my daughter would be marrying someone of wealth that would put us in such constraints."

"Neither did I! When I first met your daughter, I had no wealth, and when I found out, I concealed it from her until she consented to marry me."

Sheena's mother continued the conversation, saying, "Hans, I want you to consider me your mother-in-law, and what you say in your unguarded moments will go no further than our ears."

"What do we tell our friends and relatives," asked Sheena's father, "when they ask us what our future son-in-law does for a living?"

"You have a choice. Tell them I'm a doctor or a CEO of a company. This ends the discussion about me tonight! And before we clean up the kitchen, I have a special announcement to make. I have arranged for my sweetheart to be away from the hospital next week, and we are all going to Israel on a private jet to spend five days at a Mediterranean villa."

"Israel…on a private jet! How do we rate getting to do something like this?" said Mrs. Reznik.

"Because my mother's company owns the plane and you're part of my family."

Hans watched the excitement cover their faces. Like children, the other three jumped to their feet, pulled Hans up forming a circle, and did a traditional Jewish dance. Above the sound of singing, a voice could be heard, "Look what I've started…!"

Chapter 21

Country Without Walls

Early Monday morning two vehicles could be seen pulling up to a corporate jet warming-up its engines outside an empty hanger. One vehicle carried four passengers with its driver, the other carried luggage that would go on the well-supplied aircraft. The destination was Tel Aviv, Israel, and would be on a four-hour flight schedule.

The plane's interior had been modified to provide a greater level of comfort for its passengers than what commercial airlines offered. One section was sealed off at the rear of the plane where only the chairman, his family, and friends were allowed. It contained a private restroom with a shower, sofa, and six large first-class reclining seats. Outside the captain's quarters, as it was called, there was a small private dining room and kitchen. Between the kitchen and the cockpit were a radio room and sixteen, first-class seats. The aircraft came with the company when Hans inherited everything and was for the chairman's personal use. Up to now, it had been in storage undergoing certain modifications and never used by Hans. This flight would be its first since the renovation. When others were onboard, it was at his invitation.

The other phase of the plane's modification was in its communications system. It was made into a flying office with instant communication with Hans' headquarters. Hans had brought along one of the company's communications operators to monitor activities in the central office and provide a daily report. The operator would sleep on board the plane, and the pilots would stay at the airport hotel. Hans was on call for certain pending matters, and if an emergency came up, he would be four hours away.

Excitement filled the air when the plane lifted off. Hans had never seen Sheena's mother and father this excited. They were like canaries let out of a cage to experience freedom for the first time. They were going home. The father yelled across the aisle to Hans sitting alongside his beautiful daughter.

"Doctor, where did you pick up that gorgeous woman sitting with you?"

Hans thought Mr. Reznik was really into this trip—it had given him a new lease on life.

"It's the other way around. She picked me up in her old car and took me home, and I never let go of her."

"And I'm going to lose my beautiful girl. Sometimes one doesn't know what he has until he faces losing it."

"Pop, and you don't object to me calling you, Pop, do you? You're not losing your daughter; you're gaining a son, and eventually grandchildren!"

"Well...I like the ring that statement has about grandchildren...SON!"

Sheena leaned near Hans' ear, whispered, "Remember, three girls."

"Your father's come alive on this flight."

"It's because he's going home."

"He can stay in Israel, you know."

"He's committed to a cause, just like you, different in nature, but with the same forceful energy."

"And what might that cause be?"

212

"It's me. I'm the apple of his eye, and he will suffer anything until the rope line is cut."

"And what cuts the rope?"

"Marriage, silly!"

She saw Hans, as bright as he was, slow in picking up on the healthy relationship between a devoted father and his daughter, then realized her own lack of insight: Hans had no father, only a devoted mother. Some things could be learned only through experience. Her eyes became teary. The father who would have given him life-experience lay in the mass grave near the village where he was born. Taking his hand, she held it next to her cheek allowing her tears to roll down her face.

"Why are you crying, my love?"

The beautiful face showing ruby lips shrouded with long, wavy, black hair turned and looked at him. "Because I love you more than anything in the world."

It seemed this flight was bringing everyone to life. Now, it was the mother's turn. "Hans, this is an experience of a lifetime—what are we going to tell our relatives and friends who'll be meeting us here at the airport?"

Her statement was bittersweet. The bitter part was they had few relatives, most had been killed in the Romanian Holocaust; the sweet came from knowing that those who did survive would be there with their friends.

"Just use the normal greeting, say, 'Hello, it's nice to see you.'"

"Oh, I don't mean that! How am I going to explain getting off a private jet with all the attendants around, doing everything for us?"

"You'll be in Israel, Mom, we won't need attendants there."

"What about the private plane?"

"Tell them your future son-in-law managed a free ride with the company taking a flight to Israel. Mom, there'll be more than this to explain when they see the villa we're staying in by the seashore!"

"Oh my, what shall I do?"

"Just tell them to talk to me about it."

She stretched herself toward him leaning in front of her husband. "You won't lie to them will you?"

"No, Mom, I won't lie to them."

Sheena was laughing inside. Hans was reflecting on how this flight had changed him too: he was calling Sheena's parents, Mom and Pop.

Three hours into the flight, the teletype monitor came from the acoustically engineered radio room with a typed message for Hans, knocked on the door, saying, "Doctor Hans, I have a message from your administrative assistant."

Hans read the transcript: "Dr. Hans, there's a gentleman by the name of Cohen calling from South Africa wanting to talk to you. He said you would know his purpose for calling and would like to meet with you about the matter." Hans went to the radio room and wrote on a pad the following message: Schedule time and date to meet with Mr. Cohen in the conference room, inform the Old Man, then get back to me. He handed the message to the radio operator, saying, "Send this right away," then returned and sat alongside Sheena.

"You can take that look off your face, Miss. Beautiful"

"Does it look that bad?

"Worse than bad, and you know why?"

"Why?"

"Because it puts a wrinkle on the nose of your beautiful face."

"Are you going to be this complimentary after we're married?"

"I promise I won't fall off the wagon."

"Well, is it alright if I ask how the message will interfere with this wonderful experience?"

"You may! It was a welcomed call, and it just may be the beginning of an operation that will change a lot of lives for the better."

"I won't ask what it's about, and that way I'll not worry about it."

Sheena saw a sudden change come over Hans. She knew it had to do with his activity in the radio room. He began talking to himself: "It'll be the biggest thing since the Age of Exploration." She didn't know what it meant and didn't want to ask—then bingo! He came back to life as quickly as he had faded and was at his usual self.

When Tel Aviv came into view, they were all looking out the window. After landing, the plane came to a stop in front of its storage hanger. With the engines cut and the plane idle, a voice was overheard, saying, "I still don't know what I'm going to tell my friends about the private Jet!"

Hans looked at Sheena and smiled. "I can't wait to see her response when they reach the villa." He had rented a large villa by the Mediterranean for a week and had Sheena call and invite her mother and father's friends and relatives to spend three days relaxing in the warm waters of the sea and swimming in the private pool in the courtyard. The mother and father knew nothing of this arrangement, but Hans felt he owed it to them for what they had to endure living in their cloistered prison at home.

After clearing customs, it was a grand reunion. The mother was proud to take her new son and introduce him to everyone, hoping all the time no one would ask about the private jet.

The villa Hans had rented for the group provided bus service for its customers. There were twenty friends and relatives present, mostly elderly, some having survived the Holocaust in Romania. The driver assisted the group in boarding the bus, passed out cold bottles of water and allowed them to settle in, then made a brief speech.

"Doctor Hans has asked me to give all of you some instructions on why you're together on this bus. You have accepted his invitation to spend three days together at a luxurious, ocean-side villa with rooms located on the bottom floor. You will have a private dining room with three meals served daily. There will also be a private lounge only this group is allowed to meet in. If you have to go into the city, we have vehicles available for that. Enjoy your stay!"

As they drove to the villa, Hans could hear the Tower of Babel roaring inside the bus. He listened to Hebrew, German, Romanian, English, and Yiddish, all being spoken at the same time. One spoke in Hebrew, another would answer in Romanian. Most of the people on the bus could speak three or four languages, and Mom and Pop were having the time of their lives.

Lunch was served at one-thirty, and after Hans and Sheena were seated, her mother came over and whispered to her daughter and Hans, "I don't understand it. None of them has come up to ask us about the plane and all this flair and fete here at this fabulous place!"

Sheena saw amusement in Hans' eyes.

"Mom, they aren't asking you those things because they were told if they did, they would be sent home."

Sheena tried to keep a straight face, had to look away for Hans to finish his ploy and deliver his punch line if he had one. "You wouldn't…you couldn't do a thing like that."

"Mom, I think you want those questions asked."

She stiffened her upper lip, lifted her chin and looked down at Hans with squinted eyes like a schoolteacher disapproving of her student's behavior, held that stern look, then, cracked a smile, saying, "Son, you're smarter than I thought you were." They all cracked up laughing. She never raised concerns over that matter again.

The rest of the day Hans and Sheena went swimming in the sea, walked the beach while holding hands, and picked shells from the history-laden shore.

The party of twenty-four was in their dining room being served dinner at seven in the evening when the teletype operator came in and went to Hans' table with an unsealed envelope. Hans knew why he was there, and without discussing the matter, entered the conversation with the young man.

"Sit down Fritz and order a dinner with us."

"Thank you, Sir."

"The menu is on the table there, order a steak and lobster, or anything you want. The waiter will be by soon, just give him your order when he arrives."

"Sir, I brought this information over to you tonight…" Hans interrupted.

"We'll not talk about that right now, besides, you know what's in it—you can tell me later."

"How did you know my name, Sir?"

"I make it a point to know everyone's name who works around me, even though we have no direct contact. Where did you learn radio and all that goes into its technology?"

"In the navy, Sir. My aptitude score was high in this field, so they sent me to school."

"How long have you been working for us?"

"For one year, Sir. I've been working with the day crew in the radio room and attending class at night. They offer limited engineering classes at night, but if I can get on the evening shift, it'll give me the opportunity to increase my class load."

"What field of engineering are you going into?"

"Electrical."

The waiter came by and Hans flagged him down and motioned him over.

"Give this man the freshest and the best item you have on the menu."

"The best we can do is lobster and steak, Sir."

"Does that fit your fancy, Fritz?"

"Sounds great to me!"

Turning to Sheena, Hans asked, "What suits your fancy, my sweet?"

"I'll have what Fritz is having, but without the lobster—it's not kosher,"

"Waiter, put her lobster on my dish," then, turning to Sheena, he said, "When no one is looking, you can eat it off my plate. Waiter, bring us three orders of lobster and steak!"

Peering at Fritz, Hans continued his conversation. "So, Fritz, if you work at night, how many units can you carry?"

"Probably ten, Sir."

"That's a heavy load when one works. You must be gifted!"

"Math and physics come easy for me."

"Well, you're gifted then. I should've had you as my tutor when I was doing math in my undergraduate work."

Three waiters came from the kitchen together to serve their piping-hot orders. It was now seven-thirty, and everyone was famished with voracious appetites after swimming all afternoon.

Hans was about to offer a prayer of thanks when he looked across the table and saw Fritz bowing his head. He waited until he finished his prayer.

"Fritz, did you say grace over your dinner?"

"Yes, Sir."

"Well, let's start over; say grace for all three of us here at this table."

Hans listened to Fritz's prayer. Remorse hit him. Instead of being a Fritz in his earlier years, he had allowed the locusts and cankerworm to destroy those times. He became lost in deep, quiet introspection, and Sheena had to pick up the conversation. She knew what was going on inside him.

"When did you become a believer, Fritz?"

"About a year ago I met a girl who was very religious. She invited me to her religious activities and I attended. At first, I went because I was interested in her, and one night I saw something I had never seen before. I was told Jesus was the Messiah, and that God's greatest expression of love to man came by Him dying on a cross. I wept inside, I wept outside. My body shook with a new strange feeling, and I became changed and a new person."

"What happened to the girl?" asked Sheena.

"We're engaged to be married. I've even bought her a ring, but we haven't set a date yet."

"Well, what's holding you back?" said Hans, jumping back into the conversation.

"Money. I don't make enough to pay for my books and tuition, plus support a family. The girl with whom I'm engaged is also a student and won't graduate for another year."

"If you got a scholarship for your books and tuition," Hans said, "and had a fifty-percent increase in your salary, could you handle the marriage?"

"Oh, I would be on the gravy train, Sir."

"Tonight, when we finish eating, you're going to the office and make a call and set a date for your wedding. There will be two wedding dates set tonight, but I won't have to make a phone call!"

"I can't believe this is happening to me!" said Fritz.

"Neither can I," said Sheena.

After dinner, Hans and Fritz went to the office leaving Sheena seated at the dinner table. She went through her tote bag, found her scheduling book, and went to work with juggling her life around the most important event of her adult experience. Unknown to Hans, she already had circled prospective dates.

The next morning, Sheena lay in her bed looking at the ceiling. She had never felt this peaceful. The man of her life had agreed to any of the three dates she suggested as their wedding event. Now, she could get on with the challenge of planning everything in detail. An unexpected knock came at the door, followed by a familiar voice.

"Hello, Sleeping Beauty, your Prince is here!"

"Give me a minute!"

She scurried to her closet, found something to slip on, looked at her face in the mirror with several strokes over her hair with a brush, and opened the door.

"Are you going to look this beautiful in the morning after we get married?"

"You know how to start the day out right—why are you up so early?"

"To give you my schedule and spend the whole day with you alone, because tomorrow I have to fly back to Europe and meet with an important person who may join our company's management team. This was the news Fritz brought over last night."

"Do you want me to go with you?"

"I want you to stay here with your family. Going with me would be a punishment of fifteen hours in solitary confinement. We'll make up for it today. I'm taking you to some interesting archaeological sites—alone, just the two of us. It will be a long day so be comfortable in what you wear. I'll meet you for breakfast in thirty minutes at the dining room."

It was Wednesday morning. The plane had been in flight for three hours, scheduled to touch down local time at nine o'clock. Hans would meet with a Bernard Cohen and the Old Man in the plush, private conference room. This would be his first performance in the presence of the eagle-eyed perfectionist who stood with his mother in building this vast enterprise that was now under his control. He respected his advice and wanted him to be present.

Before disembarking the plane, Hans stuck his head inside the radio room. "Fritz, go visit the girl you're going to marry, but be back by three o'clock for our return flight."

"Thank you, Sir! Something just came over the teletype classified urgent. It's copying the last page—you may want to see it before you go."

"Put it all in a folder, and I'll take it with me," said Hans.

The driver was standing by the black limousine with the door open awaiting Hans. Underneath the image of formality and pomp that people saw was a security system in place solely for the passengers it carried. The driver was a former Special Ops member, and the vehicle he drove came equipped with its own concealed private arsenal. The folder Fritz had given him contained the resume of Bernard Cohen, the interviewee awaiting his arrival in the conference room at the headquarters building. He carefully studied the material, noting that his record of management was with a shipping line out of South Africa that had close ties with Israel. He knew the Old Man would examine carefully what he held in his hands and be on his cutting-edge mental dexterity that would match Solomon's.

When Hans arrived at the underground parking garage, the Old Man's driver had already arrived and was assisting his passenger with the wheelchair. Hans quickly moved up behind the chair, saying to the attendant, "I'll take over from here."

Hearing Han's voice from behind, a smile spread across the Old Man's face. He forced his stiff, aged torso to bend far enough around to look at the young man who had brought light to his dimming twilight years.

"What an honor," said the Old Man, "to have the Admiral of the fleet to be at the helm of this old ship going into mothballs."

"You're not going into mothballs, or else you wouldn't be here today."

"You don't mind doing the work of a hired servant, do you, Hans?"

"I learned to be a servant from the woman who became my mother. People learn to become servants by example. Isn't this the reason the Lord washed the disciples' feet? The modern educational theory of learning by doing isn't new, it's as old as time."

"Every time I see you, Hans, I see more of your mother coming out in you—she wasn't afraid of getting her hands dirty...."

"Especially when those hands picked me from the death chamber of that Romanian village, the hands that would chance the smuggling of a Jewish child into Nazi Germany as her own. That's what you call, 'Getting your hands dirty!'"

"Those are the hands pushing me now, Hans, they're Katharina's, your mother's, extended to me from where she lies. Doesn't it say, 'Their works do follow them?' Values live on inside others after we're gone, and if we ever learn anything on this treadmill of life worth remembering, it's the truth that goodness is immortal."

"And that source of goodness is God," said Hans.

"You have spoken as your mother would have said it."

Now they were in a long hallway on their way to a private conference room where they would interview a party who might become the manager of a new department. The Old Man gave Hans some thinking-out-loud advice.

"Remember, when interviewing there are times you lead, and there are times you follow. Skill shows itself when one knows when to talk and when to be silent, when to ask questions, and when to refrain. Sometimes, what is not said is more important than what is, and one must never overlook that gut feeling. *But there's a rule I have: 'Don't pay any attention to gut feelings if all the facts aren't in.'*"

Two security men stood at the entrance of the conference room like praetorian guards watching over Caesar's welfare. Upon seeing the arrival of Hans and the Old Man, they stood more at attention, opened the door as Hans rolled inside an old man in a wheelchair. It was a scene from Ironside, the crusader of truth and justice. The mental gymnastics suddenly flipped. He saw at the end of the table sitting next

223

to the assistant CEO, a small, beady-eyed, balding man that carried a look of having been bullied in life. Hans couldn't escape the humor that jumped in front of him: a picture of him and Max, the Big-One, standing side-by-side.

The assistant CEO and Mr. Cohen stood to their feet. Hans thought his diminutive stature must make him feel like a David among Goliaths. Hans was resisting the mental images being conjured up by this man of such short stature. He had grown to embellish a part of his nature that didn't fit the role of a medical doctor, and now as a chairman of a vast corporation, little had changed. Had he not become a doctor, he might have succeeded as a standup comedian. That part of his nature some would call a skill or a gift. It was always lurking, and when opportunity presented itself, he gave mental ascent frolicking in the absurd. Perhaps this was something he had perfected to escape the pain and suffering he saw every day in the hospital.

"Gentlemen," said the assistant CEO, "this is Mr. Bernard Cohen. Mr. Cohen, this is Doctor Hans Baughman, the chairman of our corporation, and the gentleman to his right, our Chairman Emeritus, Gustov Klein. Now if you will excuse me, I'll let you get down to business."

The assistant CEO left the room. Hans then took charge, saying, "Please be seated, Mr. Cohen. I trust you had a pleasant flight from South Africa?"

"It turned out to be an excellent flight. They served a nice meal, the flight attendants were pleasant, and we had good weather. The only downside was the hassle we had at the airport; otherwise, it was excellent."

When Mr. Cohen spoke, it almost knocked Hans off his chair. Out of the little man came a deep-throated, baritone-commanding voice that captured the atmosphere, followed by quick-on-the-feet responses. Hans couldn't keep the visual imagery of the opera he had recently attended out of his mind. The great male voices he had heard were those who were either large and fat or small and thin. Mr. Cohen was of the latter variety. Hans had to quickly compartmentalize his internal jest and take command of the meeting.

"Mr. Cohen, we have reviewed your resume, and you come very qualified to be a manager of a shipping line. In fact, you come recommended to us by a party who works in the intelligence department in Israel, who also tells us you are emigrating from South Africa. Is this correct?"

"Yes, that is correct."

"Can you explain why?"

"Yes, but first let me say I have been told that certain information in this interview can be revealed, so in answering your question, I will speak in generalities. I managed a fleet of cargo freighters that entered ports of call that only a ship delivering cargo could enter, ports that were of interest to Israel. I had the responsibility of making the business profitable, and at the same time, collect and pass on information."

"At what level of success did you operate in collecting information?" asked Hans. "And how does this lend itself to making Israel your permanent residence?"

"The level of success was optimal. However, suspicions, which are very easy to come by, brought the issue to the diplomatic level, and rather than attention be brought to Israel on an international scale, everyone concerned felt I should resign and leave the country of South Africa.

"You will note in my resume that the company I managed had an excellent bottom line. It's unfortunate this door of intelligence has been closed."

"Mr. Cohen, your openness allows us to respond in kind," said Hans. "We are purchasing a shipping line that has a good bottom line, but it will be used to conceal our covert operation of smuggling Jews into Israel. The Jewish people lost six million of their own in the Holocaust. A few survived and some went to Israel. Today, there is another Holocaust of a different kind: it is one of denial. Soviet bloc countries deny exit visas to Jews. We intend to use our shipping company as a front to smuggle thousands of new immigrants into Israel, many of whom will be highly trained engineers, research scientists, and physicists. This venture will be called Operation Henry. Do you know who Henry the Navigator was?"

"Of course, anyone in shipping knows he was avant-garde."

"We're going to try to be as visionary as he was but for a different reason," said Hans. "Our project carries the code name, Operation Henry."

"That's a noble venture," said Cohen. "How many ships will the shipping line operate?"

"It consists of eight vessels."

"And of the eight, how many will be given to the operation?"

"The number is yet to be determined. Right now, we're looking at two."

The Old Man up to this stage had said nothing. He was musing on how Hans was presiding over the interview, but something had passed in front of his eyes. He shifted his weight in his chair like an eagle getting ready to spring into action.

"Mr. Cohen, the manager coming into this position," said the Old Man, "will have nothing to do with this undercover effort. This position you're being interviewed for will be filled by someone who will keep a clean bottom line, and any connection with its human smuggling operation will be incidental. It will be under the manager's purview that any ship used in our rescue operation shall meet the same maintenance standards and licensures for all captains and officers."

"I understand," said the South African. "I'm assuming the operation will use ships fully loaded with cargo making discharges and pick-ups."

"Of course," replied the old man, "there's no other way to make it work. The only difference between the ships picking up people and those that aren't will be the special changes that will be made to conceal and transport those who come onboard."

"Will the captains and crews on these ships be cognizant of its operations?"

"Yes," answered the Old Man. "They will be answerable to the manager only for the commercial activities and nothing beyond that. In an Operation Henry event, the captain of the ship will always be subordinate to the one in charge of the operation."

"Mr. Cohen," said Hans, moving his eyes from the Old Man toward the South African, "your experience and difficulty, as you have described it, come to us as a bittersweet package. Your success as a manager is positive; however, your record with certain countries is a negative for our purpose. We cannot have you out front leading our shipping line with a large mark on your back—it's like waving a red flag."

"I understand perfectly."

"In your opinion," said Hans, "what would be a creative solution to this dilemma?"

"I see only two alternatives: a name change or the use of a straw man."

"You want to define and explain those actions?"

"Doctor Baughman, I think the former is out of the question, so allow me to address the latter—the straw-man. A straw-man would be a capable person who would be brought in to act in an official capacity as the manager, but in reality would only be the mouthpiece of the real manager who would be off the books."

The Old Man began to shuffle again, getting poised to strike with the grip of his talons.

"Mr. Cohen, this might make it convenient for the manager, but not for us, a company that streamlines management."

"I understand that, Sir, but if the manager were not on the books, he would be free to assist in Operation Henry without the culpability of public inspection."

The Old Man fixed his eyes on the thoughts running through his mind, turned and looked at Hans, saying, "You know Doctor, he may have a good point there."

"Mr. Cohen, have you ever worked on a freighter?" asked Hans.

"When I was twenty years old my father invested in several freighters, and he worked his entire family on them. I have done everything there's to be done on those steel tubs, and Pop made enough money to put us all through college, though I'm the only one in the family who still works in this field. I even carry a valid Masters License."

It was when the South African cited his apprenticeship onboard his father's ships that Hans knew he and the Old Man would agree on establishing this person as the director of their new shipping line.

The rest of the morning was spent asking pointed, hypothetical questions that examined the depth of his experience and knowledge. The questions centered on how he would take an Asian company, Westernize it with shipping routes over the Mediterranean and the Black Sea, the latter being the back door to countries preventing Jewish emigration to Israel.

By two o'clock, Hans and the Old Man had finished their intense interview. Mr. Cohen was requested to draw up a step-by-step plan of major actions that would be needed to make the company profitable, and at the same time adaptable to the Henry Operation. They requested his plan be submitted within one week. He was told their decision of filling this position would be decided after they read his report.

After the South African left, the Old Man and Hans had a late lunch brought in, over which they continued discussions. They agreed that if Mr. Cohen's projections looked good, they would go with someone who knew the operations onboard the ship as well as how to manage the big picture of moving ships and freight in and out of ports around the world.

The Old Man's personal attendants came and swept him out of the room like they were going to a gala, and Hans was on the phone with his administrative assistant.

"Miss Shuster, get the Public Relations Director in my office immediately. If he's not in the building, get his assistant. After Hans hung up, he went to the Human Resource Department.

A pensive-looking man dressed in a pinstriped suit stood in front of a receptionist's desk waiting to sign a log for a private meeting with the second most powerful person in Katharina Enterprises. He was nervous for a reason: he had been quickly summoned by the second in command to meet with the chairman.

The clerk took the clipboard the man had signed-in on and noticed the name.

"Oh, you're Mr. Manx?"

"That's correct."

"Miss Shuster wants you to go right in, please come with me."

The clerk led the Public Relations Director to the office of the chairman's assistant seated behind a large desk. He'd never met this person, but the rumors reaching him of her power, dress, and looks were confirmed when their eyes met.

"Please be seated, Mr. Manx." Her voice carried a tone of authority, and her words sounded more like a command than an invitation. She neither stood to her feet nor extended her hand for a formal greeting.

She had seen the man's picture in a corporate publication, but his tall, slender frame with slightly graying hair and thin mustache gave him a different image in person.

"You are the Director of our Public Relations, Mr. Manx?"

"Yes. This is somewhat sudden. Did the chairman, Mr. Baughman, indicate what the meeting was about?"

"No, he said nothing about the content or purpose of the meeting. It seemed to be an urgent request."

The lady who appeared to be cold and austere began to show a warmer, softer side. "I'm sorry I haven't had the opportunity to meet you sooner. Allow me to walk you to a more comfortable waiting area reserved for VIPs."

It was when she stood and walked away from her desk that the man felt the full impact of the rumor that she was a flamboyant dresser. It was also rumored that she had money—lots of it!

"Please have a seat. I'm sure the chairman will be here shortly, and when he arrives, you'll be called in."

He sat looking about the room noticing how up-scale everything was. His thoughts walked down the natural path of questioning why he was brought here in such an urgent manner? Was his aggressive approach in putting the corporate image out into the public too much of a good thing? Had he been too bold? He continued musing while he waited.

Hans was never enamored by luxury and affluence, but the person responsible for decorating and finishing off his office suite must have thought otherwise. It matched the elegance of nobility.

Today, he chose to enter his office the way everyone else did—through the front where Miss Shuster, his administrative assistant, acted as his gatekeeper. The public relations director was showing concerned looks. Hans was new to the corporation, and to the employees, he was an unknown. People who worked for the corporation rarely had opportunity to meet with the chairman, and seldom did any director of a department meet with him alone. For the chairman to request a meeting with him gave cause for personal concern.

An unexpected outline of a figure suddenly appeared where he was waiting. He thought the party to be someone coming to see the executive secretary until he spoke.

"And you are, Mr. Manx, our Public Relations Director?" Startled, he looked up!

"Yes, Sir."

Extending his hand, Hans said, "I'm Hans Baughman, and I don't think we have met." He was shocked that Chairman Baughman would be so informal as to meet him outside his office and that he was so young.

"Otto Manx is the name."

"You've been with us for about two years, I believe, and were a newspaperman before that."

"That's correct. I can see you've done your homework."

"I always do my homework with people I work around, Mr. Manx."

Then Hans looked at the clerk seated at her desk. "Tell Miss Shuster that I will personally escort Mr. Manx to my office."

"Yes, Sir."

Hans opened the door to his office allowing Mr. Manx to precede him. When they reached the inner office, Hans offered him a chair. Before sitting, he took in the aesthetic vibrations of the plush-ridden office he'd heard so much about. Once seated, Hans stood over him like he was his doctor attempting to find symptoms of an illness. He was intimidated and insulted at the same time—this youth-of-a-person treating him as if he were a novice. But it got worse. The chairman began asking strange questions.

"Mr. Manx, what color was Miss Shuster's dress?"

What is going on here with this man who runs this company? Where is he going with a question like this?

Hans didn't move. With the man's long pause, he was about to ask another question, when Otto said, "I believe it was blue, Sir."

The man knew enough to stay in control of himself. After all, his business was image making, and there was no image more important than his own.

"And the color of the walls, Mr. Manx?"

"Two walls were white, two were beige."

"And to move beyond the specifics to the general, Mr. Manx, what would you say the front office carried as its theme?"

232

By this time, he knew the chairman had method in this madness. He was being tested for something, and it remained to be seen what it was.

"The paintings, the décor, and the artifacts in the cases emphasize the modern state of Israel."

"Mr. Manx, the reason I have intimidated you with these inane questions is to see how observant you are about your environment. Some people can remember the physical characteristics of a room when told to do so; others have that skill as part of their nature without being told. It is this sort of person I'm looking for, someone who has natural perception and can coordinate a theme. It is evident that you are in the latter group, and I'm assigning you the most important mission of your life. It's a project that will be televised to the international community in all major languages, a story of a country that killed its own and denies it to this day. It is important you give life to what you see and hear. You will examine evidence, interview witnesses, but I will be the centerpiece of that story, for I have come from the dead to haunt the living. In the minds of millions, we will make those who lie in unmarked, mass graves come alive, and they will finally tell their stories through survivors and first-hand witnesses. History waits to be written, and we, Sir, will write it in living color for the world to see.

Chapter 22

Stolen Property Returned

When Hans' driver arrived at the airport and pulled up to the waiting jet for his return flight to Tel Aviv, he saw a food service truck at the plane site. The driver slowed and stopped, keeping a secure distance. After the service truck pulled out, he gradually moved closer. Everything appeared normal. A security officer stood guard near the entrance of the aircraft. One of the pilots was outside the plane going over the final checklist. Security protocol required the driver to open the door for Hans only after everything looked secure. The driver waited until the inspection was completed, then opened the door. With one small carry-on bag, Hans boarded the plane for his return flight, followed by the pilot closing the door to the aircraft. Hans immediately went to the radio room, saying to Fritz sitting at his desk, "Fritz, after the plane gets airborne, I'm taking a nap—wake me up in two hours and we'll have dinner together."

The plane lifted off at six o'clock. Two hours later, Hans was awakened by a knock on his door. He turned over in his reclining seat and faced the window. Greeting him was an artist's dream, a sky pulsating with the sunset of orange-glowing rays, the result of nature forcing its way through the earth's atmospheric prism. However, scenic beauty yielded to its competitor. Hans could smell what Fritz was heating in the aircraft's kitchen. The food deliveries made earlier were not of the commercial airline order but were gourmet specials. It was common knowledge among those who sought to be part of the flight crew that the best part of the job was dining on what was served in flight. Fritz had acted as a steward by preparing and serving the pilots. Hans and Fritz ate together in the dining room.

Anxiety and quietness appeared to hang over Fritz, and Hans took notice of it. Fritz quickly finished eating, excused himself, and went immediately to the radio room. In the meantime, Hans drafted an outline of the sequential steps he would take to film and record the testimonial of Mario Nicolescu, the Romanian who witnessed the mass killings in the village of Ediniti.

Lights from onshore Tel Aviv were now appearing. It was one o'clock in the morning local time, and Hans was thinking about how much he'd missed his lovely Sheena. Though he was busy, she was always in his thoughts. Fritz had opened the plane's sealed exit doorway and was waiting for Hans to emerge, but he continued to sit in the captain's quarters.

Fritz went to the door of his quarters and knocked, saying, "Doctor Hans, your taxi is waiting for you."

"The driver can wait—that's what he gets paid for."

"What do you know that I don't know, Fritz?"

"Nothing, Sir! I hope Doctor Sheena isn't upset with me."

By this time, he knew Sheena was waiting in the vehicle. He hurriedly moved to the exit, and stepping out onto the tarmac, he saw her bounding out of the vehicle toward him to be embraced with her welcome. It was freedom they enjoyed in Israel—they could go and come at will without the prison walls—and they would enjoy it while they could. For the next four hours, they rode the scenic coastal line, stopped at an all-night coffee shop, ended up having breakfast at five, arriving at their villa at six. They slept until one in the afternoon.

At two o'clock, four people sat together in the villa dining room alone without the fanfare of friends and relatives. They had all gone home and everything was now quiet and empty, a letdown for Sheena's mother and father. But it was peaceful for the other two who were reflecting on the events of the early morning.

"Sometimes, it's easier to leave your friends and relatives than it is to have them leave you," said Sheena's mother. "Reunion with the right people is always sweet, but God made the family to be nuclear. Didn't He say, 'For this cause shall a man leave his mother and father and cleave....'"

Hans noticed the father taking a quick glance at his daughter who would soon be leaving and cleaving. He was a man of few words, but when he spoke, he usually had something to say.

"I'm a diamond cutter by trade," said the father. "I have never cut a diamond from anything but a diamond, and two things happen when a diamond is cut. First, a new diamond is created; second, the part from which the new diamond is cut becomes smaller."

The old man, showing the same affectionate look he gave his wife when he first met her as a youth, said, "Mama, our diamond is being cut from the bigger stone and we will be smaller and alone."

"Don't be silly," said his spouse. "Your diamond analogy is too hard and cold. Now, if you're using diamonds to illustrate strength of character or a thing of beauty, that's something else. Leaving and cleaving has to do with the world of softness, gentility, and affection—like two new cells creating a whole new organism."

Hans and Sheena were being entertained listening to the two go at it when suddenly, the father turned and faced Hans.

"Hans, in the old days you'd have to pay me a lot of money for that beautiful woman sitting beside you. How much do you think I'd charge you for her to be your bride?"

"Pop, if you weren't her father, I'd have to give half my fortune, but since you'd be her father, and she'd be marrying out of love, I wouldn't have to pay a penny because you'd never take money from someone she married for love."

A slight grin formed on the old man's face showing pleasure at the response Hans gave. "You understand human nature—don't you?"

"Only your nature, Pop, only your nature."

"Speaking of payment for a bride," said the father, "you Lovebirds can do what you want all by yourselves this afternoon, but Mama and I are going to the Old City to experience the loneliness our Lord, the Messiah, had when He chose to leave and cleave by walking alone down the Via Dolorosa to make payment for His Bride."

The truth couldn't be missed. It was the father who knew where to place his diamond-cutting tool in conversation to get the best results. The skilled diamond cutter's words sliced it with a perfect cut. All four turned silent and reverent. Hans stared with respectful stillness. "Pop, we're going with you to remember the steps of pain He took to be a Bridegroom, and when we complete the journey, we'll renew our mission in support of a land and its people for His return."

The two seniors left the dining room leaving Hans and Sheena alone. Today, the waiter not only served in taking care of the guests, he also acted as a letter carrier by placing on the table in front of Hans an envelope addressed to him.

He knew it was from the teletype, but it was a strange way of having it delivered.

"Waiter, when were you given this?"

"Just now, Sir. The gentleman is in the lobby waiting for a confirmation that you received it."

"Tell him to come here; I want to speak to him!"

"Hans, this may be about me," said Sheena.

"About you—I don't understand—what are you talking about?"

"I'd rather Fritz tell you, or perhaps something in that envelope will explain it."

Confused, Hans opened and read the letter. It was from Max, the Big-One:

Doctor Hans,

As you know, I am the head of security and require absolute adherence to all established protocol, protocol that has been approved by the Old Man, and I trust by you also as the new chairman of Katharina Enterprises. Employees outside security are not answerable to me, but when it comes to acts or decisions that touch security, their role changes. This letter is one of commendation for someone who should be given a special award for maintaining strict adherence to the rules that govern the highest standard of security, regardless of influence put upon them. Fritz, your radioman, was approached by Doctor Sheena requesting the time of your arrival at Tel Aviv. This is forbidden and cause for dismissal according to the code of conduct. Fritz did the right thing explaining that he was not permitted to give out that info and that she should contact me, which she did, and we made adjustments for her to be taken in a hired taxi driven by our security. This information is provided so our lines of communication are maintained. If you wish a different protocol to be in place while you are in Israel, please let me know

On another subject, the Romanian family we got into this country has moved to a permanent home in a nice neighborhood and one of our companies now employs the husband. Their children are enrolled in a private school, and he's ready to be interviewed when called upon.

Max, Head of Security

Hans remembered the words spoken last night by Fritz as he exited the plane, *"I hope Doctor Sheena isn't upset with me."*

The mischievous part of Hans began to surface, the part that didn't fit the role of a doctor or the chairman of a large company. A creeping, sardonic smile started on one side of his face, and with a low, serious tone in his voice, he forced out the best histrionics he could manage, saying to Sheena, "You're a troublemaker, aren't you? You're going to make hair grow on Max's bald head doing things like you did."

Sheena was better on her stage than Hans by just looking serious and saying nothing. When a pin could be heard, if dropped, she softly said, "He'd look funny with hair on his head."

With a continued serious look on her face, Hans' stage props fell apart with the hair and baldhead remark. He caved with uncontrolled laughter, and both were beside themselves in hilarity. After they settled down and wiped the tears from their eyes, they saw Fritz standing at their table. Hans tried to be serious, saying, "Fritz, you've brought entertainment for us today."

"How is that, Sir?"

"With a baldhead growing hair."

When Hans' eye caught Sheena's, the giggles and laughter started all over again. Fritz didn't know whether to laugh with them or leave. In his mind, he'd never been around powerful people, especially powerful people who acted like this, and he knew they weren't drunk, but whatever was going on they were enjoying themselves.

In the midst of laughter, Hans pulled out a chair. "Sit down Fritz!"

"Thank you, Sir."

"Fritz, you know who Max, the Chief of Security is, don't you?"

"Yes, Sir, I deal with him a lot."

"What do you think he'd look like if he grew hair on his bald head?

"Well, if he grew a lot of it, he'd look like Samson, Sir."

Now, all three were laughing. To change the course from humor to a serious subject required a few moments of quiet. No one said anything until Fritz spoke.

"Doctor Sheena, you aren't sore with me for not giving you the confidential information on the plane's arrival time, are you?"

"Of course not, you gave me the information required, and it all worked out fine. Samson...I mean Max...brought everything together to optimize security."

Hans and Fritz were doing their best not to laugh, but as quickly as laughter came, it receded, and serious contemplations were underway.

"Fritz, when you return to your station, I want you to send a message to our Public Relations Director."

Hans wrote a memo to be sent over the teletype:

Mr. Mantz,

We will be working with a party who will give a personal account of having witnessed the Holocaust in Romania. Prepare to do your finest production ever. Spare no cost in bringing in top personnel and equipment. This will be a one-time interview and we have to get it right the first time. Between now and then, learn everything you can about the Holocaust in Romania. It will serve you well to visit the Holocaust Museum here in Israel. Your assignment is not to be an academic pursuit to fill space in books and films, but it is to fill empty space in hearts. You are Jewish, Mr. Mantz, make what you are come to life so the dead will speak from the grave!

Hans Baughman

"Fritz, see that this is sent immediately."

After Fritz departed, Hans turned to Sheena. "Shall we join your parents who are waiting for us?"

Within an hour after renting a van with a driver, they were walking the streets of the Old City of Jerusalem, now under Israeli control. It was a historic event for Hans, Sheena, and her parents. Marks of war were on display with scenes of damaged buildings, tight security, and the presence of Israeli soldiers everywhere. This was the ancient city David took from the Jebusites, the city of peace, but knew more wars, violence, and turmoil than any other city in the world. This was the city David chose to be his capital and the site where Solomon built the magnificent Temple. Today, it was again in the hands of Israel after nineteen hundred years. These were the thoughts occupying the minds of the four as they commenced the two-thousand-foot walk over the path that led the Messiah to pay the ultimate price for His bride.

The mother and father walked ahead holding hands, reflecting on how Jewish they were. They were the descendants of the Diaspora of history, and underneath their feet were the ruins of the ancients, their ancestors who rose and fell depending on how near and how far they were from God. This was the land God promised Abraham and his descendants. Today, they walked the path with pride. She saw her husband take from his pocket the Hebrew Pentateuch, then heard him read aloud the account of Abraham's journey over the same pathway of sorrow with his son, Isaac:

Abraham took the wood for the burnt offering and placed it on his son Isaac, and he himself carried the fire and the knife....

"Mama, there was a second Isaac who also carried His own wood over this path of sorrow we are now walking, and He fell beneath its weight. God laid the wood on the back of his Son to be carried to the waiting Roman soldiers with knife and fire in hand."

While the seniors walked ahead reflecting on history, the younger couple trailing behind was moved more by the present.

"Hans, how much does a person have to give to prove his love to someone?"

"Is that rhetorical, or do you want a real answer?"

242

"I want a discussion. The greatest expression of demonstrated love was done here where we are walking. It changed the direction of the world. It's an ancient bridal pathway and was used twice: first, by Abraham and his son on their way to Mount Moriah, which was a rehearsal for the one to follow—the one of God sending His Son to pay the ultimate price for His Son's espoused."

Sheena squeezed the hand she held, leaned her head on the shoulder of Hans, and asked, "Hans, what did we give up to have each other?"

"Everything!"

She stopped, looked at Hans. "My, the man of trivia answers the question with one simple word!"

"Love makes things simple," said Hans. "It's all or nothing."

"Would you give up all your wealth to have me?"

"If that were the only way I could have you, I would gladly give it in exchange for you."

"You're a darling, Hans."

"Specificity demands specificity," Hans replied as he threw Sheena a curve. "Would you give up becoming a doctor to have me?"

"Your polemics are sharp today, Mr. Hans! I would do that tomorrow, but my mother and father dream day and night of me becoming a practicing doctor, and I have two more years of residency. However, I would never put my parents ahead of you."

"There's nobility in your answer." Hans stopped walking, placed his arm around Sheena. "When we get married, you will have half of my wealth, you know!"

"I didn't intend this conversation to go in this direction. I was absorbed with the idealism and meaningfulness of this path, the principle of giving up something of great value to honor the one we love. This is what the Messiah did for His Called-Out-Ones...." Hans interrupted, saying, "We will both live a day at a time denying ourselves for the other's welfare."

"Doctor Hans, thank you for simplifying our lives." Looking up at him, she continued. "One thing I want you to remember for the rest of your life. It was on this Via Dolorosa bridal pathway where I told you that 'I loved you more than anything in the world.' I use words to say this. The Messiah, the Prince, said it by giving His body as a sacrifice."

"This is a heavy subject. Who teaches you these things?"

"That man down there in front of us holding my mother's hand. He's the family theologian."

Later, the four found themselves at the Western Wall, known as the Wailing Wall, the most visited sacred site in Israel. A few days after the Israeli army took the eastern part of the city, they bulldozed all the buildings facing the wall creating a large open courtyard. Now, devout Jews came regularly to this site to say prayers, the women at one end of the wall, the men at the other.

Hans walked up close to the wall that held some of the original massive Herodian stones, stones sculptured with King Herod's signature, a well-defined, beveled edge. The irony of history came at Hans. The most sacred place in the entire world was on the other side of this wall, and the most infamous wicked man to rule the Jews built on those grounds a temple that was a wonder in the Roman world. Herod, like a modern politician, used the people's money through taxation to ingratiate himself to the public. He stepped closer to the ancient wall. Prayers, written on small, rolled-up pieces of paper, had been stuffed in the cracks and crevices by those who had visited the site.

Someone dressed like an orthodox Jew sporting a beard and holding a prayer book stepped up alongside Hans. The prayer book was open and he was reading in English some passages from Ezekiel. Hans had learned English from his mother when he was a child:

I will now restore the fortunes of Jacob and will have compassion on all the people of Israel, and I will be zealous for my holy name. When I have brought them back from the nations and have gathered them from the countries of their enemies, I will be proved holy through them in the sight of many nations. I will gather them to their own land, not leaving any behind. I will pour out my spirit on the people of Israel.

The shuckling rhythmic motion of the worshipper continued in silence. There was no prayer and no reading, only the upper body movement of rocking back and forth. Then coming from the man's lips to break the silence was a message for someone who had moved outside his safety zone: "Doctor Baughman, don't look in my direction, look straight ahead as if you are praying," The man didn't change his movements and Hans resisted the natural impulse to turn and look at the person who knew his name.

"We know who our friends and enemies are. You should have our security with you when going to occupied territories. I'm leaving a piece of paper with an important message in the crevice in front of me. Take it with you when you leave."

Anyone watching would have seen a devout Jew leaving a prayer at the sacred wall. However, today it was used as a cover to pass on a message to someone who had made a bold proposition to certain Israeli authorities.

Hans knew Sheena and her parents had exposure he had no control over. He was a marked man, along with all the consortium members, but family members were just as vulnerable. Now he was being told that even in occupied territories the underground could have active operatives. He quickly put closure to the formalities at the Wailing Wall, placed the small, rolled-up message in his pocket, and sought the other three somewhere in the crowd of people moving about in the large courtyard. It was a Friday afternoon and people from all over the world had gathered to visit the wall that took them back to their ancestral roots. He knew Max, the Big-One, would not have approved of going into occupied territory without security, and certainly not among a crowd like this. Fortunately, he found the three of them together and said nothing about the warning he received. After crossing into the Jewish sector of Jerusalem, Hans pulled from his pocket the rolled-up piece of paper taken from the Wailing Wall. He quickly read its contents:

The department of housing and development has considered your proposal and will send a vehicle with a driver to pick you up at eight o'clock tomorrow morning at the site where you are staying. You'll be taken to an undisclosed building to meet with those in charge of the proposed project.

Hans knew the written text he held in his hand was of secondary importance—it was the verbal warning at the wall that held the higher priority. He had expected a meeting with the Department of Housing and Urban Development, but not this soon. It concerned a proposal to build three thousand housing units, providing the government could meet certain criteria. The immigrants he would bring in on the ships would need immediate housing, and the project he was offering might conflict with the government's resettlement paradigm. This could be a complicated issue.

At seven that evening, all four were seated in their private dining room at the villa being served a kosher meal. The manager of the villa came to the table holding a wrapped package. "Mr. Baughman, a young gentleman requested this be delivered to you."

"Thank you, I was expecting this." Looking at Sheena, he continued. "This was brought over by Fritz, something I requested earlier after receiving information of a meeting tomorrow. It's my file on the housing project here in Israel."

"Sounds important," said Sheena.

"It is. Pop, did you enjoy the day in the old city?"

"Mother and I had the time of our lives, and from what I saw with you two holding hands with fluttering eyes, you had a pretty good time yourself."

"How would you two like to live here permanently— without your daughter? You'd be out of the prison you live in at home and be among your own people here in Israel."

"Hans, I speak for both of us," said the father. "Thank you for the offer, but we'll not leave our darling until the knot is tied. Time will be your teacher. Someday, you'll understand that your little girl, or perhaps your little boy, will always be that to you. They may grow up, they may leave you, and they may even get married, but they will always be the little one you loved, protected, and nurtured. If your mother were alive today, the one who saved you from the Holocaust and loved you as her own child, she would feel just as we do about our daughter."

Sheena saw Hans' eyes gloss over—they stared in reflective memory. "You're right, Pop. If she were here today, she would have your feelings."

"I miss our Friday evening Shabbat dinner," said the mother.

"After we finish our dinner," said the father, "We'll all go to our room and have devotional readings."

"And on the subject of the Sabbath," said Hans, "tomorrow morning I will have an ox in the ditch. A vehicle will be picking me up in the morning at eight for a very important business conference—therefore the three of you should plan your morning together without me. Sorry if this puts a wrinkle in any schedule. I didn't know of this meeting until yesterday."

Sheena gave a puzzled look. "I was with you at all times, how were you given this information?"

"It came double-barreled at the Wailing Wall. The first was a warning in verbal form; the second was in script on paper taken from the wall. The paper contained the message about my meeting tomorrow morning. The verbal was more ominous—that we should never go into the occupied territories without security. Sorry I have to tell you these things. As long as we stay within the old borders of Israel, there will be no issue, and we can travel about freely. Now, shall we go to Mom and Pop's quarters for closure on our wonderful day together?"

───────────────

Hans and Sheena were in the dining room by seven Saturday morning. He rarely ate kosher and Sheena seldom went off kosher. There were times when no one was looking she would pinch some of his non-kosher servings. Today was one of those times. Hans had delivered Canadian bacon to the chef in the kitchen to be prepared upon his request, and today he demanded a plentiful supply along with his eggs and toast.

248

"My dear, you're looking at my beautifully prepared, luscious-tasting bacon like you want some!"

"Well, you don't have to use all those colorful, descriptive adjectives that only make it more tempting!"

Hans took two pieces of bacon from his plate, placed it alongside her order.

"You know I'll have to eat this quickly before my parents come in."

"They'll be glad if we're not in the dining room when they arrive," said Hans, "then they can feel free to order their own bacon."

"Do you really think so?"

"We should never ask them if they've ever fallen off the wagon," said Hans, "that'd just force them to give an embarrassing answer."

"I'm sure if they have, my father would justify his reason for doing so with a theological defense. He has often told us he conforms to Jewish dietary laws for the sake of his Messianic testimony to other Jews."

"That's wise and noble on his part. The nobility part shows sacrifice, especially, if he likes bacon."

The waiter came up to his table, leaned in his direction, saying, "Sir, there is a gentleman in the lobby who has sent me to inform you that the vehicle sent to pick you up is waiting outside with a driver."

Hans looked at his watch. It was ten minutes until eight. "Tell the driver I'll be out in ten minutes."

Sheena walked with Hans to the waiting vehicle. She saw two men standing near what looked like a taxi. They were dressed in regular clothes, sported no tie, and touted open-toed sandals. It was a typical kibbutz look. Being on a quasi-vacation, Hans was hardly a grade higher: what separated him were oxfords instead of sandals. He greeted the party of two with a friendly handshake, entered the vehicle, and drove away. As she walked back to her room, Sheena thought of how Hans had changed into a driven, forward-looking, forceful leader, someone who could compartmentalize issues with acute diagnostic skills.

It was the Sabbath, and few vehicles were on the roadway. Little was said between Hans and the other two, and he wasn't sure but what this was a planned strategy. At least, the government was interested enough in his offer to be willing to confer with him on the subject. This was the first experience he had dealing with people outside the military and secret service. He knew the men or women he would meet with were appointed by government leaders and the nature of its bureaucracy would show itself with a political climate in play.

After driving for twenty minutes, the taxi pulled into the parking lot of an older government building. There were five cars parked closely together. He hoped everyone on this committee had fully researched all the issues raised by his lawyers back home.

Hans walked between the two, carrying his own briefcase. They opened the door to the older building that led into a wide hallway. Hans could tell this was a typical government office building when they passed open doors to rooms that were filled with cubicles, desks, and office equipment. Finally, they reached a closed door over which was written: Conference Room.

When entering the room, he smelled coffee and saw sandwiches and pastries on a side table. Five men and two women sat at a table. When they saw the three enter, they all stood. One of the two men who picked up Hans introduced him to the group. At this point, Hans had no idea who was in charge. One of the men at the table carried a briefcase and a cylindrical tube, the kind used to store maps and drawing plans. Hans knew these people were government appointed because of their practical experience in getting their hands dirty in their fields of expertise. They were bureaucrats, but not in the traditional sense. Later, he would find that one of the seven present in the meeting was a mayor of a moderate-sized town in Israel. Considering the guidelines of his proffer, he would question why a mayor would be present.

Finally, the man at the table who carried the briefcase and cylindrical storage tube, called the meeting to order. He introduced himself as Moshe Lavai, and then formally introduced Hans to the others. Their dress code was typical Israeli: informal with sleeves rolled up and ready for work.

"Friends, we have with us today a very important person, Doctor Hans Baughman, a Zionist and friend of Israel. He's a philanthropist and has given much to the State of Israel, and is now offering to build three thousand housing units for the arrival of new immigrants. We are here to see if we can meet his prerequisites for his proposal. These matters have already been discussed at the highest levels in government and the State is eager to accept his offer. However, the government has never had to deal with issues of foreign philanthropic money coming into the country with such strings attached to it, and it is for us to examine these matters in the presence of Doctor Baughman and allow him time to present his case. Now, I yield to our invited guest."

Hans stood to his feet, took from his briefcase copies of a simplified form of a more detailed brief given to the government leaders. He handed a stack of them to the party on his right, saying, "Please take one copy, and pass the rest around the table."

Mystique already shrouded Hans. He had offered to build a community of buildings extensive enough to house

251

twelve thousand people, and those in the know had already heard of the young doctor who was in control of a vast enterprise. He startled the group by his opening statement.

"Friends, I come to you with a German name and a German look. My biological mother and father are these two people in the picture frames I'm placing here on this table. The pictures are enlargements from the two small ones inside this gold locket showing the Star of David.

"They were Jews killed in the Holocaust of our village in Romania, and today, they are buried in a mass grave just outside the town. I was one-year-old in the arms of my mother when my father and mother were shot by German and Romanian Nazi soldiers. When I was crawling over the bodies of the dead, an Angel took me into his arms and hid me in a wagon of hay, and was shortly found by the wife of a Nazi German general…." Hans continued the narrative of the account, and in conclusion, he said, "My real name is Jacob Isler. My German, Gentile mother feared the discovery of my identity and never told me I was Jewish until she passed. She left me letters telling the whole story, as well as her fortune to help the Jews of the Holocaust. This little gold locket on the table that holds the pictures of my biological mother and father was around my neck when my German mother found me in the wagon of hay."

He saw eyes glossed over with tears. They were messages speaking of personal pain. Hans continued. "Now that you know who I am we can get down to business. First, I am a Zionist, second, I'm a businessman who is also aware of human foibles, and thus you will understand why I'm as demanding in philanthropic giving as I am in a business decision.

"Notice on the paper I gave you that there are certain points that must be agreed to before I invest fifty million

252

dollars in housing." He gave them time to look over what he passed out before continuing:

1. The housing project will exist solely for new immigrants who have been in the country for less than one year.

2. The government will provide the building site for the project. It must meet with the approval of the Katharina Foundation.

3. Any member of the government or anyone working for the government who has decision-making powers to approve this project cannot own or purchase land adjoining the project for a distance of three miles. If there is existing ownership, they must recuse themselves.

4. Upon completion, it shall be administered only by the Department of Resettlement under existing policies.

5. The housing project will be independent of adjoining cities, villages, or communities.

6. The Katharina foundation will only provide completed buildings that meet state building codes and standards.

7. After an agreement is reached on the above, Hans Baughman will deposit in the Katharina escrow account the amount of fifty million dollars to be used for the construction of the stated project.

Using his assertive style, Hans took charge securing information he wanted to know, saying to the group, "Since we've all looked over the paper I passed out, I'd like to know something about you, so let's go around the table and you can tell me what you do that makes it important that you are here."

He looked to his right. "Sir, what do you do?"

"I'm in the Immigration Department."

"Are you the department head?"

"Yes, Sir."

"Would this project benefit your department in settling new immigrants?

"Most definitely!"

Hans looked across the table and randomly picked someone, trying to keep everyone on their toes. "And you, Sir, what is your portfolio?"

"I'm head of the Energy Department. Homes and energy consumption go hand-in-hand and have a direct bearing on our electrical grid."

"Considering that three thousand units will be built over a period of a couple of years, and the first hundred within four months after construction commences, will this overtax the grid system?"

"Not at all. We have all this on our planning schedule."

His attention turned to the end of the table where a smartly dressed, middle-aged woman sat. "Madam, may I ask, how you fit in with this august group?"

The lady's body language answered his question. She raised her chin slightly, forced her eyes to scan those around the table like she was looking for votes to support her cause. It was a full-blown drama scene with her prominent chin held between the thumb and index finger of her right hand, giving the image of a thinker.

"Doctor Baughman, I am proud to be here to represent the fine city that took the time to vote me in as the mayor of our outstanding town."

"Then you're the politician among us?"

Everyone looking at her saw the drama fade, several showed a slight smile, but the best was yet to come.

"Madam, I have two questions to ask you. First, who asked you to attend this meeting? Second, being an Honorable Mayor, how will this conference with me help your city?"

Those at the table now saw someone who was older than his youthful appearance, willing to be brusque when a principle was involved, but sympathetic and compassionate for his cause. Most men of wealth would send the second-in-command to do what he was doing, but today it was the big man himself.

He waited for her answer. She collected herself, realizing she was now a politician in survival mode. Her eyes caught the one who had invited her. He was squirming in his chair hoping for a good outcome.

"Madam, you don't have to answer the first question, because it's none of my business who invited you, but it is important for me to hear your answer to the second question. How will my building three thousand housing units help your city?"

Now, she was ready to pull her political trigger. "Doctor, we have a lot of vacant land around our city. There are hotels and homes that can be rented by workers, stores, and restaurants...." Hans interrupted her.

"Madam Mayor, what you're telling me about your town is a wonderful enticement for a massive operation that will be in play. However, I must ask you one more question. Do you, your relatives, or the person who invited you to this meeting, along with his relatives, own any of that land outside your city?"

When he finished with the final question, icy silence settled in. The room lost its oxygen. It reminded Hans of a patient who needed the green bottle of life. Experienced professional executives around seated around the table saw a novice kid with all the money acting as a prosecuting attorney, making a politician-turned-lobbyist into mincemeat.

"Doctor, I take offense at what you said. I had nothing but good intentions coming here today."

"Madam, you protect the interest of your city fathers—I protect the interest of those coming into this land who have nothing but the clothing on their backs. Back home, and here in Israel, it is unethical to be guilty of a conflict of interest, and sometimes punishable in a court of law."

With this last statement, the Mayor got up and walked out of the meeting, leaving Hans standing.

"Gentlemen, I can see I haven't made many friends today, and if the person who invited the Mayor to attend this meeting wishes to speak, please do so."

Everyone knew who it was—even Hans knew. The man sat looking straight ahead, hands clasped together with fingers twitching. He pulled his hands back to the edge of the table, pushed himself into a standing position. He looked down at the table, then up toward the ceiling. Tears came to his eyes. Hans gave respect by sitting. He began slowly, speaking with an uneven staccato voice.

"When I was in the concentration camp before the Americans overran the death hole, we were sometimes given one piece of bread every other day. There was this huge fellow. I remember it like it was yesterday. He would sometimes forcibly take my bread and I couldn't defend myself. I carried hate toward him for many years. Today, the stronger attempted to take bread from the weaker. I know it's not the same, but the principle is there. If I had the power to cause a decision to be made that would be a conflict of interest, and I would profit by it, it would be the same as the stronger taking bread from the weaker. Please forgive me, Doctor. Today you have saved me from myself."

Hans stood to his feet, reached across the table to the man who was still standing, took his hand, saying, "My name is Hans to you, never call me Doctor again." Both became friends from that point on.

The committee was mesmerized earlier by the report of the enormity of the young man's wealth. By the time the meeting had closed in an amicable manner, they were still mesmerized, but now for another reason: he had demonstrated prowess in understanding human nature and showed a magnetic command in making complex issues simple.

On his way to the villa where his new family awaited him, Hans yielded to the comforting thought that his mother would be smiling at him for moving the stolen millions taken from Jews in the Holocaust to the land of their ancestors in the form of housing for new arrivals.

From this meeting, the fame of the young doctor who demonstrated wisdom beyond his years would spread far and wide behind closed doors. It would be whispered news; the kind listened to, passed on, and remembered. Even those behind the impregnable high walls of government would bend their ears to hear.

Chapter 23

Renewed like the Eagle

Sunday morning after breakfast Hans had devotions with his new family, and then they all took a drive to Joppa, an ancient seacoast town. Upon returning, the manager of the villa informed Hans a letter and a package had arrived for him. He picked up the items, and the four went to their rooms before lunch.

Hans' room overlooked the beautiful Mediterranean. He chose to sit outside on the private veranda with his package and letter in hand. He noted that the letter was from Moshe Lavai, the government person who chaired the meeting the day before.

He first opened and read the letter:

Doctor Hans Baughman:

My superior had given me the authority yesterday to follow through on certain matters that would have given initial approval of your proposed housing project. However, due to the conflict of interest issues with certain parties, I was forced to postpone following through on that mandate until further research was done on the important matter you raised. After our meeting with you yesterday, we did an urgent, full-court press in our research to verify there were no primary and secondary parties that would give us conflict of interest exposure.

Sent with this letter are six land maps showing viable construction sites for your proposed project. All six sites are government-owned properties, and to the best of our knowledge are free of the above-mentioned encumbrances. Please review, select a site, and submit an overview of the architectural layout you propose that would fit with your chosen parcel. Once this is done, we'll get together and work toward the final product. I will be your direct contact person here in Israel, and for your information, we have on location highly experienced and licensed engineers and architects. You have my address, phone, and teletype numbers.

Looking forward to hearing from you.

Moshe Lavai

Hans unwrapped the package. Inside was a cylindrical storage tube holding the sitemaps Mr. Lavai mentioned. He took them to the dining room where his new family members were waiting.

"Sorry, I'm late! Been waiting long?"

"We'll forgive you since you're paying the bill," Pop said.

"Pop, how well do you know Israel?"

"I know it well enough to live here someday."

Hans took from the storage tube the six maps, handed them to Mr. Reznik, saying, "Can you examine these maps and tell me what you can about them? Each map has a penciled-in area indicating a suggested building site."

Hans could see Sheena's father's eyes brighten. He was asked to do something meaningful.

"These maps don't say a whole lot to the layman. They merely give you the topographical readings. There are major road markings, but one needs to go to each site to get the real layout."

Pop continued scanning the maps, saying, "What kind of buildings are you going to construct?"

"I have to choose one of the six buildings sites upon which there will be constructed three thousand housing units for the purpose of accommodating new immigrants coming into this country."

The old man took his eyes from the maps and stared straight ahead. He was a bright, enlightened person who had never gone to college, but an avid reader gifted with savant-like mathematical skills.

Hans could see that his brain was acting like a calculator. He looked at Hans. "That's a good chunk of money. If you're building three thousand units, and they averaged a thousand square feet per unit, that would put the figure around fifty million dollars."

Two things impressed Hans in his response: first, he made the calculations in a moment's time in his head, and he knew the current building cost per square foot. How could he use this man to make him feel useful and purposeful in life? Then it came to him...but would he be willing?

Sheena and her mother had been chatting together, oblivious of what was being said between the two males. When the waiter came by to take their order, it brought the four of them together again.

"And what would you folks like to order today?" asked the waiter. Hans was still thinking about the assignment he would request of Sheena's father when the waiter interrupted.

"Sir, what would you like to order?"

He looked at Sheena across the table. "Do you see that beautiful lady across from me? I'll order what she ordered."

After the waiter left, Hans began to lay the groundwork in making a proposal to his future father-in-law.

"Ladies and gent, I'd like to hold the floor for a few minutes if I could. I try to keep business matters from my family. However, there is a business matter that is important to me in a personal way, and it would also be very meaningful to my late mother if she were among us.

"My mother left me fifty million dollars to be returned to the Jewish people from whom it was taken by her infamous estranged husband. I have chosen to return it by constructing three thousand housing units for new immigrants coming into this country. Israel has approved of the project subject to working out all the details. I need someone to represent me here in Israel, someone to be my eyes and ears, a facilitator between my office and Israel." Hans paused, took a drink of water, looked at Sheena, then her mother. All three were waiting for him to continue. His eyes then moved to Pop—didn't say anything, just looked at him.

"You're my man for this job, Pop. You don't have to live in Israel. The job will require you to make trips to Israel at least once a week to check on its progress."

Hans looked at Sheena and her mother. Both showed smiles at the thought of what Pop was asked to do.

"Papa, you can do it, it'll be a piece of cake for you. Just think, you go to Israel once a week with Mother."

"She goes with the job?"

"No, just to Israel," said Hans.

The old man was thinking of his own experience when he arrived as a new immigrant. "Mother, remember when we first arrived in Israel? We lived in tents for months. Three thousand units will increase the population to over twelve thousand inhabitants."

"Pop, no one is to know we are related," said Hans. "If anyone finds that out, you will never hear firsthand what people are really thinking at the grassroots level. A special phone line will be installed in your home that will be used only for overseas calls. Before we get started, we'll rent an office building and carve out a place for you to use when in the country. Your only connection at the central office will be with me, not anyone else. If I need to be contacted there, I have a private line."

The old man was like an organism going through a metamorphic change. He had been along for the ride because of his beautiful daughter's engagement to a wealthy man, but now was being transformed into someone who was coming into his own. The natural river of life had not flowed favorably for his fullest expression of knowledge and talent but had now begun to change its course. The other three noticed the energy of change going on inside him.

"Hans, if I'm to carry this responsibility, we must start by doing the following: address each other in a formal manner in the presence of others; make me known to your contact person here in Israel and visit all six sites and obtain our own photos of each. These steps should be taken before returning home."

Hans' eyes swept across the dining table, found the women with fixed, jaw-dropping looks on their faces, then turned and faced Pop. "Mr. Reznik, you have spoken from your well of wisdom. We will not return home until these urgent matters are done."

The next day they met with Moshe Lavai. He elected to drive them to all six building sites. In consultation with Moshe, they narrowed it down to two sites. It was recommended that Hans take copies of architectural drawings on file of existing developments similar to his in size and see if they were adaptable. He emphasized if this were the case, it would greatly reduce cost and time. Hans considered this a good plan.

Tuesday morning the corporate plane was in flight back to their guarded way of life living inside walled residences attended to by security and caution.

Hans was busy inside the teletype room checking his office mail. The report from Bernard Cohen, the prospective director of the shipping line they were buying, had come in and there was a note from his administrative assistant saying that the Japanese company selling the line wanted to know if we're going to use their management team, or would we be bringing in our own people?

He took the time to review the report Bernard Cohen had submitted. It showed his knowledge and experience in this field. Knowing the Old Man had already looked over the report, he gave the directive to Miss Shuster that she should call the Old Man, and if he approved of the proposal, she would send the following as an overnight letter to Bernard Cohen:

Mr. Bernard Cohen,

You have been chosen to be the Managing Director of our shipping line, and your presence is being requested at the Japanese office immediately. You can use their management team until it would be appropriate to change over. Your report of projections conveyed your knowledge of the shipping industry and your experience in management. Welcome aboard! Our company will support you as you take the helm of our new venture that has as its ultimate objective, Operation Henry. You will have the responsibility of maintaining absolute secrecy on Operation Henry. In these matters, you will report to me. For everything else, report to our corporate CEO.

Hans Baughman

He instructed his executive secretary to inform him when the letter was sent. He then returned and sat next to Sheena. His thoughts were on how the lady who took him from the wagon of hay would respond to his decision on Operation Henry. In his mind, he saw her with a smile on her saintly face.

Sheena looked at Hans and her father. Their faces showed the same image: peaceful, but with subdued purpose. Her mother looked blissful sitting by one who had been given a new lease on life. She took hold of Hans' hand and both closed their eyes for a short nap.

An hour later Sheena found herself awake, Hans was gone, and her mother and father were asleep. Knowing he had been under a lot of stress, she wanted to be sure he was all right. She left the captain's quarters, went to the cockpit, opened the door, and asked, "Have you seen Doctor Baughman?"

He brought us a cup of coffee earlier," said one of the pilots.

"Thank you."

When she passed the radio room, she heard talking. After knocking on the door, it was opened. Inside were Hans and Fritz drinking coffee and eating a piece of pie.

"Am I too late to the party?"

"Come in Doctor! Fritz, get my beautiful woman a piece of that sumptuous pie with some fresh coffee." Fritz left the room leaving Hans and Sheena by themselves.

"You ran off and left me, and I came to check on you."

"I'm glad you did. We have something big coming along, and you'll have to sharpen up your Romanian. The first of this week we're doing a documentary rehearsal for a Romanian Holocaust production, and we will need you as an interpreter. Also, what do you think about using your mother and father in this production in that they are Romanian Holocaust survivors?"

"Let's think about this for a while. They are so traumatized by that part of their history, I'm not quite sure how that would go down with them emotionally. However, I will say that my father would be a better interpreter than yours truly."

Hans took her hand that held her large diamond and gently kissed it, saying, "No one can be better than you."

"What will be the run-time on a production like this, and what countries will be covered?"

Before Hans could answer, someone, knocked on the door. When Sheena opened the door, Fritz was holding a tray with a large coffee, a slice of pie, with cream and sugar on the side. Sheena took the tray from him and placed it on the table.

"Fritz, bring two more servings of coffee and pie for you and me."

"Yes, Sir."

"You know Master Hans, this pie and coffee will spoil our lunch."

"That's alright, as long as it doesn't spoil us."

"You didn't finish my question."

"Oh yes, the run-time. It will probably be no longer than thirty minutes in view that it's educational and emotionally debilitating. It will be on national TV during prime time in all Western countries. English and German will be the languages used for the original production. All other languages will be dubbed-in. It is here you and your father's Romanian voices will be helpful. Our goal in this production is to force a country through international pressure to acknowledge its record of anti-Semitism and the deaths of three hundred thousand Jews."

"Won't this production bring greater danger to you?"

"I'm concerned more about you," said Hans.

"I'd be considered just an actress doing it for money."

"The question we have to ask ourselves is, 'How much more dangerous would it be than the conditions we already live under?' If we have to, we'll move to Israel and I'll run my office from there. You could finish your internship there."

"Sounds like a good idea to me. We'll go for broke and hope for the best in this production."

"I wonder what happened to Fritz and our pie and coffee?" said Hans.

No sooner had he said this that someone knocked on the door. Hans opened it with Fritz saying, "I'm sorry I'm late with this, someone got into our last batch of freshly made, and I had to make another."

"Better fresh and late, than never! Where's yours, Fritz?"

"Oh, I wouldn't want to intrude…."

"Get yours and bring it in here with us. Our quarters are tight, but we'll manage."

"Yes, Sir."

"I can guess who the little mice were who got into Fritz's fresh coffee," Sheena said.

Hans smiled. "That's an easy one."

Fritz had just settled in when a knock came at the door. It opened slightly, and only a voice was heard.

"I smell something in there that is not coffee."

Sheena took the bait. "Are you the little mouse that took all the fresh coffee?"

"What does that little mouse have to do in the way of penance to earn a piece of what you're having?"

"Another pot of fresh coffee will clear your record."

"Sir, there is also a fresh pie in the refrigerator," said Fritz.

Sheena's father then showed his face through the door, saying, "So there are three of you in here." Then Mr. Reznik became all business. "Mr. Baughman, since I was part of the Aliyah some years ago, I believe I have a lot to offer in the way of experience in advising you of the best site to build on."

"So, Mr. Reznik, how would your experience advise us in the selection of the right building site? We only have two choices."

"Close access to public transportation is one thing. In Israel, anytime a building goes up security is of prime importance. That pie in the refrigerator is calling me. I better check it out before someone else beats me to it!"

The old man closed the door, leaving Hans and Sheena looking at each other.

"Sheena, your father will exceed our expectations."

Chapter 24

Prison of Choice

The following week everyone settled back into the routine of living behind gated walls and guarded activities. Hans was working on the Romanian Holocaust TV production, Mr. Reznik was in communication with Moshe Lavai in Israel lining up engineers and architects for the housing project, and Sheena was back at the hospital.

Sheena had been a doctor-in-training for almost one year, engaged to Hans for six months. After meeting Hans, life seemed to speed up and slow down at the same time. It was a strange world she had entered after meeting him—yet in some ways, it was as if they had always been together. The biggest adjustment for both of them was the fortune he inherited. They could no longer carry on as normal people but were sheltered, guarded, and carried about as if they were royalty. These circumstances made it difficult to work in an environment where Sheena's mentors at the hospital walked on pins and needles around her. Hans' public image and notoriety had grown in the community through the media wanting a story, invitations to ceremonial events, and those seeking to use him and his wealth for ulterior ends. She was thankful God had given them strength in all this to remain who they were.

When she returned to the hospital after spending a week in Israel, the employees, doctors, and nurses saw no change in the way she dressed and treated people. She wore no makeup and looked as common as any lady on the street.

Once in her scrubs, she blended in with everyone else. Her first day back would be a day that would rock her world.

Her assignment was with a doctor in the trauma and burn unit where a patient had been brought in with severe lacerations from an explosive device. Moving from patient to patient, she followed the doctor making notes on each patient's condition and the doctor's recommendation. When they came to the patient injured from the explosive device, they found him disoriented and speaking what appeared to be gibberish, but Sheena knew differently—it was Arabic, a language she had learned as a child in Israel. What he was saying meant nothing to her until Hans' name was mentioned. Startled, instead of taking notes from what the doctor was saying, she wrote down verbatim the words he was speaking. She knew he was talking out of his head, but the substance of what he said was harsh reality. The sentences were randomly spoken and incomplete, but he was citing names and the site where the explosive device went off. For the first time, Sheena would use the power of who she was.

"Doctor, please go to the next patient without me, I want to be with this patient by myself. I understand what he's saying."

The doctor saw the look in her eyes, heard the sternness in her command; it was something never seen in her before. He chose to comply with her request.

The patient was still speaking randomly when the doctor walked away. She moved closer to the patient's ear, attempting to induce further speech on the subject she had heard earlier. She spoke leading Arabic words that would elicit a response. A nurse came into the room to check the patient's chart for new orders and stood by the bed. Sheena knew she must secure the patient from visitors.

269

"Nurse, this patient is to have no visitors. Keep the door closed and stand outside until I'm finished here."

"Yes, Doctor."

Continuing to speak in Arabic, she elicited from the patient a few known facts: he was injured by a device intended to be attached to the Baughman vehicle, that a German had recruited him in his country and was now fearful his life was in danger. After the patient slipped into a state of semi-consciousness, she left the room and went to talk to the Chief Hospital Administrator. His secretary was seated at her desk.

"Please get the administrator here immediately—we have an emergency!"

"What's the emergency?" asked the secretary.

"This isn't a time for questions—get the administrator!"

Everyone in the hospital knew who Doctor Reznik was, and the secretary was aware she was in an awkward situation. Dare she interrupt an important conference meeting going on, jeopardizing her job, or suffer the consequences of someone whose power was greater than her superior. She yielded to the former. Sheena waited. Soon, the administrator came in. When he saw her face, he thought either he was in trouble, or there was a crisis. He found it to be the latter.

"How can I help you, Doctor Reznik?"

"First, let's go to a private room!"

When they entered the room, she closed the door, saying, "Listen to me carefully because I have time to say it only once. Room 104 has someone injured by an explosive device and should have no visitors. The surveillance cameras should be activated, and if visitors do come, get their names, and if possible, their vehicle license number."

The look on the administrator's face showed incredulity. *What was going on with this intern taking him from an important meeting, sounding and making demands like she was a patient in his mental ward?*

The administrator had known Sheena as a beautiful, compliant, and meek intern. Now, she stood in front of him neither meek nor compliant and her eyes showed it with a stern, cold stare. Something told him to walk softly.

"Doctor, why did you come to me requesting these actions?"

"Sir, the patient in room 104 is a terrorist, was injured while assembling a bomb. I understand and speak Arabic, and in his delirious and half-conscious state, I found out his name, the country he's from and his mission."

Upon hearing that she understood Arabic and the patent was a terrorist, his face turned pale, his stiff, rigid stature suddenly caved showing insecurity.

"Should we call the police?"

"For now our own security will handle this, and when they get here they will instruct you."

"Yes Doctor, I'll get right on it."

The administrator left to attend to Sheena's concerns and she went to his secretary's office to call Hans.

"Is there a private line here in this office?"

"Yes, there's one right here."

"And no one can listen in?"

"That's right."

"I'll have to ask you to leave for a few minutes and please shut the door on the way out."

Sheena described to Hans the events happening in the hospital. The conversation was short, and she elected not to interfere with the administrator's actions in carrying out her requests. She would wait in the secretary's office until Hans' security people arrived. The secretary never returned, and forty minutes later there was the sound of a helicopter overhead. It was Max, the Chief of Security. She took a deep breath—it was now someone else's burden. She had pushed herself against the tide, acting contrary to her gentle, silent nature.

Suddenly, the door to the secretary's office burst open. It was Hans. He saw she was alone, and pulled the door shut knowing they needed privacy. He held out his arms, and she welcomed an embrace that felt like a cool breeze over a dry, parched desert. There was a knock outside the door. Hans pushed it open, and standing in front of him in the doorway was big Max and the administrator.

"May we come in?" Max asked, and without waiting for an answer, he moved inside with the administrator behind him.

"Let me assure everyone that everything is under control." He looked at Sheena and shook his head, and then he shook it again. She had a flash memory of that baldhead creating humor a few days before at a dining table in Israel, but today she couldn't find any humor in it.

"Doctor Sheena," Max said, "you're something else! What you've done today by taking instant action with that patient, using your knowledge of Arabic, has given us a key to open big doors…." Sheena interrupted, "Oh, my notepad, I left it in the room, we must retrieve it!"

"No need to worry, Miss, our people have it and are already going over it. I've been informed that one visitor came to see the patient and was told, 'he was undergoing special care for his burns and to come back in two hours.' We caught his picture on camera and your administrator's secretary followed him to the parking lot and secured his license number. Today's been a lucky day—all because of you."

"Max, you haven't told the whole story. Any visitor coming to see this patient will be his executioner. He knows too much to fall into police custody." *Wow! thought the administrator, this lady knew what she was doing making demands as she did.*

"This is where we come in, Doctor Reznik. He will only go to the police if we give him up, and that would not help our cause. If we can get him back to health, we'll hide him and he'll become our talking library. In my line of work through the years, I have done a lot of this and come well qualified for the job. We have to get him to another hospital under a different name for his own protection."

Hans stepped in and took charge. "For the time being, we will carry out our Hippocratic medical oath. Police action is not warranted on our part because we have no forensic evidence that requires us to do so. No visitors will be allowed, and when he is well enough, we'll take him to another hospital where Max can give him the protection treatment. One thing we don't want to do is to hold him against his will. This is the final word. Let's all go home and let Max do his job here."

The following day Hans and Sheena returned to their routine work schedules. Sheena was back to her normal self: meek, quiet, and compliant. She took notice that the hospital administrator avoided her until he had need of her assistance. "Doctor Reznik, in view that you speak Arabic it is suggested that you be present in the transfer of the injured Arabic-speaking patient. Once he leaves this hospital, perhaps we can get back to normal."

Max was standing in the hall outside the patient's room when Sheena arrived. He showed the image of his usual self: a set jaw with a prideful glare, both hanging on a broad face that matched his immense size.

"Max, have you talked to Hans about moving this patient?"

"Yes, and his stipulation is that we must get two doctors' approval of his transfer. We already have one, and if you will check him out and sign the order, we'll be on our way."

"I can only sign this document for transfer as a resident doctor. Did you get any more info from him in his rational state?"

"Yes, and I'll be sending you and Doctor Hans a full report after we've been with him for another week. A teaser to this report will contain the information that the underground Nazi element hired this patient and his colleagues to build and plant a bomb with a magnetic device that would adhere to the side of the vehicle. A motorcyclist would have driven alongside Doctor Hans' vehicle, the device attached, and detonated after driving away."

Max saw Sheena close her eyes, cringing with pain at the thought of this being carried out.

"Give me an overview of what you have told the patient, and does he agree with what you propose?"

"He knows he's on a hit list by those who hired him, and he has been told by our people that if he gives us what we want, we'll see he is safely returned to his country with some cash in his pocket. Of course, the latter will be carried out only if he complies with agreed terms."

"What are you hoping to achieve in this?"

"The names of his contacts that are indigenous to this country and are presently under the radar. Once we know who they are, we can shine the light on them."

"Well, let's get this over with," said Sheena.

When they entered the patient's room, they found him covered with bandages, yet his face and eyes appeared to be in good condition. When he saw two figures come inside the room, he turned his head slowly, as if in pain. Fear registered on his face. Sheena spoke to him in Arabic.

"Good morning, how are you feeling today?"

When he heard his speech in his native tongue, his face brightened. She continued speaking to him in Arabic, even though his German was good. He responded in Arabic.

"Are you in agreement of being moved to another hospital under a different name?

"Yes, I have no other choice."

She checked his vital signs, then asked, "Do you feel up to making the trip?"

His reply was in the affirmative. She struggled with the conflict of having to process this patient who would have killed Hans had he been successful in his assignment.

Max and Sheena stepped outside the room. Her tense state was closely observed by Max. "What's the flight time?" she asked.

"Probably an hour by helicopter."

"He'll make the flight all right, but from this point on his issues will be psychological."

"And that's where we come in. For someone in his state of mind, massaging the psychological sensory needs outside his radical environment sometimes works wonders."

"Let's hope that will be the case," said Sheena.

She had stayed beyond her shift schedule, and after signing the release for the helicopter transfer, she went to her locker to change out of her scrubs. Circumstances and events had pushed Sheena to a point requiring deep reflection. She had come from a working-class home and by hard work was now a doctor-in-training, had fallen in love and engaged to the most wonderful person in the world, not knowing he would become one of the wealthiest men in Europe. This had turned their world, and her parents' world upside down.

Now, she was forced to live in a bastion, a prison, isolated with loss of freedom, always facing exposure to violence. *She took no comfort in the irony that the man she transferred to anonymity was in the same predicament: the need of protection. Both had something in common: they lived in a prison. His was one of darkness, created by the sword—hers was a prison of light, created by using wealth to advance the nation of Israel and her people.* Oh, that the Messiah would return and bring order and peace to the world and rule over His people as Micah, the Prophet, had promised:

> *He will judge between many peoples and will settle disputes for strong nations far and wide. They will beat their swords into plowshares and their spears into pruning hooks. Nation will not take up sword against nation, nor will they train for war anymore. Everyone will sit under their own vine.*

Chapter 25

Genocidal Exposure

Big Max, dressed in a pinstripe suit with his baldhead glistening under the overhead lights, looked the studio over inside. The background and special lighting were all in place. Those designated for specific roles in the Romanian Holocaust film production were gathered around the corporate head of public relations and two well-known film directors. On display were background-enlarged photos of gruesome Holocaust scenes, the kind one has to force himself to look at. Some consisted of photos taken at the uncovered mass burial site at Ediniti.

Among the group were the star witnesses, Mario Nicolescu, Doctor Hans, Doctor Sheena, and her father who seemed to be playing a prominent role in everything these days. Max's security men had been stationed strategically in and around the rented film studio. He thought to himself that it could be a long night knowing the perfection level of those directing the production.

Max went to look in on his people at the front doors who were responsible for checking the names of those invited to attend. This was recommended by the directors. A live audience would give greater animation in the speakers' presentation. The audience would consist mostly of older Jews who were survivors or relatives of survivors of the Holocaust.

Tonight was show time. A final recording would be made after several rehearsals. The first up was Sheena's father, a survivor, who gave a brief personal history of the Holocaust in Romania, followed by the powerful, personal testimony of Mario Nicolescu. He described watching the Nazi soldiers and civilians kill three-hundred Jews and the taking of women and young girls to be raped, some committing suicide afterward. Then came his morbid description of being forced to dig an open grave and bury the dead, while at the same time the background scene showed Hans and his team uncovering the mass grave. It was so moving the directors had to give a fifteen-minute break so those present could collect themselves.

Max gave the order that after a certain guest came in all doors were to be closed, locked, and guarded. He returned to the small auditorium, sat in the back, and noticed some of the guests were having a difficult time with the event. The last segment of production included his boss.

Hans was a convincing, articulate, public speaker. When he came before the camera, Max thought, *he was putting a mark on his back as a targeted man. If he thought security was tight under present conditions, he could only expect more of the same after the telecast of this production.*

Speaking in German, Hans began with a story-telling format: "I once knew a German woman who went to Romania in 1940 to visit her German husband who was a general stationed in that country. I want to read part of a letter she wrote about her experience while there…." It was the letter his mother had left him after she passed, and when he had finished reading the riveting letter, he looked at the camera, saying, "I am that little-orphaned boy taken from the hay wagon, reared by a righteous Gentile whose life was devoted to fighting anti-Semitism and providing support in the establishment of a homeland for the homeless and unwanted Jew. This German lady found me in the midst of a

278

Holocaust in a country whose people killed three hundred thousand Jews and to this day refuses to acknowledge it.

"Let it be said, a country that does not admit to her national crimes against humanity will never prosper in a world built on truth, peace, and justice."

The speech so moved the guests in attendance that Hans had to wait a few minutes before giving it in English for the English-speaking world. Later, other languages would be dubbed-in. When he finished with the English segment, the team went down to mingle with the guests. Hans stopped. Everyone stopped with him. From the shadows of the entry of the auditorium, he saw a wheelchair emerging, being pushed by Max. It was the Old Man.

Hans returned to the stage, and taking the microphone, said: "Ladies and gentlemen, among us, is my favorite living hero, a distinguished lawyer, a brilliant businessman, and someone who contributed to making me what I am by being a friend and business associate to my late mother. We are honored to have Gustov Klein among us."

Hans left the stage, went to where the old man rested in his chair. Tears were in his eyes.

"Hans, Your mother always told me that God would use you in a special way for Israel. Her life was spent tailoring you to that end. When you left God, she would tell me that you would someday have your Damascus-road experience. And today, her words have their fulfillment. We all have our gifts and callings from God. Your mother and I have expended ours, and now it's your turn."

"With God's help and the help of the woman I'm going to marry, we'll get it done together."

"Oh yes, the gal you're going to marry…she's something else. I'm here tonight because of her. She told

Max, 'Be sure to get the Old Man here because he's part of this'—so here I am."

Sheena joined the two, and together they went to a large lounge where guests were served refreshments.

After the tape had its final editing touches, prime time was bought and scheduled on major networks throughout the free world. The program was so gripping and well done that its promoters were successful in seeing it aired over BBC and Voice of America.

Chapter 26

An Old Table

The executive committee of the consortium had arranged a meeting in a vacated, rural farmhouse. The banker, Erhart, and William, the committee member from England, arrived together by helicopter. Gustov and Hans came in separate vehicles. They all sat around an old, common-looking, kitchen table from yesteryears. Hans sat at one end, the Old Man at the other. Showing through the table's rough appearance was the dense grain of hardwood oak, well used through years of service. The table held glaring scratches, gouges, and dents but still stood proudly functional for those who would enlist its use. The aged table never showed weakness until Hans placed his heavy briefcase on its top and leaned against it with his weight. The strong legs that held it up for years were now loose and wobbly, making creaky sounds when it moved.

The table had served poor families through the years whose livelihoods came from working the soil. Tonight, those who would use the service of the table would be the wealthy. Around the old table that measured history sat the four members of the consortium's executive committee. When it came time for Hans to give his report, he took the file from his case placing it in front of him, but an old table was his distraction. Not the one that held his briefcase that squeaked and wobbled every time he leaned against it or moved something around on its top. It was the face of another old table sitting among them with weak legs and a well-worn surface. He saw oak-hardness underneath the scars, dents, and abrasions of life. This was what the Old Man was made of—hard, enduring oak. He had given years of service to his mother and the consortium for the cause of the State of Israel. He had been the silent kingmaker helping to create a homeland for destitute Jews after the war. Tonight, Hans thought his mortality was peering through his frail exterior much beyond what he'd seen before. He was slower speaking, his eyes more sunken, narrowed, and more unsteady on his feet, much like the table they sat around. However, unlike the old oak table that would end up on the garbage heap, the Old Man's faith assured him that the table of his life, which had served others through the years, would undergo a change that would make him better than new.

Hans struggled to finish his report on the progress of the newly acquired shipping line and the proposed refitting of two ships that would accommodate the new migratory pick-ups for Israel. Upon leaving their cloistered meeting site, Hans pushed the Old Man's wheelchair outside to his waiting attendant, and together they helped him onto the special handicap ramp. They drove away with the Old Man giving a certain wave to Hans that seemed to say, *"I'm leaving, but when I return, I'll not be the old rickety table you put your briefcase on tonight."*

By the time Hans reached home, he had the news that the Old Man had passed. He wept, then, called Sheena. He had lost a family member. *He and the Old Man had two things in common: both lost their families in the Holocaust, and each had derived strength from the noble Lady who had given him life.*

On his way to his office the next morning, Hans was wondering who would be handling the Old Man's affairs. There was his funeral, his estate, and personal issues that had to be administered. He entered his office through his private access door and found a voice message from Miss Shuster. "Mr. Baughman, a Joseph Muller, one of the lawyers who worked closely with the Old Man is trying to get an appointment to see you. He says, 'It's an urgent matter.'"

He called Miss Shuster. "Please get Mr. Muller to my office immediately."

When the gentleman arrived, he was led to Hans' plush office. They had never met, but between the time of Hans' arrival and the introduction, he had reviewed his file.

"Mr. Joseph Muller, I presume."

"That's correct, Sir."

Hans saw a man in his early 50s with a receding hairline that went unnoticed because attention was drawn to his dress. There wasn't a wrinkle in his pinstripe suit, giving the appearance it had been molded to fit his torso. *Hans thought, for the first time someone of the male gender had graced his office with equal elegance.*

"And you have been Gustov's assistant for four years?"

"Yes, Sir."

"To what extent were you with him in administrative meetings and decision-making?"

"In all legal matters, I was the first to review and offer up suggested changes and alternatives. I also drew up the original legal drafts going out to our legal panel for final review.

"Regarding the administrative end, I was in most meetings with Mr. Klein, and before your mother passed, she would sometimes deal with me because she didn't want to overtax her beloved friend."

When Hans heard him refer to his mother dealing with him instead of Gustov, his prejudiced view of his dress changed.

"Did you know my mother personally?"

"Only to the extent of being with her in business meetings."

"How many meetings would that be?"

"Off the top of my head, I don't know, maybe ten, but if you want to know the actual number I can get the record from our minutes."

"Did she ever discuss me in any of your meetings?"

"She never discussed you in my presence. She only answered questions Gustov raised about you. I heard enough to know the sun rose and set with you. She was proud of you for becoming a doctor."

Hans was becoming emotional and had the need to move on. "And what is it you wish to discuss with me?"

Hans noticed he had brought a small attaché case with him and kept it on his lap. "Mr. Baughman, I have come here representing Mr. Klein's legal affairs. The Old Man had no living relatives—all were lost in the Holocaust. He considered you and your mother his only living kin. It fell to me, his close legal confidant, to handle his personal affairs. So, this morning, I'm representing him as his attorney. He assigned me the responsibility of handling all funeral arrangements and act as the executor of his estate.

"Mr. Klein was a very wealthy man. I didn't know this until I gained access to his confidential files. In those files, I found a note stating that 'his wealth was garnered by investing where Katharina put her money.' He has commissioned me to arrange his private religious interment as he did for your mother, and he has requested you to be the main speaker at his public memorial service."

The lawyer paused, reached inside his case, and took out a folder, saying, "Mr. Baughman, in this folder is a sealed confidential letter to you and a copy of his last will and testament. When you review this, you will see he has left everything to you as his sole heir."

The lawyer saw Hans look off into space. Tears moistened his eyes. "I wish he could have been around in my youth; he would've been a wonderful grandfather."

"Sir, he would have been that and more."

"Mr. Muller, have you been compensated for your time and effort?"

"You can be assured that the Old Man has left me well-compensated."

"Please remember that Mr. Klein's memorial event will require the highest level of security, and Max, our Chief Security Officer, stands ready to work with you in this important matter."

"Yes, his reputation is well known, and I have already discussed security with him. In fact, he has checked out the site I selected for the memorial service and has given approval providing the luncheon being served afterward is onsite."

"It appears you have everything under control. It's quite inappropriate to discuss this matter now, but necessary. I want you to assume the responsibility of directing our legal department. Your salary will be adjusted accordingly."

"Thank you, sir. We will continue to operate on the same professional level following the example left us by the Old Man."

The lawyer left Hans' elegant office pondering that for the first time someone junior to him in age had the authority to give him a promotion.

Hans, now alone in his office, opened the packet delivered to him by the lawyer from the Old Man. He first read a personal letter addressed to him:

Dear Hans,

I am now out of my wheelchair visiting with my dear wife and Kathy. What we are in life tends to live on in others after we're gone. Your mother and I have passed on to you a heavy burden only men of certain moral and spiritual fiber can handle. Life is a proving ground. It has tested you with good success, and because you have proven yourself, I have left my entire estate to you knowing it will be used to continue the work of supporting a people and their land for the coming Messiah.

My life has been shrouded with a lot of mystery because of the events that came my way. This letter will attempt to tell the story only your mother knew.

My wife and I were born Jews in the country of Holland where I practiced law until I went to work for Kathy's father who had expanded his industry into that country. He and I had attended boarding school together and remained friends until he and his wife were killed.

Your mother inherited everything in Holland and Germany and kept me on to help run the business in Holland. In 1940, the Nazis invaded Holland and began shipping Jews to concentration camps. My wife and I went underground, and with the help of your mother, escaped to Switzerland, changed our identity, and from there worked with your mother in expanding her business.

At the end of the war, we moved to Germany and joined forces with your mother in sponsoring efforts of returning Jews to their homeland. It was in those days right after the war your mother led us into a personal faith and belief that the historical Jesus was the Messiah, and that He would be returning to earth to rule over the world.

All my family in Holland perished in the Holocaust, but God gave us a new family with you and your mother. Oh yes, my wife and I both knew you as a child. You and your mother would visit us in Switzerland when you were in arms. We held you in our embrace when you were but two and three years old.

When we return to earth with the Messiah in our mystical form, we'll continue the work of supporting His kingdom rule on earth.

Goodbye, my dear boy, you have been a friend indeed.

Uncle Gustov, formally known as the Old Man

That evening Hans and Sheena went to the mortuary for the viewing. Visitors waiting in line to view the mortal remains of the man who influenced their lives reached outside the building onto the sidewalk. Security personnel stood close by the two as they joined others waiting in line. After entering the front door, Hans saw Sonje Shuster standing with her staff waiting to place a floral arrangement at the foot of the bier. From where he stood, he saw her wiping tears from her eyes, and upon reaching the open casket, she leaned over and kissed the honored man on his forehead. Without speaking to anyone, she left her flowers and walked away sobbing.

Hans knew he had seen drama in play with hidden mystery. *What would cause that kind of emotional display from someone who only had a professional connection in the workplace? Then he remembered she gave the same response at his mother's funeral. Mystery hung over Miss Shuster, and he would let time tell the whole story.*

Hans and Sheena stepped up together to give their final farewell. A soft, delicate hand holding a large diamond engagement ring placed a rose on the chest of the departed. Eyes that bore the rose remained fixed on hands folded together until another deep crimson flower was laid alongside, followed by the words, "Uncle Gustov, give these roses to my mother when you see her."

Before moving from the scene, Hans' attention was drawn to the flower arrangement Sonje Shuster had placed at the foot of the bier. Contained in the spray was a species of roses laced with greenery that opened his memory. He had seen that exact arrangement bearing that species of flower in his home. His inquisitive, precocious nature couldn't resist reading the card that came with it:

Gustov, I am at a loss of words to express my appreciation of your acts of kindness to me when I was taken from the death camp and nurtured back to life by you and Katharina. You have always been a father figure to me, and when your voyage reaches its final port of call, please greet your dear wife for me. Thank you for everything.

Sonje

Hans left the mortuary that night with two things hanging over him: guilt for having read the personal note left by Miss Shuster, and the question of her historical connection with the Old Man and his mother. *He knew she wasn't Jewish, so why the reference of a death camp?*

Following Gustov Klein's instructions, Mr. Muller arranged his religious burial interment to be performed under the supervision of his Messianic Rabbi, his final resting place being alongside his late wife. The private interment would be unannounced, allowing only those who were close to him to be in attendance.

The morning following the public viewing of the Old Man, four large limousines were seen pulling into the Jewish sector of the cemetery. Nearby, underneath a large awning rested a closed casket covered with an array of beautiful flowers.

Those in attendance of the graveside service followed the Messianic Rabbi onto the soft green mat covering the sacred grounds of the departed. Left behind, were Max's security people stationing themselves strategically with watchful eyes for any eventuality? In attendance for the private ceremony were four of the Old Man's close friends: Hans Isler, Sonje Shuster, Erhart, the banker and William, the Brit. Each placed a traditional small stone on top of the closed casket.

In death, the Old Man demonstrated his penchant for detail. He requested his executor to adhere to written instructions if there were a memorial service in his honor. Such an event would include Hans Isler and Sonje Shuster as principal speakers.

The passing of Gustov Klein weighed heavily on Hans. Now, he carried the total load without the wise old sage at his side, and being fraught with doubts and fears, he would lean into the cool breezes of knowing that he was saved out of the Holocaust for such an hour.

The latter days of Gustov showed the man's level of character, insight, and wisdom. He knew when he was gone the success of Katharina Enterprises would be attributed to him by the professionals who invariably assigned success to those in charge, and being chairman, he was perceived to be in control. This matter had been settled long before the aging senescent decline of the Old Man. It was in the interest of the invisible lady who owned the company that her dear friend be assigned that honored status. The honor she desired was to be perceived as a loving mother of the child she saved from the Holocaust. Both had a common mission. They had signed an agreement, not with pen and paper, but with the heart—all for the greater cause of helping Israel to be a people and a nation in their land for the coming Messianic Ruler. Inside the inner circle of the company, it was common knowledge that the chairman listened to the voice of an invisible face, an invisible face that cared little about who was assigned the credit of the company's success. Her success would be measured, not by the company she built, but by the child she was rearing outside the domain of wealth and privilege.

The Old Man was a lawyer known for detail. Mr. Muller, his executor, had to reference often his typical wordy request of everything pertaining to his demise, but when it came to his memorial celebration, he was glaringly brief. He put no prohibitions on the company's celebration of his life and accomplishments; however, he made two important inclusions: Hans Isler would be the main speaker and Sonje Shuster would do his eulogy.

Though a very private person, he knew the public relations people of the company would see to it that his picture was in every newspaper and business magazine. For this, he had no objections if it served to promote the company's bottom line. In the end, Israel would be the beneficiary. With Hans at the helm of the ship, he knew things would come off well.

It wasn't incumbent on Mr. Muller to keep the new chairman of the company informed of the Old Man's final requests. The only time personal contact was made with the chairman following his initial conference in his office was when a delivery was made in the form of a sealed envelope containing a program copy of the Old Man's memorial ceremony. Attached to the program was a note in his own handwriting: "Enclosed is the program schedule as outlined by the venerable, Gustov Klein."

When Hans looked over the program, he found the Old Man had requested only two things: Sonje Shuster would do his eulogy, and Hans Isler would be the main spokesperson. Mr. Muller had selected two additional speakers pertinent to the occasion: the city mayor and an Israeli intelligence officer. Seeing the name of Miss Shuster deepened the mystery surrounding her. *He knew she was not given the assignment of doing the Old Man's eulogy because of her status in the finance world. Suspicion of hidden history continued to etch itself in the back of Hans' mind.*

Ten days following the private graveside interment, Max found himself working over-time for the big event of securing the safety of those who would be in attendance of the Old Man's public memorial service, a man of international prominence whose influence was renown in Jewish circles.

The auditorium used to honor the life and work of Gustov Klein would be the prestigious performing arts building in downtown Munich. Doors were scheduled to open at nine a.m. with the showing of the life-story video as a prelude to the main event. Max made the decision to disperse consortium members among the audience alongside two civilian-dressed security personnel. Reporters and TV technicians were required to arrive at eight o'clock to register and set-up.

Employees of Katharina Enterprises at the central headquarters building were given the morning off to attend the ceremony of the company's venerable legend. Following the event, refreshment would be served downstairs in the large dining room.

Sheena sat in the audience with her mother and father. Hans was with others on the stage. The building was packed with some standing in the large entryway. Hans was allocated the closing fifteen minutes of the memorial event. The first to speak was the mayor, followed by the Israeli intelligence officer and Sonje Shuster.

Hans brought closure to his memorial speech:

... "Friends, we bid farewell to a man who will be measured more by what he did than what he said. Gustov was a silent philanthropist, giving to the needy in anonymity. A survivor of the Holocaust, he became a bridge over which many walked to find safety in their homeland. Bread that he cast upon the waters in silence returned when common people filed by his bier leaving flowers, notes, and tears. Gustov was a brilliant lawyer by training, but an engineer by vision. He knew how to put things together to make them last, whether it was legalese in documents or systems of management. It was his bright, erudite-piercing blue eyes that characterized who and what he was. He could see what others couldn't. When in his presence, his eyes seem to tell you what you were thinking; they spoke as clearly as words and gave expression of his level of intelligence. Though his frame weathered with age, and his gnarled, swollen hands lost their grip, his path was always straight because his vision was clear. He lived his entire life never having the need of eyewear, and like Moses at the end of his life, Gustov viewed from his own mountaintop with clear vision the future, the Promised Land, the hope of the world. Today, we bid farewell to the man who left us a company with a strong bottom line and straight paths to walk down. "

After Hans finished speaking, he returned to his chair behind the podium and left it for others to make further announcements. In the audience, Sheena's father saw his daughter wiping her teary eyes, and reaching over, he took hold of one of her hands. She welcomed his hand's rough feel. It spoke of having made things beautiful in life: the garden of flowers he grew and harvested, the diamonds he cut and polished, and even her own life bore the marks of his workmanship. However, the roughness didn't register on his hand—it was carried in his heart.

At the luncheon following the memorial event, Hans sat with Sheena and her family at a table that included others that were part of the memorial production. The consortium members chose not to stay because of security issues; however, two of the executive committee members remained to discuss a business matter with Hans.

The conversation around the table was spirited with a display of formal reservation. Hans noticed that Sonje

Shuster was going out of her way to be friendly with Sheena, something he hadn't noticed before. Then he realized they'd never been formally introduced and were now taking it upon themselves to become acquainted.

The somber one at the table was the Israeli intelligence officer. He kept conversation in check and used silence to keep his skill up by studying human behavior.

Of those around the table, the Israeli was the only one who saw three members withdraw to another part of the room where they huddled together. Erhart, a member of the executive committee had requested a private conversation. He led the conversation.

"This year has been devastating for the consortium with the loss of Gustov and Chuck. This leaves us without a chairman for our fifteen-member consortium and no one to lead the executive committee."

The banker, Erhart, paused. The brief silence was an invitation for others to get involved. Of the three, William spoke first.

"In view that Hans has excellent public relations skills and has been well-received by others, I would recommend that he be appointed chairman to fulfill the Old Man's term of office."

"I concur with that," responded Erhart. "We need someone to hold us together until a formal election is held, Hans' youthful vision would be a plus."

"Well, what do you say, Hans?" asked William.

"Gentlemen, I now have three burdens to carry: my mother's, the estate of the Old Man, and the one you just assigned me. In view that we use only consortium members for retaining and handling confidential matters, I'll need one of you to act as secretary to call a special meeting with the consortium."

All three returned to the table they'd vacated. Before Hans sat, he was met by the intelligence officer, handed a sealed letter with the words: "This letter is from my senior officer and does not require a reply. Needless to say, we are indebted to you, your company, and the consortium members for what you do for our nation and our people."

Hans stuffed the letter in his vest-suit pocket, walked Sheena and her parents to their waiting vehicle in the VIP parking section where their driver was seated behind the wheel. Up to this point, the swirling movement of crowds prevented the opportunity for private words between the two. After the senior Rezniks boarded, the husband to the front seat with the driver and the wife to the rear, it left Hans and Sheena standing alone.

"Hans, Gustov Klein knew what he was doing when he requested you to be the closing speaker today. You have a way with words. Like an artist who works his colors to produce a masterpiece, you use words to paint pictures that stimulate feeling and thought. You did a masterful job."

"If people were moved, it was because I spoke truth of the Old Man's life."

"That's true," said Sheena, "but when the tires are fully inflated, the ride is smoother."

"Now, look at the one who has a way with words! Someday, you'll be my speechwriter!"

At this point, they were interrupted by the senior, Mrs. Reznik, knocking on the window signaling they should be on their way. Looking at Hans, Sheena retorted with slight disdain: "I promise when I reach my mother's age, I'll be more patient with our daughters!"

"I'll see everyone at my place tonight. After my driver drops me off at my office, he's going to pick up my favorite chef for this evening's gourmet delights."

The two kissed, said goodbye. Sheena sat beside her mother now showing a control scowl.

"Why are you so irritable today, Mother?"

"It is not you, my dear. I feel like a prisoner having to live behind gated walls under the watchful eyes of others who do everything for us.

"Hans has offered to get you a place in Israel, you know."

"And that's my dilemma. The human psyche carries two powerful entities. We know them as reason and emotion. Hans' offer is emotion knocking at my door. On the musical strings of feelings, I am told it would be the solution to my anxieties, but then I hear another voice using the argument of reason.

"Sheena, look at your father in the front seat talking to our driver. He's happy as a lark doing what Hans has assigned him. He is the voice of reason I hear. Emotion pulls the heartstrings of unproven hypotheticals. Reason addresses the whole picture—the inclusion of others, and because God in marriage makes two people one, it would be selfish to act against reason. My frustration, my dear, comes from forcing myself to do what is right, rather than what my feelings tell me.

"Now, my doctor-daughter, I have given you my symptoms. What is the antidote for my choice of living under the law of reason."

"Well, mother, confession is good for the soul. The fact that you see the big picture and are able to identify your problem means you can create pathways out of your depression."

"My doctor-daughter pulls no punches! She used the big D word."

"Mother, your depression is not clinical, but situational. You have the power to create situations that turnoff those voices that titillate with hypotheticals. If, is always contrary to fact, and you are to be commended for your insightful self-review.

"Now, let me give you a daughter's suggestions for action. First, is your intense reading used as an escape mechanism? Perhaps your pleasure of reading should involve others. You could start a book club and bring different genres into a group discussion.

"Secondly, make an effort to attend and arrange social outings. The fact that you have a driver who takes you about puts distance between you and those you wish to befriend; however, that will change once they are visitors to your home and they see who you really are. The result of these efforts will be invitations to homes otherwise never visited.

"Next, consult with your Messianic Rabbi and offer your services in areas of need. He'll probably interview you and give you assignments that best fit your experience and interest. Do you remember Hans' speech describing the Old Man? He lived a life just like you behind gated walls, but he was busy, something that's missing in your life!"

"Mother, to put closure on this subject for today, I'll give my closing commentary: Hypothetical emotional feelings without logic are to be treated like fictional novels—for entertainment alone!

"And may I also add, tonight is a special evening at Hans' place. He's bringing in a special chef and his assistant to do the evening dinner and it's a big deal for Hans because we're all that he has."

"Your father is excited about tonight. He has already packed the drawings he wants to review with Hans.

"Hans gave Papa something that surged new life in him with that project in Israel," added Sheena

"Well, Hans needs to give me something that would bring new life!"

"Mother, look at me." The daughter reached for her mother's face, turned it toward her, saying, "Mother, Hans gave you more than you could ever wish for: he gave you the gift of a marriage proposal to your daughter.

The father in the front seat heard sobbing. Unobtrusively, he turned down his overhead sun visor that held a mirror, and then quickly flipped it up, leaned back in his seat with closed eyes and a broad smile. He would let the picture of his daughter's arms around her sobbing mother linger on the wall of memory. He knew something beautiful was being formed out of hurt.

Chapter 27

Loneliness in Wealth

Hans had spent the afternoon in his downtown office and looked forward to the evening's activities with Sheena and her parents. When his driver pulled into his walled compound, he was instructed to drop him off at the tool shed. It was there he stored his homeless-looking clothes, clothes he wore on the streets to escape his world of isolation. Tonight, they would be used to work in his flower garden and remember the life of a man who made it possible for his late adoptive mother to be a full-time parent.

The driver stopped in front of the tool shed. The chairman got out, watched the vehicle drive away. Hans stood facing the building used to store his soup-kitchen attire. Though he appeared to be alone, he knew there were attendants on the compound watching from the shadows. Max, the company's chief security officer, maintained strict rules governing attendants inside the large compound. They were never to approach the chairman without cause and were to make themselves inconspicuous when he was outside walking about.

His busy schedule rarely gave him time to enjoy his well-kept compound, and tonight nature was demonstrating its elegance with the setting sun cutting through earth's atmospheric prism leaving a beautiful orange glow looming overhead. He wished Sheena was there to enjoy the scene, then, reminded himself that in two months she would be with him permanently in a state of marriage.

Nostalgia for his former life without wealth gripped him. He remembered the days when he came home from the hospital dressed in scrubs. It was another world, another time, a time when he was everybody's friend. Those were the days when people went out of their way to greet him, to ask him out to lunch, to attend a party, and even requested advice.

Hans stepped toward the windowed front door of the tool shed and froze. Reflected in the glass section of the door was a dull outline of his image showing the fitted, upscale pinstriped suit worn today for the Old Man's memorial event. It was a picture of his new world of wealth, one that came with a wall of separation, behind which was his prison of loneliness and isolation.

Hans remembered the efforts he and Sheena made to break down barriers because of wealth—then came the assassination attempts forcing them behind higher walls and less social interaction. Wealth had created a prison of loneliness and isolation. However, people outside his world thought differently. From the outside looking in, they saw what could be measured: the walled residence, large vehicles with darkened windows ushering him about with attendants and drivers. They never saw him at small events, and he never went out of his way to attend public functions unless there was a cadre of security people around him. Though the people who worked and moved with him wore civilian clothes, everyone knew they were security people. The public didn't know it was his support of Israel and her people that forced him into a controlled environment.

Sheena had survived better than Hans. At the hospital, She was now accepted as one the group. She went through the routine of being with the same people on a daily basis. Even doctors with whom she worked had come to respect her in her professional role. But with Hans, it was different. He was the target of those who hated Israel, and his forced, cloistered life kept him isolated. He walked up to his neck in money, but none of it could buy his freedom from his prison of separation. Now he understood why some people of wealth engaged in unseemly behavior, abused their bodies with drugs, alcohol, and engaged in wild parties. It was the voice of loneliness they were trying to drown. Had it not been for God and the companionship of Sheena, he might have taken the road that led to self-destruction. Sheena went to work with others as an equal. He went to work as a superior in rank, but more importantly, a very wealthy one.

Hans' position of wealth had taken him from his old world. He no longer belonged anywhere. In anonymity, he had more friends in the soup kitchens than in his boardroom where it was all about finance and power. There was one exception: Karl, his pediatrician colleague. They remained close, and with Karl's known administrative skills, Hans had appointed him chairman of his mother's health industry.

Tonight, Hans would put closure on today's celebration of the Old Man's life with cuttings from his own flower garden. His soup kitchen street clothes awaited his attention.

In removing his upscale suit, he found in the vest pocket the letter from the Israeli intelligence officer. While the chef was busy in the kitchen, and his guests still on their way, he moved under the single overhead light in the tool shed and read the special message from the Israeli intelligence officer:

Your proposal to pick up Jews at ports and on open seas has been given to our intelligence team, and they will use their contacts through our embassies to lay the groundwork for moving people to your ships. A priority list will be created to first move what Israel needs: aerospace engineers, research chemists, and physicists just to name a few. As you know, we will always maintain plausible deniability for any and all actions. These are dangerous times that create clandestine situations. Israel exists because of the idealism of people like you.

No signature was attached, and normal protocol was followed: the note was destroyed.

When Hans entered the back entrance to his home, one arm held a large bundle of freshly cut flowers; the other carried his pinstriped suit. After hanging his suit in his walk-in wardrobe closet, the flowers were placed in the middle of the dining table as a centerpiece in memory of the Old Man. Hans refused to order flowers from a florist. He had the need to do a physical act in showing respect to a special person instead of using money to pay for someone else's labor.

Hans went to his bedroom, disrobed and dressed for a casual evening. His street clothes were placed on the dresser and alongside he laid an old, brimmed hat, violin, and bow. They would be put to use later tonight.

He was anxious for the arrival of his special guests for the evening. They were his family, the only people in the world who loved him for what he was. Waiting for his guests to arrive provoked memories of those times when as a child certain events brought euphoric feelings. The difference was that now the experience was in an adult body.

The sound of a vehicle heard inside his compound riveted pleasure through him. He quickly went to the kitchen and asked the chef: "Is everything ready to be served?"

"Yes, Sir, it's ready to be put in serving dishes and is piping hot. The apple pie is just out of the oven."

"Wonderful, fill the serving dishes, pour four glasses of water—then you can leave! We'll make this a weekly event, but with a different menu."

Sheena didn't knock on the door—she just opened it and walked in. When she saw Hans, her face brightened.

"Since I'm going to be living here with you shortly, I thought I would just make myself at home. Do you mind?"

"Do I mind?" He grabbed her, pulled her next to him, whispering, "I've been waiting all day to be with the one who'll soon be with me permanently"

"We have two months to go and I'm counting the days," said Sheena.

Coming through the door, he heard Sheena's father say, "We're not getting any attention over here, Mr. Baughman? That woman you're holding seems to be getting it all!"

Hans looked over Sheena's shoulder. Standing in the doorway was Mr. Reznik clutching an armload of blueprints and drawings of his special project in Israel. Behind him stood his gallant wife, effervescent as ever.

"Pop, don't you get enough attention from that lady behind you?"

"In Bible times, you'd wash our feet before we came into your house, and now you just look at me and call me Pop."

"Yes, but those were the days before the automobile and oxford shoes."

"Oh yes, the automobile…it changed everything didn't it!"

"What are you carrying in your arms? Tonight's not supposed to be a night for work," said Hans.

"Hans, he's become a workaholic with that project you assigned him," added his wife.

The old man shuffled over to the coffee table, laid his bundle of rolled-up drawings down, saying, "We've come a long way on this project since we started. I want to show you how far."

"First, let's eat before it gets cold—ladies, lend me your hands in the kitchen!"

They all sat at the table, and Hans was about to offer a prayer of thanks when Mr. Reznik made a request. "Mr. Baughman, let's read a verse from Amos as our prayer of thanksgiving."

"A splendid suggestion, Pop."

Being addressed as Pop, Mr. Reznik looked at Hans over the top rims of his sagging glasses, showed a warm smile at the man soon to be his son-in-law. He first read from the Hebrew text, then, read the German translation. Wrinkled hands holding his Hebrew Bible told the story of his length of years, and when his melodious voice was heard without faint or quiver, he became the picture of vitality in his sunset years. He was a Jew who had made it home and was now helping others find the way. He was one of the people Amos talked about:

I will bring my people back from exile. They will build the ruined cities and live in them. I will plant Israel in their own land, never again to be uprooted.

Hans was quick to say, "That prophecy is being fulfilled before our eyes and we are very much a part of it."

"Wait until you see our plans that have been submitted," said Mr. Reznik. "The committee of architects and engineers you put together has completed its work and is at the point of being approved by the building department. Everyone living near the proposed project is excited about the economic activity it will bring."

"Speaking of economic impact," said Hans, "I'm considering moving to Israel one of our manufacturing plants located in South America. This would help provide a source of employment for new immigrants. It can't be done overnight because a trained and skilled labor force is required, but everything will come in its time."

"The prophet, Zachariah, speaks of this," said Mr. Reznik, "*"My towns will again overflow with prosperity...and the Lord will again choose Jerusalem.'"*

It didn't take long until Hans was back to his playful self, sending flirtatious signals to Sheena, acting younger than his years.

The fixation and attention Hans and Sheena were giving each other with whispers, winks, and certain looks seemed to short-circuit Mr. Reznik's need to discuss the housing project in Israel. He was hyper-focused, wanting to discuss it at the table, but Hans had little interest with his daughter present. With a look of frustration, he stopped eating and stared at the two of them before he spoke.

"Look, you two lovebirds, conversation seems to be going only one way. Why don't you two get married tomorrow and then we can have a two-way conversation?"

"Papa, are you telling me that after you married Mother you stopped flirting with her?"

"Sheena, your father does a lot of flirting these days, but it's not with me, it's with those plans he brought over. I haven't heard anything around my house beyond these building plans. He can give you the dimensions of each room in every designed model going up. Add to this the length of the underground piping for the wastewater for the whole project."

"Mama," said Mr. Reznik, "I've been with you a lot—you've been to Israel twice with me. You even went first-class."

"I have spent a lot of time with you up in the clouds, Mr. Reznik, a place you stay a lot these days—up in the clouds."

Hans quickly turned serious. "Mrs. Reznik, I want to commend your husband for his tenacity. Word has reached me that he's memorized the building code manual and knows it better than the officers in the Planning Commission, and they say if he doesn't stop quoting it to them they'll have to hire him to do their work."

"So that's what he's been mumbling in his sleep at night—it's the building code! Mr. Reznik, why do you have to know the building code? You can't remember flowers on my birthday, but you can memorize the building code!"

"I've never forgotten your birthday!"

"And that's only because our birthdates fall on the same day."

Mrs. Reznik was never one to leave a negative statement hanging without putting a closing positive note to it. She reached over, took his hand and looked him in the eyes, saying, "I would marry you a thousand times again just to be with you in the clouds and listen to your recitations of the building code at night—that's easier to take than your snoring!"

Mr. Reznik looked at Hans. "Mr. Baughman, you see what you're getting into when you get married? You get old and crabby like us! But it's a fun journey, especially, when you're madly in love."

"But it would be more fun," said Hans, "if you remembered flowers and avoided talking in your sleep?"

"Hans, don't take my mother and father seriously, they entertain themselves, and others, talking like this. Squinting her eyes, she put her face in front of Hans. "Do you snore at night? When I was still at home, I heard my father snoring from my bedroom."

Her father's eyes lit up with mischief. "I see it now—there's trouble already in paradise."

"Papa, let Hans speak for himself."

"First, let me say," said Hans, "I don't know if I snore at night because I never stay awake to find out! Miss beautiful here will find her answer in about five weeks when she starts sleeping with me."

Sheena's face turned beet-red. The three around her stared at her flushed face. "Hans, you embarrassed me." The theologian father jumped in the middle of it, saying, "My sweetie pie, my adorable lovely daughter, Hans is talking about living with you in the union of marriage—something God created, a mystical state where two become one. Besides, you led Hans down that path for him to give you that answer."

"Papa, I welcomed the answer he gave me, but to have you and mother hear him say it is another matter. Don't you always tell me I'm your little girl?"

Hans put his arm around Sheena. "I promise two things to my innocent bride tonight: I won't embarrass her again, and I'll not snore."

"Peace has returned to paradise!" said Mr. Reznik, "so this calls for a celebration by taking on that good-smelling apple pie. Then we can go over those plans."

"We'll look over those plans," said Hans, "providing you won't talk to your wife about them in your sleep."

"I'll agree to that if you cut me a big piece of pie."

Hans suddenly stood to his feet, saying, "About the pie, I'll ask Sheena if she would serve it with coffee while I step outside for a minute. Pop, if you are served before I return, don't wait for me!"

"I'll consider that, Son, and if you're late returning, I'll start on your piece."

When Hans gave Sheena a wink-of-the-eye and dimmed the lights in the large dining room, she knew whatever he was doing was planned.

Though today had been a sobering event remembering the Old Man, Hans chose to put a touch of levity and jest on its closure. After all, the senior Rezniks did their entertainment shtick around the dining table tonight, and it was opportune for him to show others a glimpse of the old Hans.

Whether he was motivated from a desire to measure Sheena's family's acceptance of him using a shock method or his need to express in creative form his frustrated life of living in a bubble, only time would tell. His experience in playing the violin in the high school orchestra and recent rehearsals would optimize his shtick for the evening.

At the dining table, the pie and coffee had been served, and all three were seated waiting for Hans when they heard the sound of a violin. The sound came closer. The three around the table looked at each other in wonderment. They recognized the tune as part of a world classic musical now in its sixth year on Broadway.

Expecting to see a performer Hans had brought in for entertainment, jaws dropped when a tattered figure with scruffy clothes and a pointed hat swaggered in rhythmic movement mimicking the figure of a fiddler walking precariously on a tin roof.

The guests' state of catatonia was short lived. Hans had rehearsed his part and soon all three joined in with clapping to the music. When he stopped, they applauded. However, in the middle of the laudation, Hans began singing the number most identified with Fiddler on the Roof but would change the words in the middle of the song that gave meaning to the cause of his lonely and isolated world. His audience of three gave respect as if he were on stage with a thousand in attendance:

If I were a rich man,

Ya ha deedle deedle, bubba bubba deedle deedle dum.

All day long I'd biddy biddy bum.

If I were a wealthy man

I wouldn't have to work hard.

Ya ha deedle deedle, bubba bubba deedle deedle dum.

If I were a biddy biddy rich,

Yidle-diddle-didle-didle man.

The three seated around the dinner table never knew this side of Hans. Unknown to his special guests, the performance being given was intended to show the bigger picture of how wealth had isolated him from his old world. The lyrics he changed told the whole story:

I wish a was a poor man

Ya ha deedle deedle, bubba bubba deedle deedle dum.

All day long I'd have friends biddy biddy bum.

If I were a poor man,

I wouldn't have to live behind high walls.

Ya ha deedle deedle, bubba bubba deedle deedle dum.

If I were a biddy biddy poor,

Yidle-diddle-didle-didle man.

When Hans finished the performance, he bowed to his audience of three, they clapped and sat in hush. Each felt the weight of what wealth had done to them. Their lives had been changed in ways others would never understand. First, to speak was the father, the family priest.

"Hans, God gave you a mission with a cross to bear, the kind of cross only those of us around this table can understand because we are part of it, but we will all grow from it and become better by it if we keep the vision of why God gave you wealth.

To the surprise of others, Mrs. Reznik took from Hans the violin and faced her daughter playing and singing:

Sunrise, sunset

Is this the little girl I carried

I don't remember growing older, when did they

When did she become so beautiful

Then turning to Hans, she sang the words:

When did he grow to be so tall?

310

Next was her husband who heard the words:

Wasn't it yesterday that they were small

Sunrise, sunset

When Mrs. Reznik finished singing, introspective silence hung in the air. The father was first to speak.

"Music releases the feelings of the soul, and tonight Hans has used his hidden talent to tell his story. Added to this is a reminder of where I first met my devoted wife. She was a gifted violinist who played in an orchestra that I frequented and history tells the rest of the story."

Hans interrupted Mr. Reznik, saying, "Let's not let her talent go into dormancy. Fiddler on the Roof is already a classic, and it tells the story of the Jewish struggle before the rise of Nazism. I would like to see it performed here in Munich and am willing to sponsor that effort if Mrs. Reznik is up to being in charge of the project."

The devoted mother and wife said nothing. They watched her walk over where Hans stood, handed him the violin, and bow. "Hans, you have given me two gifts! The first being a marriage proposal to my daughter and the other is the one you are now offering me."

"This calls for a celebration," said the father. Let's make some fresh coffee and finish the pie so Hans and I can go over the building plans for the new immigrants coming to Israel."

The evening closed with Hans carrying an armload of blueprints and drawings to the vehicle where their driver was waiting. When his arms were emptied of his bundle, he kissed his bride-to-be goodnight, whispering in her ear something she would think about through the night.

Chapter 28

For the Greater Good

The next morning Hans got out of bed to begin his day with thoughts of the lady he was going to marry. He made his way to his kitchen, a much further walk than in his old cottage near the hospital, found it spic-and-span from the evening before—thanks to the women. He put on his coffee and prepared to dress for his day at the office.

Though Hans had security acting as personal attendants when away from his sealed compound, they were never inside his home. He still had his cleaning lady come once a week, but he prepared his own breakfast and made his own coffee as he had always done. His large corporate office building that maintained several hundred employees provided a small coffee shop that served sandwiches, fruit, salads, and desserts. Because of security issues, he frequented the shop and came to know those who worked in the coffee shop better than those in executive positions who made major decisions half-a-world away. This was Hans' day-to-day schedule. However, today it would begin differently with Max calling on his private line.

"Hello."

"Mr. Baughman, this is Max. I have some important reports to give you. Can you give me a few minutes of your time today?"

"Bring two lunches to my office at twelve and we'll discuss your issues."

"I'll be there," said Max.

Why the urgency, Hans thought? He could've called one of the secretaries in the front office.

The first thing Hans did when arriving at his office was to review any urgent overnight mail, which might require his attention. He studied a memo from Bernard Cohen, the senior director of the newly acquired shipping line who was attempting to move its headquarters from Japan to Europe. A copy of the memo had been sent to the CEO suggesting they consider Stockholm, Sweden. Hans needed an update on the two ships undergoing retrofitting for the Henry Operation, which was not in the purview of the CEO. He dictated a letter to Bernard Cohen requesting a full report. The matter of a European site relocation for the shipping line would be determined by those on the administrative team. His primary interest now was in moving Jews across the waters to Israel.

Max was on time. When he came through Hans' office door, his girth was of such that he almost had to turn sideways to get through. He wasn't fat—just big. Behind him were two security people carrying a folding table, linen tablecloth, and a package of silverware. After everything was set up, another security person came in pushing a cart with three gourmet-style lunches.

"Mr. Baughman, I ordered these from one of your favorite restaurants."

"There are three orders here, is someone joining us?"

"No, I ordered two for myself. My mass requires more calories than most people."

The security people brought in a chair without wings to it so Max's girth could spread without restriction. Hans got out of the habit of sizing up people's physical condition by going every day to his office instead of the hospital. Today he took time to notice that Max seemed to be growing. For a moment, he considered suggesting he get tested for acromegaly, a condition of a malfunctioning hormone gland that caused abnormal bone growth. His cranium didn't show the physical characteristics of this disease, he just had a large head. *Hans thought it was sometimes a curse to be a doctor when it made him worry about someone he cared for.* He took his place on one side of the table, Max, the other side.

Max was waiting for Hans to take the lead in offering thanks when he handed him a Bible, saying, "Max, would you read Zechariah, chapter two, verses ten and eleven?"

"Sure," said Max. His large hands reached across the table, took the Sacred Book, almost making it disappear in his palms.

"I'm coming and will live among you…Many nations will be joined with the Lord in that day and will become my people." He closed the Bible and handed it to Hans.

Max was eyeing his two gourmet lunches when Hans gave commentary on the Scripture reading. "The prophet is speaking of the time when the Messiah will return to rule over Israel and other nations, and we are part of that effort by giving support to Israel and assisting the people of the land."

At this point, Max was more interested in his over-sized lunches and found it difficult to talk and eat at the same time. Hans, who could juggle eating and talking, began the exchange.

"Max, I am in need of a special type of person who can head up an organization that will pick up Jews in ports and in small boats, smuggle them onboard a freighter and deliver them to Israel. He will be connected to an agent in Israel whose intelligence will be passed on for times and locations of pick-ups. The number of pick-ups will vary from place-to-place. Our company has bought eight ships, two of which are presently being retrofitted to accommodate hidden stowaways."

Max stopped eating, swallowed, and then took a deep breath.

"When do you need this person to start?"

"Right away," said Hans.

"It's interesting you brought this up to me at this time. I know a colonel who just retired from Special Ops who might be interested. He would certainly bring to the table the experience and background for this kind of operation."

"He is to be vetted thoroughly before being approached and must fit into our philosophical paradigm. His religious beliefs may fall short of ours, but he must be an ardent supporter of Israel."

"I'll get right onto this, and if this person I have in mind doesn't work out, I'll find someone who will. Now, if you're through with this subject, I'd like to segue to another matter.

"First, the injured bomb-maker we removed from the hospital for his own protection has recovered from his injuries, and his rehab is a success. As the director of security for our corporation, I checked in with our contact person in the country we defend, a person who deals with terrorism on a daily basis. He has intelligence that could lead to a major disruption inside our enemies' camp. He tells me that the bomb-maker and his cohorts are from the same clan. Please bear with me.

"Doctor Baughman, you know the classroom science of consanguinity, close cousin marriages. I have seen what it does outside the classroom having worked in the Middle East and observed it firsthand. The Middle East is composed of clans. Marriage outside the clan is forbidden and those who perpetuate cousin marriages condemn their people to a backward society. I am told there are two things going for us:

the terrorists are from the same clan and that money in the form of bribery will transcend ideology."

"Max, where are we going with this?"

"In the Middle East, the cornerstone of loyalty comes through cousin marriages. Grouped together, we call them clans. Generally, a clan has strong central control over the large extended family, and because of the common bond of blood marriages, loyalty is a cardinal principle. It imposes a forced rigid allegiance and forbids independent thinking and acting. Loyalty is first to the clan, not to the state, and if one defies the clan, an honor killing is in order."

"Get to your point, Max. I appreciate the history lesson...remember, brevity is the soul of what?

"If you want an answer," Max said, "it's wit, and cited in Shakespeare's Hamlet."

"Very good! Are you a student of English literature?"

"I'm a student of human nature, especially, the bad side. Now, if you will allow me to continue where I left off? It is recommended by our friend in Israel that because our bomb-maker is of the same clan as his cohorts, we should offer them a bribe to purloin the Nazi's records."

"Max, if I didn't know you, I'd say you're a loose cannon."

"Stay with me on this for a bit until you hear me out. The shadowy Nazi movement, the superior Aryan group, lacks the knowledge of this culture we've been discussing. Israel has frequently used this filial social structure when gathering intelligence by paying money to same-clan members. The tight-knit fabric within their community guarantees no one will rat, and for this reason, they are open to negotiating information for money. Had the Nazis been smart, they would have brought in people from different clans."

By this time, Max's polemics had moved Han's resistance to the neutral zone—one of listening with an open mind.

"You see, Mr. Baughman, these people know the Nazi office compound, been at their headquarters, met with the key people. If offered the right amount of money, they may be willing to purloin their files—all for a price—and because they're from the same clan, they will have no fear of disloyalty among their own—honor will carry the day."

Hans said nothing, put his fork on the table, and leaned back in his chair staring at the ceiling. What was going through his mind was the wealth of information hidden in those locked filing cabinets: names and addresses of membership, businesses that supported them, planned operations, and even financial records. It would be a treasure trove of information.

"Max, we're dealing with two devils, and the only difference between them is that one works one side of the street, and the other works both sides. We can get whacked more easily that way. I prefer them both working just one side of the street. If they are no more proficient than the injured bomb-builder, then we are guaranteed to be whacked. Even if maximum success is achieved, the underground will continue to use their own Aryan hit men as they have in recent months."

"Mr. Baughman, there's a basic tactic used in war where the enemy's supply line is interrupted or destroyed reducing the capacity to make war. Secrecy, operating below the radar and the use of hired terrorists are their weapons of war. Breaking one or two of the links in this chain weakens their ability to cause havoc. In our vulnerable position, we have to fight behind their lines to stay ahead of them."

Max paused to gulp down a glass of water, then, continued. "Let me give you the bigger picture. Not one of our people will have their fingerprints on anything. We pay the money, and the highly trained agents in Israel will handle the supervision of the operation."

"You make it sound easy, Max, with others doing the dangerous part. What's all this going to cost us?"

"Whatever the cost, It'll be a fraction of the value of your life or your family's. All I need is the guarantee of the funds, and I'll see that it's done."

Max saw Hans' face give the message of needing trivia while he postured for what he really wanted to say.

"By the way, Max, before the Christian church spread to Europe, it was divided by clans and tribalism just like the Middle East is today. What brought about change was the action the church took in forbidding marriages closer than the fourth cousin. This caused clans to cross over and intermarry, from which statehoods evolved."

Max started eating again, but now his jaws were in slow motion—his attention was divided—his boss knew all about clans—yet, let him believe he knew nothing.

"Are you a student of history?" asked Max.

"Only the history I need to know," said Hans. "Our ships may be picking up people from these regions and I try to keep abreast of the thinking patterns of different cultures we might be moving in and around?"

"I'm very impressed with your knowledge on this subject," Max said.

"Not as much as I'm impressed with your experience. Experience will always provide an advantage. Survival requires both, and I carry just one. Max, I'm going to a meeting tomorrow in England, and I want you to go with me and present this to the consortium. If they approve, we'll go for it!"

Max's broad face showed a stoic look. *We're almost there, he thought, but not quite.*

"Before we break up, Doctor Baughman, there's a matter that has come up you need to know about. Your film on the Holocaust in Romania that is being played around the world has caused some very deep reactions, and I want to remind you to be very cautious about your personal safety. Also, there is a Romanian who says he's a Holocaust survivor, says he saw the film and wants to meet with you. He keeps coming around, and I've run all kinds of checks on him and come up with nothing. I'm advising you not to meet with him alone, and if he moves beyond our front security desk, which we've not allowed, he would have to be searched."

"Tell him to put everything in writing and have a security person hand-deliver the letter to my administrative assistant in the front office, and if she's not in, leave it with one of her office workers."

Max left, leaving Hans to mull over their discussions—an operation that would violate the law for the greater good. Germany had outlawed the existence of the Nazi party, and yet they operated under the radar. The rule of law protected private property. Did that protection extend to an illegal entity whose primary objective was to destroy Israel? Where was the rule of law protecting private property and human life during the Holocaust? For now, he would let the sleeping dog lie.

Chapter 29

The Consortium's Choice

It was seven in the morning when Hans' driver pulled next to the hanger where the crew of two pilots was waiting aboard the corporate jet. He carried a briefcase and was dressed casually. Already onboard were Fritz, the radio operator, and the Big Man, Max, along with three of his security men who would be working the grounds at the site of the meeting. The flight into Manchester would take ninety minutes, and from there they would drive to a country estate where he would meet with consortium members. As Chairman of the Executive Committee, he would conduct the business on the agenda, the first being the election of officers. William, one of the committee members, had arranged the meeting site. Max would be called upon later to present his clandestine proposal.

Present were ten men of influential wealth whose belief system was consistent with the teaching of the Scriptures, that the Messiah would return and rule the world from Jerusalem, and that it was their calling to use wealth to support the nation of Israel and her people.

Hans first eulogized the late Gustov Klein, known as the Old Man. In opening the meeting, he invited the treasurer to give his report, which included the newly acquired shipping line, held in legal title to Katharina Enterprises. He was surprised when his name stood alone in nomination for the chairmanship of the organization. He wasn't sure if he should be the one to lead the consortium. Others were more experienced, and then there was the matter of his upcoming marriage. Even during the history of the first Jewish nation, there was a law on the books that kept a newly married man home with his bride for a year before he entered the army. Considering what his soon-to-be-bride would want, he acquiesced and gave an acceptance speech.

Hans had brought a copy of the Romanian Holocaust film production for private viewing and intended to have Max submit his project to the group immediately after its showing. However, with the emotional impact of seeing the film again with the memory of his dream of the little boy crawling over the dead, the mass grave they uncovered at the village of his birth and the description of the village killings by the man who worked for his father, he changed his mind. The energy these images created would forbid him to enlist the crutches of others to support the proposed action against the underground Nazis. He would stand alone as a single pillar to bear the burden, and whatever the outcome, he would own it. Max was left to wonder what happened. After the film, Hans addressed the group.

"This production was put together as an effort to expose a country to the world that has not acknowledged the deaths of three hundred thousand of my people. We often think of the Holocaust being in other parts of Europe, but anti-Semitism was just as systemic in Romania as in other areas. The parents of the beautiful lady I'm soon to marry are survivors of that Holocaust. Her father is working with me to build three thousand new housing units for new immigrants arriving in Israel. Friends, the Jews are going home and this is what we're a part of. Speaking to us today are the words of Zechariah, '*I will save my people from the countries of the East and the West, I will bring them back to live in Jerusalem; they will be my people.*'"

William had prepared a luncheon for the consortium members and the security people they brought. When Max saw Hans, he addressed the issue of not being called to speak to the consortium.

"In view, you didn't call me in, Mr. Baughman, I assume you changed your mind about going through with the matter."

"On the contrary! After viewing the film, I decided we'll go it alone. Therefore, when we get back put everything in motion. Remind the invisible people who work with us that the less we spend on the payoff, the more we can send to their efforts."

Hans saw a big grin stretch across Max's broad face. It was news he welcomed.

"Yes, Sir! As soon as we reach the plane, I'll send them word."

The corporate jet was in the air by three o'clock and was scheduled to arrive at four-thirty. Fritz had handed Hans a folder of mail when he boarded and was in his quarters going through it when someone knocked on the door.

"Come in."

The door opened halfway with a voice saying, "Sir, Doctor Sheena is on the radio and she wishes to speak with you."

What a pleasant surprise, Hans thought. "I'll be right there, Fritz."

Unless instructed to do otherwise, Fritz always left the room when the chairman used the radio. As with any two lovers who planned a lifetime together, Hans and Sheena were discovering the mystery of their symbiotic relationship, a condition where a part of one's life enhances the development and growth of another. Today, the process was in motion on a different level, and knowing others could be listening, they used illusive, arcane symbolic language.

"This is the captain speaking," said Hans.

"This is first mate in the launch nearing the big ship in harbor. Were the waters you sailed over today smooth?"

"My waters were calm and blissful. And your waters were…?"

"Likewise. I am reporting to the captain that his presence is requested tonight at the big ship to be the judge between two vying competitors. After the judging ceremony, your other discriminating skills will be requested for the final event."

"Will there be other judges present to give their opinions on the competition?"

"Only at the captain's invitation."

"The captain will board your vessel at eighteen hundred hours and will handle the judging ceremony all by himself if that is alright with the first mate."

"The captain's order will be carried out as he has requested. Bon voyage."

"Ditto."

Fritz noticed when Hans came from the radio room he had more spring in his steps, even whistled a tune on his way back to the captain's quarters. Hans was thinking more about the evening he'd spend with Sheena without her mother and father than the two meat dishes she'd be serving up. He wasn't quite sure about the main event. Making plans for the wedding was a woman's job, and he just might recuse himself as a judge in that matter.

Chapter 30

Avenger's Letter

Hans was seated at his desk in his opulent office trying to decide which thoughts in his mind would be the victor: the memories of last evening with Sheena, or the decision to offer money in exchange for information, and the process by which it would be obtained.

Hans had reservations about the decision he'd made with Max, was aware that wealth gave men power others did not have and that there were two ways to use it: for good or evil. But why couldn't there be a third, a neutral one, a halfway switch, one that didn't leave the sound of a screech on a chalkboard? He thought he had made the right decision when he approved Max's clandestine operation, but the screeching continued. It was after deep reflection on his marriage to Sheena and the exposure she would have to these people operating freely that the screeching lost its grip and faded into the background.

The intercom was giving the signal that Miss Shuster wanted to speak to him. He switched on the speaker.

"What is it, Miss Shuster?"

"Mr. Baughman, there's a security person here in my office who has something to give you that you requested."

"Send him in please."

The man was delivering a letter from a Romanian Holocaust survivor as requested. The chairman was seated behind his desk, and after being handed the letter, he addressed the man: "Please wait until I read this—have a seat if you wish."

The men Max used as security were mature, experienced, and former professionals. Most of them had been in the military or had served on the police force. The man waited, noticed that the chairman was moved by what he read, got up and went to another room. He felt awkward sitting in the large office all by himself, but he was told to wait. Ten minutes later the chairman returned, moving now at a slower gait. He sat behind his desk with eyes riveted on the letter. Without looking at the security officer, he asked, "Have you seen the gentleman who wrote this letter?"

The officer knew something strange was going on inside the chairman—the letter was turning his world upside down and he was at the ringside to see it firsthand.

"Yes, Sir, I've seen him several times."

"Can you describe him to me?"

"He has light hair, about your height, and speaks with a strong accent. His dress is a little shabby, but there's a...how shall I say it...there's something in his eyes that carries a determined, fearless look."

"Do what you do with people to clear them, and have Max bring him to the conference room downstairs immediately. Call me when you're there."

The officer left knowing something big was going on with the chairman when he would leave his busy schedule to meet with someone off the street, and it had to do with the letter he delivered.

Hans wished Sheena was present to stand by his side. It seemed the Holocaust in Romania would never end. It had a continuum of bleak despair. History had returned to haunt his wounded memory. He hoped he could keep himself together.

Interrupting his thoughts was a message from his administrative assistant. "Yes, what is it?"

"They are waiting for you in the conference room, Mr. Baughman."

"Thank you, tell them I'll be right down."

Max had taken precautionary security measures. When Hans arrived, two men were standing guard outside the boardroom. Upon entering, he saw three men seated at the large conference table. They stood to their feet. Hans' eyes were laser-fixed on the stranger who was now standing between Max and another security person. The man's face showed more than the pain of a Holocaust survivor—it was etched with a hardened, self-confident look of steel.

Without looking at Max, Hans said, "You gentleman can now leave. Thank you."

The security person walked away leaving Max standing by himself. With a sharp tone in his voice, he heard Hans say, "Max, wait for me outside."

Hans took several steps toward the stranger, extended his hand, saying," I'm Hans Baughman, and you are Michael Pencovich...."

"Yes, Sir."

"Please sit down."

The stranger saw Hans turn and walk to the other side of the room stopping in front of a new painting just put up in the boardroom. Looking at the painting with his back facing the visitor, Hans asked, "How many immediate family members did you lose in Ediniti?"

Hans continued staring at the painting, waiting for an answer. He knew it was difficult for the stranger, was about to turn around and face him, when he said, "As I mentioned in the letter I gave you, I lost my mother, father, and a sister

326

with a one-year-old who had married into the Isler family. Also, I lost the beautiful girl I was to marry."

"What was your sister's name?"

"Rachael, her name was Rachael. She was a beautiful lady, and she had a handsome lad—about a year old. I remember pulling him around in his little wagon."

Hans couldn't respond. He remembered his dream, the little boy, and the man in white who carried him to a wagon, where a German lady found him....

"Doctor Baughman, this is why executions come easy for me. My losses demand justice, and requitement will not be satisfied until the last one receives his due."

"How many did you kill in Romania?" asked Hans.

"Mr. Bauman, there is a difference between killings and executions. In war, the enemy is killed and little remembered in terms of numbers or who they were. However, executions carry numbers with a face. In answer to your question, I have personally executed fifteen who were guilty of murder, theft, and rape. Several were guilty of all three.

"How many of these were killed in Ediniti?"

"Seven in Ediniti, eight from different areas of the country, the latter consisting mostly of Iron Guard army officers. I assisted my two friends in the executions they carried out. Of these, I kept no record."

"How were they executed?"

"By gunshot and knife to the throat. In some cases, they were hanged."

"What determined the method of execution?"

"The location and proximity of others. In the woods, guns were used. Inside the villages, quietness had to be maintained."

"Did they know why they were dying?"

"We told them in a slow deliberate manner while we held our family pictures in their faces."

"How many proclaimed their innocence?"

"All of them."

"Do you feel vindicated by your actions?"

"I feel justice has been carried out—vindication will happen when the rest of the war criminals are judged."

"Who were these people you executed?"

"Collaborators with the Nazis and the Romanian Iron Guard. Some were Romanian citizens who joined in the killings, rape, and plunder. After the communists took over in 1944, they went underground and gave a show of loyalty to the new regime. The same thing happened here in Germany, and there are probably Nazi sleeper cells still active in this country."

"Where were you when the Nazis forces moved into Ediniti?"

"My family owned and operated a lumber mill, and I was sent to the mountains to assess the harvestable trees on a section of land we leased. I had taken two friends of mine with me, and everything happened while we were away in the mountains."

Hans was still looking at the new painting on the wall, but all he could see was pain in the man's voice and his image that spoke of a damaged life. Hans was using the painting as an excuse not to turn around and look at the stranger.

"Doctor Baughman, did you read my letter? My signature on the letter is my real name. In Romania, I am known by another name."

"How did that come about?"

"Three days after the killings, a man who worked for us at the mill came up to where we were camped and gave us the news. He wasn't Jewish but was a loyal employee and friend. He carried with him the names of those who killed my family and abused the girl I was to marry. He also brought a letter she wrote before taking her own life. It took us a couple of weeks to accept what happened, and from that point on we did what we had to do.

"All three of us knew how to survive in the forest. Every year we had gone camping in the mountains, each with fishing gear and a rifle. We knew how to track and hunt big game, little game, and set traps. The forest was our friend, and we knew how to survive in it. Others were not as fortunate. We lived off the land retrieving arms from small Nazi Iron Guard patrols. We took no prisoners making it difficult to be identified. We became mountain men living off the land and survived very well.

"It was when we moved to the low country we had greater difficultly. However, that soon changed when we apprehended an officer targeted for execution and found in his possession a briefcase full of stolen Jewish money, gold, and diamonds. With the cache of money now in our possession, we could help Jews in hiding as well as the sympathetic Romanians willing to risk their lives doing so.

"A notable war criminal, a colonel, was being sought by our group, and in pursuit of him, we found a fortune of money hidden on his estate that he had stolen from Jews. We used that wealth to continue our efforts in helping Jews in hiding. The colonel eluded us, disappeared from his family and relatives, but is still at the top of my list for execution.

"Living and surviving in the wild can cause one to develop the skill of a jungle predator. We were that when we went out to execute justice in a land where there was no justice. Because I had blond hair and blue eyes, I changed my Jewish name to a common Romanian name so I could move about freely, slipping through patrols to gain information for nighttime operations. We were predators of the night in a jungle of genocide.

"In 1944 things changed when the Soviets occupied Romania. That was when I became Doctor Jekyll and Mr. Hyde. My changed name, blond hair, and blue eyes helped me get a Job on a freighter. It gave me a livelihood as a seafaring worker, a dependable, respectable person who would come home for a week or two before going back to sea. On the ship, I was Doctor Jekyll. Onshore, I would get together with my other two colleagues, and together we would go over the execution list. Mr. Hyde would then carry out justice on those who killed my family and the love of my life. Even to this day when I go to bed, I see her beautiful face looking down on me."

Hans forced himself not to turn around. The stranger must not see his face, else he would see the pain he had the night he found the mass grave where the stranger's family and his own biological mother and father lay buried, a grave created by the darkness of hell. Still pretending to look at the painting, Hans fought back something that was trying to surface: admiration for someone who avenged the genocidal deaths of family and people.

Hans struggled to create conversation. "I'm sorry for your continued anguish…I don't know what to say…how did you get to this country?"

"I still work the freighters. When our ship was in port I saw your production of the Romania Holocaust on TV, and it so moved me that I had to see someone who survived the Holocaust in our village and see if help could be given in sponsoring the cause of bringing justice to the guilty. I jumped ship and entered this country illegally. Doctor

Baughman, you didn't answer my question—did you read my letter?"

The letter...he had to mention his letter again! Hans swung around, walked over to the large conference table, forced himself to look across its flat, shiny surface at a person who had been destroyed. *But he was more than a damaged Holocaust survivor. The man was his uncle, a brother to his own mother, born in his village, someone who had pulled him about in a little wagon!*

Hans felt like a Joseph about to reveal himself to his family, but even Joseph took time in making that final step. Here was a sick man whose profession had become that of an executioner, performing his own kind of individual justice.

"Mr. Pencovich, I read your letter at least three times. I want you to know my schedule doesn't permit me to sit down with you today to discuss what you wrote about, but I assure you that in a couple of days my driver will pick you up and we will have a long talk. Please don't discuss your letter with anyone or what you've told me in this room—not even with the security people here at this building. You and I are the only ones to know what you stated in your letter."

"I didn't come here today to ask for anything that would benefit me personally."

"I know you didn't, but for you to move about in this building we're going to have to fix you up a bit so as to not draw attention to yourself. A driver will take you to a men's clothing store, a barbershop, and a hotel. Meals will be provided at the hotel, and you can stay there until I contact you. Our meeting is to be kept confidential. Discuss nothing with the drivers taking you about."

"Yes, Sir, I fully understand."

Hans noticed that the short period of time he had been with him his countenance had lifted with more spirited demeanor. Hopefully, these were signs of better things to come.

"You wait here, I'll be right back."

Hans went to the security personnel outside the conference room, called Max to the side.

"Max, assign to this man a driver who will see that he goes to the barbershop, a men's clothing store for three changes of clothes, and is booked into a medium-class hotel where meals are served. Register one of our people next door to his room without his knowledge so a report can be given to me of his activities. Everything we do with and for him is to be confidential."

Hans couldn't wait to get to his office to make several urgent calls. One would be to Sheena, the other to her parents. Of all evenings, tonight he would need his family as never before. He would send his driver to his favorite restaurant to pick up the evening dinner.

Chapter 31

Holstering the Sword

Hans was outside waiting for Sheena and her parents when they pulled into the driveway. He had not spoken to either of them about the matter of the letter. Mr. Reznik was reminded that it was not a work evening and that there would be no discussions about the housing project in Israel. Standard greetings were done outside the vehicle where it was parked, overshadowed by the beautiful, low-hanging, foliage-filled tree branches.

The moment Sheena saw Hans she knew he was troubled about something. "What's wrong?" she whispered.

"We'll talk about it later," answered Hans.

Hans opened the front door and followed them inside, invited them to sit. He immediately got down to the business of why they were there.

"I've invited you here tonight because you are Holocaust survivors and I have need of your sound advice."

Hans gave each a copy of the letter he received from the man he met with today, saying, "I received this letter from someone who survived the Holocaust in Romania. I would like you to read it over carefully while I put everything on the table for dinner."

The table had already been set, and it didn't take long for the hot food to be put in serving dishes and drinks poured. Hans heard no discussion among them. When he glanced in their direction, he thought if the atmosphere could be morphed into human form, it would show itself with a distinct ghostly pallor. He did notice Mr. Reznik looking at the Holy Book he always carried on his person.

With a light touch to break the silence, Hans said, "Shall we come to the table?"

Not one word had been spoken between them since they were given copies of the letter. The first to speak was Mr. Reznik.

"For our thanksgiving prayer, I'd like to read something found in the sacred writings of one of the Messiah's disciples: *"Then Simon Peter, who had a sword, drew it and struck the high priest's servant, cutting off his right ear. Jesus commanded Peter, put your sword away! Shall I not drink the cup the Father has given me?"*"

Mr. Reznik continued. "The gentleman who wrote that moving letter must sheath the sword he carries. God will judge the living and the dead, and it is for us to judge ourselves before that great day."

Sheena was tearing-up, the mother had her face covered with her hands, and the father looked off into space as if he had seen this picture before.

Sheena, taking Hans by his hand, said, "Oh, what a horrible thing for that man to experience, the girl he was to marry, taken and raped, then hearing she committed suicide."

The family theologian who had been lost in his personal Holocaust history made the transition back, offering commentary on the purpose of the letter.

"Only people who've been in his shoes can understand why he has come to you asking for financial support in his cause of justice. He acted on his principle of justice when justice was lacking, and he will continue to do so because he is driven by that part of him the Holocaust has made dead. Do I believe he executed guilty people...? Yes! A Holocaust victim can smell guilt."

"He told me today that he had executed fifteen individuals. I asked him, 'Were they guilty?' 'Yes, they were guilty, and before they were executed photos of the victims were held in front of their faces.'"

The insightful father was beginning to hear the clamor and rattling of the cellar door of his past, voices reminding him of those dark, evil times. With pain written on his face, he said, "When this man heard the love of his life, the one he was to marry, was dead by her own hands after being raped, he died to this world, and the raging animal we all have the potential of becoming, possessed him. This was why he survived in the mountains and others died. He was on a mission of death, and as long as he's alive his mission is not finished. The darkest chamber of despair and hopelessness is being dead while still living. Inside, he carries the paradox of a dead man who is kept alive by living off revenge."

Sheena had calmed herself enough to ask, "So, Hans, this man saw the Romanian Holocaust TV production, found out that both of you were from the same village and thought you would finance the cause of his justice on Romanians who participated in the Holocaust?"

"Exactly, and now I want everyone to hold on to their seats. The gentleman we have been speaking of who lost all his family doesn't know this, but he has one surviving nephew, and he is here among you tonight. Michael Pencovich is my biological mother's younger brother."

Everyone's jaw dropped. Confused emotions were bouncing around the room. "What are you telling us?" asked Mrs. Reznik.

"I am telling you that the person who wrote that letter is my uncle, the younger brother of my mother. He was away in the mountains on a project for the family for several days when it all happened. A friend of the family took the news to him while still in the mountains. From that point on he began to die a day at a time and is now a very sick man. His mental health will have to be evaluated."

Silence hung so heavy one could cut it with a knife. But after the initial shock, a spirit of lightness settled over the room. Sheena was first to show the winds of change.

"This is a miracle," said Sheena, "God has brought him to you, Hans. Does he know who you are?"

"For his health, that information should come in stages. He first needs a friend to help him find his way, then, he can discover answers for himself, rather than someone forcing them on him. He must learn to reach for something that gives life because what is inside is dead. It will be a challenge for him and for me."

"I chose the Scripture reading earlier," said Mr. Reznik, "because it shows the choice of two worlds: the sword and the cup. The cup speaks of another world—the sword addresses this world. The Lord told Pilate, *'My kingdom is not of this world, if it were, my servants would fight. But my kingdom is from another place.'* Hans, it will only be when your uncle sheathes his sword and chooses the cup that he will find healing. Our prayers tonight will support you in this weight that is now on your shoulders."

"Papa, the man your daughter is going to marry has big, strong shoulders."

The thoughts of the letter hung heavily on Hans when he went to work the next morning. Instead of using his private entrance to access his office, he used the front where his administrative assistant maintained an office.

"Miss Shuster, get Max, the Director of Security, to my office right away!"

336

"I'll get right on that."

"Oh yes, also get Bernard Cohen on the phone."

"I'll see that it's done, Mr. Baughman."

Hans could have used the phone for his directive for Max, but this, being a highly confidential matter, using the phone gave the potential for someone to listen in. Hans had just sat and settled in at his desk when the intercom light came on.

"Yes, Miss Shuster, what is it?"

"The director of security is here."

"Send him in."

In normal fashion, Max came through the door as big as life itself showing his typical aura of confidence, whose nature was to push beyond his space if not kept in check.

Hans always drew the line.

"Morning, Mr. Baughman."

"Hello, Max! You can sit down if you like. Have you heard anything about yesterday's visitor?"

"My man tells me you won't recognize him with his haircut and new wardrobe."

"I thought as much," said Hans. "Now, to the matter of you being here. I am going to trust you to keep everything you hear confidential. The stranger we have among us is from my village in Romania. He told me all his family was killed in the Holocaust along with the girl he was to marry. He works on ships sailing from Romanian ports, and when docked here, he saw our Holocaust production on TV, jumped ship, and is in this country illegally. I want you to get on this and see that he becomes an Israeli resident, a member of the Aliyah. All papers he's required to sign will go through me."

Upon hearing the background of the stranger, Hans saw Max's demeanor change. He had been adversarial, almost hostile toward him. Now, his eyes and face displayed a relaxed stance, even a look of compassion.

"It goes to show you that experiences like he's been through can really mess one up," Max said.

"Just do all the gopher work, Max; I'll be with him in any document signing and personal appearances he'll have to make. Be sure the local immigration authorities don't grab him before he's properly documented."

"Just don't you worry about it, Mr. Baughman, I'll take care of it."

"Remember the confidentiality!"

"I want to tell you before I leave," added Max, "our purloining operation with those who work both sides of the street is underway with an agreed amount."

Hans was smitten with a burst of feelings that were confusing: he was glad it was happening but fearful of the downsides it might bring.

"Remind them," said Hans, "if anyone gets hurt, no payment will be made."

As soon as Max closed the door to the office, Hans' thoughts returned to the stranger among them who had spent several years plying the waters and ports of Soviet Bloc countries. He had been onshore, knew the streets, the layout, the strengths, and weaknesses of their security. Perhaps he could redeem himself by saving life instead of taking it.

The intercom light came on.

"What is it?" asked Hans

"Mr. Bernard Cohen is on the line."

"Mr. Cohen, I would like an update on the retrofitting of those two ships for our Henry Project."

"You'll be pleased to know that the work is underway. Also, the report I just submitted to our CFO shows a good bottom line, and will even show more positive results when we get everything moved to Europe."

"That's good news! And the ships are in the harbor at Haifa?"

"That is correct. There have been no problems. Skilled workers are available and materials are on site."

"Tell your people I'll be making an appearance there this week for an inspection. Be sure your lead man in Haifa keeps in touch with my office so I can apprise him of my arrival."

"Will do, and I'm sure you'll be pleased with what you see. I was there two weeks ago and found it coming along fine."

Hans couldn't free himself of the stranger that had entered his life. He quickly wrote a note to Sheena, sealed it in an envelope, and called his driver. "Come to my office via the private entrance."

"Yes, Sir, I'll be right there."

Hans then called his executive secretary, Miss Shuster. "I'm flying out of the country tomorrow morning. My destination is Tel Aviv, Israel. Get Max on the security detail for our departure and arrival. He knows what to do."

There was a knock on his private entrance door. Knowing it was the driver, he opened the door holding the sealed envelope.

"Driver, get Max to inform the stranger we put up at the hotel that someone will pick him up within the hour out in front. He is to keep one of our people with him at all times. When you finish with Max, take this envelope, and deliver it only to Doctor Sheena at the hospital. After delivering the envelope, return for further instructions."

Hans was always discreet with instructions to his driver. It was his policy not to tell the driver the destination until he boarded the vehicle, a vehicle specially equipped with bulletproof windows and armor-protected doors.

When Hans and his driver neared the hotel, he saw two men standing at the sidewalk edge. He recognized one being a security person dressed in street clothes, the other bore little resemblance of the man he had been with the day before. When the door was opened for him, he was reluctant to enter until he saw Hans in the back seat.

Hans was first to speak. "Good morning, how was your stay at the hotel? Are you having your meals in the dining room?"

The stranger was more interested in the vehicle he was riding in than responding to his questions. He paid special attention to the heavy, thick, frosted glass window that sealed off the rear seat from the front. This was a world he'd only read about and seen in movies.

"Oh yes, the room! It was more than satisfactory, and the food was quite good. It does lack some of the spices we're used to in Romania."

"You mean like garlic."

"Yes, that's the main one."

"Do you follow the kosher diet?"

Hans noticed he was slow, almost reluctant to answer his question.

"I no longer follow Jewish religious customs and teachings. If there is a God, why did He allow the Holocaust?"

Now, it was Hans who was slow to respond. He needed wisdom and appropriateness, knowing that the latter was dependent on the former.

"It was an era when evil won a battle," said Hans, "and like most battle losses, it awakens the spirit to change tactics. From the battle loss, we gained the state of Israel, a homeland, a fulfillment of prophecy. Israel will win the war in the end when the Messiah returns to rule in Jerusalem."

"The polemics of religious idealism I avoid," said the stranger. "I have lost all my family, and for me, I live only to bring justice on those who have destroyed them. There is only one law I believe in: an eye for an eye, tooth for a tooth, and a life for a life."

The air that Hans breathed pulsed with compassion and sympathy—he wanted to tell him there was a survivor—that he had a living nephew—but now was not the time.

"Tell me about your work aboard the freighters. What ports have you visited? Romania is a member of the Soviet bloc; you must have been in most of the ports?"

Moving from the discussions of the Holocaust had a calming effect on the stranger who was becoming less strange the longer he talked with Hans. Instead of answering questions with succinct replies, he launched into a resume of his work experience.

"I feel secure on a ship. I started out as a deckhand doing the heavy lifting of manual work. After several years, I knew everything about the operations of a vessel. I studied and move up the ranks to the level of first mate, then acquired a captain's License, but I had the need to exercise Mr. Hyde's role and didn't need the notoriety, so I rarely signed on as a captain.

"Regarding the ports, I know them all. I've been to their bars, visited their entertainment centers, and even made friends with some dock workers."

"Ever meet any Jews in these ports?"

"There are two things one never talks about in a communist country: the government and religion. If you single out Jews, it falls on the side of religion. As you know, Jews try to fit into the cultural landscape but fall short unless they convert to Christianity, or adopt atheism. The latter became my position and station in life. I visited a synagogue once when I was in port and the only people I saw there were the elderly, and they were few in number. This is not to say they didn't have secret meeting sites."

"Mr. Pencovich, you know your immigration status puts you at risk with the government here in this country?"

"I am very much aware of that, and I'll have to stay hidden as long as I'm here."

"We are working on obtaining a legal standing for you with the state of Israel with the Aliyah program. Would you be interested?"

Hans waited for an answer. It was slow coming. He noticed this calculated, methodical man showing a nervous edge, something displayed for the first time. He was in conflict, a person who lived a double life—a Doctor Jekyll and Mr. Hyde. *He struggled with the answer knowing Israel would change his life. He would lose half of himself, the half that kept the memory of the girl he loved alive. Did he want to throw this spirit of revenge and justice to the wind? He had jumped ship, abandoned his duties, and could be in trouble with the authorities in Romania!*

"I only know the trade of working on ships," said the stranger, "and have a livelihood in Romania. Going to Israel is an unknown."

"I can assure you that employment will be the least of your concerns."

Hans had told the driver to go wherever he wished until instructed otherwise. Being a doctor, he knew the best therapy for this emotionally challenged man was to get him to talk about himself, his life before his tragedy. He was headed for the edge of a cliff and needed to find himself before he reached the precipice.

"Mr. Pencovich, having been taken from our village as a small child, I know nothing. Tell me about your life in the village while growing up, about your parents and sister, especially your sister."

It was difficult for the stranger to begin, but with Hans interjecting questions now and then to keep him on track, he slowly began to unwrap his life, releasing feelings and experiences that had meaning and purpose, things long been forgotten. When discussing his sister, Hans had to look away and with all the energy he could find, he forced himself not to break down.

For an hour they rode in a moving, fortified vehicle, one made to protect life, but today it was a womb where two opposites would come together to create a new beginning of a different life form, and like a zygote itself at conception, the early stage would bear no resemblance to its final form.

The driver stopped in front of the hotel. For the first time in many years, the stranger had reconnected with his past in a cathartic way. He had turned back the clock to a time of his life that allowed a different perspective to compete with his energy for revenge. Before getting out of the vehicle, he was surprised to hear what Hans asked him.

"I'd like to hire you to go with me to look over a couple of freighters that are being retrofitted for special projects. The pay is good, and it will help tide you over until you decide what you want to do."

"That sounds interesting and challenging. I think I would like that. Where are the ships located?"

"In Israel—in the Haifa harbor. Someone will pick you up tomorrow morning at seven-thirty and take you to the plane."

Chapter 32

Finding the Way Home

Hans' driver pulled into Sheena's compound at seven in the morning and found her, and her parents, packed and ready to go for the flight to Israel.

Sheena gave Hans a hug, saying, "Thank you for your sweet letter yesterday inviting us to go with you to Israel!"

"Yeah, my boy," said Sheena father, "glad you're taking us with you. It beats flying first class on a commercial. Maybe I can have you to myself to discuss the housing project without this woman to flirt with."

"Now Dad, that's what he's supposed to do, and I hope he continues that good behavior after we're married."

Hans leaned close to her ear, whispering, "You can depend on it Pipse."

She turned around with widened eyes. "Whoa…is that my new name?"

"It's your new secret sobriquet, known only to us!"

"I love it!"

The father, already in his jovial mood, responded, "You're already at it—at this early hour! I can't imagine what it's going to be like later in the day."

"Mother, remind Papa what he was like when he was courting you!"

"I'm afraid he'll embarrass himself."

The plane was parked outside the hanger when their two vehicles pulled up. One vehicle carried passengers, the other, luggage. The food service truck had just left, and the

344

pilots were doing their external inspections of the airplane. Fritz, the radio operator who always went on flights, helped Hans and the two drivers load the luggage. When Mr. Reznik saw the amount of luggage being taken on board, he asked Hans, "How many pieces of baggage did you bring, Mr. Baughman?"

"None, just my briefcase. Anything I need is already packed in closets and drawers on the plane."

"Ladies, you have six pieces of luggage for a three-day stay, and you need this much stuff?"

"Papa, you're going to get into trouble if you're not careful. Mother was just telling me how cluttered you've made the garage with your hobby stuff."

"That's because I've been so busy with the housing project in Israel, I've had no time. Besides, what does that have to do with all this luggage?"

"That can best be answered with the old adage, 'People who live in glass houses shouldn't throw stones.'"

The old man forced a grin across his wrinkled face. "My dear, you are as smart and witty as your mother."

"I want all of us inside the captain's quarters right away!" said Hans. "There are some things you need to know before we take off."

Hans was last to climb the stairs, and when he passed Fritz in the doorway of the plane he gave him instructions that went beyond his normal duties. "Someone will be coming on board shortly and will be my guest. If you like, you can show him the radio room, the kitchen, and tell him to help himself, but only after my family and I have had breakfast."

"I'll do that, Sir."

After everyone settled in the captain's quarters, Hans gave instructions on the treatment of the stranger flying with them.

"I want everyone to understand that Mr. Pencovich, my uncle, will be onboard our plane and is to be treated only as a guest. Don't be overly friendly, and only discuss subjects he brings up. I think it best that you do not speak of your relationship with me, and above all, he is not to know that he's related to me. If the opportunity comes up, it would be a positive thing for Mr. Reznik to speak to him in Romanian."

"And if he probes us?" asked Mr. Reznik.

"Be as wise as serpents and harmless as doves. Now everyone stays here until I get back."

They looked at each other. The mother asked, "Where did he get that?"

"I'll give you two guesses," said the father, "it came from his mother, or from his Sunday School class when he was a child."

Outside the captain's quarters, Fritz was meeting the stranger who had boarded after being met by Hans. He appeared well dressed, carrying one small luggage piece.

"Mr. Pencovich," Hans said, "Fritz, our radio operator, will take care of you. If you want or need anything, just let him know."

"Oh, a radio person, radio technology is one of my specialties, so we should get along fine."

By this time the engines were on, then came the pilot's voice, "They've given us the clearance to line up for flight, everyone please be seated and fasten your seat belts."

The plane was in the air, Hans and his family were finishing breakfast in the kitchen, and Fritz had the stranger in his radio room showing him the operation.

"Hans, we are all anxious to meet the stranger," said Sheena.

"As soon as we finish breakfast and clean up, we'll go out and meet him. Remember not to stare. Think of him as an employee, and, in reality, he is."

Hans opened the door to the radio room, saw the stranger talking to Fritz.

"Mr. Pencovich, I want you to meet some of my guests onboard the craft," said Hans, "come, let's go to our lobby. Fritz will get you breakfast after we meet these people."

The lobby consisted of two sofa pieces with several wood-finished armchairs. Included were two magazine racks that held the early morning newspapers. When Hans and the stranger entered the area, the three family members stood.

"Mr. Pencovich, I would like you to meet some of my guests on this flight."

They did what Hans had asked them not to do: they stared. With jaws almost hanging, they were mesmerized with the two standing side-by-side. It was the hair, the eyes, the facial structure—if the stranger were twenty years younger, the two could pass as twins.

"This is Mr. and Mrs. Reznik, and alongside them is their lovely daughter, Doctor Sheena. You folks visit and I'll put on some fresh coffee."

They found the stranger uninhibited in conversation, something they didn't expect knowing his background. He was performing his Doctor Jekyll role very well.

"Mr. Reznik, do you work for Mr. Baughman?"

"He has asked me to coordinate the housing project we have going on in Israel with the home office. We're constructing three thousand housing units for new immigrants coming into Israel. May I ask what your project assignment is?"

347

"My experience is on freighters, loading, and unloading—even charting and sailing them. I've been asked to inspect two that are being refurbished in the Haifa harbor. I detect a Romanian accent in your speech. Have you spent time in that country?"

Before he could answer, Sheena said, "Mother and I have something to do, so if you two will excuse us, we'll visit later. Come, Mother!"

Reluctantly, the mother followed her daughter, quietly asking, "Why did you pull us away? It was just getting interesting!"

"Intuition Mother…intuition."

The two women found Hans and Fritz in the kitchen drinking coffee and engaged in what seemed like a serious conversation. They sat and listened-in. Fritz was speaking.

"He knows a lot about radio, the international laws that govern its use, and some of the latest technology coming out, which will revolutionize the industry. The country he's from is certainly not an advanced country, so he must have gotten his information from reading books and technical magazines."

"Did he mention anything about Romania, his friends, or his family?"

"Nothing, Sir."

"Did he say anything about me?"

"He did say you had been very kind and generous, and it was because both of you were from the same village."

"Sir, what is his special skill that enables him to be brought along on this trip?"

Hans looked at Sheena and her mother. He knew the question was above Fritz's rank, that under different circumstances, he would receive a rebuke, but he had invited conversation in a neutral zone creating a climate of no-holds-barred. It was as much his fault as Fritz's.

"Fritz, I'm giving you an assignment. You'll be around Mr. Pencovich during our stay here in Haifa for three days. If you can find the answer to your question without asking him directly, I'll give you an invitation to my wedding."

"I already got one, Sir, you even signed it."

Sheena quickly came to his rescue. "Captain Hans, don't you remember coming over to the First Mate's big ship for the final event where you signed all those wedding invitations."

"Okay, okay…so I'm mortal! I'll change the prize to a front-row seat at our wedding."

"I accept the challenge!" said Fritz.

The coastal breezes coming from the ancient waters that floated vessels in history cooled the brows of three men whose eyes were fastened on a ship they would board. Their launch slowed and yielded to the swells as it edged itself up against an immense solid wall of steel. Hanging nearby was the lowered boarding ramp holding two men prepared to assist the visitors. The stranger allowed Hans and the old man to step onto the ramp first. It was a ramp for dockworkers and the ship's crew, not delicate passengers who paid handsome prices for a vacation cruise. These ships weren't made for pleasure but for moving freight from one port to another.

Mr. Reznik and Hans reached the top and stepped onto the starboard side of the ship. The guardrail now stood between them and the water below. They watched the stranger slowly step upward, his eyes taking in everything about the ship. Both saw confidence impale itself on the face of the stranger—the ship was his friend.

Mr. Reznik had something to say and waited until the stranger reached where he stood. "Gentleman, before us is the port of Haifa. In the background are the ascending mountains leading up to a point called Mount Carmel. Who can tell me what famous event in history happened on that mountain?"

The stranger quickly said, "It was the battle between Elijah and the prophets of Baal," then, he turned and walked to the other side of the ship and stared out over the vast Mediterranean facing west. It was the scene of emptiness, a mirror of his soul, water everywhere, but none to quench the parched desert he had made of himself.

"You stay here, Hans," said the old man, "I think our stranger is trying to say something."

Hans watched the family theologian walk slowly over to where a Doctor Jekyll stood with a fixed gaze. He wished he could listen to the dialogue.

The stranger saw the old man coming toward him alone—he was prepared to talk. "Mr. Reznik, the other side of this ship shows one of the many pillars of Jewish history. I used to live on that side of the ship. I believed in what I saw. It was tangible, touchable, and real. But life's events pushed me to live on this side of the ship. And this is the view I wake up to every morning—a vast sea of nothingness as far as the eye can reach. These are the distant, deep waters I sail over."

"Mr. Pencovich, it's not far to the other side of this ship, and you really don't have to take any steps, just turn around and you'll get the same view. It's not the side of the ship you're on—it's the direction you're facing. God wants you to turn and face Him, and He will heal your hurt. Vicissitudes may determine where we're placed on the ship of life, but passengers onboard always have a choice in the direction they choose to look."

"Sir, you narrow truth down to where one lives. I commend you for that talent. Regardless of where one stands on this ship, he must have clarity of sight. My eyes are filled with cataracts from the searing images I see every night when I go to bed."

"Mr. Pencovich, this ship is being retrofitted to pick up stranded Jews, descendants of the Diaspora, people who want to return to a place of freedom in their fathers' land. They've had lots of pain too, and to reach the ship it will take struggle, they'll have to fight and claw their way to get here."

The stranger turned and looked into the eyes of a man who knew his pain. "That's a long journey for me to make, one that will take time. I was a good boy when I was small. My folks sent me to study Hebrew at the synagogue. I was a gifted, clever student. I can still read the Hebrew text."

"Did you ever read Isaiah fifty-three?"

The old man saw the stranger try to avoid the question. His feet shuffled, his face grimaced, then, suddenly became peaceful.

"Yes, I have read that passage in the original language. I remember reading it when I was a child, and it made me cry to see the record of a man suffering from cruel punishment and abuse."

"The man you read about in Isaiah fifty-three was God's Son, the Jewish Messiah. He knew pain. He knew loss of family. He looked down from the cross and saw the pain his mother carried. But in His pain, he saw life coming from it. He would live again—without pain.

"If you can look beyond your pain, you'll find life."

"Sir, I am guilty of being an executioner without the authority of the court. The executed were guilty of heinous crimes against my people. I violated the law of the Scripture by not having witnesses to testify against them, and to be truthful, I took pleasure in taking the lives of those who killed my own in acts of genocide. Can forgiveness be found when pleasure is derived from taking life? Nazism not only killed my family, it killed my soul. I am as dead inside as those who lie in unmarked graves"

"There is no sin or act that God cannot forgive," said the old man. "On the day the Messiah died, He forgave not an executioner, but a murderer, saying, 'You will be with me today in Paradise.'"

"Sir, you have shown me how my ship can be safe in the harbor. My eyesight is poor, my strength is weak, but I want what you have that has taken you from the same Holocaust in Romania and given you life."

From across the deck of the ship, Hans stood watching the interactions of two people who had been through the fires of the Holocaust. One was a survivor with life inside, though scarred in memory; the other was a pillar of stone, dead and lifeless, made that way by his court of justice. When he saw the old man put his arm around the stranger, he knew he was saying a prayer. Han's bowed his head thinking how the patriarch had passed through the fire of the Holocaust himself and was now reaching back into the flames, extending a hand to a fellow traveler.

Breaking into his thoughts was a voice calling his name, "Doctor Baughman!" He looked up. Standing nearby was the person in charge of the retrofit project, and coming from the other side of the ship was a modern-day prophet being followed by someone who was struggling to climb aboard another kind of ship.

Like students under the tutorship of a master teacher, they all trailed after the stranger as he began his inspection tour. The old patriarch was preoccupied with his reflections on how the ship had already rescued its first victim from a stormy sea.

The stranger had never lauded the extent of his knowledge of ships, but Hans would soon be favorably impressed with the inspections he made and the questions he asked. They found themselves down in the belly of the ship where the stowaways would be kept. Additional bathrooms and showers had been installed and everything was made portable so it could be moved, stacked, and stored. The only stationary items were showers and bathrooms and they were put in at locations that made it appear they accommodated the crew.

"Mr. Pencovich," asked Hans, "how would you smuggle Jews onboard this freighter?"

"Human smuggling is done all the time on a small scale. The easiest and simplest is bribery. Ten crewmembers go ashore, twenty return while certain people look the other way. Sometimes, obfuscation is used. After the bribery is paid, the electrical power goes down, which is a normal thing in these countries anyway, and the parties merely find their way onboard using flashlights. In an operation where all the crew is part of the process, it can be done quickly and smoothly.

"Another method is to have an air-vented box container delivered to the dock that contains the human cargo. It is stored in the hold where the stowaways are released and stay hidden on the ship. This can be a dangerous operation if protocol isn't followed. Only the ship's crew and equipment are used with this method. Safety goes with your own people and equipment. Nighttime coastal departures also can be effective taking people on board who come from the shoreline in small boats. This, of course, would be done at night after leaving port.

"It is important that whatever is done to accommodate passengers or stowaways, that it be designed in such a way it can be easily modified. It is inevitable that trial and error adjustments will have to be made."

While the men were onboard the ship, the women were in Haifa shopping. The wedding was on Sheena's mind and bolts of cloth were purchased for the gowns to be worn by her attendants in the ceremony.

The evening was spent in the hotel dining room where the airline crew and guests were booked. The following day, the pilots would service the plane, oversee a cleaning crew, and prepare for a fly-out the day after. The women would indulge themselves doing more shopping for the wedding while the stranger completed his inspection of the freighters anchored in the bay. Mr. Reznik would have Hans all to himself so he could show him the extent of the progress of the housing complex.

The morning started early. Breakfast was served at seven in the dining room, and everyone was on their way for the day's activities by eight. When Hans' driver stopped in front of what had been open land when he was last here, all he could see were rows and rows of framed units with men everywhere busy with construction.

"Come on, Mr. Baughman, I want you to meet the site superintendent I'm working with," said Sheena's father.

The old man was as proud as a peacock with the work he had put into the project. Hans was pleased with himself having selected this gifted person to help with its development.

The two walked over to the construction-site office. Inside, were several desks with a large central table in the middle of the room. He saw two draftsmen at their tables and two secretaries answering and placing calls. Three workers with hardhats were standing together at the large table going over some plans. One of them saw the old gentleman and stopped everything.

"Mr. Reznik! I wasn't expecting you here until next week! What a surprise! We're well underway as you can see, and who is this gentleman you've brought along?"

Again, Hans felt pride swelling inside over his decision to use Sheena's father as a liaison between the people here on the field and his office. His reception by those in charge validated his decision.

"Mr. Riznor, I want you to meet the big man of this whole project. This is Mr. Hans Baughman."

"It can't be! Am I given the privilege of meeting the person who made this housing project possible? It is an honor, Mr. Baughman, to have you visit the project site."

"The honor is mine, Mr. Riznor. I would like you to show me around."

"It is the gentleman standing with you who should do that. He knows more about the work here than I do."

"Oh no, I insist you do the honors," said Mr. Reznik. "Doctor Baughman hears enough from me at home."

For the next hour, Hans was given an overview of the plans for the first phase of the project, then spent another hour outside inspecting the foundations and framing.

It was on the return trip to the hotel that the talkative Mr. Reznik became subdued and quiet. They were both weary in the back seat of their taxi from their efforts of inspecting the buildings under construction and were anxious to get to the hotel, cleaned up, and ready for dinner.

Hans was almost dozing off when he heard someone say, "When are you going to tell him?" He opened his eyes and looking straight at him was the old man.

"Tell who, what?" asked Hans.

"When are you going to tell Mr. Pencovich you're his nephew?"

"Soon…but first there's a question I have to ask him before the curtain is raised on that scene."

The dining table at the hotel where the party of eight had gathered carried a festive atmosphere of unity. Even the stranger showed signs of pleasure. Hans noticed a lot of talking going on between Fritz and the stranger, and he knew the motive in that activity.

When everyone began to leave the table for the evening, Hans moved near the stranger who now seemed part of the group.

"Will you be in your room at eight-thirty tonight, Mr. Pencovich?"

"Yes."

"Do you mind if Sheena and I drop in at that time?"

"Please do. I usually read late anyway."

Hans and Sheena went out together; the others were on their own. Outside the hotel, they took a taxi and drove the coastal route, found an ice cream parlor and sat outside under the stars and discussed their wedding plans.

Inside the stranger's room at the hotel, the man who had jumped ship hoping to get support for his private war for justice, sat in a chair reading a book he'd borrowed from Mr. Reznik. When he heard a knock at his door, he looked at his watch, laid the book on the bed, and opened the door. Standing in front of him was a very wealthy man and a beautiful woman, a lady who could dress with all the elegance of Europe, but chose to be plain. The only affluence showing was her large diamond ring. She reminded him of someone he once knew.

"Come in please."

The room had a small lounge with a sofa and four chairs. After sitting, Hans opened the conversation.

"There are two matters I want to discuss with you. First, I appreciate the work you did aboard the freighters. When we get back, I would like you to give me a written report so we can have it on file. A secretary will be provided for dictation if you like."

"If it's alright with you," said the stranger, "I would prefer a desk and a typewriter. I'm a writer and have compiled a lot of notes and will create the format I'm familiar with."

"Whatever you wish," said Hans. "The next matter concerns the need we have of getting the right person to direct and supervise the collection of Jews from the different ports, and in some cases, the open seas. Knowing your experience and knowledge, you would be the right person for the job. You will be paid a handsome salary and will bring life to thousands who will board these ships."

"Doctor Baughman, are you trying to give me life?"

"Only God can give life, all I do is hand out tickets for the trip."

"You have a way of sharpening the edge of truth. Both of you impact me tonight with words and beauty."

His eye contact with Hans and Sheena was lost when he turned his face downward, his slumped-over shoulders showing his personal burden of history, but the passion of his voice kept pace with the flow of his words.

"I once had a beautiful young lady I was going to marry. She dressed simply and was intelligent like you, Doctor Sheena. She's no longer by my side, but if she were, she would be whispering in my ear that I should accept the ticket you're offering for the ride on a trip in finding my way back home, a home that's empty without any living relative, but I will learn to be strong as others have and make the journey with the help of God."

He looked up, saw Hans and Sheena with tears on their cheeks. *He was confused. Why were these powerful people showing all this compassion to someone off the street, someone most people would look down upon if they knew he'd been a self-appointed executioner.*

Hans and Sheena saw a man who had survived the Holocaust, someone whose face showed the scars and pain of a life that had lived on the energy of hurt and anger, a man who had the strength of a lion to survive in a jungle, but was now unsure of himself in the new world he had entered. He was unprepared for what he was about to hear. *He saw them both stand and move toward him.*

"Michael, I'm here tonight to tell you that you have one family member still alive, and he is the son of your sister, Rachael...I, Hans Baughman, am your nephew, the son of your sister, Rachael, the lad you pulled around in the little wagon."

Any life showing on the stranger's face suddenly vanished. His face became stone. Wild thoughts were surging through him. *What was this man saying? It was common knowledge all his family had been killed.*

Hans and Sheena saw his confusion and dismay—like he'd seen the grim reaper. Then, they heard him whisper to himself, *"No, no, it can't be...it can't be! How could it be?"*

"Michael, you saw on TV the documentary film of the Romanian Holocaust. Remember the German lady who found the little boy in the wagon of hay, took him to Germany and adopted him. I was that little boy in the arms of your sister, Rachael, when she fell to the ground. An angel in white picked me up in his arms and carried me to safety."

The stone-fixed face in front of Hans and Sheena began to show life. Tears formed in sockets of blue eyes, tears foreign to his nature. The surge of emotional energy pushed from his lips the words, *"I didn't know...I didn't know. Oh, if I had only known. My dear sister, Rachael, has left me something of her...I can't believe it! It's a miracle! Part of Rachael, my beautiful sister, is with me."*

Michael stood to his feet, grabbed Hans, saying, "This is a miracle...I can't believe it!" All three were embraced together weeping like children. The reunion marked a new beginning for both of them.

Michael didn't sleep that night. Hans never slept better, and Sheena awoke the next morning reflecting on the biblical account of Joseph revealing himself to his brothers. She was proud of the man she was going to marry. He had demonstrated wisdom in the steps he'd taken to help Michael find his way home.

At the breakfast table in the hotel dining room, Sheena sat on one side of Hans, Michael on the other, and Mr. Reznik flirted with his wife sporting a broad grin on his face.

Chapter 33

The Wedding

Aboard the return flight, Michael was in the captain's quarters connecting with people who had become his family, and Hans was on the radio transacting business with Max who had requested a live call.

"Max, you requested a call?"

"Yes, my report concerns two matters: the director of operation H and the matter of operation P."

In addressing the subject of H, Max was referencing the Henry Operation and the need for a director. The subject of P was more clandestine. It involved the purloining of documents and records of the underground Nazis. Using quasi-steganography over the radio meant leaving no trail to follow.

Max continued the conversation. "The gentleman I mentioned for the position of Operation H feels the job would be too stressful. I will continue to look further for someone suitable."

"Max, cancel this directive. I have already filled this position with a very capable person."

"Glad to hear that!" said Max. "I have good news with a report from our friends at the big I. Your contribution toward the P operation has reaped a bountiful harvest of intelligence. A complete report of the assayer's findings will be on your desk tomorrow. Everyone came out in good health."

"Needless to say, Max, I'm ecstatic! I'll celebrate this with you at my house over dinner at which time I will

360

introduce to you a long-lost relative I never knew I had. Thank you for your work!"

When Hans signed off, he paused for a moment to thank God that violence was avoided in the successful purloin operation in the deep chambers of the Nazi secret underground. He would consult with his attorneys on how to use the intelligence to thwart and prosecute the underground Nazi movement.

Hans was on his way to the captain's quarters when he saw Fritz in the kitchen. "Well Fritz, your time is up. Can you tell me why Mr. Pencovich was brought along on this flight?"

"Unfortunately, I can't, he knows a lot about everything which made it difficult to focus on his area of expertise. He wouldn't be here if he didn't have a specialty. May I ask what he specializes in, Doctor Hans?"

He had a specialty all right, Hans thought, he specialized in executions. But now he was reversing the course. Hans remembered another executioner who gave up the life of executions to be a follower of the Messiah. Not much was said about his former life other than he was called Simeon, the zealot, an equivalent of a self-appointed executioner.

"Fritz, his specialty is ships. He was assigned to assess some work being done on a couple of our vessels. Even though you failed in your assignment, I have a special role for you at our wedding."

"Thank you, Sir."

Hans returned to the captain's quarters and found four people interacting like a family who had always been around.

Seeing Hans, Mrs. Reznik asked, "Hans, where is Michael going to stay? He's welcome to move in with us. We have plenty of room."

"I think he'd prefer to stay with me, but that's up to Michael. He can carry on at the hotel where he's now booked if he likes. However, with the conditions we live under, he should stay in a well-secured compound."

"After you and Sheena are married, her place will be vacant and he could move in there."

"A splendid idea, Mom, providing Michael would want to do that. Right now, he'll move in with me, and I'll hire a cook and housekeeper. He'll be provided a vehicle, driver, and an office."

Michael surprised everyone. He broke into the conversation with the need to talk about himself. He addressed Hans by the name his mother and father gave him at birth.

"God has been good in giving me a family when I thought I had no family. When Jacob asked me to save life instead of taking it, it was a hard move to make, but I knew I had to do this for the memory of the one taken from me. It was a decision she would want.

"There is no one more qualified than I am to do what Hans has asked of me because of my experience. I've been in the shoes of those who will board the ships. I know what they will have to go through to get there. They will have to hide, practice subterfuge, travel with little to eat, and learn to bear up under stress and pain. I hope they never have to experience violence as I did. I will stay with Jacob until the ships are ready to go, then, move to Israel, the base of operations."

Everyone in the room knew enough to refrain from interrupting his discourse. Two were doctors, and the mother saw her daughter place her index finger to her lips requesting silence. Silence brought further speech.

"I need two skilled people with my experience aboard those two ships taking on the Diaspora, people who've been through what I've been through."

At this point, he turned and looked at Hans, saying, "These two people I need are my colleagues in Romania. They would be loyal, committed to the cause, and perhaps saved as I have been saved."

Michael had returned home from a war, his own war, a war of his own making. Though it was a different kind of war, it would still carry all the downsides of what soldiers experienced after returning from the battlefield.

Hans placed his hand on his shoulder to reassure him, saying, "We'll get these people out of that country if this is what you want. Give Max all the information you have on them. Are you sure they'll want to come and join you?"

"When they hear what the mission is, and that I'm in charge, they'll come. We'll put our energies together for the good of Israel."

The following day everyone was adjusting to the new swirling events going on around them, and the wedding in three weeks was one of them. Sheena would be away from the hospital working on the greatest event of her life. Because Hans had provided a limitless budget, she was able to hire professional people who specialized in large weddings. The tedious details left to her were the most important: arranging the format of a Jewish wedding with adjustments that included Messianic theology. Her father and the Shul's Messianic Rabbi came to her aid. The ceremony would picture the future event of the mystical wedding between the Messiah and His chosen bride, the finality of an espousal relationship.

The elaborate ceremony would include the long walk down the aisle at her father's side, joining her bridegroom in front of the Chuppah, the Bridal Canopy, a tradition dating back to tent-dwelling days in the desert. When the ceremony commenced, they would enter the canopy together where the bride would circle the groom seven times for the seven days of creation and rest. It would show that the groom was to be the center of her life. Her Maid of Honor and attendants had all been selected.

In the meantime, Hans had to comply with wedding protocol: the selection of male honor attendants to balance out the wedding party. He would need four men. Selecting the best man was an easy call. It fell on his uncle, Michael, who was now staying with him in one of the five bedrooms in his home, and who was given a driver and vehicle with an office to begin his management of the Prince Henry operation. The next in line was a special person who stood by his side when he was alone at his mother's passing. Karl was the only special friend Hans had. They were both doctors, had similar backgrounds and Karl modeled what he wanted to become—a devoted father.

Hans would keep his promise to Max for a dinner invitation by mixing business with a social event. He brought in his favorite chef to prepare a sumptuous dinner for those he would ask to be in his wedding party. The invitations would be extended to Max, Karl, Fritz, and Michael. When Max rang the doorbell for the special event, everyone else had already arrived.

The big man, Max, was always as large as life. His imposing size and strict security standards created a daunting image. Few in the company dared to cross the line with him, and most considered him an aggressive guard dog in an enclosed fenced yard. But tonight, the gate to his fenced yard would be left open, and without boundaries, he would lose his bark and bite. Right off, when he came through the front door, the guests saw a trait in his nature never seen before: nervousness with a look of insecurity.

Though Fritz was smaller than Max, both were of equal size in their sense of being out-of-place. Fritz came to know Hans as a radio operator on the company plane, and the doctor had been overly generous to him by increasing his pay and providing a scholarship. It was one thing to be with the chairman in the workplace and quite another to be in the man's home.

Everyone was stiff and formal in the beginning. Michael was a good storyteller and could quickly give a narrative of an event that happened on a sea voyage or in a port of call. He was careful to talk about the event and not himself. He sensed the insecurity of the other two guests and his storytelling became a charitable contribution just to fill in the gaps.

Michael knew why he was present at the dinner table—he now lived with Hans—was part of his family. Max thought he was there because of success in the purloin operation that was now in the hands of the corporation's legal team and the government. Fritz considered himself a charity case. Though Max had lost his bark and growl, the guests noticed he still hadn't lost his appetite to put away the gourmet challenge on his plate.

Halfway through dinner, Hans abruptly interrupted the conversation. "Gentlemen, you have been invited here for a very special reason. Four men are needed to stand with me on my wedding day, and after giving much thought to this, I have chosen you four to be the ones in my wedding party. I have been blessed to have found a lost relative, my Uncle Michael, and he will be my best man. Karl, Max, and Fritz will be my other attendants. If you don't wish to serve, let me know, but if you choose to do so, I will be honored."

Everyone's jaw dropped, even Max's came to a slow grind. Hands holding forks and spoons became paralyzed on the starched, white, linen tablecloth. Eyes that had been entertained with the help of taste buds gave momentary stares at half-filled plates of epicurean delights. Michael was first to speak.

"Who would ever think that the little boy I pulled around in his wagon would someday ask me to be his best man at his wedding? Life has returned to me in a special way."

Tears came to his eyes. He looked away from those seated at the table as if he were seeing something. "I was dressed in my best suit when your mother, Rachael, my beautiful sister, and your father, Isaac, were married. Oh, how beautiful they were as a couple!"

Cold, eerie silence chilled the room. It was as if they'd visited a sacred place in history, a place that demanded reverential silence.

Hans was moved by two inner forces: emotion and reason. His emotions were tearing him apart inside, but he was a doctor and knew this was a vital therapeutic step Michael had taken in his healing, a healthy reconnection with his past. He had remembered his history without the need for revenge.

Hans closed his eyes for a moment to show honor and respect for the past. He was part of that history, created by those two beautiful people, and here at this table was someone who was present at their wedding. *Wisdom was justified by her children, Hans thought, and if Fritz and Max remained mute, their silence would be the fruit of wisdom.*

Michael had led those around the table into a sobering room of history, and it was incumbent on him to find the way back. Hans resisted the temptation to talk. He had the need to follow.

Finally, Michael returned and connected to the subject Hans introduced. "My dear nephew, we are the ones to be honored. Marriage is the most joyous celebration of all institutions of life. It is the central part of creation, the first being performed by God Himself."

Hans gave a long pause before he segued to the next subject. "You four have no choice in what's to be worn, Sheena has all the colors picked out, and the suits you're to wear are available at a chosen men's clothing store. Well, Fritz, Max….I haven't heard from you two!"

"They can't fit me," said Max, "my suits have to be custom made."

"Well, you better get on it right away so it'll be ready for the grand event. The men's shop will bill me for any cost. And you, Fritz, shouldn't be difficult to fit.

"Oh, no, Sir, that'll be no problem."

Through the evening Karl acted like the statesman among the group. Hans had already discussed with him the matter of him being part of his wedding team.

For three weeks, Hans and Sheena worked with professionals whose business it was to put together high-end weddings. They handled everything, gown and suit fittings, floral arrangements, seating logistics, publicity, photos, and the minutia of a hundred other things that fell under the purview of their professional services. Finally, the day, the hour, and the event were upon them. Some of the members of the consortium were in attendance. Greater freedom to move about was the results of the successful purloin operation.

The final part of most traditional weddings was celebrated by showering the bride and bridegroom with rice as the couple left in a vehicle decorated with posters and tin cans hanging from the back bumper. But today, the public would see an upscale traditional departure from that scene. After the ceremony and fanfare of cake-cutting, pomp, and speeches. Rice covered them as they boarded a waiting limousine that would be escorted by the entourage of four additional limos holding the wedding party, family, and friends. Everyone assumed the bride and groom would be driven to the airport from which they would leave for an undisclosed location. Max would drive the lead limo. Only the bride and groom, and Max, the head of security, knew the place of departure. The wedding party inside the string of limousines saw onlookers straining to see what was going on as they cruised along the highway anticipating a drive to the airport for the waiting corporate jet.

Everyone was surprised when the leading limo pulled into the cordoned-off parking lot of the general hospital. In plain view in the middle of the lot sat a helicopter. It was the couple's decision to make their flight to their honeymoon location from the site where they met and came to know each other. They wanted something to symbolize what their lives stood for in marriage.

Standing near the helicopter, Hans made a brief speech.

"Friends, we have chosen to leave from the site where we first met. It can be said that the death of my mother brought us together. One life was given that two might live together in happiness. In one week we shall return to continue our work with an ancient people in an ancient land."

The beautiful lady who always dressed in a common, simple manner now stood gorgeously adorned in a white wedding dress artistically designed to compliment her natural, stunning features. She didn't have to add anything to what Hans said; her radiant face of joy and happiness said it all. Her mother and father stood proudly in front of the wedding party. Sheena gave each of them an embraced kiss.

The wedding party saw the blades of the copter start to turn. The bride and groom boarded, and the door was shut. The swirling breeze around them measured the defiance of gravity. They ascended while the group watched the figure of a craft become smaller in the distance.

The old man, the bride's father, continued his role as the family theologian. Today, he carried the look of an old prophet with eyes set in wrinkled stone, the nature of what he was. Time had weathered him on the outside, but the message he had for those standing and watching the departure was neither old nor wrinkled.

"Ladies and gentlemen, I have been poor in life, but God blessed us with a beautiful daughter who fell in love with someone she would later discover was of great wealth. This is the story of the Messiah's Bride, born poor, but made rich, an heir, and joint heir."

Silence blanketed the group as they watched the nuptial couple fade in flight. Then came the booming voice of the old man, "You see that craft! It'll return just like it left, and the two of them will finish the work of moving Jews to Israel from the countries of the world."

The wedding party began to move at the command of the old seer leading the way. He put his arm around his wife, saying, "Mama, though the cord has been cut, I think I'll hang around here and help my new son-in-law. Life is getting interesting."

His wife thought he was mumbling to himself. She stopped, looked into his bright, crystal-blue eyes, and said, "Mr. Reznik, stop talking to yourself, it makes you look older than you are."

I will return to Zion and dwell in Jerusalem
(Zech. 8:3)